DANGER ZONE

The Art of Deception

and

Risky Business

Sign of Seven Trilogy
Blood Brothers • *The Hollow* • *The Pagan Stone*

Bride Quartet
Vision in White • *Bed of Roses* • *Savor the Moment* • *Happy Ever After*

The Inn Boonsboro Trilogy
The Next Always • *The Last Boyfriend* • *The Perfect Hope*

The Cousins O'Dwyer Trilogy
Dark Witch • *Shadow Spell* • *Blood Magick*

The Guardians Trilogy
Stars of Fortune • *Bay of Sighs* • *Island of Glass*

Chronicles of The One
Year One • *Of Blood and Bone* • *The Rise of Magicks*

The Dragon Heart Legacy
The Awakening • *The Becoming* • *The Choice*

EBOOKS BY NORA ROBERTS

Cordina's Royal Family
Affaire Royale • *Command Performance* • *The Playboy Prince* • *Cordina's Crown Jewel*

The Donovan Legacy
Captivated • *Entranced* • *Charmed* • *Enchanted*

The O'Hurleys
The Last Honest Woman • *Dance to the Piper* • *Skin Deep* • *Without a Trace*

Night Tales
Night Shift • *Night Shadow* • *Nightshade* • *Night Smoke* • *Night Shield*

• *Witness in Death* • *Judgment in Death* • *Betrayal in Death*
• *Seduction in Death* • *Reunion in Death* • *Purity in Death*
• *Portrait in Death* • *Imitation in Death* • *Divided in Death*
• *Visions in Death* • *Survivor in Death* • *Origin in Death*
• *Memory in Death* • *Born in Death* • *Innocent in Death* •
Creation in Death • *Strangers in Death* • *Salvation in Death*
• *Promises in Death* • *Kindred in Death* • *Fantasy in Death* •
Indulgence in Death • *Treachery in Death* • *New York to Dallas*
• *Celebrity in Death* • *Delusion in Death* • *Calculated in Death*
• *Thankless in Death* • *Concealed in Death* • *Festive in Death* •
Obsession in Death • *Devoted in Death* • *Brotherhood in Death*
• *Apprentice in Death* • *Echoes in Death* • *Secrets in Death* •
Dark in Death • *Leverage in Death* • *Connections in Death* •
Vendetta in Death • *Golden in Death* • *Shadows in Death* •
Faithless in Death • *Forgotten in Death* • *Abandoned in Death*
• *Desperation in Death* • *Encore in Death*

ANTHOLOGIES

From the Heart • *A Little Magic* • *A Little Fate*

Moon Shadows
(with Jill Gregory, Ruth Ryan Langan, and Marianne Willman)

The Once Upon Series
(with Jill Gregory, Ruth Ryan Langan, and Marianne Willman)
Once Upon a Castle • *Once Upon a Star* • *Once Upon a
Dream* • *Once Upon a Rose* • *Once Upon a Kiss* • *Once Upon
a Midnight*

Silent Night
(with Susan Plunkett, Dee Holmes, and Claire Cross)

Out of This World
(with Laurell K. Hamilton, Susan Krinard, and Maggie Shayne)

Bump in the Night
(with Mary Blayney, Ruth Ryan Langan, and Mary Kay McComas)

DANGER ZONE

The Art of Deception

and

Risky Business

TWO NOVELS IN ONE

NORA ROBERTS

St. Martin's Paperbacks

This is a work of fiction. All of the characters, organizations, and events portrayed in this book are either products of the author's imagination or are used fictitiously.

Published in the United States by St. Martin's Paperbacks, an imprint of St. Martin's Publishing Group.

DANGER ZONE: THE ART OF DECEPTION copyright © 1986 by Nora Roberts and RISKY BUSINESS copyright © 1986 by Nora Roberts.

For information, address St. Martin's Publishing Group, 120 Broadway, New York, NY 10271.

www.stmartins.com

ISBN: 978-1-250-89007-8

Our books may be purchased in bulk for promotional, educational, or business use. Please contact your local bookseller or the Macmillan Corporate and Premium Sales Department at 1-800-221-7945, ext. 5442, or by email at MacmillanSpecialMarkets@macmillan.com.

Printed in the United States of America

St. Martin's Paperbacks edition / June 2023

10 9 8 7 6 5 4 3 2 1

The Art of Deception

CHAPTER 1

It was more like a castle than a house. The stone was gray, but beveled at the edges, Herodian-style, so that it shimmered with underlying colors. Towers and turrets jutted toward the sky, joined together by a crenellated roof. Windows were mullioned, long and narrow with diamond-shaped panes.

The structure—Adam would never think of it as anything so ordinary as a house—loomed over the Hudson, audacious and eccentric and, if such things were possible, pleased with itself. If the stories were true, it suited its owner perfectly.

All it required, Adam decided as he crossed the flagstone courtyard, was a dragon and a moat.

Two grinning gargoyles sat on either side of the wide stone steps. He passed by them with a reservation natural to a practical man. Gargoyles and turrets could be accepted in their proper place—but not in rural New York, a few hours' drive out of Manhattan.

Deciding to reserve judgment, he lifted the heavy brass knocker and let it fall against a door of thick Honduras mahogany. After a third pounding, the door creaked open. With strained patience, Adam looked down at a small woman with huge gray eyes, black braids and a soot-streaked face.

She wore a rumpled sweatshirt and jeans that had seen better days. Lazily, she rubbed her nose with the back of her hand and stared back.

"Hullo."

He bit back a sigh, thinking that if the staff ran to half-witted maids, the next few weeks were going to be very tedious. "I'm Adam Haines. Mr. Fairchild is expecting me," he enunciated.

Her eyes narrowed with curiosity or suspicion, he couldn't be sure. "Expecting you?" Her accent was broad New England. After another moment of staring, she frowned, shrugged, then moved aside to let him in.

The hall was wide and seemingly endless. The paneling gleamed a dull deep brown in the diffused light. Streaks of sun poured out of a high angled window and fell over the small woman, but he barely noticed. Paintings. For the moment, Adam forgot the fatigue of the journey and his annoyance. He forgot everything else but the paintings.

Van Gogh, Renoir, Monet. A museum could claim no finer exhibition. The power pulled at him. The hues, the tints, the brush strokes, and the overall magnificence they combined to create, tugged at his senses. Perhaps, in some strange way, Fairchild had been right to house them in something like a fortress. Turning, Adam saw the maid with her hands loosely folded, her huge gray eyes on his face. Impatience sprang back.

"Run along, will you? Tell Mr. Fairchild I'm here."

"And who might you be?" Obviously impatience didn't affect her.

"Adam Haines," he repeated. He was a man accustomed to servants—and one who expected efficiency.

"Ayah, so you said."

How could her eyes be smoky and clear at the same time? he wondered fleetingly. He gave a moment's thought to the fact that they reflected a maturity and intelligence at odds with her braids and smeared face. "Young lady . . ." He paced the words, slowly and distinctly. "Mr. Fairchild is expecting me. Just tell him I'm here. Can you handle that?"

A sudden dazzling smile lit her face. "Ayah."

The smile threw him off. He noticed for the first time that she had an exquisite mouth, full and sculpted. And there was something . . . something under the soot. Without thinking, he lifted a hand, intending to brush some off. The tempest hit.

"I can't do it! I tell you it's impossible. A travesty!" A man barreled down the long, curved stairs at an alarming rate. His face was shrouded in tragedy, his voice croaked with doom. "This is all your fault." Coming to a breathless stop, he pointed a long, thin finger at the little maid. "It's on your head, make no mistake."

Robin Goodfellow, Adam thought instantly. The man was the picture of Puck, short with a spritely build, a face molded on cherubic lines. The spare thatch of light hair nearly stood on end. He seemed to dance. His thin legs lifted and fell on the landing as he waved the long finger at the dark-haired woman. She remained serenely undisturbed.

"Your blood pressure's rising every second, Mr. Fairchild. You'd better take a deep breath or two before you have a spell."

"Spell!" Insulted, he danced faster. His face glowed pink with the effort. "I don't have spells, girl. I've never had a spell in my life."

"There's always a first time." She nodded, keeping her fingers lightly linked. "Mr. Adam Haines is here to see you."

"Haines? What the devil does Haines have to do with it? It's the end, I tell you. The climax." He placed a hand dramatically over his heart. The pale blue eyes watered so that for one awful moment, Adam thought he'd weep. "Haines?" he repeated. Abruptly he focused on Adam with a brilliant smile. "I'm expecting you, aren't I?"

Cautiously Adam offered his hand. "Yes."

"Glad you could come, I've been looking forward to it."

Still showing his teeth, he pumped Adam's hand. "Into the parlor," he said, moving his grip from Adam's hand to his arm. "We'll have a drink." He walked with the quick bouncing stride of a man who hadn't a worry in the world.

In the parlor Adam had a quick impression of antiques and old magazines. At a wave of Fairchild's hand he sat on a horsehair sofa that was remarkably uncomfortable. The maid went to an enormous stone fireplace and began to scrub out the hearth with quick, tuneful little whistles.

"I'm having Scotch," Fairchild decided, and reached for a decanter of Chivas Regal.

"That'll be fine."

"I admire your work, Adam Haines." Fairchild offered the Scotch with a steady hand. His face was calm, his voice moderate. Adam wondered if he'd imagined the scene on the stairs.

"Thank you." Sipping Scotch, Adam studied the little genius across from him.

Small networks of lines crept out from Fairchild's eyes and mouth. Without them and the thinning hair, he might have been taken for a very young man. His aura of youth seemed to spring from an inner vitality, a feverish energy. The eyes were pure, unfaded blue. Adam knew they could see beyond what others saw.

Philip Fairchild was, indisputably, one of the greatest living artists of the twentieth century. His style ranged from the flamboyant to the elegant, with a touch of everything in between. For more than thirty years, he'd enjoyed a position of fame, wealth and respect in artistic and popular circles, something very few people in his profession achieved during their lifetime.

Enjoy it he did, with a temperament that ranged from pompous to irascible to generous. From time to time he invited other artists to his house on the Hudson, to spend weeks or months working, absorbing or simply relaxing. At other times, he barred everyone from the door and went into total seclusion.

"I appreciate the opportunity to work here for a few weeks, Mr. Fairchild."

"My pleasure." The artist sipped Scotch and sat, gesturing with a regal wave of his hand—the king granting benediction.

Adam successfully hid a smirk. "I'm looking forward to studying some of your paintings up close. There's such incredible variety in your work."

"I live for variety," Fairchild said with a giggle. From the hearth came a distinct snort. "Disrespectful brat," Fairchild muttered into his drink. When he scowled at her, the maid tossed a braid over her shoulder and plopped her rag noisily into the bucket. "Cards!" Fairchild bellowed, so suddenly Adam nearly dumped the Scotch in his lap.

"I beg your pardon?"

"No need for that," Fairchild said graciously and shouted again. At the second bellow the epitome of butlers walked into the parlor.

"Yes, Mr. Fairchild." His voice was grave, lightly British. The dark suit he wore was a discreet contrast to the white hair and pale skin. He held himself like a soldier.

"See to Mr. Haines's car, Cards, and his luggage. The Wedgwood guest room."

"Very good, sir," the butler agreed after a slight nod from the woman at the hearth.

"And put his equipment in Kirby's studio," Fairchild added, grinning as the hearth scrubber choked. "Plenty of room for both of you," he told Adam before he scowled. "My daughter, you know. She's doing sculpture, up to her elbows in clay or chipping at wood and marble. I can't cope with it." Gripping his glass in both hands, Fairchild bowed his head. "God knows I try. I've put my soul into it. And for what?" he demanded, jerking his head up again. "For what?"

"I'm afraid I—"

"Failure!" Fairchild moaned, interrupting him. "To have to deal with failure at my age. It's on your head," he told the little brunette again. "You have to live with it—if you can."

Turning, she sat on the hearth, folded her legs under her and rubbed more soot on her nose. "You can hardly blame me if you have four thumbs and your soul's lost." The accent was gone. Her voice was low and smooth, hinting of European finishing schools. Adam's eyes narrowed. "You're determined to be better than I," she went on. "Therefore, you were doomed to fail before you began."

"Doomed to fail! Doomed to fail, am I?" He was up and dancing again, Scotch sloshing around in his glass. "Philip Fairchild will overcome, you heartless brat. He shall triumph! You'll eat your words."

"Nonsense." Deliberately, she yawned. "You have your medium, Papa, and I have mine. Learn to live with it."

"Never." He slammed a hand against his heart again. "Defeat is a four-letter word."

"Six," she corrected, and, rising, commandeered the rest of his Scotch.

He scowled at her, then at his empty glass. "I was speaking metaphorically."

"How clever." She kissed his cheek, transferring soot.

"Your face is filthy," Fairchild grumbled.

Lifting a brow, she ran a finger down his cheek. "So's yours."

They grinned at each other. For a flash, the resemblance was so striking, Adam wondered how he'd missed it. Kirby Fairchild, Philip's only child, a well-respected artist and eccentric in her own right. Just what, Adam wondered, was the darling of the jet set doing scrubbing out hearths?

"Come along, Adam." Kirby turned to him with a casual smile. "I'll show you to your room. You look tired. Oh, Papa," she added as she moved to the door, "this week's issue of

People came. It's on the server. That'll keep him entertained," she said to Adam as she led him up the stairs.

He followed her slowly, noting that she walked with the faultless grace of a woman who'd been taught how to move. The pigtails swung at her back. Jeans, worn white at the stress points, had no designer label on the back pocket. Her canvas Nikes had broken shoelaces.

Kirby glided along the second floor, passing half a dozen doors before she stopped. She glanced at her hands, then at Adam. "You'd better open it. I'll get the knob filthy."

He pushed open the door and felt like he was stepping back in time. Wedgwood blue dominated the color scheme. The furniture was all Middle Georgian—carved armchairs, ornately worked tables. Again there were paintings, but this time, it was the woman behind him who held his attention.

"Why did you do that?"

"Do what?"

"Put on that act at the door." He walked back to where she stood at the threshold. Looking down, he calculated that she barely topped five feet. For the second time he had the urge to brush the soot from her face to discover what lay beneath.

"You looked so polished, and you positively glowered." She leaned a shoulder against the doorjamb. There was an elegance about him that intrigued her, because his eyes were sharp and arrogant. Though she didn't smile, the amusement in her expression was soft and ripe. "You were expecting a dimwitted parlor maid, so I made it easy for you. Cocktails at seven. Can you find your way back, or shall I come for you?"

He'd make do with that for now. "I'll find it."

"All right. *Ciao,* Adam."

Unwillingly fascinated, he watched her until she'd turned the corner at the end of the hall. Perhaps Kirby Fairchild would be as interesting a nut to crack as her father. But that was for later.

Adam closed the door and locked it. His bags were already set neatly beside the rosewood wardrobe. Taking the brief-case, Adam spun the combination lock and drew up the lid. He pulled out a small transmitter and flicked a switch.

"I'm in."

"Password," came the reply.

He swore, softly and distinctly. "Seagull. And that is, with-out a doubt, the most ridiculous password on record."

"Routine, Adam. We've got to follow routine."

"Sure." There'd been nothing routine since he'd stopped his car at the end of the winding uphill drive. "I'm in, McIntyre, and I want you to know how much I appreciate your dump-ing me in this madhouse." With a flick of his thumb, he cut McIntyre off.

*   *   *

Without stopping to wash, Kirby jogged up the steps to her father's studio. She opened the door, then slammed it so that jars and tubes of paint shuddered on their shelves.

"What have you done this time?" she demanded.

"I'm starting over." Wispy brows knit, he huddled over a moist lump of clay. "Fresh start. Rebirth."

"I'm not talking about your futile attempts with clay. Adam Haines," she said before he could retort. Like a small tank, she advanced on him. Years before, Kirby had learned size was of no consequence if you had a knack for intimidation. She'd developed it meticulously. Slamming her palms down on his worktable, she stood nose to nose with him. "What the hell do you mean by asking him here and not even telling me?"

"Now, now, Kirby." Fairchild hadn't lived six decades with-out knowing when to dodge and weave. "It simply slipped my mind."

Better than anyone else, Kirby knew nothing slipped his mind. "What're you up to now, Papa?"

"Up to?" He smiled guilelessly.

"Why did you ask him here now, of all times?"

"I've admired his work. So've you," he pointed out when her mouth thinned. "He wrote such a nice letter about *Scarlet Moon* when it was exhibited at the Metropolitan last month."

Her brow lifted, an elegant movement under a layer of soot. "You don't invite everyone who compliments your work."

"Of course not, my sweet. That would be impossible. One must be . . . selective. Now I must get back to my work while the mood's flowing."

"Something's going to flow," she promised. "Papa, if you've a new scheme after you promised—"

"Kirby!" His round, smooth face quivered with emotion. His lips trembled. It was only one of his talents. "You'd doubt the word of your own father? The seed that spawned you?"

"That makes me sound like a gardenia, and it won't work." She crossed her arms over her chest. Frowning, Fairchild poked at the unformed clay.

"My motives are completely altruistic."

"Hah."

"Adam Haines is a brilliant young artist. You've said so yourself."

"Yes, he is, and I'm sure he'd be delightful company under different circumstances." She leaned forward, grabbing her father's chin in her hand. "Not now."

"Ungracious," Fairchild said with disapproval. "Your mother, rest her soul, would be very disappointed in you."

Kirby ground her teeth. "Papa, the Van Gogh!"

"Coming along nicely," he assured her. "Just a few more days."

Knowing she was in danger of tearing out her hair, she stalked to the tower window. "Oh, bloody murder."

Senility, she decided. It had to be senility. How could he consider having that man here now? Next week, next month, but now? That man, Kirby thought ruthlessly, was nobody's fool.

At first glance she'd decided he wasn't just attractive—very attractive—but sharp. Those big camel's eyes gleamed with intelligence. The long, thin mouth equaled determination. Perhaps he was a bit pompous in his bearing and manner, but he wasn't soft. No, she was certain instinctively that Adam Haines would be hard as nails.

She'd like to do him in bronze, she mused. The straight nose, the sharp angles and planes in his face. His hair was nearly the color of deep, polished bronze, and just a tad too long for convention. She'd want to capture his air of arrogance and authority. But not now!

Sighing, she moved her shoulders. Behind her back, Fairchild grinned. When she turned back to him, he was studiously intent on his clay.

"He'll want to come up here, you know." Despite the soot, she dipped her hands in her pockets. They had a problem; now it had to be dealt with. For the better part of her life, Kirby had sorted through the confusion her father gleefully created. The truth was, she'd have had it no other way. "It would seem odd if we didn't show him your studio."

"We'll show him tomorrow."

"He mustn't see the Van Gogh." Kirby planted her feet, prepared to do battle on this one point, if not the others. "You're not going to make this more complicated than you already have."

"He won't see it. Why should he?" Fairchild glanced up briefly, eyes wide. "It has nothing to do with him."

Though she realized it was foolish, Kirby was reassured. No, he wouldn't see it, she thought. Her father might be a little . . . unique, she decided, but he wasn't careless. Neither was she. "Thank God it's nearly finished."

"Another few days and off it goes, high into the mountains of South America." He made a vague, sweeping gesture with his hands.

Moving over, Kirby uncovered the canvas that stood on an

easel in the far corner. She studied it as an artist, as a lover of art and as a daughter.

The pastoral scene was not peaceful but vibrant. The brush strokes were jagged, almost fierce, so that the simple setting had a frenzied kind of motion. No, it didn't sit still waiting for admiration. It reached out and grabbed by the throat. It spoke of pain, of triumph, of agonies and joys. Her lips tilted because she had no choice. Van Gogh, she knew, could have done no better.

"Papa." When she turned her head, their eyes met in perfect understanding. "You are incomparable."

* * *

By seven, Kirby had not only resigned herself to their house guest, but was prepared to enjoy him. It was a basic trait of her character to enjoy what she had to put up with. As she poured vermouth into a glass, she realized she was looking forward to seeing him again, and to getting beneath the surface gloss. She had a feeling there might be some fascinating layers in Adam Haines.

She dropped into a high-backed chair, crossed her legs and tuned back in to her father's rantings.

"It hates me, fails me at every turn. Why, Kirby?" He spread his hands in an impassioned plea. "I'm a good man, loving father, faithful friend."

"It's your attitude, Papa." She shrugged a shoulder as she drank. "Your emotional plane's faulty."

"There's nothing wrong with my emotional plane." Sniffing, Fairchild lifted his glass. "Not a damn thing wrong with it. It's the clay that's the problem, not me."

"You're cocky," she said simply. Fairchild made a sound like a train straining up a long hill.

"Cocky? *Cocky?* What the devil kind of word is that?"

"Adjective. Two syllables, five letters."

Adam heard the byplay as he walked toward the parlor. After a peaceful afternoon, he wondered if he was ready to cope with another bout of madness. Fairchild's voice was rising steadily, and as Adam paused in the doorway, he saw that the artist was up and shuffling again.

McIntyre was going to pay for this, Adam decided. He'd see to it that revenge was slow and thorough. When Fairchild pointed an accusing finger, Adam followed its direction. For an instant he was totally and uncharacteristically stunned.

The woman in the chair was so completely removed from the grimy, pigtailed chimney sweep, he found it nearly impossible to associate the two. She wore a thin silk dress as dark as her hair, draped at the bodice and slit up the side to show off one smooth thigh. He studied her profile as she watched her father rant. It was gently molded, classically oval with a very subtle sweep of cheekbones. Her lips were full, curved now in just a hint of a smile. Without the soot, her skin was somewhere between gold and honey with a look of luxurious softness. Only the eyes reminded him this was the same woman—gray and large and amused. Lifting one hand, she tossed back the dark hair that covered her shoulders.

There was something more than beauty here. Adam knew he'd seen women with more beauty than Kirby Fairchild. But there was something . . . He groped for the word, but it eluded him.

As if sensing him, she turned—just her head. Again she stared at him, openly and with curiosity, as her father continued his ravings. Slowly, very slowly, she smiled. Adam felt the power slam into him.

Sex, he realized abruptly. Kirby Fairchild exuded sex the way other women exuded perfume. Raw, unapologetic sex.

With a quick assessment typical of him, Adam decided she wouldn't be easy to deceive. However he handled Fairchild, he'd have to tread carefully with Fairchild's daughter. He decided as well that he already wanted to make love to her. He'd have to tread *very* carefully.

"Adam." She spoke in a soft voice that nonetheless carried over her father's shouting. "You seem to have found us. Come in, Papa's nearly done."

"Done? I'm undone. And by my own child." Fairchild moved toward Adam as he entered the room. "Cocky, she says. I ask you, is that a word for a daughter to use?"

"An aperitif?" Kirby asked. She rose with a fluid motion that Adam had always associated with tall, willowy women.

"Yes, thank you."

"Your room's agreeable?" His face wreathed in smiles again, Fairchild plopped down on the sofa.

"Very agreeable." The best way to handle it, Adam decided, was to pretend everything was normal. Pretenses were, after all, part of the game. "You have an . . . exceptional house."

"I'm fond of it." Content, Fairchild leaned back. "It was built near the turn of the century by a wealthy and insane English lord. You'll take Adam on a tour tomorrow, won't you, Kirby?"

"Of course." As she handed Adam a glass, she smiled into his eyes. Diamonds, cold as ice, glittered at her ears. He could feel the heat rise.

"I'm looking forward to it." Style, he concluded. Whether natural or developed, Miss Fairchild had style.

She smiled over the rim of her own glass, thinking precisely the same thing about Adam. "We aim to please."

A cautious man, Adam turned to Fairchild again. "Your art collection rivals a museum's. The Titian in my room is fabulous."

The Titian, Kirby thought in quick panic. How could she have forgotten it? What in God's name could she do about it? No difference. It made no difference, she reassured herself. It couldn't, because there was nothing to be done.

"The Hudson scene on the west wall—" Adam turned to her just as Kirby was telling herself to relax "—is that your work?"

"My . . . Oh, yes." She smiled as she remembered. She'd

deal with the Titian at the first opportunity. "I'd forgotten that. It's sentimental, I'm afraid. I was home from school and had a crush on the chauffeur's son. We used to neck down there."

"He had buck teeth," Fairchild reminded her with a snort.

"Love conquers all," Kirby decided.

"The Hudson River bank is a hell of a place to lose your virginity," her father stated, suddenly severe. He swirled his drink, then downed it.

Enjoying the abrupt paternal disapproval, she decided to poke at it. "I didn't lose my virginity on the Hudson River bank." Amusement glimmered in her eyes. "I lost it in a Renault in Paris."

Love conquers all, Adam repeated silently.

"Dinner is served," Cards announced with dignity from the doorway.

"And about time, too." Fairchild leaped up. "A man could starve in his own home."

With a smile at her father's retreating back, Kirby offered Adam her hand. "Shall we go in?"

In the dining room, Fairchild's paintings dominated. An enormous Waterford chandelier showered light over mahogany and crystal. A massive stone fireplace thundered with flame and light. There were scents of burning wood, candles and roasted meat. There was Breton lace and silver. Still, his paintings dominated.

It appeared he had no distinct style. Art was his style, whether he depicted a sprawling, light-filled landscape or a gentle, shadowy portrait. Bold brush strokes or delicate ones, oils streaked on with a pallet knife or misty watercolors, he'd done them all. Magnificently.

As varied as his paintings were his opinions on other artists. While they sat at the long, laden table, Fairchild spoke of each artist personally, as if he'd been transported back in time and had developed relationships with Raphael, Goya, Manet.

His theories were intriguing, his knowledge was impressive. The artist in Adam responded to him. The practical part, the part that had come to do a job, remained cautious. The opposing forces made him uncomfortable. His attraction to the woman across from him made him itchy.

He cursed McIntyre.

Adam decided the weeks with the Fairchilds might be interesting despite their eccentricities. He didn't care for the complications, but he'd allowed himself to be pulled in. For now, he'd sit back and observe, waiting for the time to act.

The information he had on them was sketchy. Fairchild was just past sixty, a widower of nearly twenty years. His art and his talent were no secrets, but his personal life was veiled. Perhaps due to temperament. Perhaps, Adam mused, due to necessity.

About Kirby, he knew almost nothing. Professionally, she'd kept a low profile until her first showing the year before. Though it had been an unprecedented success, both she and her father rarely sought publicity for their work. Personally, she was often written up in the glossies and tabloids as she jetted to Saint Moritz with this year's tennis champion or to Martinique with the current Hollywood golden boy. He knew she was twenty-seven and unmarried. Not for lack of opportunity, he concluded. She was the type of woman men would constantly pursue. In another century, duels would have been fought over her. Adam thought she'd have enjoyed the melodrama.

From their viewpoint, the Fairchilds knew of Adam only what was public knowledge. He'd been born under comfortable circumstances, giving him both the time and means to develop his talent. At the age of twenty, his reputation as an artist had begun to take root. A dozen years later, he was well established. He'd lived in Paris, then in Switzerland, before settling back in the States.

Still, during his twenties, he'd traveled often while painting. With Adam, his art had always come first. However, under the poised exterior, under the practicality and sophistication, there was a taste for adventure and a streak of cunning. So there had been McIntyre.

He'd just have to learn control, Adam told himself as he thought of McIntyre. He'd just have to learn how to say no, absolutely no. The next time Mac had an inspiration, he could go to hell with it.

When they settled back in the parlor with coffee and brandy, Adam calculated that he could finish the job in a couple of weeks. True, the place was immense, but there were only a handful of people in it. After his tour he'd know his way around well enough. Then it would be routine.

Satisfied, he concentrated on Kirby. At the moment she was the perfect hostess—charming, personable. All class and sophistication. She was, momentarily, precisely the type of woman who'd always appealed to him—well-groomed, well-mannered, intelligent, lovely. The room smelled of hothouse roses, wood smoke and her own tenuous scent, which seemed to blend the two. Adam began to relax with it.

"Why don't you play, Kirby?" Fairchild poured a second brandy for himself and Adam. "It helps clear my mind."

"All right." With a quick smile for Adam, Kirby moved to the far end of the room, running a finger over a wing-shaped instrument he'd taken for a small piano.

It took only a few notes for him to realize he'd been wrong. A harpsichord, he thought, astonished. The tinny music floated up. Bach. Adam recognized the composer and wondered if he'd fallen down the rabbit hole. No one—no one normal—played Bach on a harpsichord in a castle in the twentieth century.

Fairchild sat, his eyes half closed, one thin finger tapping, while Kirby continued to play. Her eyes were grave, her mouth was faintly moist and sober. Suddenly, without missing a note or moving another muscle, she sent Adam a slow wink. The notes flowed into Brahms. In that instant, Adam knew he was not only going to take her to bed. He was going to paint her.

"I've got it!" Fairchild leaped up and scrambled around the room. "I've got it. Inspiration. The golden light!"

"Amen," Kirby murmured.

"I'll show you, you wicked child." Grinning like one of his gargoyles, Fairchild leaned over the harpsichord. "By the end of the week, I'll have a piece that'll make anything you've ever done look like a doorstop."

Kirby raised her brows and kissed him on the mouth. "Goat droppings."

"You'll eat your words," he warned as he dashed out of the room.

"I sincerely hope not." Rising, she picked up her drink. "Papa has a nasty competitive streak." Which constantly pleased her. "More brandy?"

"Your father has a . . . unique personality." An emerald flashed on her hand as she filled her glass again. He saw her hands were narrow, delicate against the hard glitter of the stone. But there'd be strength in them, he reminded himself as he moved to the bar to join her. Strength was indispensable to an artist.

"You're diplomatic." She turned and looked up at him. There was the faintest hint of rose on her lips. "You're a very diplomatic person, aren't you, Adam?"

He'd already learned not to trust the nunlike expression. "Under some circumstances."

"Under most circumstances. Too bad."

"Is it?"

Because she enjoyed personal contact during any kind of confrontation, she kept her eyes on his while she drank. Her irises were the purest gray he'd ever seen, with no hint of other colors. "I think you'd be a very interesting man if you didn't bind yourself up. I believe you think everything through very carefully."

"You see that as a problem?" His voice had cooled. "It's a remarkable observation after such a short time."

No, he wouldn't be a bore, she decided, pleased with his annoyance. It was lack of emotion Kirby found tedious. "I could've come by it easily enough after an hour, but I'd already seen your work. Besides talent, you have self-control, dignity and a strong sense of the conventional."

"Why do I feel as though I've been insulted?"

"Perceptive, too." She smiled, that slow curving of lips that was fascinating to watch. When he answered it, she made up her mind quickly. She'd always found it the best way. Still watching him, she set down her brandy. "I'm impulsive," she explained. "I want to see what it feels like."

Her arms were around him, her lips on his, in a move that caught him completely off balance. He had a very brief impression of wood smoke and roses, of incredible softness and strength, before she drew back. The hint of a smile remained as she picked up her brandy and finished it off. She'd enjoyed the brief kiss, but she'd enjoyed shocking him a great deal more.

"Very nice," she said with borderline approval. "Breakfast is from seven on. Just ring for Cards if you need anything. Good night."

She turned to leave, but he took her arm. Kirby found herself whirled around. When their bodies collided, the surprise was hers.

"You caught me off guard," he said softly. "I can do much better than nice."

He took her mouth swiftly, molding her to him. Soft to hard, thin silk to crisp linen. There was something primitive in her taste, something . . . ageless. She brought to his mind the woods on an autumn evening—dark, pungent and full of small mysteries.

The kiss lengthened, deepened without plan on either side. Her response was instant, as her responses often were. It was boundless as they often were. She moved her hands from his shoulders, to his neck, to his face, as if she were already sculpting. Something vibrated between them.

For the moment, blood ruled. She was accustomed to it; he wasn't. He was accustomed to reason, but he found none here. Here was heat and passion, needs and desires without questions or answers.

Ultimately, reluctantly, he drew back. Caution, because he was used to winning, was his way.

She could still taste him. Kirby wondered, as she felt his breath feather over her lips, how she'd misjudged him. Her head was spinning, something new for her. She understood heated blood, a fast pulse, but not the clouding of her mind.

Not certain how long he'd have the advantage, Adam smiled at her. "Better?"

"Yes." She waited until the floor became solid under her feet again. "That was quite an improvement." Like her father, she knew when to dodge and weave. She eased herself away and moved to the doorway. She'd have to do some thinking, and some reevaluating. "How long are you here, Adam?"

"Four weeks," he told her, finding it odd she didn't know.

"Do you intend to sleep with me before you go?"

Torn between amusement and admiration, he stared at her. He respected candor, but he wasn't used to it in quite so blunt a form. In this case, he decided to follow suit. "Yes."

She nodded, ignoring the little thrill that raced up her spine. Games—she liked to play them. To win them. Kirby sensed one was just beginning between her and Adam. "I'll have to think about that, won't I? Good night."

CHAPTER 2

Shafts of morning light streamed in the long windows of the dining room and tossed their diamond pattern on the floor. Outside the trees were touched with September. Leaves blushed from salmon to crimson, the colors mixed with golds and rusts and the last stubborn greens. The lawn was alive with fall flowers and shrubs that seemed caught on fire. Adam had his back to the view as he studied Fairchild's paintings.

Again, Adam was struck with the incredible variety of styles Fairchild cultivated. There was a still life with the light and shadows of a Goya, a landscape with the frantic colors of a Van Gogh, a portrait with the sensitivity and grace of a Raphael. Because of its subject, it was the portrait that drew him.

A frail, dark-haired woman looked out from the canvas. There was an air of serenity, of patience, about her. The eyes were the same pure gray as Kirby's, but the features were gentler, more even. Kirby's mother had been a rare beauty, a rare woman who looked like she'd had both strength and understanding. While she wouldn't have scrubbed at a hearth, she would have understood the daughter who did. That Adam could see this, be certain of it, without ever having met Rachel Fairchild, was only proof of Fairchild's genius. He created life with oil and brush.

The next painting, executed in the style of Gainsborough,

was a full-length portrait of a young girl. Glossy black curls
fell over the shoulders of a white muslin dress, tucked at the
bodice, belled at the skirt. She wore white stockings and neat
black buckle shoes. Touches of color came from the wide
pink sash around her waist and the dusky roses she carried
in a basket. But this was no demure *Pinky*.

The girl held her head high, tilting it with youthful
arrogance. The half smile spoke of devilment while the
huge gray eyes danced with both. No more than eleven
or twelve, Adam calculated. Even then, Kirby must have
been a handful.

"An adorable child, isn't she?" Kirby stood at the doorway
as she had for five full minutes. She'd enjoyed watching and
dissecting him as much as Adam had enjoyed dissecting the
painting.

He stood very straight—prep school training, Kirby decided. Yet his hands were dipped comfortably in his pockets. Even in a casual sweater and jeans, there was an air of
formality about him. Contrasts intrigued her, as a woman
and as an artist.

Turning, Adam studied her as meticulously as he had her
portrait. The day before, he'd seen her go from grubby urchin
to sleek sophisticate. Today she was the picture of the bohe-
mian artist. Her face was free of cosmetics and unframed as
her hair hung in a ponytail down her back. She wore a shapeless black sweater, baggy, paint-streaked jeans and no shoes.
To his annoyance, she continued to attract him.

She turned her head and, by accident or design, the sunlight fell over her profile. In that instant, she was breathtak-
ing. Kirby sighed as she studied her own face. "A veritable
angel."

"Apparently her father knew better."

She laughed, low and rich. His calm, dry voice pleased her
enormously. "He did at that, but not everyone sees it." She
was glad he had, simply because she appreciated a sharp eye
and a clever mind. "Have you had breakfast?"

He relaxed. She'd turned again so that the light no longer illuminated her face. She was just an attractive, friendly woman. "No, I've been busy being awed."

"Oh, well, one should never be awed on an empty stomach. It's murder on the digestion." After pressing a button, she linked her arm through his and led him to the table. "After we've eaten, I'll take you through the house."

"I'd like that." Adam took the seat opposite her. She wore no fragrance this morning but soap—clean and sexless. It aroused nonetheless.

A woman clumped into the room. She had a long bony face, small mud-brown eyes and an unfortunate nose. Her graying hair was scraped back and bundled at the nape of her neck. The deep furrows in her brow indicated her pessimistic nature. Glancing over, Kirby smiled.

"Good morning, Tulip. You'll have to send a tray up to Papa, he won't budge out of the tower." She drew a linen napkin from its ring. "Just toast and coffee for me, and don't lecture. I'm not getting any taller."

After a grumbling disapproval, Tulip turned to Adam. His order of bacon and eggs received the same grumble before she clumped back out again.

"Tulip?" Adam cocked a brow as he turned to Kirby.

"Fits beautifully, doesn't it?" Lips sober, eyes amused, she propped her elbows on the table and dropped her face in her hands. "She's really a marvel as far as organizing. We've had a running battle over food for fifteen years. Tulip insists that if I eat, I'll grow. After I hit twenty, I figured I'd proved her wrong. I wonder why adults insist on making such absurd statements to children."

The robust young maid who'd served dinner the night before brought in coffee. She showered sunbeam smiles over Adam.

"Thank you, Polly." Kirby's voice was gentle, but Adam caught the warning glance and the maid's quick blush.

"Yes, ma'am." Without a backward glance, Polly scurried from the room. Kirby poured the coffee herself.

"Our Polly is very sweet," she began. "But she has a habit of becoming, ah, a bit too matey with two-thirds of the male population." Setting down the silver coffee urn, Kirby smiled across the table. "If you've a taste for slap and tickle, Polly's your girl. Otherwise, I wouldn't encourage her. I've even had to warn her off Papa."

The picture of the lusty young Polly with the Pucklike Fairchild zipped into Adam's mind. It lingered there a moment with perfect clarity until he roared with laughter.

Well, well, well, Kirby mused, watching him. A man who could laugh like that had tremendous potential. She wondered what other surprises he had tucked away. Hopefully she'd discover quite a few during his stay.

Picking up the cream pitcher, he added a stream to his coffee. "You have my word, I'll resist temptation."

"She's built stupendously," Kirby observed as she sipped her coffee black.

"Really?" It was the first time she'd seen his grin—quick, crooked and wicked. "I hadn't noticed."

Kirby studied him while the grin did odd things to her nervous system. Surprise again, she told herself, then reached for her coffee. "I've misjudged you, Adam," she murmured. "A definite miscalculation. You're not precisely what you seem."

He thought of the small transmitter locked in his dignified briefcase. "Is anyone?"

"Yes." She gave him a long and completely guileless look. "Yes, some people are precisely what they seem, for better or worse."

"You?" He asked because he suddenly wanted to know badly who and what she was. Not for McIntyre, not for the job, but for himself.

She was silent a moment as a quick, ironic smile moved

over her face. He guessed, correctly, that she was laughing at herself. "What I seem to be today is what I am—today." With one of her lightning changes, she threw off the mood. "Here's breakfast."

They talked a little as they ate, inconsequential things, polite things that two relative strangers speak about over a meal. They'd both been raised to handle such situations—small talk, intelligent give-and-take that skimmed over the surface and meant absolutely nothing.

But Kirby found herself aware of him, more aware than she should have been. More aware than she wanted to be.

Just what kind of man was he, she wondered as he sprinkled salt on his eggs. She'd already concluded he wasn't nearly as conventional as he appeared to be—or perhaps as he thought himself to be. There was an adventurer in there, she was certain. Her only annoyance stemmed from the fact that it had taken her so long to see it.

She remembered the strength and turbulence of the kiss they'd shared. He'd be a demanding lover. And a fascinating one. Which meant she'd have to be a great deal more careful. She no longer believed he'd be easily managed. Something in his eyes . . .

Quickly she backed off from that line of thought. The point was, she had to manage him. Finishing off her coffee, she sent up a quick prayer that her father had the Van Gogh well concealed.

"The tour begins from bottom to top," she said brightly. Rising, she held out her hand. "The dungeons are marvelously morbid and damp, but I think we'll postpone that in respect of your cashmere sweater."

"Dungeons?" He accepted her offered arm and walked from the room with her.

"We don't use them now, I'm afraid, but if the vibrations are right, you can still hear a few moans and rattles." She said it so casually, he nearly believed her. That, he realized, was one of her biggest talents. Making the ridiculous sound plausible. "Lord Wickerton, the original owner, was quite dastardly."

"You approve?"

"Approve?" She weighed this as they walked. "Perhaps not, but it's easy to be intrigued by things that happened nearly a hundred years ago. Evil can become romantic after a certain period of time, don't you think?"

"I've never looked at it quite that way."

"That's because you have a very firm grip on what's right and what's wrong."

He stopped and, because their arms were linked, Kirby stopped beside him. He looked down at her with an intensity that put her on guard. "And you?"

She opened her mouth, then closed it again before she could say something foolish. "Let's just say I'm flexible. You'll enjoy this room," she said, pushing open a door. "It's rather sturdy and staid."

Taking the insult in stride, Adam walked through with her. For nearly an hour they wandered from room to room. It occurred to him that he'd underestimated the sheer size of the place. Halls snaked and angled, rooms popped up where they were least expected, some tiny, some enormous. Unless he got very, very lucky, Adam concluded, the job would take him a great deal of time.

Pushing open two heavy, carved doors, Kirby led him into the library. It had two levels and was the size of an average two-bedroom apartment. Faded Persian rugs were scattered over the floor. The far wall was glassed in the small diamond panes that graced most of the windows in the house. The rest of the walls were lined floor to ceiling with books. A glance showed Chaucer standing beside D. H. Lawrence. Stephen King leaned against Milton. There wasn't even the pretense of organization, but there was the rich smell of leather, dust and lemon oil.

The books dominated the room and left no space for paintings. But there was sculpture.

Adam crossed the room and lifted a figure of a stallion carved in walnut. Freedom, grace, movement, seemed to vibrate in his hands. He could almost hear the steady heartbeat against his palm.

There was a bronze bust of Fairchild on a high, round stand. The artist had captured the puckishness, the energy, but more, she'd captured a gentleness and generosity Adam had yet to see.

In silence, he wandered the room, examining each piece as Kirby looked on. He made her nervous, and she struggled against it. Nerves were something she felt rarely, and never acknowledged. Her work had been looked at before, she reminded herself. What else did an artist want but recognition? She linked her fingers and remained silent. His opinion hardly mattered, she told herself, then moistened her lips.

He picked up a piece of marble shaped into a roaring mass of flames. Though the marble was white, the fire was real. Like every other piece he'd examined, the mass of marble flames was physical. Kirby had inherited her father's gift for creating life.

For a moment, Adam forgot all the reasons he was there and thought only of the woman and the artist. "Where did you study?"

The flip remark she'd been prepared to make vanished from her mind the moment he turned and looked at her with those calm brown eyes. "École des Beaux-Arts formally. But Papa taught me always."

He turned the marble in his hands. Even a pedestrian imagination would've felt the heat. Adam could all but smell it. "How long have you been sculpting?"

"Seriously? About four years."

"Why the hell have you only had one exhibition? Why are you burying it here?"

Anger. She lifted her brow at it. She'd wondered just what sort of a temper he'd have, but she hadn't expected to see it break through over her work. "I'm having another in the spring," she said evenly. "Charles Larson's handling it." Abruptly uncomfortable, she shrugged. "Actually, I was pressured into having the other. I wasn't ready."

"That's ridiculous." He held up the marble as if she hadn't seen it before. "Absolutely ridiculous."

Why should it make her feel vulnerable to have her work in the palm of his hand? Turning away, Kirby ran a finger down her father's bronze nose. "I wasn't ready," she repeated, not sure why, when she never explained herself to anyone, she was explaining such things to him. "I had to be sure, you see. There are those who say—who'll always say— that I rode on Papa's coattails. That's to be expected." She blew out a breath, but her hand remained on the bust of her father. "I had to know differently. *I* had to know."

He hadn't expected sensitivity, sweetness, vulnerability. Not from her. But he'd seen it in her work, and he'd heard it in her voice. It moved him, every bit as much as her passion had. "Now you do."

She turned again, and her chin tilted. "Now I do." With an odd smile, she crossed over and took the marble from him. "I've never told anyone that before—not even Papa." When she looked up, her eyes were quiet, soft and curious. "I wonder why it should be you."

He touched her hair, something he'd wanted to do since he'd seen the morning sun slant on it. "I wonder why I'm glad it was."

She took a step back. There was no ignoring a longing so quick and so strong. There was no forgetting caution. "Well, we'll have to think about it, I suppose. This concludes the first part of our tour." She set the marble down and smiled easily. "All comments and questions are welcome."

He'd dipped below the surface, Adam realized, and she didn't care for it. That he understood. "Your home's . . . overwhelming," he decided, and made her smile broaden into a grin. "I'm disappointed there isn't a moat and dragon."

"Just try leaving your vegetables on your plate and you'll see what a dragon Tulip can be. As to the moat . . ." She started to shrug an apology, then remembered. "Toadstools, how could I have forgotten?"

Without waiting for an answer, she grabbed his hand and dashed back to the parlor. "No moat," she told him as she went directly to the fireplace. "But there are secret passageways."

"I should've known."

"It's been quite a while since I—" She broke off and began to mutter to herself as she pushed and tugged at the carved oak mantel. "I swear it's one of the flowers along here—there's a button, but you have to catch it just right." With an annoyed gesture, she flicked the ponytail back over her shoulder. Adam watched her long, elegant fingers push and prod. He saw that her nails were short, rounded and unpainted. A schoolgirl's nails, or a nun's. Yet the impression of sexual vitality remained. "I know it's here, but I can't quite . . . *Et voil*à." Pleased with herself, Kirby stepped back as a section of paneling slid creakily aside. "Needs some oil," she decided.

"Impressive," Adam murmured, already wondering if he'd gotten lucky. "Does it lead to the dungeons?"

"It spreads out all over the house in a maze of twists and turns." Moving to the entrance with him, she peered into the dark. "There's an entrance in nearly every room. A button on the other side opens or closes the panel. The passages are horribly dark and moldy." With a shudder, she stepped back. "Perhaps that's why I forgot about them." Suddenly cold, she rubbed her hands together. "I used to haunt them as a child, drove the servants mad."

"I can imagine." But he saw the quick dread in her eyes as she looked back into the dark.

"I paid for it, I suppose. One day my flashlight went out on me and I couldn't find my way out. There're spiders down there as big as schnauzers." She laughed, but took another step back. "I don't know how long I was in there, but when Papa found me I was hysterical. Needless to say, I found other ways to terrorize the staff."

"It still frightens you."

She glanced up, prepared to brush it off. For the second time the quiet look in his eyes had her telling the simple truth. "Yes. Yes, apparently it does. Well, now that I've confessed my neurosis, let's move on."

The panel closed, grumbling in protest as she pushed the control. Adam felt rather than heard her sigh of relief. When he took her hand, he found it cold. He wanted to warm it, and her. Instead he concentrated on just what the passages could mean to him. With them he'd have access to every room without the risk of running into one of the staff or one of the Fairchilds. When an opportunity was tossed in your lap, you took it for what it was worth. He'd begin tonight.

"A delivery for you, Miss Fairchild."

Both Kirby and Adam paused on the bottom landing of the stairs. Kirby eyed the long white box the butler held in his hands. "Not again, Cards."

"It would appear so, miss."

"Galoshes." Kirby sniffed, scratched a point just under her jaw and studied the box. "I'll just have to be more firm."

"Just as you say, miss."

"Cards . . ." She smiled at him, and though his face remained inscrutable, Adam would have sworn he came to attention. "I know it's rude, but give them to Polly. I can't bear to look at another red rose."

"As you wish, miss. And the card?"

"Details," she muttered, then sighed. "Leave it on my desk, I'll deal with it. Sorry, Adam." Turning, she started up the stairs again. "I've been bombarded with roses for the last three weeks. I've refused to become Jared's mistress, but he's persistent." More exasperated than annoyed, she shook her head as they rounded the first curve. "I suppose I'll have to threaten to tell his wife."

"Might work," Adam murmured.

"I ask you, shouldn't a man know better by the time he hits sixty?" Rolling her eyes, she bounced up the next three steps. "I can't imagine what he's thinking of."

She smelled of soap and was shapeless in the sweater and jeans. Moving behind her to the second story, Adam could imagine very well.

The second floor was lined with bedrooms. Each was unique, each furnished in a different style. The more Adam saw of the house, the more he was charmed. And the more he realized how complicated his task was going to be.

"The last room, my boudoir." She gave him the slow, lazy smile that made his palms itchy. "I'll promise not to compromise you as long as you're aware my promises aren't known for being kept." With a light laugh, she pushed open the door and stepped inside. "Fish fins."

"I beg your pardon?"

"Whatever for?" Ignoring him, Kirby marched into the room. "Do you see that?" she demanded. In a gesture remarkably like her father's, she pointed at the bed. A scruffy dog lay like a lump in the center of a wedding ring quilt. Frowning, Adam walked a little closer.

"What is it?"

"A dog, of course."

He looked at the gray ball of hair, which seemed to have no front or back. "It's possible."

A stubby tail began to thump on the quilt.

"This is no laughing matter, Montique. I take the heat, you know."

Adam watched the bundle shift until he could make out a head. The eyes were still hidden behind the mop of fur, but there was a little black nose and a lolling tongue. "Somehow I'd've pictured you with a brace of Afghan hounds."

"What? Oh." Giving the mop on the bed a quick pat, she turned back to Adam. "Montique doesn't belong to me, he belongs to Isabelle." She sent the dog an annoyed glance. "She's going to be very put out."

Adam frowned at the unfamiliar name. Had McIntyre missed someone? "Is she one of the staff?"

"Good grief, no." Kirby let out a peal of laughter that had Montique squirming in delight. "Isabelle serves no one. She's . . . Well, here she is now. There'll be the devil to pay," she added under her breath.

Shifting his head, Adam looked toward the doorway. He started to tell Kirby there was no one there when a movement caught his eye. He looked down on a large buff-colored Siamese. Her eyes were angled, icily blue and, though he hadn't considered such things before, regally annoyed. The cat crossed the threshold, sat and stared up at Kirby. .

"Don't look at me like that," Kirby tossed out. "I had nothing to do with it. If he wanders in here, it has nothing to do with me." Isabelle flicked her tail and made a low, dangerous sound in her throat. "I won't tolerate your threats, and I will not keep my door locked." Kirby folded her arms and tapped a foot on the Aubusson carpet. "I refuse to change a habit of a lifetime for your convenience. You'll just have to keep a closer eye on him."

As he watched silently, Adam was certain he saw genuine temper in Kirby's eyes—the kind of temper one person aims toward another person. Gently he placed a hand on her arm and waited for her to look at him. "Kirby, you're arguing with a cat."

"Adam." Just as gently, she patted his hand. "Don't worry. I can handle it." With a lift of her brow, she turned back to Isabelle. "Take him, then, and put him on a leash if you don't want him wandering. And the next time, I'd appreciate it if you'd knock before you come into my room."

With a flick of her tail, Isabelle moved to the bed and stared up at Montique. He thumped his tail, tongue lolling, before he leaped clumsily to the floor. With a kind of jiggling trot, he followed the gliding cat from the room.

"He went with her," Adam murmured.

"Of course he did," Kirby retorted. "She has a beastly temper."

Refusing to be taken for a fool, Adam gave Kirby a long, uncompromising look. "Are you trying to tell me that the dog belongs to that cat?"

"Do you have a cigarette?" she countered. "I rarely smoke, but Isabelle affects me that way." She noted that his eyes never lost their cool, mildly annoyed expression as he took one out and lit it for her. Kirby had to swallow a chuckle. Adam was, she decided, remarkable. She drew on the cigarette and blew out the smoke without inhaling. "Isabelle maintains that Montique followed her home. I think she kidnapped him. It would be just like her."

Games, he thought again. Two could play. "And to whom does Isabelle belong?"

"Belong?" Kirby's eyes widened. "Isabelle belongs to no one but herself. Who'd want to lay claim to such a wicked creature?"

And he could play as well as anyone. Taking the cigarette from her, Adam drew in smoke. "If you dislike her, why don't you just get rid of her?"

She nipped the cigarette from his fingers again. "I can hardly do that as long as she pays the rent, can I? There, that's enough," she decided after another drag. "I'm quite calm again." She handed him back the cigarette before she walked to the door. "I'll take you up to Papa's studio. We'll just skip over the third floor, everything's draped with dustcovers."

Adam opened his mouth, then decided that some things were best left alone. Dismissing odd cats and ugly dogs, he followed Kirby back into the hall again. The stairs continued up in a lazy arch to the third floor, then veered sharply and became straight and narrow. Kirby stopped at the transition point and gestured down the hall.

"The floor plan is the same as the second floor. There's a set of stairs at the opposite side that lead to my studio. The rest of these rooms are rarely used." She gave him the slow smile as she linked hands. "Of course, the entire floor's haunted."

"Of course." He found it only natural. Without a word, he followed her to the tower.

CHAPTER 3

Normalcy. Tubes of paint were scattered everywhere, brushes stood in jars. The scent of oil and turpentine hung in the air. This Adam understood—the debris and the sensuality of art.

The room was rounded with arching windows and a lofty ceiling. The floor might have been beautiful at one time, but now the wood was dull and splattered and smeared with paints and stains. Canvases were in the corners, against the walls, stacked on the floor.

Kirby gave the room a swift, thorough study. When she saw all was as it should be, the tension eased from her shoulders. Moving across the room, she went to her father.

He sat, motionless and unblinking, staring down at a partially formed mound of clay. Without speaking, Kirby walked around the worktable, scrutinizing the clay from all angles. Fairchild's eyes remained riveted on his work. After a few moments, Kirby straightened, rubbed her nose with the back of her hand and pursed her lips.

"Mmm."

"That's only your opinion," Fairchild snapped.

"It certainly is." For a moment, she nibbled on her thumbnail. "You're entitled to another. Adam, come have a look."

He sent her a killing glance that caused her to grin. Trapped by manners, he crossed the studio and looked down at the clay.

It was, he supposed, an adequate attempt—a partially formed hawk, talons exposed, beak just parted. The power, the life, that sung in his paints, and in his daughter's sculptures, just wasn't there. In vain, Adam searched for a way out.

"Hmm," he began, only to have Kirby pounce on the syllable.

"There, he agrees with me." Kirby patted her father's head and looked smug.

"What does he know?" Fairchild demanded. "He's a painter."

"And so, darling Papa, are you. A brilliant one."

He struggled not to be pleased and poked a finger into the clay. "Soon, you hateful brat, I'll be a brilliant sculptor, as well."

"I'll get you some Play-Doh for your birthday," she offered, then let out a shriek as Fairchild grabbed her ear and twisted. "Fiend." With a sniff, she rubbed at the lobe.

"Mind your tongue or I'll make a Van Gogh of you."

As Adam watched, the little man cackled; Kirby, however, froze—face, shoulders, hands. The fluidity he'd noticed in her even when she was still vanished. It wasn't annoyance, he thought, but . . . fear? Not of Fairchild. Kirby, he was certain, would never be afraid of a man, particularly her father. *For* Fairchild was more feasible, and just as baffling.

She recovered quickly enough and tilted her chin. "I'm going to show Adam my studio. He can settle in."

"Good, good." Because he recognized the edge to her voice, Fairchild patted her hand. "Damn pretty girl, isn't she, Adam?"

"Yes, she is."

As Kirby heaved a gusty sigh, Fairchild patted her hand again. The clay on his smeared onto hers. "See, my sweet, aren't you grateful for those braces now?"

"Papa." With a reluctant grin, Kirby laid her cheek against his balding head. "I never wore braces."

"Of course not. You inherited your teeth from me." He gave Adam a flashing smile and a wink. "Come back when you've gotten settled, Adam. I need some masculine company." He pinched Kirby's cheek lightly. "And don't think Adam's going to sniff around your ankles like Rick Potts."

"Adam's nothing like Rick," Kirby murmured as she picked up a rag and wiped the traces of clay from her hands. "Rick is sweet."

"She inherited her manners from the milkman," Fairchild observed.

She shot a look at Adam. "I'm sure Adam can be sweet, too." But there was no confidence in her voice. "Rick's forte is watercolor. He's the sort of man women want to mother. I'm afraid he stutters a bit when he gets excited."

"He's madly in love with our little Kirby." Fairchild would've cackled again, but for the look his daughter sent him.

"He just thinks he is. I don't encourage him."

"What about the clinch I happened in on in the library?" Pleased with himself, Fairchild turned back to Adam. "I ask you, when a man's glasses are steamed, isn't there a reason for it?"

"Invariably." He liked them, damn it, whether they were harmless lunatics or something more than harmless. He liked them both.

"You know very well that was totally one-sided." Barely shifting her stance, she became suddenly regal and dignified. "Rick lost control, temporarily. Like blowing a fuse, I suppose." She brushed at the sleeve of her sweater. "Now that's quite enough on the subject."

"He's coming to stay for a few days next week." Fairchild dropped the bombshell as Kirby walked to the door. To her credit, she barely broke stride. Adam wondered if he was watching a well-plotted game of chess or a wild version of Chinese checkers.

"Very well," Kirby said coolly. "I'll tell Rick that Adam

and I are lovers and that Adam's viciously jealous, and keeps a stiletto in his left sock."

"Good God," Adam murmured as Kirby swept out of the door. "She'll do it, too."

"You can bank on it," Fairchild agreed, without disguising the glee in his voice. He loved confusion. A man of sixty was entitled to create as much as he possibly could.

* * *

The structure of the second tower studio was identical to the first. Only the contents differed. In addition to paints and brushes and canvases, there were knives, chisels and mallets. There were slabs of limestone and marble and lumps of wood. Adam's equipment was the only spot of order in the room. Cards had stacked his gear personally.

A long wooden table was cluttered with tools, wood shavings, rags and a crumpled ball of material that might've been a paint smock. In a corner was a high-tech stereo component system. An ancient gas heater was set into one wall with an empty easel in front of it.

As with Fairchild's tower, Adam understood this kind of chaos. The room was drenched with sun. It was quiet, spacious and instantly appealing.

"There's plenty of room," Kirby told him with a sweeping gesture. "Set up where you're comfortable. I don't imagine we'll get in each other's way," she said doubtfully, then shrugged. She had to make the best of it. Better for him to be here, in her way, than sharing her father's studio with the Van Gogh. "Are you temperamental?"

"I wouldn't say so," Adam answered absently as he began to unpack his equipment. "Others might. And you?"

"Oh, yes." Kirby plopped down behind the worktable and lifted a piece of wood. "I have tantrums and fits of melancholia. I hope it won't bother you." He turned to answer, but she was staring down at the wood in her hands, as if searching

for something hidden inside. "I'm doing my emotions now.
I can't be held responsible."

Curious, Adam left his unpacking to walk to the shelf behind her. On it were a dozen pieces in various stages. He
chose a carved piece of fruitwood that had been polished.
"Emotions," he murmured, running his fingers over the
wood.

"Yes, that's—"

"Grief," he supplied. He could see the anguish, feel the
pain.

"Yes." She wasn't sure if it pleased her or not to have him
so in tune—particularly with that one piece that had cost her
so much. "I've done *Joy* and *Doubt,* as well. I thought to save
Passion for last." She spread her hands under the wood she
held and brought it to eye level. "This is to be *Anger.*" As if
to annoy it, she tapped the wood with her fingers. "One of
the seven deadly sins, though I've always thought it misla-
beled. We need anger."

He saw the change in her eyes as she stared into the wood.
Secrets, he thought. She was riddled with them. Yet as she
sat, the sun pouring around her, the unformed wood held aloft
in her hands, she seemed to be utterly, utterly open, completely readable, washed with emotion. Even as he began to
see it, she shifted and broke the mood. Her smile when she
looked up at him was teasing.

"Since I'm doing *Anger,* you'll have to tolerate a few bouts
of temper."

"I'll try to be objective."

Kirby grinned, liking the gloss of politeness over the sar-
casm. "I bet you have bundles of objectivity."

"No more than my share."

"You can have mine, too, if you like. It's very small."
Still moving the wood in her hands, she glanced toward his
equipment. "Are you working on anything?"

"I was." He walked around to stand in front of her. "I've
something else in mind now. I want to paint you."

Her gaze shifted from the wood in her hands to his face. With some puzzlement, he saw her eyes were wary. "Why?"

He took a step closer and closed his hand over her chin. Kirby sat passively as he examined her from different angles. But she felt his fingers, each individual finger, as it lay on her skin. Soft skin, and Adam didn't bother to resist the urge to run his thumb over her cheek. The bones seemed fragile under his hands, but her eyes were steady and direct.

"Because," he said at length, "your face is fascinating. I want to paint that, the translucence, and your sexuality."

Her mouth heated under the careless brush of his fingers. Her hands tightened on the fruitwood, but her voice was even. "And if I said no?"

That was another thing that intrigued him, the trace of hauteur she used sparingly—and very successfully. She'd bring men to their knees with that look, he thought. Deliberately he leaned over and kissed her. He felt her stiffen, resist, then remain still. She was, in her own way, in her own defense, absorbing the feelings he brought to her. Her knuckles had whitened on the wood, but he didn't see. When he lifted his head, all Adam saw was the deep, pure gray of her eyes.

"I'd paint you anyway," he murmured. He left the room, giving them both time to think about it.

* * *

She did think about it. For nearly thirty minutes, Kirby sat perfectly still and let her mind work. It was a curious part of her nature that such a vibrant, restless woman could have such a capacity for stillness. When it was necessary, Kirby could do absolutely nothing while she thought through problems and looked for answers. Adam made it necessary.

He stirred something in her that she'd never felt before. Kirby believed that one of the most precious things in life was the original and the fresh. This time, however, she wondered if she should skirt around it.

She appreciated a man who took the satisfaction of his own desires for granted, just as she did. Nor was she averse to pitting herself against him. But . . . She couldn't quite get past the *but* in Adam's case.

It might be safer—smarter, she amended—if she concentrated on the awkwardness of Adam's presence with respect to the Van Gogh and her father's hobby. The attraction she felt was ill-timed. She touched her tongue to her top lip and thought she could taste him. Ill-timed, she thought again. And inconvenient.

Her father had better be prudent, she thought, then immediately sighed. Calling Philip Fairchild prudent was like calling Huck Finn studious. The blasted, brilliant Van Gogh was going to have to make a speedy exit. And the Titian, she remembered, gnawing on her lip. She still had to handle that.

Adam was huddled with her father, and there was nothing she could do at the moment. Just a few more days, she reminded herself. There'd be nothing more to worry about. The smile crept back to her mouth. The rest of Adam's visit might be fun. She thought of him, the serious brown eyes, the strong, sober mouth.

Dangerous fun, she conceded. But then, what was life without a bit of danger? Still smiling, she picked up her tools.

She worked in silence, in total concentration. Adam, her father, the Van Gogh were forgotten. The wood in her hand was the center of the universe. There was life there; she could feel it. It only waited for her to find the key to release it. She would find it, and the soaring satisfaction that went hand in hand with the discovery.

Painting had never given her that. She'd played at it, enjoyed it, but she'd never possessed it. She'd never been possessed by it. Art was a lover that demanded complete allegiance. Kirby understood that.

As she worked, the wood seemed to take a tentative breath. She felt suddenly, clearly, the temper she sought pushing against the confinement. Nearly—nearly free.

At the sound of her name, she jerked her head up. "Bloody murder!"

"Kirby, I'm so sorry."

"Melanie." She swallowed the abuse, barely. "I didn't hear you come up." Though she set down her tools, she continued to hold the wood. She couldn't lose it now. "Come in. I won't shout at you."

"I'm sure you should." Melanie hesitated at the doorway. "I'm disturbing you."

"Yes, you are, but I forgive you. How was New York?" Kirby gestured to a chair as she smiled at her oldest friend.

Pale blond hair was elegantly styled around a heartshaped face. Cheekbones, more prominent than Kirby's, were tinted expertly. The Cupid's-bow mouth was carefully glossed in deep rose. Kirby decided, as she did regularly, that Melanie Burgess had the most perfect profile ever created.

"You look wonderful, Melly. Did you have fun?"

Melanie wrinkled her nose as she brushed off the seat of her chair. "Business. But my spring designs were well received."

Kirby brought up her legs and crossed them under her. "I'll never understand how you can decide in August what we should be wearing next April." She was losing the power of the wood. Telling herself it would come back, she set it on the table, within reach. "Have you done something nasty to the hemlines again?"

"You never pay any attention anyway." She gave Kirby's sweater a look of despair.

"I like to think of my wardrobe as timeless rather than trendy." She grinned, knowing which buttons to push. "This sweater's barely twelve years old."

"And looks every day of it." Knowing the game and Kirby's skill, Melanie switched tactics. "I ran into Ellen Parker at 21."

"Did you?" After lacing her hands, Kirby rested her chin on them. She never considered gossiping rude, particularly if it was interesting. "I haven't seen her for months. Is she still spouting French when she wants to be confidential?"

"You won't believe it." Melanie shuddered as she pulled a long, slender cigarette from an enameled case. "I didn't believe it myself until I saw it with my own eyes. Jerry told me. You remember Jerry Turner, don't you?"

"Designs women's underwear."

"Intimate apparel," Melanie corrected with a sigh. "Really, Kirby."

"Whatever. I appreciate nice underwear. So what did he tell you?"

Melanie pulled out a monogrammed lighter and flicked it on. She took a delicate puff. "He told me that Ellen was having an affair."

"There's news," Kirby returned dryly. With a yawn, she stretched her arms to the ceiling and relieved the stiffness in her shoulder blades. "Is this number two hundred and three, or have I missed one?"

"But, Kirby—" Melanie tapped her cigarette for emphasis as she leaned forward "—she's having this one with her son's orthodontist."

It was the sound of Kirby's laughter that caused Adam to pause on his way up the tower steps. It rang against the stone walls, rich, real and arousing. He stood as it echoed and faded. Moving quietly, he continued up.

"Kirby, really. An orthodontist." Even knowing Kirby as well as she did, Melanie was stunned by her reaction. "It's so—so middle-class."

"Oh, Melanie, you're such a wonderful snob." She smothered another chuckle as Melanie gave an indignant huff. When Kirby smiled, it was irresistible. "It's perfectly acceptable for Ellen to have any number of affairs, as long as she keeps her choice socially prominent but an orthodontist goes beyond good taste?"

"It's not acceptable, of course," Melanie muttered, finding

herself caught in the trap of Kirby's logic. "But if one is discreet, and . . ."

"Selective?" Kirby supplied good-naturedly. "Actually, it is rather nasty. Here's Ellen carrying on with her son's orthodontist, while poor Harold shells out a fortune for the kid's overbite. Where's the justice?"

"You say the most astonishing things."

"Orthodonture work is frightfully expensive."

With an exasperated sigh, Melanie tried another change of subject. "How's Stuart?"

Though he'd been about to enter, Adam stopped in the doorway and kept his silence. Kirby's smile had vanished. The eyes that had been alive with humor were frigid. Something hard, strong and unpleasant came into them. Seeing the change, Adam realized she'd make a formidable enemy. There was grit behind the careless wit, the raw sexuality and the eccentric-rich-girl polish. He wouldn't forget it.

"Stuart," Kirby said in a brittle voice. "I really wouldn't know."

"Oh, dear." At the arctic tone, Melanie caught her bottom lip between her teeth. "Have you two had a row?"

"A row?" The smile remained unpleasant. "One might put it that way." Something flared—the temper she'd been prodding out of the wood. With an effort, Kirby shrugged it aside. "As soon as I'd agreed to marry him, I knew I'd made a mistake. I should've dealt with it right away."

"You'd told me you were having doubts." After stubbing out her cigarette, Melanie leaned forward to take Kirby's hands. "I thought it was nerves. You'd never let any relationship get as far as an engagement before."

"It was an error in judgment." No, she'd never let a relationship get as far as an engagement. Engagements equaled commitment. Commitments were a lock, perhaps the only lock, Kirby considered sacred. "I corrected it."

"And Stuart? I suppose he was furious."

The smile that came back to Kirby's lips held no humor. "He gave me the perfect escape hatch. You know he'd been pressuring me to set a date?"

"And I know that you'd been putting him off."

"Thank God," Kirby murmured. "In any case, I'd finally drummed up the courage to renege. I think it was the first time in my life I've felt genuine guilt." Moving her shoulders restlessly, she picked up the wood again. It helped to steady her, helped her to concentrate on temper. "I went by his place, unannounced. It was a now-or-never sort of gesture. I should've seen what was up as soon as he answered the door, but I was already into my neat little speech when I noticed a few—let's say articles of intimate apparel tossed around the room."

"Oh, Kirby."

Letting out a long breath, Kirby went on. "That part of it was my fault, I suppose. I wouldn't sleep with him. There was just no driving urge to be intimate with him. No . . ." She searched for a word. "Heat," she decided, for lack of anything better. "I guess that's why I knew I'd never marry him. But, I was faithful." The fury whipped through her again. "I was faithful, Melly."

"I don't know what to say." Distress vibrated in her voice. "I'm so sorry, Kirby."

Kirby shook her head at the sympathy. She never looked for it. "I wouldn't have been so angry if he hadn't stood there, telling me how much he loved me, when he had another woman keeping the sheets warm. I found it humiliating."

"You have nothing to be humiliated about," Melanie returned with some heat. "He was a fool."

"Perhaps. It would've been bad enough if we'd stuck to the point, but we got off the track of love and fidelity. Things got nasty."

Her voice trailed off. Her eyes clouded over. It was time for secrets again. "I found out quite a bit that night," she murmured. "I've never thought of myself as a fool, but it seems I'd been one."

Again, Melanie reached for her hand. "It must have been a dreadful shock to learn Stuart was unfaithful even before you were married."

"What?" Blinking, Kirby brought herself back. "Oh, that. Yes, that, too."

"Too? What else?"

"Nothing." With a shake of her head, Kirby swept it all aside. "It's all dead and buried now."

"I feel terrible. Damn it, I introduced you."

"Perhaps you should shave your head in restitution, but I'd advise you to forget it."

"Can you?"

Kirby's lips curved up, her brow lifted. "Tell me, Melly, do you still hold André Fayette against me?"

Melanie folded her hands primly. "It's been five years."

"Six, but who's counting?" Grinning, Kirby leaned forward. "Besides, who expects an oversexed French art student to have any taste?"

Melanie's pretty mouth pouted. "He was very attractive."

"But base." Kirby struggled with a new grin. "No class, Melly. You should thank me for luring him away, however unintentionally."

Deciding it was time to make his presence known, Adam stepped inside. Kirby glanced up and smiled without a trace of the ice or the fury. "Hello, Adam. Did you have a nice chat with Papa?"

"Yes."

Melanie, he decided as he glanced in her direction, was even more stunning at close quarters. Classic face, classic figure draped in a pale rose dress cut with style and simplicity. "Am I interrupting?"

"Just gossip. Melanie Burgess, Adam Haines. Adam's our guest for a few weeks."

Adam accepted the slim rose-tipped hand. It was soft and

pampered, without the slight ridge of callus that Kirby's had just under the fingers. He wondered what had happened in the past twenty-four hours to make him prefer the untidy artist to the perfectly groomed woman smiling up at him. Maybe he was coming down with something.

"*The* Adam Haines?" Melanie's smile warmed. She knew of him, the irreproachable lineage and education. "Of course you are," she continued before he could comment. "This place attracts artists like a magnet. I have one of your paintings."

"Do you?" Adam lit her cigarette, then one of his own. "Which one?"

"*A Study in Blue.*" Melanie tilted her face to smile into his eyes, a neat little feminine trick she'd learned soon after she'd learned to walk.

From across the table, Kirby studied them both. Two extraordinary faces, she decided. The tips of her fingers itched to capture Adam in bronze. A year before, she'd done Melanie in ivory—smooth, cool and perfect. With Adam, she'd strive for the undercurrents.

"I wanted the painting because it was so strong," Melanie continued. "But I nearly let it go because it made me sad. You remember, Kirby. You were there."

"Yes, I remember." When she looked up at him, her eyes were candid and amused, without the traces of flirtation that flitted in Melanie's. "I was afraid she'd break down and disgrace herself, so I threatened to buy it myself. Papa was furious that I didn't."

"Uncle Philip could practically stock the Louvre already," Melanie said with a casual shrug.

"Some people collect stamps," Kirby returned, then smiled again. "The still life in my room is Melanie's work, Adam. We studied together in France."

"No, don't ask," Melanie said quickly, holding up her hand. "I'm not an artist. I'm a designer who dabbles."

"Only because you refuse to dig your toes in."

Melanie inclined her head, but didn't agree or refute. "I must go. Tell Uncle Philip I said hello. I won't risk disturbing him, as well."

"Stay for lunch, Melly. We haven't seen you in two months."

"Another time." She rose with the grace of one who'd been taught to sit and stand and walk. Adam stood with her, catching the drift of Chanel. "I'll see you this weekend at the party." With another smile, she offered Adam her hand. "You'll come, too, won't you?"

"I'd like that."

"Wonderful." Snapping open her bag, Melanie drew out thin leather gloves. "Nine o'clock, Kirby. Don't forget. Oh!" On her way to the door, she stopped, whirling back. "Oh, God, the invitations were sent out before I . . . Kirby, Stuart's going to be there."

"I won't pack my derringer, Melly." She laughed, but it wasn't quite as rich or quite as free. "You look as though someone's just spilled caviar on your Saint Laurent. Don't worry about it." She paused, and the chill passed quickly in and out of her eyes. "I promise you, I won't."

"If you're sure . . ." Melanie frowned. It was, however, not possible to discuss such a thing in depth in front of a guest. "As long as you won't be uncomfortable."

"I won't be the one who suffers discomfort." The careless arrogance was back.

"Saturday, then." Melanie gave Adam a final smile before she slipped from the room.

"A beautiful woman," Adam commented, coming back to the table.

"Yes, exceptional." The simple agreement had no undertones of envy or spite.

"How do two women, two exceptional women, of totally different types, remain friends?"

"By not attempting to change one another." She picked up the wood again and began to roll it around in her hands. "I overlook what I see as Melanie's faults, and she overlooks mine." She saw the pad and pencil in his hand and lifted a brow. "What're you doing?"

"Some preliminary sketches. What are your faults?"

"Too numerous to mention." Setting the wood down again, she leaned back.

"Any good points?"

"Dozens." Perhaps it was time to test him a bit, to see what button worked what switch. "Loyalty," she began breezily. "Sporadic patience and honesty."

"Sporadic?"

"I'd hate to be perfect." She ran her tongue over her teeth. "And I'm terrific in bed."

His gaze shifted to her bland smile. Just what game was Kirby Fairchild playing? His lips curved as easily as hers. "I bet you are."

Laughing, she leaned forward again, chin cupped in her hands. "You don't rattle easily, Adam. It makes me all the more determined to keep trying."

"Telling me something I'd already concluded isn't likely to rattle me. Who's Stuart?"

The question had her stiffening. She'd challenged him, Kirby conceded, now she had to meet one of his. "A former fiancé," she said evenly. "Stuart Hiller."

The name clicked, but Adam continued to sketch. "The same Hiller who runs the Merrick Gallery?"

"The same." He heard the tightening in her voice. For a moment he wanted to drop it, to leave her to her privacy and her anger. The job came first.

"I know him by reputation," Adam continued. "I'd planned to see the gallery. It's about twenty miles from here, isn't it?"

She paled a bit, which confused him, but when she spoke her voice was steady. "Yes, it's not far. Under the circumstances, I'm afraid I can't take you."

"You may mend your differences over the weekend." Prying wasn't his style. He had a distaste for it, particularly when it involved someone he was beginning to care about.

When he lifted his gaze, however, he didn't see discomfort. She was livid.

"I think not." She made a conscious effort to relax her hands. Noting the gesture, Adam wondered how much it cost her. "It occurred to me that my name would be Fairchild-Hiller." She gave a slow, rolling shrug. "That would never do."

"The Merrick Gallery has quite a reputation."

"Yes. As a matter of fact, Melanie's mother owns it, and managed it until a couple of years ago."

"Melanie? Didn't you say her name was Burgess?"

"She was married to Carlyse Burgess—Burgess Enterprises. They're divorced."

"So, she's Harriet Merrick's daughter." The cast of players was increasing. "Mrs. Merrick's given the running of the gallery over to Hiller?"

"For the most part. She dips her hand in now and then."

Adam saw that she'd relaxed again, and concentrated on the shape of her eyes. Round? Not quite, he decided. They were nearly almond shaped, but again, not quite. Like Kirby, they were simply unique.

"Whatever my personal feelings, Stuart's a knowledgeable dealer." She gave a quick, short laugh. "Since she hired him, she's had time to travel. Harriet's just back from an African safari. When I phoned her the other day, she told me she'd brought back a necklace of crocodile teeth."

To his credit, Adam closed his eyes only briefly. "Your families are close, then. I imagine your father's done a lot of dealing through the Merrick Gallery."

"Over the years. Papa had his first exhibition there, more than thirty years ago. It sort of lifted his and Harriet's careers off at the same time." Straightening in her chair, Kirby frowned across the table. "Let me see what you've done."

"In a minute," he muttered, ignoring her outstretched hand.

"Your manners sink to my level when it's convenient, I see." Kirby plopped back in her chair. When he didn't comment, she screwed her face into unnatural lines.

"I wouldn't do that for long," Adam advised. "You'll hurt yourself. When I start in oil, you'll have to behave or I'll beat you."

Kirby relaxed her face because her jaw was stiffening. "Corkscrews, you wouldn't beat me. You have the disadvantage of being a gentleman, inside and out."

Lifting his head, he pinned her with a look. "Don't bank on it."

The look alone stopped whatever sassy rejoinder she might have made. It wasn't the look of a gentleman, but of a man who made his own way however he chose. Before she could think of a proper response, the sound of shouting and wailing drifted up the tower steps and through the open door. Kirby made no move to spring up and investigate. She merely smiled.

"I'm going to ask two questions," Adam decided. "First, what the hell is that?"

"Which that is that, Adam?" Her eyes were dove gray and guileless.

"The sound of mourning."

"Oh, that." Grinning, she reached over and snatched his sketch pad. "That's Papa's latest tantrum because his sculpture's not going well—which of course it never will. Does my nose really tilt that way?" Experimentally she ran her finger down it. "Yes, I guess it does. What was your other question?"

"Why do you say 'corkscrews' or something equally ridiculous when a simple 'hell' or 'damn' would do?"

"It has to do with cigars. You really must show these sketches to Papa. He'll want to see them."

"Cigars." Determined to have her full attention, Adam grabbed the pad away from her.

"Those big, nasty, fat ones. Papa used to smoke them by the carload. You needed a gas mask just to come in the door. I begged, threatened, even tried smoking them myself." She swallowed on that unfortunate memory. "Then I came up with the solution. Papa is a sucker."

"Is that so?"

"That is, he just can't resist a bet, no matter what the odds." She touched the wood again, knowing she'd have to come back to it later. "My language was, let's say, colorful. I can swear eloquently in seven languages."

"Quite an accomplishment."

"It has its uses, believe me. I bet Papa ten thousand dollars that I could go longer without swearing than he could without smoking. Both my language and the ozone layer have been clean for three months." Rising, Kirby circled the table. "I have the gratitude of the entire staff." Abruptly she dropped in his lap. Letting her head fall back, she wound her arms around his neck. "Kiss me again, will you? I can't resist."

There can't be another like her, Adam thought as he closed his mouth over hers. With a low sound of pleasure, Kirby melted against him, all soft demand.

Then neither of them thought, but felt only.

Desire was swift and sharp. It built and expanded so that they could wallow in it. She allowed herself the luxury, for such things were too often brief, too often hollow. She wanted the speed, the heat, the current. A risk, but life was nothing without them. A challenge, but each day brought its own. He made her feel soft, giddy, senseless. No one else had. If she could be swept away, why shouldn't she be? It had never happened before.

She needed what she'd never realized she needed from a man before: strength, solidity.

Adam felt the initial stir turn to an ache—something deep and dull and constant. It wasn't something he could resist, but something he found he needed. Desire had always been basic and simple and painless. Hadn't he known she was a woman who would make a man suffer? Knowing it, shouldn't he have been able to avoid it? But he hurt. Holding her soft and pliant in his arms, he hurt. From wanting more.

"Can't you two wait until after lunch?" Fairchild demanded from the doorway.

With a quiet sigh, Kirby drew her lips from Adam's. The taste lingered as she knew now it would. Like the wood behind her, it would be something that pulled her back again and again.

"We're coming," she murmured, then brushed Adam's mouth again, as if in promise. She turned and rested her cheek against his in a gesture he found impossibly sweet. "Adam's been sketching me," she told her father.

"Yes, I can see that." Fairchild gave a quick snort. "He can sketch you all he chooses after lunch. I'm hungry."

CHAPTER 4

Food seemed to soothe Fairchild's temperament. As he plowed his way through poached salmon, he went off on a long, technical diatribe on surrealism. It appeared breaking conventional thought to release the imagination had appealed to him to the extent that he'd given nearly a year of his time in study and application. With a good-humored shrug, he confessed that his attempts at surrealistic painting had been poor, and his plunge into abstraction little better.

"He's banished those canvases to the attic," Kirby told Adam as she poked at her salad. "There's one in shades of blue and yellow, with clocks of all sizes and shapes sort of melting and drooping everywhere and two left shoes tucked in a corner. He called it *Absence of Time*."

"Experimental," Fairchild grumbled, eyeing Kirby's uneaten portion of fish.

"He refused an obscene amount of money for it and locked it, like a mad relation, in the attic." Smoothly she transferred her fish to her father's plate. "He'll be sending his sculpture to join it before long."

Fairchild swallowed a bite of fish, then ground his teeth. "Heartless brat." In the blink of an eye he changed from amiable cherub to gnome. "By this time next year, Philip Fairchild's name will be synonymous with sculpture."

"Horse dust," Kirby concluded, and speared a cucumber.

"That shade of pink becomes you, Papa." Leaning over, she placed a loud kiss on his cheek. "It's very close to fuchsia."

"You're not too old to forget my ability to bring out the same tone on your bottom."

"Child abuser." As Adam watched, she stood and wrapped her arms around Fairchild's neck. In the matter of love for her father, the enigma of Kirby Fairchild was easily solvable. "I'm going out for a walk before I turn yellow and dry up. Will you come?"

"No, no, I've a little project to finish." He patted her hand as she tensed. Adam saw something pass between them before Fairchild turned to him. "Take her for a walk and get on with your . . . sketching," he said with a cackle. "Have you asked Kirby if you can paint her yet? They all do." He stabbed at the salmon again. "She never lets them."

Adam lifted his wine. "I told Kirby I was going to paint her."

The new cackle was full of delight. Pale blue eyes lit with the pleasure of trouble brewing. "A firm hand, eh? She's always needed one. Don't know where she got such a miserable temper." He smiled artlessly. "Must've come from her mother's side."

Adam glanced up at the serene, mild-eyed woman in the portrait. "Undoubtedly."

"See that painting there?" Fairchild pointed to the portrait of Kirby as a girl. "That's the one and only time she modeled for me. I had to pay the brat scale." He gave a huff and a puff before he attacked the fish again. "Twelve years old and already mercenary."

"If you're going to discuss me as if I weren't here, I'll go fetch my shoes." Without a backward glance, Kirby glided from the room.

"Hasn't changed much, has she?" Adam commented as he drained his wine.

"Not a damn bit," Fairchild agreed proudly. "She'll lead

you a merry chase, Adam, my boy. I hope you're in condition."

"I ran track in college."

Fairchild's laugh was infectious. Damn it, Adam thought again, I like him. It complicated things. From the other room he heard Kirby in a heated discussion with Isabelle. He was beginning to realize complication was the lady's middle name. What should've been a very simple job was developing layers he didn't care for.

"Come on, Adam." Kirby poked her head around the doorway. "I've told Isabelle she can come, but she and Montique have to keep a distance of five yards at all times. Papa—" she tossed her ponytail back "—I really think we ought to try raising the rent. She might look for an apartment in town."

"We should never have agreed to a long-term lease," Fairchild grumbled, then gave his full attention to Kirby's salmon.

Deciding not to comment, Adam rose and went outside.

It was warm for September, and breezy. The grounds around the house were alive with fall. Beds of zinnias and mums spread out helter-skelter, flowing over their borders and adding a tang to the air. Near a flaming maple, Adam saw an old man in patched overalls. With a whimsical lack of dedication, he raked at the scattered leaves. As they neared him, he grinned toothlessly.

"You'll never get them all, Jamie."

He made a faint wheezing sound that must've been a laugh. "Sooner or later, missy. There be plenty of time."

"I'll help you tomorrow."

"Ayah, and you'll be piling them up and jumping in 'em like always." He wheezed again and rubbed a frail hand over his chin. "Stick to your whittling and could be I'll leave a pile for you."

With her hands hooked in her back pockets, she scuffed at a leaf. "A nice big one?"

"Could be. If you're a good girl."

"There's always a catch." Grabbing Adam's hand, she pulled him away.

"Is that little old man responsible for the grounds?" Three acres, he calculated. Three acres if it was a foot.

"Since he retired."

"Retired?"

"Jamie retired when he was sixty-five. That was before I was born." The breeze blew strands of hair into her face and she pushed at them. "He claims to be ninety-two, but of course he's ninety-five and won't admit it." She shook her head. "Vanity."

Kirby pulled him along until they stood at a dizzying height above the river. Far below, the ribbon of water seemed still. Small dots of houses were scattered along the view. There was a splash of hues rather than distinct tones, a melding of textures.

On the ridge where they stood there was only wind, river and sky. Kirby threw her head back. She looked primitive, wild, invincible. Turning, he looked at the house. It looked the same.

"Why do you stay here?" Blunt questions weren't typical of him. Kirby had already changed that.

"I have my family, my home, my work."

"And isolation."

Her shoulders moved. Though her lashes were lowered, her eyes weren't closed. "People come here. That's not isolation."

"Don't you want to travel? To see Florence, Rome, Venice?"

From her stance on a rock, she was nearly eye level with him. When she turned to him, it was without her usual arrogance. "I'd been to Europe five times before I was twelve. I spent four years in Paris on my own when I was studying."

She looked over his shoulder a moment, at nothing or at everything, he couldn't be sure. "I slept with a Breton count

in a chateau, skied in the Swiss Alps and hiked the moors
in Cornwall. I've traveled, and I'll travel again. But . . ." He
knew she looked at the house now, because her lips curved.
"I always come home."

"What brings you back?"

"Papa." She stopped and smiled fully. "Memories, famil-
iarity. Insanity."

"You love him very much." She could make things impossibly complicated or perfectly simple. The job he'd come to
do was becoming more and more of a burden.

"More than anything or anyone." She spoke quietly, so that
her voice seemed a part of the breeze. "He's given me everything of importance: security, independence, loyalty, friend-
ship, love—and the capability to give them back. I'd like to
think someday I'll find someone who wants that from me. My
home would be with him then."

How could he resist the sweetness, the simplicity, she could
show so unexpectedly? It wasn't in the script, he reminded
himself, but reached a hand to her face, just to touch. When
she brought her hand to his, something stirred in him that
wasn't desire, but was just as potent.

She felt the strength in him, and sensed a confusion that
might have been equal to her own. Another time, she thought.
Another time, it might have worked. But now, just now, there
were too many other things. Deliberately she dropped her
hand and turned back to the river. "I don't know why I tell
you these things," she murmured. "It's not in character. Do
people usually let you in on their personal thoughts?"

"No. Or maybe I haven't been listening."

She smiled and, in one of her lightning changes of mood,
leaped from the rock. "You're not the type people would con-
fide in." Casually she linked her arm through his. "Though
you seem to have strong, sturdy shoulders. You're a little
aloof," she decided. "And just a tad pompous."

"Pompous?" How could she allure him one instant and infuriate him the next? "What do you mean, pompous?"

Because he sounded dangerously like her father, she swallowed. "Just a tad," she reminded him, nearly choking on a laugh. "Don't be offended, Adam. Pomposity certainly has its place in the world." When he continued to scowl down at her, she cleared her throat of another laugh. "I like the way your left brow lifts when you're annoyed."

"I'm not pompous." He spoke very precisely and watched her lips tremble with fresh amusement.

"Perhaps that was a bad choice of words."

"It was a completely incorrect choice." Just barely, he caught himself before his brow lifted. Damn the woman, he thought, and swore he wouldn't smile.

"Conventional." Kirby patted his cheek. "I'm sure that's what I meant."

"I'm sure those two words mean the same thing to you. I won't be categorized by either."

Tilting her head, she studied him. "Maybe I'm wrong," she said, to herself as much as him. "I've been wrong before. Give me a piggyback ride."

"What?"

"A piggyback ride," Kirby repeated.

"You're crazy." She might be sharp, she might be talented, he'd already conceded that, but part of her brain was permanently on holiday.

With a shrug, she started back toward the house. "I knew you wouldn't. Pompous people never give or receive piggyback rides. It's the law."

"Damn." She was doing it to him, and he was letting her. For a moment, he stuck his hands in his pockets and stood firm. Let her play her games with her father, Adam told himself. He wasn't biting. With another oath, he caught up to her. "You're an exasperating woman."

"Why, thank you."

They stared at each other, him in frustration, her in amusement, until he turned his back. "Get on."

"If you insist." Nimbly she jumped on his back, blew the hair out of her eyes and looked down. "Wombats, you're tall."

"You're short," he corrected, and hitched her to a more comfortable position.

"I'm going to be five-seven in my next life."

"You'd better add pounds as well as inches to your fantasy." Her hands were light on his shoulders, her thighs firm around his waist. Ridiculous, he thought. Ridiculous to want her now, when she's making a fool of both of you. "What do you weigh?"

"An even hundred." She sent a careless wave to Jamie.

"And when you take the ball bearings out of your pocket?"

"Ninety-six, if you want to be technical." With a laugh, she gave him a quick hug. Her laughter was warm and distracting at his ear. "You might do something daring, like not wearing socks."

"The next spontaneous act might be dropping you on your very attractive bottom."

"Is it attractive?" Idly she swung her feet back and forth. "I see so little of it myself." She held him for a moment longer because it felt so right, so good. Keep it light, she reminded herself. And watch your step. As long as she could keep him off balance, things would run smoothly. Leaning forward, she caught the lobe of his ear between her teeth. "Thanks for the lift, sailor."

Before he could respond, she'd jumped down and dashed into the house.

* * *

It was night, late, dark and quiet, when Adam sat alone in his room. He held the transmitter in his hand and found he wanted to smash it into little pieces and forget it had ever existed. No personal involvements. That was rule number one, and he'd always followed it. He'd never been tempted not to.

He'd wanted to follow it this time, he reminded himself. It just wasn't working that way. Involvement, emotion, conscience; he couldn't let any of it interfere. Staring at Kirby's painting of the Hudson, he flicked the switch.

"McIntyre?"

"Password."

"Damn it, this isn't a chapter of Ian Fleming."

"Procedure," McIntyre reminded him briskly. After twenty seconds of dead air, he relented. "Okay, okay, what've you found out?"

I've found out I'm becoming dangerously close to being crazy about a woman who makes absolutely no sense to me, he thought. "I've found out that the next time you have a brainstorm, you can go to hell with it."

"Trouble?" McIntyre's voice snapped into the receiver. "You were supposed to call in if there was trouble."

"The trouble is I like the old man and the daughter's . . . unsettling." An apt word, Adam mused. His system hadn't settled since he'd set eyes on her.

"It's too late for that now. We're committed."

"Yeah." He let out a breath between his teeth and blocked Kirby from his mind. "Melanie Merrick Burgess is a close family friend and Harriet Merrick's daughter. She's a very elegant designer who doesn't seem to have any deep interest in painting. At a guess I'd say she'd be very supportive of the Fairchilds. Kirby recently broke off her engagement to Stuart Hiller."

"Interesting. When?"

"I don't have a date," Adam retorted. "And I didn't like pumping her about something that sensitive." He struggled with himself as McIntyre remained silent. "Sometime during the last couple months, I'd say, no longer. She's still smoldering." And hurting, he said to himself. He hadn't forgotten the look in her eyes. "I've been invited to a party this weekend. I should meet both Harriet Merrick and Hiller. In the meantime, I've had a break here. The place is riddled with secret passages."

"With what?"

"You heard me. With some luck, I'll have easy access throughout the house."

McIntyre grunted in approval. "You won't have any trouble recognizing it?"

"If he's got it, and if it's in the house, *and* if by some miracle I can find it in this anachronism, I'll recognize it." He switched off and, resisting the urge to throw the transmitter against the wall, dropped it back in the briefcase.

Clearing his mind, Adam rose and began to search the fireplace for the mechanism.

It took him nearly ten minutes, but he was rewarded with a groaning as a panel slid halfway open. He squeezed inside with a flashlight. It was both dank and musty, but he played the light against the wall until he found the inside switch. The panel squeaked closed and left him in the dark.

His footsteps echoed and he heard the scuttering sound of rodents. He ignored both. For a moment he stopped at the wall of Kirby's room. Telling himself he was only doing his job, he took the time to find the switch. But he wondered if she was already sleeping in the big four-poster bed, under the wedding ring quilt.

He could press the button and join her. The hell with McIntyre and the job. The hell with everything but what lay beyond the wall. Procedure, he thought on an oath. He was sick to death of procedure. But Kirby had been right. Adam had a very firm grip on what was right and what was wrong.

He turned and continued down the passage.

Abruptly the corridor snaked off, with steep stone steps forking to the left. Mounting them, he found himself in another corridor. A spider scrambled on the wall as he played his light over it. Kirby hadn't exaggerated much about the size. The third story, he decided, was as good a place to start as any.

He turned the first mechanism he found and slipped through the opening. Dust and dustcovers. Moving quietly, he began a slow, methodical search.

Kirby was restless. While Adam had been standing on the other side of the wall, fighting back the urge to open the panel, she'd been pacing her room. She'd considered going up to her studio. Work might calm her—but any work she did in this frame of mind would be trash. Frustrated, she sank down on the window seat. She could see the faint reflection of her own face and stared at it.

She wasn't completely in control. Almost any other flaw would've been easier to admit. Control was essential and, under the current circumstances, vital. The problem was getting it back.

The problem was, she corrected, Adam Haines.

Attraction? Yes, but that was simple and easily dealt with. There was something more twisted into it that was anything but simple. He could involve her, and once involved, nothing would be easily dealt with.

Laying her hands on the sill, she rested her head on them. He could hurt her. That was a first—a frightening first. Not a superficial blow to the pride or ego, Kirby admitted, but a hurt down deep where it counted; where it wouldn't heal.

Obviously, she told herself, forewarned was forearmed. She just wouldn't let him involve her, therefore she wouldn't let him hurt her. And that little piece of logic brought her right back to the control she didn't have. While she struggled to methodically untangle her thoughts, the beam of headlights distracted her.

Who'd be coming by at this time of night? she wondered without too much surprise. Fairchild had a habit of asking people over at odd hours. Kirby pressed her nose to the glass. A sound, not unlike Isabelle's growl, came from her throat.

"Of all the nerve," she muttered. "Of all the bloody nerve."

Springing up, she paced the floor three times before she grabbed a robe and left the room.

Above her head, Adam was about to reenter the passageway when he, too, saw the beams. Automatically he switched
off his flashlight and stepped beside the window. He watched
the man step from a late-model Mercedes and walk toward
the house. Interesting, Adam decided. Abandoning the passageway, he slipped silently into the hall.

The sound of voices drifted up as he eased himself into
the cover of a doorway and waited. Footsteps drew nearer.
From his concealment, Adam watched Cards lead a slim,
dark man up to Fairchild's tower studio.

"Mr. Hiller to see you, sir." Cards gave the information
as if it were four in the afternoon rather than after midnight.

"Stuart, so nice of you to come." Fairchild's voice boomed
through the doorway. "Come in, come in."

After counting to ten, Adam started to move toward the
door Cards had shut, but just then a flurry of white scrambled up the stairs. Swearing, he pressed back into the wall as
Kirby passed, close enough to touch.

What the hell is this? he demanded, torn between frustration and the urge to laugh. Here he was, trapped in a doorway, while people crept up tower steps in the middle of the
night. While he watched, Kirby gathered the skirt of her robe
around her knees and tiptoed up to the tower.

It was a nightmare, he decided. Women with floating hair
sneaking around drafty corridors in filmy white. Secret passages. Clandestine meetings. A normal, sensible man wouldn't
be involved in it for a minute. Then again, he'd stopped being
completely sensible when he'd walked in the front door.

After Kirby reached the top landing, Adam moved closer.
Her attention was focused on the studio door. Making a
quick calculation, Adam moved up the steps behind her, then
melted into the shadows in the corner. With his eyes on her,
he joined Kirby in the eavesdropping.

"What kind of fool do you think I am?" Stuart demanded.
He stood beside Adam with only the wall separating them.

"Whatever kind you prefer. Makes no difference to me. Have a seat, my boy."

"Listen to me, we had a deal. How long did you think it would take before I found out you'd double-crossed me?"

"Actually I didn't think it would take you quite so long." Smiling, Fairchild rubbed a thumb over his clay hawk. "Not as clever as I thought you were, Stuart. You should've discovered the switch weeks ago. Not that it wasn't superb," he added with a touch of pride. "But a smart man would've had the painting authenticated."

Because the conversation confused her, Kirby pressed even closer to the door. She tucked her hair behind her ear as if to hear more clearly. Untended, her robe fell open, revealing a thin excuse for a nightgown and a great deal of smooth golden skin. In his corner, Adam shifted and swore to himself.

"We had a deal—" Stuart's voice rose, but Fairchild cut him off with no more than a wave of his hand.

"Don't tell me you believe in that nonsense about honor among thieves? Time to grow up if you want to play in the big leagues."

"I want the Rembrandt, Fairchild."

Kirby stiffened. Because his attention was now fully focused on the battle in the tower, Adam didn't notice. By God, he thought grimly, the old bastard did have it.

"Sue me," Fairchild invited. Kirby could hear the shrug in his voice.

"Hand it over, or I'll break your scrawny neck."

For a full ten seconds, Fairchild watched calmly as Stuart's face turned a deep, dull red. "You won't get it that way. And I should warn you that threats make me irritable. You see . . ." Slowly he picked up a rag and began to wipe some excess clay from his hands. "I didn't care for your treatment of Kirby. No, I didn't care for it at all."

Abruptly he was no longer the harmless eccentric. He was neither cherub nor gnome, but a man. A dangerous one. "I knew she'd never go as far as marrying you. She's far too bright. But your threats, once she told you off, annoyed me. When I'm annoyed, I tend to be vindictive. A flaw," he said amiably. "But that's just the way I'm made." The pale eyes were cold and calm on Stuart's. "I'm still annoyed, Stuart. I'll let you know when I'm ready to deal. In the meantime, stay away from Kirby."

"You're not going to get away with this."

"I hold all the cards." In an impatient gesture, he brushed Stuart aside. "I have the Rembrandt, and only I know where it is. If you become a nuisance, which you're dangerously close to becoming, I may decide to keep it. Unlike you, I have no pressing need for money." He smiled, but the chill remained in his eyes. "One should never live above one's means, Stuart. That's my advice."

Impotent, intimidated, Stuart loomed over the little man at the worktable. He was strong enough, and furious enough, to have snapped Fairchild's neck with his hands. But he wouldn't have the Rembrandt, or the money he so desperately needed. "Before we're done, you'll pay," Stuart promised. "I won't be made a fool of."

"Too late," Fairchild told him easily. "Run along now. You can find your way out without disturbing Cards, can't you?"

As if he were already alone, Fairchild went back to his hawk.

Swiftly, Kirby looked around for a hiding place. For one ridiculous moment, Adam thought she'd try to ease herself into the corner he occupied. The moment she started to cross the hall toward him, the handle of the door turned. She'd left her move too late. With her back pressed against the wall, Kirby closed her eyes and pretended to be invisible.

Stuart wrenched open the door and stalked from the room, blind with rage. Without a backward glance he plunged down the steps. His face, Adam noted as he passed, was murderous. At the moment, he lacked a weapon. But if he found one, he wouldn't hesitate.

Kirby stood, still and silent, as the footsteps receded. She sucked in a deep breath, then let it out on a huff. What now? *What now?* she thought, and wanted to just bury her face in her hands and surrender. Instead, she straightened her shoulders and went in to confront her father.

"Papa." The word was quiet and accusing. Fairchild's head jerked up, but his surprise was quickly masked by a genial smile.

"Hello, love. My hawk's beginning to breathe. Come have a look."

She took another deep breath. All of her life she'd loved him, stood by him. Adored him. None of that had ever stopped her from being angry with him. Slowly, keeping her eyes on him, she crossed the front panels of her robe and tied the sash. As she approached, Fairchild thought she looked like a gunslinger buckling on his six-gun. She wouldn't, he thought with a surge of pride, intimidate like Hiller.

"Apparently you haven't kept me up to date," she began. "A riddle, Papa. What do Philip Fairchild, Stuart Hiller and Rembrandt have in common?"

"You've always been clever at riddles, my sweet."

"*Now,* Papa."

"Just business." He gave her a quick, hearty smile as he wondered just how much he'd have to tell her.

"Let's be specific, shall we?" She moved so that only the table separated them. "And don't give me that blank, foolish look. It won't work." Bending over, she stared directly into his eyes. "I heard quite a bit while I was outside. Tell me the rest."

"Eavesdropping." He made a disapproving tsk-tsk. "Rude."

"I come by it honestly. Now tell me or I'll annihilate your hawk." Sweeping up her arm, she held her palm three inches above his clay.

"Vicious brat." With his bony fingers, he grabbed her wrist, each knowing who'd win if it came down to it. He gave a windy sigh. "All right."

With a nod, Kirby removed her hand then folded her arms under her breasts. The habitual gesture had him sighing again.

"Stuart came to me with a little proposition some time ago. You know, of course, he hasn't a cent to his name, no matter what he pretends."

"Yes, I know he wanted to marry me for my money." No one but her father would've detected the slight tightening in her voice.

"I didn't bring that up to hurt you." His hand reached for hers in the bond that had been formed when she'd taken her first breath.

"I know, Papa." She squeezed his hand, then stuck both of hers in the pockets of her robe. "My pride suffered. It has to happen now and again, I suppose. But I don't care for humiliation," she said with sudden fierceness. "I don't care for it one bloody bit." With a toss of her head, she looked down at him. "The rest."

"Well." Fairchild puffed out his cheeks, then blew out the breath. "Among his other faults, Stuart's greedy. He needed a large sum of money, and didn't see why he had to work for it. He decided to help himself to the Rembrandt self-portrait from Harriet's gallery."

"He *stole* it?" Kirby's eyes grew huge. "Great buckets of bedbugs! I wouldn't have given him credit for that much nerve."

"He thought himself clever." Rising, Fairchild walked to the little sink in the corner to wash off his hands. "Harriet was going on her safari, and there'd be no one to question the disappearance for several weeks. Stuart's a bit dictatorial with the staff at the gallery."

"It's such a treat to flog underlings."

"In any case—" lovingly, Fairchild draped his hawk for the night "—he came to me with an offer—a rather paltry offer, too—if I'd do the forgery for the Rembrandt's replacement."

She hadn't thought he could do anything to surprise her.

Certainly nothing to hurt her. "Papa, it's Harriet's Rembrandt," she said in shock.

"Now, Kirby, you know I'm fond of Harriet. Very fond." He put a comforting arm around her shoulders. "Our Stuart has a very small brain. He handed over the Rembrandt when I said I needed it to do the copy." Fairchild shook his head. "There wasn't any challenge to it, Kirby. Hardly any fun at all."

"Pity," she said dryly and dropped into a chair.

"Then I told him I didn't need the original any longer, and gave him the copy instead. He never suspected." Fairchild linked his hands behind his back and stared up at the ceiling. "I wish you'd seen it. It was superlative. It was one of Rembrandt's later works, you know. Rough textures, such luminous depth—"

"Papa!" Kirby interrupted what would've become a lecture.

"Oh, yes, yes." With an effort, Fairchild controlled himself. "I told him it'd take just a little more time to complete the copy and treat it for the illusion of age. He bought it. Gullibility," Fairchild added and clucked his tongue. "It's been almost three weeks, and he just got around to having the painting tested. I made certain it wouldn't stand up to the most basic of tests, of course."

"Of course," Kirby murmured.

"Now he has to leave the copy in the gallery. And I have the original."

She gave herself a moment to absorb all he'd told her. It didn't make any difference in how she felt. Furious. "Why, Papa? Why did you do this! It isn't like all the others. It's Harriet."

"Now, Kirby, don't lose control. You've such a nasty temper." He did his best to look small and helpless. "I'm much too old to cope with it. Remember my blood pressure."

"Blood pressure be hanged." She glared up at him with

fury surging into her eyes. "Don't think you're going to get around me with that. Old?" she tossed back. "You're still your youngest child."

"I feel a spell coming on," he said, inspired by Kirby's own warning two days before. He pressed a trembling hand to his heart and staggered. "I'll end up a useless heap of cold spaghetti. Ah, the paintings I might have done. The world's losing a genius."

Clenching her fists, Kirby beat them on his worktable. Tools bounced and clattered while she let out a long wail. Protective, Fairchild placed his hands around his hawk and waited for the crisis to pass. At length, she slumped back in the chair, breathless.

"You used to do better than that," he observed. "I think you're mellowing."

"Papa." Kirby clamped her teeth to keep from grinding them. "I know I'll be forced to beat you about the head and ears, then I'll be arrested for patricide. You know I've a terror of closed-in places. I'd go mad in prison. Do you want that on your conscience?"

"Kirby, have I ever given you cause for one moment's worry?"

"Don't force me into a recital, Papa, it's after midnight. What have you done with the Rembrandt?"

"Done with it?" He frowned and fiddled with the cover of his hawk. "What do you mean, done with it?"

"Where is it?" she asked, carefully spacing the words. "You can't leave a painting like that lying around the house, particularly when you've chosen to have company."

"Company? Oh, you mean Adam. Fine boy. I'm fond of him already." His eyebrows wiggled twice. "You seem to be finding him agreeable."

Kirby narrowed her eyes. "Leave Adam out of this."

"Dear, dear, dear." Fairchild grinned lavishly. "And I thought you'd brought him up."

"Where *is* the Rembrandt?" All claim to patience disintegrated. Briefly, she considered banging her head on the table, but she'd given up that particular ploy at ten.

"Safe and secure, my sweet." Fairchild's voice was calm and pleased. "Safe and secure."

"Here? In the house?"

"Of course." He gave her an astonished look. "You don't think I'd keep it anywhere else?"

"Where?"

"You don't need to know everything." With a flourish, he whipped off his painting smock and tossed it over a chair. "Just content yourself that it's safe, hidden with appropriate respect and affection."

"Papa."

"Kirby." He smiled—a gentle father's smile. "A child must trust her parent, must abide by the wisdom of his years. You do trust me, don't you?"

"Yes, of course, but—"

He cut her off with the first bars of "Daddy's Little Girl" in a wavering falsetto.

Kirby moaned and lowered her head to the table. When would she learn? And how was she going to deal with him this time? He continued to sing until the giggles welled up and escaped. "You're incorrigible." She lifted her head and took a deep breath. "I have this terrible feeling that you're leaving out a mountain of details and that I'm going to go along with you anyway."

"Details, Kirby." His hand swept them aside. "The world's too full of details, they clutter things up. Remember, art reflects life, and life's an illusion. Come now, I'm tired." He walked to her and held out his hand. "Walk your old papa to bed."

Defeated, she accepted his hand and stood. Never, never would she learn. And always, always would she adore him. Together they walked from the room.

Adam watched as they started down the steps, arm in arm.

"Papa . . ." Only feet away from Adam's hiding place, Kirby stopped. "There is, of course, a logical reason for all this?"

"Kirby." Adam could see the mobile face move into calm, sober lines. "Have I ever done anything without a sensible, logical reason?"

She started with a near-soundless chuckle. In moments, her laughter rang out, rich and musical. It echoed back, faint and ghostly, until she rested her head against her father's shoulder. In the half-light, with her eyes shining, Adam thought she'd never looked more alluring. "Oh, my papa," she began in a clear contralto. "To me he is so wonderful." Linking her arm through Fairchild's, she continued down the steps.

Rather pleased with himself, and with his offspring, Fairchild joined her in his wavery falsetto. Their mixed voices drifted over Adam until the distance swallowed them.

Leaving the shadows, he stood at the head of the stairway. Once he heard Kirby's laugh, then there was silence.

"Curiouser and curiouser," he murmured.

Both Fairchilds were probably mad. They fascinated him.

CHAPTER 5

In the morning the sky was gray and the rain sluggish. Adam was tempted to roll over, close his eyes and pretend he was in his own well-organized home, where a housekeeper tended to the basics and there wasn't a gargoyle in sight. Partly from curiosity, partly from courage, he rose and prepared to deal with the day.

From what he'd overheard the night before, he didn't count on learning much from Kirby. Apparently she'd known less about the matter of the Rembrandt than he. Adam was equally sure that no matter how much he prodded and poked, Fairchild would let nothing slip. He might look innocent and harmless, but he was as shrewd as they came. And potentially dangerous, Adam mused, remembering how cleanly Fairchild had dealt with Hiller.

The best course of action remained the nightly searches with the aid of the passages. The days he determined for his own sanity to spend painting.

I shouldn't be here in the first place, Adam told himself as he stood in the shower under a strong cold spray of water. If it hadn't been for the fact that Mac tantalized me with the Rembrandt, I *wouldn't* be here. The last time, he promised himself as he toweled off. The very last time.

Once the Fairchild hassle was over, painting would not

only be his first order of business, it would be his only business.

Dressed, and content with the idea of ending his secondary career in a few more weeks, Adam walked down the hallway thinking of coffee. Kirby's door was wide open. As he passed, he glanced in. Frowning, he stopped, walked back and stood in the doorway.

"Good morning, Adam. Isn't it a lovely day?" She smiled, upside down, as she stood on her head in the corner.

Deliberately he glanced at the window to make sure he was on solid ground. "It's raining."

"Don't you like the rain? I do." She rubbed her nose with the back of her hand. "Look at it this way, there must be dozens of places where the sun's shining. It's all relative. Did you sleep well?"

"Yes." Even in her current position, Adam could see that her face glowed, showing no signs of a restless night.

"Come in and wait a minute, I'll go down to breakfast with you."

He walked over to stand directly in front of her. "Why are you standing on your head?"

"It's a theory of mine." She crossed her ankles against the wall while her hair pooled onto the carpet. "Could you sit down a minute? It's hard for me to talk to you when your head's up there and mine's down here."

Knowing he'd regret it, Adam crouched. Her sweater had slipped up, showing a thin line of smooth midriff.

"Thanks. My theory is that all night I've been horizontal, and most of the day I'll be right side up. So . . ." Somehow she managed to shrug. "I stand on my head in the morning and before bed. That way the blood can slosh around a bit."

Adam rubbed his nose between his thumb and forefinger. "I think I understand. That terrifies me."

"You should try it."

"I'll just let my blood stagnate, thanks."

"Suit yourself. You'd better stand back, I'm coming up."

She dropped her feet and righted herself with a quick athletic agility that surprised him. Facing him, she pushed at the hair that floated into her eyes. As she tossed it back she gave him a long, slow smile.

"Your face is red," he murmured, more in his own defense than for any other reason.

"Can't be helped, it's part of the process." She'd spent a good many hours arguing with herself the night before. This morning she'd decided to let things happen as they happened. "It's the only time I blush," she told him. "So, if you'd like to say something embarrassing . . . or flattering . . . ?"

Against his better judgment, he touched her, circling her waist with his hands. She didn't move back, didn't move forward, but simply waited. "Your blush is already fading, so it seems I've missed my chance."

"You can give it another try tomorrow. Hungry?"

"Yes." Her lips made him hungry, but he wasn't ready to test himself quite yet. "I want to go through your clothes after breakfast."

"Oh, really?" She drew out the word, catching her tongue between her teeth.

His brow lifted, but only she was aware of the gesture. "For the painting."

"You don't want to do a nude." The humor in her eyes faded into boredom as she drew away. "That's the usual line."

"I don't waste my time with lines." He studied her—the cool gray eyes that could warm with laughter, the haughty mouth that could invite and promise with no more than a smile. "I'm going to paint you because you were meant to be painted. I'm going to make love with you for exactly the same reason."

Her expression didn't change, but her pulse rate did. Kirby wasn't foolish enough to pretend even to herself it was anger. Anger and excitement were two different things. "How decisive and arrogant of you," she drawled. Strolling over to her dresser, she picked up her brush and ran it quickly through her hair. "I haven't agreed to pose for you, Adam, nor have I agreed to sleep with you." She flicked the brush through a last time then set it down. "In fact, I've serious doubts that I'll do either. Shall we go?"

Before she could get to the door, he had her. The speed surprised her, if the strength didn't. She'd hoped to annoy him, but when she tossed her head back to look at him, she didn't see temper. She saw cool, patient determination. Nothing could have been more unnerving.

Then he had her close, so that his face was a blur and his mouth was dominant. She didn't resist. Kirby rarely resisted what she wanted. Instead she let the heat wind through her in a slow continuous stream that was somehow both terrifying and peaceful.

Desire. Wasn't that how she'd always imagined it would be with the right man? Wasn't that what she'd been waiting for since the first moment she'd discovered herself a woman? It was here now. Kirby opened her arms to it.

His heartbeat wasn't steady, and it should have been. His mind wasn't clear, and it had to be. How could he win with her when he lost ground every time he was around her? If he followed through on his promise—or threat—that they'd be lovers, how much more would he lose? And gain, he thought as he let himself become steeped in her. The risk was worth taking.

"You'll pose for me," he said against her mouth. "And you'll make love with me. There's no choice."

That was the word that stopped her. That was the phrase that forced her to resist. She'd always have a choice. "I don't—"

"For either of us," Adam finished as he released her. "We'll decide on the clothes after breakfast." Because he didn't want to give either of them a chance to speak, he propelled her from the room.

An hour later, he propelled her back.

She'd been serene during the meal. But he hadn't been

fooled. Livid was what she was, and livid was exactly how
he wanted her. She didn't like to be outmaneuvered, even on
a small point. It gave him a surge of satisfaction to be able to
do so. The defiant, sulky look in her eyes was exactly what
he wanted for the portrait.

"Red, I think," he stated. "It would suit you best."

Kirby waved a hand at her closet and flopped backward
onto her bed. Staring up at the ceiling, she thought through
her position. It was true she'd always refused to be painted,
except by her father. She hadn't wanted anyone else to get
that close to her. As an artist, she knew just how intimate the
relationship was between painter and subject, be the subject
a person or a bowl of fruit. She'd never been willing to share
herself with anyone to that extent.

But Adam was different. She could, if she chose, tell herself it was because of his talent, and because he wanted to
paint her, not flatter her. It wasn't a lie, but it wasn't quite the
truth. Still, Kirby was comfortable with partial truths in certain cases. If she was honest, she had to admit that she was
curious to see just how she'd look from his perspective, and
yet she wasn't entirely comfortable with that.

Moving only her eyes, she watched him as he rummaged
through her closet.

He didn't have to know what was going on in her head.
Certainly she was skilled in keeping her thoughts to herself.
It might be a challenge to do so under the sharp eyes of an
artist. It might be interesting to see just how difficult she
could make it for him. She folded her hands demurely on her
stomach.

While Kirby was busy with her self-debate, Adam looked
through an incredible variety of clothes. Some were perfect
for an orphan, others for an eccentric teenager. He wondered
if she'd actually worn the purple miniskirt and just how she'd
looked in it. Elegant gowns from Paris and New York hung
haphazardly with army surplus. If clothes reflected the person,

there was more than one Kirby Fairchild. He wondered just how many she'd show him.

He discarded one outfit after another. This one was too drab, that one too chic. He found a pair of baggy overalls thrown over the same hanger with a slinky sequin dress with a two-thousand-dollar label. Pushing aside a three-piece suit perfect for an assistant D.A., he found it.

Scarlet silk. It was undoubtedly expensive, but not chic in the way he imagined Melanie Burgess would design. The square-necked bodice tapered to a narrow waist before the material flared into a full skirt. There were flounces at the hem and underskirts of white and black and fuchsia. The sleeves were short and puffed, running with stripes of the same colors. It was perfect.

"This." Adam carried it to the bed and stood over Kirby. With a frown, she continued to stare up at the ceiling. "Put it on and come up to the studio. I'll do some sketches."

She spoke without looking at him. "Do you realize that not once have you asked me to pose for you? You told me you wanted to paint me, you told me you were going to paint me, but you've never *asked* if you could paint me." With her hands still folded, one finger began to tap. "Instinct tells me you're basically a gentleman, Adam. Perhaps you've just forgotten to say please."

"I haven't forgotten." He tossed the dress across the bottom of the bed. "But I think you hear far too many pleases from men. You're a woman who brings men to their knees with the bat of an eye. I'm not partial to kneeling." No, he wasn't partial to kneeling, and it was becoming imperative that he handle the controls, for both of them. Bending over, he put his hands on either side of her head then sat beside her. "And I'm just as used to getting my own way as you are."

She studied him, thinking over his words and her position. "Then again, I haven't batted my eyes at you yet."

"Haven't you?" he murmured.

He could smell her, that wild, untamed fragrance that was suited to isolated winter nights. Her lips pouted, not by design, but mood. It was that that tempted him. He had to taste them. He did so lightly, as he'd intended. Just a touch, just a taste, then he'd go about his business. But her mouth yielded to him as the whole woman hadn't. Or perhaps it conquered.

Desire scorched him. Fire was all he could relate to. Flames and heat and smoke. That was her taste. Smoke and temptation and a promise of unreasonable delights.

He tasted, but it was no longer enough. He had to touch.

Her body was small, delicate, something a man might fear to take. He did, but no longer for her sake. For his own. Small and delicate she might be, but she could slice a man in two. Of that he was certain. But as he touched, as he tasted, he didn't give a damn.

Never had he wanted a woman more. She made him feel like a teenager in the back seat of a car, like a man paying for the best whore in a French bordello, like a husband nuzzling into the security of a wife. Her complexities were more erotic than satin and lace and smoky light—the soft, agile mouth, the strong, determined hands. He wasn't certain he'd ever escape from either. In possessing her, he'd invite an endless cycle of complications, of struggles, of excitement. She was an opiate. She was a dive from a cliff. If he wasn't careful, he was going to overdose and hit the rocks.

It cost him more than he would have believed to draw back. She lay with her eyes half closed, her mouth just parted. Don't get involved, he told himself frantically. Get the Rembrandt and walk away. That's what you came to do.

"Adam . . ." She whispered his name as if she'd never said it before. It felt so beautiful on her tongue. The only thought that stayed with her was that no one had ever made her feel like this. No one else ever would. Something was opening inside her, but she wouldn't fight it. She'd give. The innocence in her eyes was real, emotional not physical. Seeing it, Adam felt desire flare again.

She's a witch, he told himself. Circe. Lorelei. He had to pull back before he forgot that. "You'll have to change."

"Adam . . ." Still swimming, she reached up and touched his face.

"Emphasize your eyes." He stood before he could take the dive.

"My eyes?" Mind blank, body throbbing, she stared up at him.

"And leave your hair loose." He strode to the door as she struggled up to her elbows. "Twenty minutes."

She wouldn't let him see the hurt. She wouldn't allow herself to feel the rejection. "You're a cool one, aren't you?" she said softly. "And as smooth as any I've ever run across. You might find yourself on your knees yet."

She was right—he could've strangled her for it. "That's a risk I'll have to take." With a nod, he walked through the door. "Twenty minutes," he called back.

Kirby clenched her fists together then slowly relaxed them. "On your knees," she promised herself. "I swear it."

* * *

Alone in Kirby's studio, Adam searched for the mechanism to the passageway. He looked mainly from curiosity. It was doubtful he'd need to rummage through a room that he'd been given free run in, but he was satisfied when he located the control. The panel creaked open, as noisily as all the others he'd found. After a quick look inside, he shut it again and went back to the first order of business—painting.

It was never a job, but it wasn't always a pleasure. The need to paint was a demand that could be soft and gentle, or sharp and cutting. Not a job, but work certainly, sometimes every bit as exhausting as digging a trench with a pick and shovel.

Adam was a meticulous artist, as he was a meticulous

man. Conventional, as Kirby had termed him, perhaps. But he
wasn't rigid. He was as orderly as she wasn't, but his creative
process was remarkably similar to hers. She might stare at
a piece of wood for an hour until she saw the life in it. He
would do the same with a canvas. She would feel a jolt, a
physical release the moment she saw what she'd been searching for. He'd feel that same jolt when something would leap
out at him from one of his dozens of sketches.

Now he was only preparing, and he was as calm and ordered as his equipment. On an easel he set the canvas, blank
and waiting. Carefully, he selected three pieces of charcoal.
He'd begin with them. He was going over his first informal
sketches when he heard her footsteps.

She paused in the doorway, tossed her head and stared at
him. With deliberate care, he set his pad back on the worktable.

Her hair fell loose and rich over the striped silk shoulders.
At a movement, the gold hoops at her ears and the half-dozen
gold bracelets on her arm jangled. Her eyes, darkened and
sooty, still smoldered with temper. Without effort, he could
picture her whirling around an open fire to the sound of violins and tambourines.

Aware of the image she projected, Kirby put both hands
on her hips and walked into the room. The full scarlet skirt
flowed around her legs. Standing in front of him, she whirled
around twice, turning her head each time so that she watched
him over her shoulder. The scent of wood smoke and roses
flowed into the room.

"You want to paint Katrina's picture, eh?" Her voice lowered into a sultry Slavic accent as she ran a fingertip down
his cheek. Insolence, challenge, and then a laugh that skid-
ded warm and dangerous over his skin. "First you cross her
palm with silver."

He'd have given her anything. What man wouldn't? Fighting her, fighting himself, he pulled out a cigarette. "Over by
the east window," he said easily. "The light's better there."

No, he wouldn't get off so easy. Behind the challenge and the insolence, her body still trembled for him. She wouldn't let him know it. "How much you pay?" she demanded, swirling away in a flurry of scarlet and silk. "Katrina not come free."

"Scale." He barely resisted the urge to grab her by the hair and drag her back. "And you won't get a dime until I'm finished."

In an abrupt change, Kirby brushed and smoothed her skirts. "Is something wrong?" she asked mildly. "Perhaps you don't like the dress after all."

He crushed out his cigarette in one grinding motion. "Let's get started."

"I thought we already had," she murmured. Her eyes were luminous and amused. He wanted to choke her every bit as much as he wanted to crawl for her. "You insisted on painting."

"Don't push me too far, Kirby. You have a tendency to bring out my baser side."

"I don't think I can be blamed for that. Maybe you've locked it up too long." Because she'd gotten precisely the reaction she'd wanted, she became completely cooperative. "Now, where do you want me to stand?"

"By the east window."

Tie score, she thought with satisfaction as she obliged him.

He spoke only when he had to—tilt your chin higher, turn your head. Within moments he was able to turn the anger and the desire into concentration. The rain fell, but its sound was muffled against the thick glass windows. With the tower door nearly closed, there wasn't another sound.

He watched her, studied her, absorbed her, but the man and the artist were working together. Perhaps by putting her on canvas, he'd understand her . . . and himself. Adam swept the charcoal over the canvas and began.

Now she could watch him, knowing that he was turned inward. She'd seen dozens of artists work; the old, the young, the talented, the amateur. Adam was, as she'd suspected, different.

He wore a sweater, one he was obviously at home in, but no smock. Even as he sketched he stood straight, as though his nature demanded that he remain always alert. That was one of the things she'd noticed about him first. He was always watching. A true artist did, she knew, but there seemed to be something more.

She called him conventional, knowing it wasn't quite true. Not quite. What was it about him that didn't fit into the mold he'd been fashioned for? Tall, lean, attractive, aristocratic, wealthy, successful, and . . . daring? That was the word that came to mind, though she wasn't completely sure why.

There was something reckless about him that appealed to her. It balanced the maturity, the dependability she hadn't known she'd wanted in a man. He'd be a rock to hold on to during an earthquake. And he'd be the earthquake. She was, Kirby realized, sinking fast. The trick would be to keep him from realizing it and making a fool of herself. Still, beneath it all, she liked him. That simple.

Adam glanced up to see her smiling at him. It was disarming, sweet and uncomplicated. Something warned him that Kirby without guards was far more dangerous than Kirby with them. When she let hers drop, he put his in place.

"Doesn't Hiller paint a bit?"

He saw her smile fade and tried not to regret it. "A bit."

"Haven't you posed for him?"

"No."

"Why not?"

The ice that came into her eyes wasn't what he wanted for the painting. The man and artist warred as he continued to sketch. "Let's say I didn't care much for his work."

"I suppose I can take that as a compliment to mine."

She gave him a long, neutral look. "If you like."

Deceit was part of the job, he reminded himself. What he'd

heard in Fairchild's studio left him no choice. "I'm surprised he didn't make an issue of it, being in love with you."

"He wasn't." She bit off the words, and ice turned to heat.

"He asked you to marry him."

"One hasn't anything to do with the other."

He looked up and saw she said exactly what she meant. "Doesn't it?"

"I agreed to marry him without loving him."

He held the charcoal an inch from the canvas, forgetting the painting. "Why?"

While she stared at him, he saw the anger fade. For a moment she was simply a woman at her most vulnerable. "Timing," she murmured. "It's probably the most important factor governing our lives. If it hadn't been for timing, Romeo and Juliet would've raised a half-dozen children."

He was beginning to understand, and understanding only made him more uncomfortable. "You thought it was time to get married?"

"Stuart's attractive, very polished, charming, and I'd thought harmless. I realized the last thing I wanted was a polished, charming, harmless husband. Still, I thought he loved me. I didn't break the engagement for a long time because I thought he'd make a convenient husband, and one who wouldn't demand too much." It sounded empty. It had been empty. "One who'd give me children."

"You want children?"

The anger was back, quickly. "Is there something wrong with that?" she demanded. "Do you think it strange that I'd want a family?" She made a quick, furious movement that had the gold jangling again. "This might come as a shock, but I have needs and feelings almost like a real person. And I don't have to justify myself to you."

She was halfway to the door before he could stop her. "Kirby, I'm sorry." When she tried to jerk out of his hold, he tightened it. "I *am* sorry."

"For what?" she tossed back.

"For hurting you," he murmured. "With stupidity."

Her shoulders relaxed under his hands, slowly, so that he knew it cost her. Guilt flared again. "All right. You hit a nerve, that's all." Deliberately she removed his hands from her shoulders and stepped back. He'd rather she'd slapped him. "Give me a cigarette, will you?"

She took one from him and let him light it before she turned away again. "When I accepted Stuart's proposal—"

"You don't have to tell me anything."

"I don't leave things half done." Some of the insolence was back when she whirled back to him. For some reason it eased Adam's guilt. "When I accepted, I told Stuart I wasn't in love with him. It didn't seem fair otherwise. If two people are going to have a relationship that means anything, it has to start out honestly, don't you think?"

He thought of the transmitter tucked into his briefcase. He thought of McIntyre waiting for the next report. "Yes."

She nodded. It was one area where she wasn't flexible. "I told him that what I wanted from him was fidelity and children, and in return I'd give him those things and as much affection as I could." She toyed with the cigarette, taking one of her quick, nervous drags. "When I realized things just wouldn't work for either of us that way, I went to see him. I didn't do it carelessly, casually. It was very difficult for me. Can you understand that?"

"Yes, I understand that."

It helped, she realized. More than Melanie's sympathy, more even than her father's unspoken support, Adam's simple understanding helped. "It didn't go well. I'd known there'd be an argument, but I hadn't counted on it getting so out of hand. He made a few choice remarks on my maternal abilities and my track record. Anyway, with all the blood and bone being strewn about, the real reason for him wanting to marry me came out."

She took a last puff on the cigarette and crushed it out

before she dropped into a chair. "He never loved me. He'd been unfaithful all along. I don't suppose it mattered." But she fell silent, knowing it did. "All the time he was pretending to care for me, he was using me." When she looked up again, the hurt was back in her eyes. She didn't know it—she'd have hated it. "Can you imagine how it feels to find out that all the time someone was holding you, talking with you, he was thinking of how you could be useful?" She picked up the piece of half-formed wood that would be her anger. "Useful," she repeated. "What a nasty word. I haven't bounced back from it as well as I should have."

He forgot McIntyre, the Rembrandt and the job he still had to do. Walking over, he sat beside her and closed his hand over hers. Under them was her anger. "I can't imagine any man thinking of you as useful."

When she looked up, her smile was already spreading. "What a nice thing to say. The perfect thing." Too perfect for her rapidly crumbling defenses. Because she knew it would take so little to have her turning to him now and later, she lightened the mood. "I'm glad you're going to be there Saturday."

"At the party?"

"You can send me long, smoldering looks and everyone'll think I jilted Stuart for you. I'm fond of petty revenge."

He laughed and brought her hands to his lips. "Don't change," he told her with a sudden intenseness that had her uncertain again.

"I don't plan on it. Adam, I— Oh, chicken fat, what're you doing here? This is a private conversation."

Wary, Adam turned his head and watched Montique bounce into the room. "He won't spread gossip."

"That isn't the point. I've told you you're not allowed in here."

Ignoring her, Montique scurried over and with an awkward leap plopped into Adam's lap. "Cute little devil," Adam decided as he scratched the floppy ears.

"Ah, Adam, I wouldn't do that."

"Why?"

"You're only asking for trouble."

"Don't be absurd. He's harmless."

"Oh, yes, he is. *She* isn't." Kirby nodded her head toward the doorway as Isabelle slinked through. "Now you're in for it. I warned you." Tossing back her head, Kirby met Isabelle's cool look equally. "I had nothing to do with it."

Isabelle blinked twice, then shifted her gaze to Adam. Deciding her responsibility had ended, Kirby sighed and rose. "There's nothing I can do," she told Adam and patted his shoulder. "You asked for it." With this, she swept out of the room, giving the cat a wide berth.

"I didn't ask him to come up here," Adam began, scowling down at Isabelle. "And there can't be any harm in— Oh, God," he murmured. "She's got me doing it."

CHAPTER 6

Let's walk," Kirby demanded when the afternoon grew late and Fairchild had yet to budge from his studio. Nor would he budge, she knew, until the Van Gogh was completed down to the smallest detail. If she didn't get out and forget about her father's pet project for a while, she knew she'd go mad.

"It's raining," Adam pointed out as he lingered over coffee.

"You mentioned that before." Kirby pushed away her own coffee and rose. "All right then, I'll have Cards bring you a lap robe and a nice cup of tea."

"Is that a psychological attack?"

"Did it work?"

"I'll get a jacket." He strode from the room, ignoring her quiet chuckle.

When they walked outside, the fine misting rain fell over them. Leaves streamed with it. Thin fingers of fog twisted along the ground. Adam hunched inside his jacket, thinking it was miserable weather for a walk. Kirby strolled along with her face lifted to the sky.

He'd planned to spend the afternoon on the painting, but perhaps this was better. If he was going to capture her with colors and brush strokes, he should get to know her better. No easy task, Adam mused, but a strangely appealing one.

The air was heavy with the fragrance of fall, the sky

gloomy. For the first time since he'd met her, Adam sensed a
serenity in Kirby. They walked in silence, with the rain flowing over them.

She was content. It was an odd feeling for her to identify
as she felt it so rarely. With her hand in his, she was content
to walk along as the fog moved along the ground and the
chilly drizzle fell over them. She was glad of the rain, of
the chill and the gloom. Later, there would be time for a
roaring fire and warm brandy.

"Adam, do you see the bed of mums over there?"

"Hmm?"

"The mums, I want to pick some. You'll have to be the
lookout."

"Lookout for what?" He shook wet hair out of his eyes.

"For Jamie, of course. He doesn't like anyone messing with
his flowers."

"They're your flowers."

"No, they're Jamie's."

"He works for you."

"What does that have to do with it?" She put a hand on his
shoulder as she scanned the area. "If he catches me, he'll get
mad, then he won't save me any leaves. I'll be quick—I've
done this before."

"But if you—"

"There's no time to argue. Now, you watch that window
there. He's probably in the kitchen having coffee with Tulip.
Give me a signal when you see him."

Whether he went along with her because it was simpler,
or because he was getting into the spirit of things despite himself, Adam wasn't sure. But he walked over to the window
and peeked inside. Jamie sat at a huge round table with a mug
of coffee in both frail hands. Turning, he nodded a go-ahead
to Kirby.

She moved like lightning, dashing to the flower bed and
plucking at stems. Dark and wet, her hair fell forward to

curtain her face as she loaded her arms with autumn flowers. She should be painted like this, as well, Adam mused. In the fog, with her arms full of wet flowers. Perhaps it would be possible to capture those odd little snatches of innocence in the portrait.

Idly he glanced back in the window. With a ridiculous jolt of panic, he saw Jamie rise and head for the kitchen door. Forgetting logic, Adam dashed toward her.

"He's coming."

Surprisingly swift, Kirby leaped over the bed of flowers and kept on going. Even though he was running full stride, Adam didn't catch her until they'd rounded the side of the house. Giggling and out of breath, she collapsed against him.

"We made it!"

"Just," he agreed. His own heart was thudding—from the race? Maybe. He was breathless—from the game? Perhaps. But they were wet and close and the fog was rising. It didn't seem he had a choice any longer.

With his eyes on hers, he brushed the dripping hair back from her face. Her cheeks were cool, wet and smooth. Yet her mouth, when his lowered to it, was warm and waiting.

She hadn't planned it this way. If she'd had the time to think, she'd have said she didn't want it this way. She didn't want to be weak. She didn't want her mind muddled. It didn't seem she had a choice any longer.

He could taste the rain on her, fresh and innocent. He could smell the sharp tang of the flowers that were crushed between them. He couldn't keep his hands out of her hair, the soft, heavy tangle of it. He wanted her closer. He wanted all of her, not in the way he'd first wanted her, but in every way. The need was no longer the simple need of a man for woman, but of him for her. Exclusive, imperative, impossible.

She'd wanted to fall in love, but she'd wanted to plan it out in her own way, in her own time. It wasn't supposed to happen in a crash and a roar that left her trembling. It wasn't supposed to happen without her permission. Shaken, Kirby drew back. It wasn't going to happen until she was ready. That was that. Nerves taut again, she made herself smile.

"It looks like we've done a good job of squashing them." When he would've drawn her back, Kirby thrust the flowers at him. "They're for you."

"For me?" Adam looked down at the mums they held between them.

"Yes, don't you like flowers?"

"I like flowers," he murmured. However unintentionally, she'd moved him as much with the gift as with the kiss. "I don't think anyone's given me flowers before."

"No?" She gave him a long, considering look. She'd been given floods of them over the years, orchids, lilies, roses and more roses, until they'd meant little more than nothing. Her smile came slowly as she touched a hand to his chest. "I'd've picked more if I'd known."

Behind them a window was thrown open. "Don't you know better than to stand in the rain and neck?" Fairchild demanded. "If you want to nuzzle, come inside. I can't stand sneezing and sniffling!" The window shut with a bang.

"You're terribly wet," Kirby commented, as if she hadn't noticed the steadily falling rain. She linked her arm with his and walked to the door that was opened by the ever-efficient Cards.

"Thank you." Kirby peeled off her soaking jacket. "We'll need a vase for the flowers, Cards. They're for Mr. Haines's room. Make sure Jamie's not about, will you?"

"Naturally, miss." Cards took both the dripping jackets and the dripping flowers and headed back down the hall.

"Where'd you find him?" Adam wondered aloud. "He's incredible."

"Cards?" Like a wet dog, Kirby shook her head. "Papa brought him back from England. I think he was a spy, or maybe it was a bouncer. In either case, it's obvious he's seen everything."

"Well, children, have you had a nice holiday?" Fairchild bounced out of the parlor. He wore a paint-streaked shirt and a smug smile. "My work's complete, and now I'm free to give my full attention to my sculpting. It's time I called Victor Alvarez," he murmured. "I've kept him dangling long enough."

"He'll dangle until after coffee, Papa." She sent her father a quick warning glance Adam might've missed if he hadn't been watching so closely. "Take Adam in the parlor and I'll see to it."

She kept him occupied for the rest of the day. Deliberately, Adam realized. Something was going on that she didn't want him getting an inkling of. Over dinner, she was again the perfect hostess. Over coffee and brandy in the parlor, she kept him entertained with an in-depth discussion on baroque art. Though her conversations and charm were effortless, Adam was certain there was an underlying reason. It was one more thing for him to discover.

She couldn't have set the scene better, he mused. A quiet parlor, a crackling fire, intelligent conversation. And she was watching Fairchild like a hawk.

When Montique entered, the scene changed. Once again, the scruffy puppy leaped into Adam's lap and settled down.

"How the hell did he get in here?" Fairchild demanded.

"Adam encourages him," Kirby stated as she sipped at her brandy. "We can't be held responsible."

"I should say not!" Fairchild gave both Adam and Montique a steely look. "And if that—that creature threatens to sue again, Adam will have to retain his own attorney. I won't be involved in a legal battle, particularly when I have my business with Senhor Alvarez to complete. What time is it in Brazil?"

"Some time or other," Kirby murmured.

"I'll call him immediately and close the deal before we find ourselves slapped with a summons."

Adam sat back with his brandy and scratched Montique's

ears. "You two don't seriously expect me to believe you're worried about being sued by a cat?"

Kirby ran a fingertip around the rim of her snifter. "I don't think we'd better tell him about what happened last year when we tried to have her evicted."

"No!" Fairchild leaped up and shuffled before he darted to the door. "I won't discuss it. I won't remember it. I'm going to call Brazil."

"Ah, Adam . . ." Kirby trailed off with a meaningful glance at the doorway.

Adam didn't have to look to know that Isabelle was making an entrance.

"I won't be intimidated by a cat."

"I'm sure that's very stalwart of you." Kirby downed the rest of her drink then rose. "Just as I'm sure you'll understand if I leave you to your courage. I really have to reline my dresser drawers."

For the second time that day, Adam found himself alone with a dog and cat.

A half hour later, after he'd lost a staring match with Isabelle, Adam locked his door and contacted McIntyre. In the brief, concise tones that McIntyre had always admired, Adam relayed the conversation he'd overheard the night before.

"It fits," McIntyre stated. Adam could almost see him rubbing his hands together. "You've learned quite a bit in a short time. The check on Hiller reveals he's living on credit and reputation. Both are running thin. No idea where Fairchild's keeping it?"

"I'm surprised he doesn't have it hanging in full view." Adam lit a cigarette and frowned at the Titian across the room. "It would be just like him. He mentioned a Victor Alvarez from Brazil a couple of times. Some kind of deal he's cooking."

"I'll see what I can dig up. Maybe he's selling the Rembrandt."

"He hardly needs the money."

"Some people never have enough."

"Yeah." But it didn't fit. It just didn't fit. "I'll get back to you."

Adam brooded, but only for a few moments. The sooner he had something tangible, the sooner he could untangle himself. He opened the panel and went to work.

* * *

In the morning, Kirby posed for Adam for more than two hours without the slightest argument. If he thought her cooperation and her sunny disposition were designed to confuse him, he was absolutely right. She was also keeping him occupied while Fairchild made the final arrangements for the disposal of the Van Gogh.

Adam had worked the night before until after midnight, but had found nothing. Wherever Fairchild had hidden the Rembrandt, he'd hidden it well. Adam's search of the third floor was almost complete. It was time to look elsewhere.

"Hidden with respect and affection," he remembered. In all probability that would rule out the dungeons and the attic. Chances were he'd have to give them some time, but he intended to concentrate on the main portion of the house first. His main objective would be Fairchild's private rooms, but when and how he'd do them he had yet to determine.

After the painting session was over and Kirby went back to her own work, Adam wandered around the first floor. There was no one to question his presence. He was a guest and he was trusted. He was supposed to be, he reminded himself when he became uncomfortable. One of the reasons McIntyre had drafted him for this particular job was because he would have easy access to the Fairchilds and the house. He was, socially and professionally, one of them. They'd have no reason to be suspicious of a well-bred, successful artist whom they'd welcomed into their own home. And the more Adam tried to justify his actions, the more the guilt ate at him.

Enough, he told himself as he stared out at the darkening sky. He'd had enough for one day. It was time he went up and changed for Melanie Burgess's party. There he'd meet Stuart Hiller and Harriet Merrick. There were no emotional ties there to make him feel like a spy and a thief. Swearing at himself, he started up the stairs.

"Excuse me, Mr. Haines." Impatient, Adam turned and looked down at Tulip. "Were you going up?"

"Yes." Because he stood on the bottom landing blocking her way, he stood aside to let her pass.

"You take this up to her then, and see she drinks it." Tulip shoved a tall glass of milky white liquid into his hand. "All," she added tersely before she clomped back toward the kitchen.

Where did they get their servants? Adam wondered, frowning down at the glass in his hands. And why, for the love of God, had he let himself be ordered around by one? When in Rome, he supposed, and started up the steps again.

The *she* obviously meant Kirby. Adam sniffed doubtfully at the glass as he knocked on her door.

"You can bring it in," she called out, "but I won't drink it. Threaten all you like."

All right, he decided, and pushed her door open. The bedroom was empty, but he could smell her.

"Do your worst," she invited. "You can't intimidate me with stories of intestinal disorders and vitamin deficiencies. I'm healthy as a horse."

The warm, sultry scent flowed over him. Glass in hand, he walked through and into the bathroom where the steam rose up, fragrant and misty as a rain forest. With her hair pinned on top of her head, Kirby lounged in a huge sunken tub. Overhead, hanging plants dripped down, green and moist. White frothy bubbles floated in heaps on the surface of the water.

"So she sent you, did she?" Unconcerned, Kirby rubbed a loofah sponge over one shoulder. The bubbles, she concluded, covered her with more modesty than most women at the party that night would claim. "Well, come in then, and stop scowling at me. I won't ask you to scrub my back."

He thought of Cleopatra, floating on her barge. Just how many men other than Caesar and Antony had she driven mad? He glanced at the long mirrored wall behind the sink. It was fogged with the steam that rose in visible columns from her bath. "Got the water hot enough?"

"Do you know what that is?" she demanded, and plucked her soap from the dish. The cake was a pale, pale pink and left a creamy lather on her skin. "It's a filthy-tasting mixture Tulip tries to force on me periodically. It has raw eggs in it and other vile things." Making a face she lifted one surprisingly long leg out of the bath and soaped it. "Tell me the truth, Adam, would you voluntarily drink raw eggs?"

He watched her run soap and fingertips down her calf. "I can't say I would."

"Well, then." Satisfied, she switched legs. "Down the drain with it."

"She told me to see that you drank it. All," he added, beginning to enjoy himself.

Her lower lip moved forward a bit as she considered. "Puts you in an awkward position, doesn't it?"

"A position in any case."

"Tell you what, I'll have a sip. Then when she asks if I drank it, I can say I did. I'm trying to cut down on my lying."

Adam handed her the glass, watching as she sipped and grimaced. "I'm not sure you're being truthful this way."

"I said cutting down, not eliminating. Into the sink," she added. "Unless you'd care for the rest."

"I'll pass." He poured it out then sat on the lip of the tub.

Surprised by the move, she tightened her fingers on the soap. It plopped into the water. "Hydrophobia," she muttered. "No, don't bother, I'll find it." Dipping her hand in, she began to search. "You'd think they could make a soap that wasn't forever leaping out of your hands." Grateful for the distraction, she gripped the soap again. "Aha. I appreciate your bringing me that revolting stuff, Adam. Now if you'd like to run along . . ."

"I'm in no hurry." Idly he picked up her loofah. "You mentioned something about scrubbing your back."

"Robbery!" Fairchild's voice boomed into the room just ahead of him. "Call the police. Call the FBI. Adam, you'll be a witness." He nodded, finding nothing odd in the audience to his daughter's bath.

"I'm so glad I have a large bathroom," she murmured. "Pity I didn't think to serve refreshments." Relieved by the interruption, she ran the soap down her arm. "What's been stolen, Papa? The Monet street scene, the Renoir portrait? I know, your sweat socks."

"My black dinner suit!" Dramatically he pointed a finger to the ceiling. "We'll have to take fingerprints."

"Obviously stolen by a psychotic with a fetish for formal attire," Kirby concluded. "I love a mystery. Let's list the suspects." She pushed a lock of hair out of her eyes and leaned back—a naked, erotic Sherlock Holmes. "Adam, have you an alibi?"

With a half smile, he ran the damp abrasive sponge through his hands. "I've been seducing Polly all afternoon."

Her eyes lit with amusement. She'd known he had potential. "That won't do," she said soberly. "It wouldn't take above fifteen minutes to seduce Polly. You have a black dinner suit, I suppose."

"Circumstantial evidence."

"A search warrant," Fairchild chimed in, inspired. "We'll get a search warrant and go through the entire house."

"Time-consuming," Kirby decided. "Actually, Papa, I think we'd best look to Cards."

"The butler did it." Fairchild cackled with glee, then immediately sobered. "No, no, my suit would never fit Cards."

"True. Still, as much as I hate to be an informer, I overheard Cards telling Tulip he intended to take your suit."

"Trust," Fairchild mumbled to Adam. "Can't trust anyone."

"His motive was sponging and pressing, I believe." She sank down to her neck and examined her toes. "He'll crumble like a wall if you accuse him. I'm sure of it."

"Very well." Fairchild rubbed his thin, clever hands together. "I'll handle it myself and avoid the publicity."

"A brave man," Kirby decided as her father strode out of the room. Relaxed and amused, she smiled at Adam. "Well, my bubbles seem to be melting, so we'd better continue this discussion some other time."

Reaching over, Adam yanked the chain and drew the old-fashioned plug out of the stupendous tub. "The time's coming when we're going to start—and finish—much more than a conversation."

Wary, Kirby watched her water level and last defense recede. When cornered, she determined, it was best to be nonchalant. She tried a smile that didn't quite conceal the nerves. "Let me know when you're ready."

"I intend to," he said softly. Without another word, he rose and left her alone.

* * *

Later, when he descended the stairs, Adam grinned when he heard her voice.

"Yes, Tulip, I drank the horrid stuff. I won't disgrace you by fainting in the Merrick living room from malnutrition." The low rumble of response that followed was dissatisfied. "Cricket wings, I've been walking in heels for half my life. They're not six inches, they're three. And I'll still have to look up at everyone over twelve. Go bake a cake, will you?"

He heard Tulip's mutter and sniff before she stomped out of the room and passed him.

"Adam, thank God. Let's go before she finds something else to nag me about."

Her dress was pure, unadorned white, thin and floaty. It covered her arms, rose high at the throat, as modest as a nun's habit, as sultry as a tropical night. Her hair fell, black and straight over the shoulders.

Tossing it back, she picked up a black cape and swirled it around her. For a moment she stood, adjusting it while the light from the lamps flitted over the absence of color. She looked like a Manet portrait—strong, romantic and timeless.

"You're a fabulous-looking creature, Kirby."

They both stopped, staring. He'd given compliments before, with more style, more finesse, but he'd never meant one more. She'd been flattered by princes, in foreign tongues and with smooth deliveries. It had never made her stomach flutter.

"Thank you," she managed. "So're you." No longer sure it was wise, she offered her hand. "Are you ready?"

"Yes. Your father?"

"He's already gone," she told him as she walked toward the door. And the sooner they were, the better. She needed a little more time before she was alone with him again. "We don't drive to parties together, especially to Harriet's. He likes to get there early and usually stays longer, trying to talk Harriet into bed. I've had my car brought around." She shut the door and led him to a silver Porsche. "I'd rather drive than navigate, if you don't mind."

But she didn't wait for his response as she dropped into the driver's seat. "Fine," Adam agreed.

"It's a marvelous night." She turned the key in the ignition. The power vibrated under their feet. "Full moon, lots of stars." Smoothly she released the brake, engaged the clutch and pressed the accelerator. Adam was tossed against the seat as they roared down the drive.

"You'll like Harriet," Kirby continued, switching gears as Adam stared at the blurring landscape. "She's like a mother to me." When they came to the main road, Kirby downshifted and swung to the left, tires squealing. "You met Melly, of course. I hope you won't desert me completely tonight after seeing her again."

Adam braced his feet against the floor. "Does anyone notice her when you're around?" And would they make it to the Merrick home alive?

"Of course." Surprised by the question, she turned to look at him.

"Good God, watch where you're going!" None too gently, he pushed her head around.

"Melly's the most perfectly beautiful woman I've ever known." Downshifting again, Kirby squealed around a right turn then accelerated. "She's a very clever designer and very, very proper. Wouldn't even take a settlement from her husband when they divorced. Pride, I suppose, but then she wouldn't need the money. There's a marvelous view of the Hudson coming up on your side, Adam." Kirby leaned over to point it out. The car swerved.

"I prefer seeing it from up here, thanks," Adam told her as he shoved her back in her seat. "Do you always drive this way?"

"Yes. There's the road you take to the gallery," she continued. She waved her hand vaguely as the car whizzed by an intersection. Adam glanced down at the speedometer.

"You're doing ninety."

"I always drive slower at night."

"There's good news." Muttering, he flicked on the lighter.

"There's the house up ahead." She raced around an ess curve. "Fabulous when it's all lit up this way."

The house was white and stately, the type you expected to see high above the riverbank. It glowed with elegance from dozens of windows. Without slackening pace, Kirby sped up the circular drive. With a squeal of brakes, and a muttered curse from Adam, she stopped the Porsche at the front entrance.

Reaching over, Adam pulled the keys from the ignition and pocketed them. "I'm driving back."

"How thoughtful." Offering her hand to the valet, Kirby stepped out. "Now I won't have to limit myself to one drink. Champagne," she decided, moving up the steps beside him. "It seems like a night for it."

The moment the door opened, Kirby was enveloped by a flurry of dazzling, trailing silks. "Harriet." Kirby squeezed the statuesque woman with flaming red hair. "It's wonderful to see you, but I think I'm being gnawed by the denture work of your crocodile."

"Sorry, darling." Harriet held her necklace and drew back to press a kiss to each of Kirby's cheeks. She was an impressive woman, full-bodied in the style Rubens had immortalized. Her face was wide and smooth, dominated by deep green eyes that glittered with silver on the lids. Harriet didn't believe in subtlety. "And this must be your houseguest," she continued with a quick sizing up of Adam.

"Harriet Merrick, Adam Haines." Kirby grinned and pinched Harriet's cheek. "And behave yourself, or Papa'll have him choosing weapons."

"Wonderful idea." With one arm still linked with Kirby's, Harriet twined her other through Adam's. "I'm sure you have a fascinating life story to tell me, Adam."

"I'll make one up."

"Perfect." She liked the look of him. "We've a crowd already, though they're mostly Melanie's stuffy friends."

"Harriet, you've got to be more tolerant."

"No, I don't." She tossed back her outrageous hair. "I've been excruciatingly polite. Now that you're here, I don't have to be."

"Kirby." Melanie swept into the hall in an ice-blue sheath. "What a picture you make. Take her cloak, Ellen, though it's a pity to spoil that effect." Smiling, she held out a hand to Adam as the maid slipped Kirby's cloak off her shoulders. "I'm so glad you came. We've some mutual acquaintances here, it seems. The Birminghams and Michael Towers from New York. You remember Michael, Kirby?"

"The adman who clicks his teeth?"

Harriet let out a roar of laughter while Adam struggled to control his. With a sigh, Melanie led them toward the party. "Try to behave, will you?" But Adam wasn't certain whether she spoke to Kirby or her mother.

This was the world he was used to—elegant people in elegant clothes having rational conversations. He'd been raised in the world of restrained wealth where champagne fizzed quietly and dignity was as essential as the proper alma mater. He understood it, he fit in.

After fifteen minutes, he was separated from Kirby and bored to death.

"I've decided to take a trek through the Australian bush," Harriet told Kirby. She fingered her necklace of crocodile teeth. "I'd love you to come with me. We'd have such fun brewing a billy cup over the fire."

"Camping?" Kirby asked, mulling it over. Maybe what she needed was a change of scene, after her father settled down.

"Give it some thought," Harriet suggested. "I'm not planning on leaving for another six weeks. Ah, Adam." Reaching out, she grabbed his arm. "Did Agnes Birmingham drive you to drink? No, don't answer. It's written all over your face, but you're much too polite."

He allowed himself to be drawn between her and Kirby, where he wanted to be. "Let's just say I was looking for more stimulating conversation. I've found it."

"Charming." She decided she liked him, but would reserve judgment a bit longer as to whether he'd suit her Kirby. "I admire your work, Adam. I'd like to put the first bid in on your next painting."

He took glasses from a passing waiter. "I'm doing a portrait of Kirby."

"She's posing for you?" Harriet nearly choked on her champagne. "Did you chain her?"

"Not yet." He gave Kirby a lazy glance. "It's still a possibility."

"You have to let me display it when it's finished." She might've been a woman who ran on emotion on many levels, but the bottom line was art, and the business of it. "I can promise to cause a nasty scene if you refuse."

"No one does it better," Kirby toasted her.

"You'll have to see the portrait of Kirby that Philip painted for me. She wouldn't sit for it, but it's brilliant." She toyed with the stem of her glass. "He painted it when she returned from Paris—three years ago, I suppose."

"I'd like to see it. I'd planned on coming by the gallery."

"Oh, it's here, in the library."

"Why don't you two just toddle along then?" Kirby suggested. "You've been talking around me, you might as well desert me physically, as well."

"Don't be snotty," Harriet told her. "You can come, too. And I . . . Well, well," she murmured in a voice suddenly lacking in warmth. "Some people have no sense of propriety."

Kirby turned her head, just slightly, and watched Stuart walk into the room. Her fingers tightened on the glass, but she shrugged. Before the movement was complete, Melanie was at her side.

"I'm sorry, Kirby. I'd hoped he wouldn't come after all."

In a slow, somehow insolent gesture, Kirby pushed her hair behind her back. "If it had mattered, I wouldn't have come."

"I don't want you to be embarrassed," Melanie began, only to be cut off by a quick and very genuine laugh.

"When have you ever known me to be embarrassed?"

"Well, I'll greet him, or it'll make matters worse." Still, Melanie hesitated, obviously torn between loyalty and manners.

"I'll fire him, of course," Harriet mused when her daughter went to do her duty. "But I want to be subtle about it."

"Fire him if you like, Harriet, but not on my account." Kirby drained her champagne.

"It appears we're in for a show, Adam." Harriet tapped a coral fingertip against her glass. "Much to Melanie's distress, Stuart's coming over."

Without saying a word, Kirby took Adam's cigarette.

"Harriet, you look marvelous." The smooth, cultured voice wasn't at all like the tone Adam had heard in Fairchild's studio. "Africa agreed with you."

Harriet gave him a bland smile. "We didn't expect to see you."

"I was tied up for a bit." Charming, elegant, he turned to Kirby. "You're looking lovely."

"So are you," she said evenly. "It seems your nose is back in joint." Without missing a beat, she turned to Adam. "I don't believe you've met. Adam, this is Stuart Hiller. I'm sure you know Adam Haines's work, Stuart."

"Yes, indeed." The handshake was polite and meaningless. "Are you staying in our part of New York long?"

"Until I finish Kirby's portrait," Adam told him and had the dual satisfaction of seeing Kirby grin and Stuart frown. "I've agreed to let Harriet display it in the gallery."

With that simple strategy, Adam won Harriet over.

"I'm sure it'll be a tremendous addition to our collection." Even a man with little sensitivity wouldn't have missed the waves of resentment. For the moment, Stuart ignored them. "I wasn't able to reach you in Africa, Harriet, and things have been hectic since your return. The Titian woman has been sold to Ernest Myerling."

As he lifted his glass, Adam's attention focused on Kirby. Her color drained, slowly, degree by degree until her face was as white as the silk she wore.

"I don't recall discussing selling the Titian," Harriet countered. Her voice was as colorless as Kirby's skin.

"As I said, I couldn't reach you. As the Titian isn't listed under your personal collection, it falls among the saleable paintings. I think you'll be pleased with the price." He lit a cigarette with a slim silver lighter. "Myerling did insist on having it tested. He's more interested in investment than art, I'm afraid. I thought you'd want to be there tomorrow for the procedure."

Oh, God, oh, my God! Panic, very real and very strong, whirled through Kirby's mind. In silence, Adam watched the fear grow in her eyes.

"Tested!" Obviously insulted, Harriet seethed. "Of all the gall, doubting the authenticity of a painting from my gallery. The Titian should not have been sold without my permission, and certainly not to a peasant."

"Testing isn't unheard-of, Harriet." Seeing a hefty commission wavering, Stuart soothed, "Myerling's a businessman, not an art expert. He wants facts." Taking a long drag, he blew out smoke. "In any case, the paperwork's already completed and there's nothing to be done about it. The deal's a fait accompli, hinging on the test results."

"We'll discuss this in the morning." Harriet's voice lowered as she finished off her drink. "This isn't the time or place."

"I—I have to freshen my drink," Kirby said suddenly. Without another word, she spun away to work her way through the crowd. The nausea, she realized, was a direct result of panic, and the panic was a long way from over. "Papa." She latched on to his arm and pulled him out of a discussion on Dali's versatility. "I have to talk to you. Now."

Hearing the edge in her voice, he let her drag him from the room.

CHAPTER 7

Kirby closed the doors of Harriet's library behind her and leaned back against them. She didn't waste any time. "The Titian's being tested in the morning. Stuart sold it."

"Sold it!" Fairchild's eyes grew wide, his face pink. "Impossible. Harriet wouldn't sell the Titian."

"She didn't. She was off playing with lions, remember?" Dragging both hands through her hair, she tried to speak calmly. "Stuart closed the deal, he just told her."

"I told you he was a fool, didn't I? Didn't I?" Fairchild repeated as he started dancing in place. "I told Harriet, too. Would anyone listen? No, not Harriet." He whirled around, plucked up a pencil from her desk and broke it in two. "She hires the idiot anyway and goes off to roam the jungle."

"There's no use going over that again!" Kirby snapped at him. "We've got to deal with the results."

"There wouldn't be any results if I'd been listened to. Stubborn woman falling for a pretty face. That's all it was." Pausing, he took a deep breath and folded his hands. "Well," he said in a mild voice, "this is a problem."

"Papa, this isn't an error in your checkbook."

"But it can be handled, probably with less effort. Any way out of the deal?"

"Stuart said the paperwork had been finalized. And it's Myerling," she added.

"That old pirate." He scowled a moment and gave Harriet's desk a quick kick. "No way out of it," Fairchild concluded. "On to the next step. We exchange them." He saw by Kirby's nod that she'd already thought of it. There was a quick flash of pride before anger set in. The round, cherubic face tightened. "By God, Stuart's going to pay for making me give up that painting."

"Very easily said, Papa." Kirby walked into the room until she stood toe to toe with him. "But who was it who settled Adam in the same room with the painting? Now we're going to have to get it out of his room, then get the copy from the gallery in without him knowing there's been a switch. I'm sure you've noticed Adam's not a fool."

Fairchild's eyebrows wiggled. His lips curved. He rubbed his palms together. "A plan."

Knowing it was too late for regrets, Kirby flopped into a chair. "We'll phone Cards and have him put the painting in my room before we get back."

He approved this with a brief nod. "You have a marvelous criminal mind, Kirby."

She had to smile. A sense of adventure was already spearing through the panic. "Heredity," she told her father. "Now, here's my idea. . . ." Lowering her voice, she began the outline.

"It'll work," Fairchild decided a few moments later.

"That has yet to be seen." It sounded plausible enough, but she didn't underestimate Adam Haines. "So there's nothing to be done but to do it."

"And do it well."

Her agreement was a careless shrug of her shoulders. "Adam should be too tired to notice that the Titian's gone, and after I make the exchange at the gallery, I'll slip it back into his room. Sleeping pills are the only way." She stared down at her hands, dissatisfied, but knowing it was the only way out. "I don't like doing this to Adam."

"He'll just get a good night's sleep." Fairchild sat on the arm of her chair. "We all need a good night's sleep now and again. Now we'd better go back or Melanie'll send out search parties."

"You go first." Kirby let out a deep breath. "I'll phone Cards and tell him to get started."

Kirby waited until Fairchild had closed the doors again before she went to the phone on Harriet's desk. She didn't mind the job she had to do, in fact she looked forward to it. Except for Adam's part. It couldn't be helped, she reminded herself, and gave Cards brief instructions.

Now, she thought as she replaced the receiver, it was too late to turn back. The die, so to speak, had been cast. The truth was, the hastily made plans for the evening would prove a great deal more interesting than a party. While she hesitated a moment longer, Stuart opened the door, then closed it softly behind him.

"Kirby." He crossed to her with a half smile on his face. His patience had paid off now that he'd found her alone. "We have to talk."

Not now, she thought on a moment's panic. Didn't she have enough to deal with? Then she thought of the way he'd humiliated her. The way he'd lied. Perhaps it was better to get everything over with at once.

"I think we said everything we had to say at our last meeting."

"Not nearly everything."

"Redundancy bores me," she said mildly. "But if you insist, I'll say this. It's a pity you haven't the money to suit your looks. Your mistake, Stuart, was in not making me want you—not the way you wanted me." Deliberately her voice dropped, low and seductive. She hadn't nearly finished paying him back. "You could deceive me about love, but not about lust. If you'd concentrated on that instead of greed, you might've had a chance. You are," she continued softly, "a liar and a cheat, and while that might've been an interesting diversion for a short time, I thank God you never got your hands on me or my money."

Before she could sweep around him, he grabbed her arm. "You'd better remember your father's habits before you sling mud."

She dropped her gaze to his hand, then slowly raised it again. It was a look designed to infuriate. "Do you honestly compare yourself with my father?" Her fury came out on a laugh, and the laugh was insult itself. "You'll never have his style, Stuart. You're second-rate, and you'll always be second-rate."

He brought the back of his hand across her face hard enough to make her stagger. She didn't make a sound. When she stared up at him, her eyes were slits, very dark, very dangerous slits. The pain meant nothing, only that he'd caused it and she had no way to pay him back in kind. Yet.

"You prove my point," Kirby said evenly as she brushed her fingers over her cheek. "Second-rate."

He wanted to hit her again, but balled his hands into fists. He needed her, for the moment. "I'm through playing games, Kirby. I want the Rembrandt."

"I'd take a knife to it before I saw Papa hand it over to you. You're out of your class, Stuart." She didn't bother to struggle when he grabbed her arms.

"Two days, Kirby. You tell the old man he has two days or it's you who'll pay."

"Threats and physical abuse are your only weapons." Abruptly, with more effort than she allowed him to see, Kirby turned her anger to ice. "I've weapons of my own, Stuart, infinitely more effective. And if I chose to drop to gutter tactics, you haven't the finesse to deal with me." She kept her eyes on his, her body still. He might curse her, but Stuart knew the truth when he heard it. "You're a snake," she added quietly. "And you can't stay off your belly for long. The fact that you're stronger than I is only a temporary advantage."

"Very temporary," Adam said as he closed the door at his back. His voice matched Kirby's chill for chill. "Take your hands off her."

Kirby felt the painful grip on her arms relax and watched Stuart struggle with composure. Carefully he straightened his tie. "Remember what I said, Kirby. It could be important to you."

"You remember how Byron described a woman's revenge," she countered as she rubbed the circulation back into her arms. "'Like a tiger's spring—deadly, quick and crushing.'" She dropped her arms to her sides. "It could be important to you." Turning, she walked to the window and stared out at nothing.

Adam kept his hand on the knob as Stuart walked to the door. "Touch her again and you'll have to deal with me." Slowly Adam turned the knob and opened the door. "That's something else for you to remember." The sounds of the party flowed in, then silenced again as he shut the door at Stuart's back.

"Well," he began, struggling with his own fury. "I guess I should be grateful I don't have an ex-fiancée hanging around." He'd heard enough to know that the Rembrandt had been at the bottom of it, but he pushed that aside and went to her. "He's a poor loser, and you're amazing. Most women would have been weeping or pleading. You stood there flinging insults."

"I don't believe in pleading," she said as lightly as she could. "And Stuart would never reduce me to tears."

"But you're trembling," he murmured as he put his hands on her shoulders.

"Anger." She drew in a deep breath and let it out slowly. She didn't care to show a weakness, not to anyone. "I appreciate the white-knight routine."

He grinned and kissed the top of her head. "Any time. Why don't we . . ." He trailed off as he turned her to face him. The mark of Stuart's hand had faded to a dull, angry red, but it was unmistakable. When Adam touched his fingers to her cheek, his eyes were cold. Colder and more dangerous than she'd ever seen them. Without a word, he spun around and headed for the door.

"No!" Desperation wasn't characteristic, but she felt it now as she grabbed his arm. "No, Adam, don't. Don't get involved." He shook her off, but she sprinted to the door ahead of him and stood with her back pressed against it. The tears she'd been able to control with Stuart now swam in her eyes. "Please, I've enough on my conscience without dragging you into this. I live my life as I choose, and what I get from it is of my own making."

He wanted to brush her aside and push through the crowd outside the door until he had his hands on Stuart. He wanted, more than he'd ever wanted anything, the pleasure of smelling the other man's blood. But she was standing in front of him, small and delicate, with tears in her eyes. She wasn't the kind of woman tears came easily to.

"All right." He brushed one from her cheek and made a promise on it. Before it was over, he would indeed smell Stuart Hiller's blood. "You're only postponing the inevitable."

Relieved, she closed her eyes a moment. When she opened them again, they were still damp, but no longer desperate. "I don't believe in the inevitable." She took his hand and brought it to her cheek, holding it there a moment until she felt the tension drain from both of them. "You must've come in to see my portrait. It's there, above the desk."

She gestured, but he didn't take his eyes from hers. "I'll have to give it a thorough study, right after I give my attention to the original." He gathered her close and just held her. It was, though neither one of them had known it, the perfect gesture of support. Resting her head against his shoulder, she thought of peace, and she thought of the plans that had already been put into motion.

"I'm sorry, Adam."

He heard the regret in her voice and brushed his lips over her hair. "What for?"

"I can't tell you." She tightened her arms around his waist and clung to him as she had never clung to anyone. "But I am sorry."

* * *

The drive away from the Merrick estate was more sedate than the approach. Kirby sat in the passenger seat. Under most circumstances, Adam would've attributed her silence and unease to her scene with Hiller. But he remembered her reaction at the mention of the sale of a Titian.

What was going on in that kaleidoscope brain of hers? he wondered. And how was he going to find out? The direct approach, Adam decided, and thought fleetingly that it was a shame to waste the moonlight. "The Titian that's been sold," he began, pretending he didn't see Kirby jolt. "Has Harriet had it long?"

"The Titian." She folded her hands in her lap. "Oh, years and years. Your Mrs. Birmingham's shaped like a zucchini, don't you think?"

"She's not my Mrs. Birmingham." A new game, he concluded, and relaxed against the seat. "It's too bad it was sold before I could see it. I'm a great admirer of Titian. The painting in my room's exquisite."

Kirby let out a sound that might have been a nervous giggle. "The one at the gallery is just as exquisite," she told him. "Ah, here we are, home again. Just leave the car out front," she said, half relieved, half annoyed, that the next steps were being put into play. "Cards will see to it. I hope you don't mind coming back early, Adam. There's Papa," she added as she stepped from the car. "He must've struck out with Harriet. Let's have a nightcap, shall we?"

She started up the steps without waiting for his agreement.

Knowing he was about to become a part of some hastily conceived plan, he went along. It's all too pat, he mused as Fairchild waited at the door with a genial smile.

"Too many people," Fairchild announced. "I much prefer small parties. Let's have a drink in the parlor and gossip."

Don't look so bloody anxious, Kirby thought, and nearly scowled at him. "I'll go tell Cards to see to the Rolls and my car." Still, she hesitated as the men walked toward the parlor. Adam caught the indecision in her eyes before Fairchild cackled and slapped him on the back.

"And don't hurry back," he told Kirby. "I've had enough of women for a while."

"How sweet." The irony and strength came back into her voice. "I'll just go in and eat Tulip's lemon trifle. All," she added as she swept past.

Fairchild thought of his midnight snack with regret. "Brat," he muttered. "Well, we'll have Scotch instead."

Adam dipped his hands casually in his pockets and watched every move Fairchild made. "I had a chance to see Kirby's portrait in Harriet's library. It's marvelous."

"One of my best, if I say so myself." Fairchild lifted the decanter of Chivas Regal. "Harriet's fond of my brat, you know." In a deft move, Fairchild slipped two pills from his pocket and dropped them into the Scotch.

Under normal circumstances Adam would've missed it. Clever hands, he thought as intrigued as he was amused. Very quick, very agile. Apparently they wanted him out of the way. He was going to find it a challenge to pit himself against both of them. With a smile, he accepted the drink, then turned to the Corot landscape behind him.

"Corot's treatment of light," Adam began, taking a small sip. "It gives all of his work such deep perspective."

No ploy could've worked better. Fairchild was ready to roll. "I'm very partial to Corot. He had such a fine hand with details without being finicky and obscuring the over-all painting. Now the leaves," he began, and set down his drink to point them out. While the lecture went on, Adam set down his own drink, picked up Fairchild's and enjoyed the Scotch.

Upstairs Kirby found the Titian already wrapped in heavy paper. "Bless you, Cards," she murmured. She checked her watch and made herself wait a full ten minutes before she picked up the painting and left the room. Quietly she moved down the back stairs and out to where her car waited.

In the parlor, Adam studied Fairchild as he sat in the corner of the sofa, snoring. Deciding the least he could do was to make his host more comfortable, Adam started to swing Fairchild's legs onto the couch. The sound of a car engine stopped him. Adam was at the window in time to see Kirby's Porsche race down the drive.

"You're going to have company," he promised her. Within moments, he was behind the wheel of the Rolls.

The surge of speed added to Kirby's sense of adventure. She drove instinctively while she concentrated on her task for the evening. It helped ease the guilt over Adam, a bit.

A quarter mile from the gallery, she stopped and parked on the side of the road. Grateful that the Titian was relatively small, though the frame added weight, she gathered it up again and began to walk. Her heels echoed on the asphalt.

Clouds drifted across the moon, obscuring the light then freeing it again. With her cape swirling around her, Kirby walked into the cover of trees that bordered the gallery. The light was dim, all shadows and secrets. Up ahead came the low moan of an owl. Tossing back her hair, she laughed.

"Perfect," she decided. "All we need is a rumble of thunder and a few streaks of lightning. Skulking through the woods on a desperate mission," she mused. "Surrounded by the sounds of night." She shifted the bundle in her arms and continued on. "What one does for those one loves."

She could see the stately red brick of the gallery through the trees. Moonlight slanted over it. Almost there, she thought with a quick glance at her watch. In an hour she'd be back home—and perhaps she'd have the lemon trifle after all.

A hand fell heavily on her shoulder. Her cape spread out like wings as she whirled. Great buckets of blood, she thought as she stared up at Adam.

"Out for a stroll?" he asked her.

"Why, hello, Adam." Since she couldn't disappear, she had to face him down. She tried a friendly smile. "What are you doing out here?"

"Following you."

"Flattering. But wasn't Papa entertaining you?"

"He dozed off."

She stared up at him a moment, then let out a breath. A wry smile followed it. "I suppose he deserved it. I hope you left him comfortable."

"Enough. Now what's in the package?"

Though she knew it was useless, she fluttered her lashes. "Package?"

He tapped his finger on the wrapping.

"Oh, this package. Just a little errand I have to run. It's getting late, shouldn't you be starting back?"

"Not a chance."

"No." She moved her shoulders. "I thought not."

"What's in the package, Kirby, and what do you intend to do with it?"

"All right." She thrust the painting into his arms because hers were tiring. When the jig was up, you had to make the best of it. "I suppose you deserve an explanation, and you won't leave until you have one anyway. It has to be the condensed version, Adam, I'm running behind schedule." She laid a hand on the package he held. "This is the Titian woman, and I'm going to put it in the gallery."

He lifted a brow. He didn't need Kirby to tell him that he held a painting. "I was under the impression that the Titian woman was in the gallery."

"No . . ." She drew out the word. If she could have thought

of a lie, a half-truth, a fable, she'd have used it. She could only think of the truth. "This is a Titian," she told him with a nod to the package. "The painting in the gallery is a Fairchild."

He let the silence hang a moment while the moonlight filtered over her face. She looked like an angel . . . or a witch. "Your father forged a Titian and palmed it off on the gallery as an original?"

"Certainly not!" Indignation wasn't feigned. Kirby bit back on it and tried to be patient. "I won't tell you any more if you insult my father."

"I don't know what came over me."

"All right then." She leaned back against a tree. "Perhaps I should start at the beginning."

"Good choice."

"Years ago, Papa and Harriet were vacationing in Europe. They came across the Titian, each one swearing they'd seen it first. Neither one would give way, and it would've been criminal to let the painting go altogether. They compromised." She gestured at the package. "Each paid half, and Papa painted a copy. They rotate ownership of the original every six months, alternating with the copy, if you get the drift. The stipulation was that neither of them could claim ownership. Harriet kept hers in the gallery—not listing it as part of her private collection. Papa kept it in a guest room."

He considered for a moment. "That's too ridiculous for you to have made up."

"Of course I didn't make it up." As it could, effectively, her bottom lip pouted. "Don't you trust me?"

"No. You're going to do a lot more explaining when we get back."

Perhaps, Kirby thought. And perhaps not.

"Now just how do you intend to get into the gallery?"

"With Harriet's keys."

"She gave you her keys?"

Kirby let out a frustrated breath. "Pay attention, Adam. Harriet's furious about Stuart selling the painting, but until

she studies the contracts there's no way to know how binding
the sale is. It doesn't look good, and we can't take a chance
on having the painting tested—my father's painting, that is.
If the procedure were sophisticated enough, it might prove
that the painting's not sixteenth-century."

"Harriet's aware that a forgery's hanging in her gallery?"

"An emulation, Adam."

"And are there any other . . . emulations in the Merrick
Gallery?"

She gave him a long, cool look. "I'm trying not to be annoyed. All of Harriet's paintings are authentic, as is her half
of the Titian."

"Why didn't she replace it herself?"

"Because," Kirby began and checked her watch. Time was
slipping away from her. "Not only would it have been difficult
for her to disappear from the party early as we did, but it
would've been awkward altogether. The night watchman could
report to Stuart that she came to the gallery in the middle of
the night carrying a package. He might put two and two together. Yes, even he might add it up."

"So what'll the night watchman have to say about Kirby
Fairchild coming into the gallery in the middle of the night?"

"He won't see us." Her smile was quick and very, very
smug.

"Us?"

"Since you're here." She smiled at him again, and meant
it. "I've told you everything, and being a gentleman you'll
help me make the switch. We'll have to work quickly. If we're
caught, we'll just brazen it out. You won't have to do anything,
I'll handle it."

"You'll handle it." He nodded at the drifting clouds. "We
can all sleep easy now. One condition." He stopped her before she could speak. "When we're done, if we're not in jail
or hospitalized, I want to know it all. If we are in jail, I'll murder you as slowly as possible."

"That's two conditions," she muttered. "But all right."

They watched each other a moment, one wondering how much would have to be divulged, one wondering how much could be learned. Both found the deceit unpleasant.

"Let's get it done." Adam gestured for her to go first.

Kirby walked across the grass and went directly to the main door. From the deep pocket of her cloak, she drew out keys.

"These two switch off the main alarm," she explained as she turned keys in a series of locks. "And these unbolt the door." She smiled at the faint click of tumblers. Turning, she studied Adam, standing behind her in his elegant dinner suit. "I'm so glad we dressed for it."

"Seems right to dress formally when you're breaking into a distinguished institution."

"True." Kirby dropped the keys back in her pocket. "And we do make a rather stunning couple. The Titian hangs in the west room on the second floor. The watchman has a little room in the back, here on the main floor. I assume he drinks black coffee laced with rum and reads pornographic magazines. I would. He's supposed to make rounds hourly, though there's no way to be certain he's diligent."

"And what time does he make them, if he does?"

"On the hour—which gives us twenty minutes." She glanced at her watch and shrugged. "That's adequate, though if you hadn't pressed me for details we'd've had more time. Don't scowl," she added. She pressed her finger to her lips and slipped through the door.

From out of the depths of her pocket came a flashlight. They followed the narrow beam over the carpet. Together they moved up the staircase.

Obviously she knew the gallery well. Without hesitation, she moved through the dark, turning on the second floor and marching down the corridor without breaking rhythm. Her cape swirled out as she pivoted into a room. In silence she played her light over paintings until it stopped on the copy of the Titian that had hung in Adam's room.

"There," Kirby whispered as the light shone on the sunset hair Titian had immortalized. The light was too poor for Adam to be certain of the quality, but he promised himself he'd examine it minutes later.

"It's not possible to tell them apart—not even an expert." She knew what he was thinking. "Harriet's a respected authority, and she couldn't. I'm not sure the tests wouldn't bear it out as authentic. Papa has a way of treating the paints." She moved closer so that her light illuminated the entire painting. "Papa put a red circle on the back of the copy's frame so they could be told apart. I'll take the package now," she told him briskly. "You can get the painting down." She knelt and began to unwrap the painting they'd brought with them. "I'm glad you happened along," she decided. "Your height's going to be an advantage when it comes to taking down and putting up again."

Adam paused with the forgery in his hands. Throttling her would be too noisy at the moment, he decided. But later . . . "Let's have it then."

In silence they exchanged paintings. Adam replaced his on the wall, while Kirby wrapped the other. After she'd tied the string, she played the light on the wall again. "It's a bit crooked," she decided. "A little to the left."

"Look, I—" Adam broke off at the sound of a faint, tuneless whistle.

"He's early!" Kirby whispered as she gripped the painting. "Who expects efficiency from hired help these days?"

In a quick move, Adam had the woman, the painting and himself pressed against the wall by the archway. Finding herself neatly sandwiched, and partially smothered, Kirby held back a desperate urge to giggle. Certain it would annoy Adam, she held her breath and swallowed.

The whistle grew louder.

In her mind's eye, Kirby pictured the watchman strolling down the corridor, pausing to shine his light here and there as he walked. She hoped, for the watchman's peace of mind and Adam's disposition, the search was cursory.

Adam felt her trembling and held her tighter. Somehow he'd manage to protect her. He forgot that she'd gotten him into the mess in the first place. Now his only thought was to get her out of it.

A beam of light streamed past the doorway, with the whistle close behind. Kirby shook like a leaf. The light bounced into the room, sweeping over the walls in a curving arch. Adam tensed, knowing discovery was inches away. The light halted, rested a moment, then streaked away over its original route. And there was darkness.

They didn't move, though Kirby wanted to badly, with the frame digging into her back. They waited, still and silent, until the whistling receded.

Because her light trembling had become shudder after shudder, Adam drew her away to whisper reassurance. "It's all right. He's gone."

"You were wonderful." She covered her mouth to muffle the laughter. "Ever thought about making breaking and entering a hobby?"

He slid the painting under one arm, then took a firm grip on hers. When the time was right, he'd pay her back for this one. "Let's go."

"Okay, since it's probably a bad time to show you around. Pity," she decided. "There are some excellent engravings in the next room, and a really marvelous still life Papa painted."

"Under his own name?"

"Really, Adam." They paused at the hallway to make certain it was clear. "That's tacky."

They didn't speak again until they were hidden by the trees. Then Adam turned to her. "I'll take the painting and follow you back. If you go over fifty, I'll murder you."

She stopped when they reached the cars, then threw him off balance with suddenly serious eyes. "I appreciate everything, Adam. I hope you don't think too badly of us. It matters."

He ran a finger down her cheek. "I've yet to decide what I think of you."

Her lips curved up at the corners. "That's all right then. Take your time."

"Get in and drive," he ordered before he could forget what had to be resolved. She had a way of making a man forget a lot of things. Too many things.

The trip back took nearly twice the time, as Kirby stayed well below the speed limit. Again she left the Porsche out front, knowing Cards would handle the details. Once inside, she went straight to the parlor.

"Well," she mused as she looked at her father. "He seems comfortable enough, but I think I'll just stretch him out."

Adam leaned against the doorjamb and waited as she settled her father for the night. After loosening his tie and pulling off his shoes, she tossed her cape over him and kissed his balding head. "Papa," she murmured. "You've been outmaneuvered."

"We'll talk upstairs, Kirby. Now."

Straightening, Kirby gave Adam a long, mild look. "Since you ask so nicely." She plucked a decanter of brandy and two glasses from the bar. "We may as well be sociable during the inquisition." She swept by him and up the stairs.

CHAPTER 8

Kirby switched on the rose-tinted bedside lamp before she poured brandy. After handing Adam a snifter, she kicked off her shoes and sat cross-legged on the bed. She watched as he ripped off the wrapping and examined the painting.

Frowning, he studied the brush strokes, the use of color, the Venetian technique that had been Titian's. Fascinating, he thought. Absolutely fascinating. "This is a copy?"

She had to smile. She warmed the brandy between her hands but didn't drink. "Papa's mark's on the frame."

Adam saw the red circle but didn't find it conclusive. "I'd swear it was authentic."

"So would anyone."

He propped the painting against the wall and turned to her. She looked like an Indian priestess—the nightfall of hair against the virgin white silk. With an enigmatic smile, she continued to sit in the lotus position, the brandy cupped in both hands.

"How many other paintings in your father's collection are copies?"

Slowly she lifted the snifter and sipped. She had to work at not being annoyed by the question, telling herself he was entitled to ask. "All of the paintings in Papa's collection are authentic. Excepting now this Titian." She moved her shoulders carelessly. It hardly mattered at this point.

"When you spoke of his technique in treating paints for age, you didn't give the impression he'd only used it on one painting."

What had given her the idea he wouldn't catch on to a chance remark like that one? she wondered. The fat's in the fire in any case, she reminded herself. And she was tired of trying to dance around it. She swirled her drink and red and amber lights glinted against the glass.

"I trust you," she murmured, surprising them both. "But I don't want to involve you, Adam, in something you'll regret knowing about. I really want you to understand that. Once I tell you, it'll be too late for regrets."

He didn't care for the surge of guilt. Who was deceiving whom now? his conscience demanded of him. And who'd pay the price in the end? "Let me worry about that," he stated, dealing with Kirby now and saving his conscience for later. He swallowed brandy and let the heat ease through him. "How many copies has your father done?"

"Ten—no, eleven," she corrected, and ignored his quick oath. "Eleven, not counting the Titian, which falls into a different category."

"A different category," he murmured. Crossing the room, he splashed more brandy into his glass. He was certain to need it. "How is this different?"

"The Titian was a personal agreement between Harriet and Papa. Merely a way to avoid bad feelings."

"And the others?" He sat on a fussily elegant Queen Anne chair. "What sort of arrangements did they entail?"

"Each is individual, naturally." She hesitated as she studied him. If they'd met a month from now, would things have been different? Perhaps. Timing again, she mused and sipped the warming brandy. "To simplify matters, Papa painted them, then sold them to interested parties."

"Sold them?" He stood because he couldn't be still. Wishing it had been possible to stop her before she'd begun, he started to pace the room. "Good God, Kirby. Don't you understand what he's done? What he's doing? It's fraud, plain and simple."

"I wouldn't call it fraud," she countered, giving her brandy a contemplative study. It was, after all, something she'd given a great deal of thought to. "And certainly not plain or simple."

"What then?" If he'd had a choice, he'd have taken her away then and there—left the Titian, the Rembrandt and her crazy father in the ridiculous castle and taken off. Somewhere. Anywhere.

"Fudging," Kirby decided with a half smile.

"Fudging," he repeated in a quiet voice. He'd forgotten she was mad as well. "Fudging. Selling counterfeit paintings for large sums of money to the unsuspecting is fudging? Fixing a parking ticket's fudging." He paced another moment, looking for answers. "Damn it, his work's worth a fortune. Why does he do it?"

"Because he can," she said simply. She spread one hand, palm out. "Papa's a genius, Adam. I don't say that just as his daughter, but as a fellow artist. With the genius comes a bit of eccentricity, perhaps." Ignoring the sharp sound of derision, she went on. "To Papa, painting's not just a vocation. Art and life are one, interchangeable."

"I'll go along with all that, Kirby, but it doesn't explain why—"

"Let me finish." She had both hands on the snifter again, resting it in her lap. "One thing Papa can't tolerate is greed, in any form. To him greed isn't just the worship of money, but the hoarding of art. You must know his collection's constantly being lent out to museums and art schools. Though he has strong feelings that art belongs in the private sector, as well as public institutions, he hates the idea of the wealthy buying up great art for investment purposes."

"Admirable, Kirby. But he's made a business out of selling fraudulent paintings."

"Not a business. He's never benefited financially." She set her glass aside and clasped her hands together. "Each prospective buyer of one of Papa's emulations is first researched thoroughly." She waited a beat. "By Harriet."

He nearly sat back down again. "Harriet Merrick's in on all of this?"

"All of this," she said mildly, "has been their joint hobby for the last fifteen years."

"Hobby," he murmured and did sit.

"Harriet has very good connections, you see. She makes certain the buyer is very wealthy and that he or she lives in a remote location. Two years ago, Papa sold an Arabian sheik a fabulous Renoir. It was one of my favorites. Anyway—" she continued, getting up to freshen Adam's drink, then her own "—each buyer would also be known for his or her attachment to money, and/or a complete lack of any sense of community spirit or obligation. Through Harriet, they'd learn of Papa's ownership of a rare, officially undiscovered artwork."

Taking her own snifter, she returned to her position on the bed while Adam remained silent. "At the first contact, Papa is always uncooperative without being completely dismissive. Gradually he allows himself to be worn down until the deal's made. The price, naturally, is exorbitant, otherwise the art fanciers would be insulted." She took a small sip and enjoyed the warm flow of the brandy. "He deals only in cash, so there's no record. Then the paintings float off to the Himalayas or Siberia or somewhere to be kept in seclusion. Papa then donates the money anonymously to charity."

Taking a deep breath at the end of her speech, Kirby rewarded herself with more brandy.

"You're telling me that he goes through all that, all the work, all the intrigue, for nothing?"

"I certainly am not." Kirby shook her head and leaned

forward. "He gets a great deal. He gets satisfaction, Adam. What else is necessary after all?"

He struggled to remember the code of right and wrong. "Kirby, he's stealing!"

Kirby tilted her head and considered. "Who caught your support and admiration, Adam? The Sheriff of Nottingham or Robin Hood?"

"It's not the same." He dragged a hand through his hair as he tried to convince them both. "Damn it, Kirby, it's not the same."

"There's a newly modernized pediatric wing at the local hospital," she began quietly. "A little town in Appalachia has a new fire engine and modern equipment. Another, in the dust bowl, has a wonderful new library."

"All right." He rose again to cut her off. "In fifteen years I'm sure there's quite a list. Maybe in some strange way it's commendable, but it's also illegal, Kirby. It has to stop."

"I know." Her simple agreement broke his rhythm. With a half smile, Kirby moved her shoulders. "It was fun while it lasted, but I've known for some time it had to stop before something went wrong. Papa has a project in mind for a series of paintings, and I've convinced him to begin soon. It should take him about five years and give us a breathing space. But in the meantime, he's done something I don't know how to cope with."

She was about to give him more. Even before she spoke, Adam knew Kirby was going to give him all her trust. He sat in silence, despising himself, as she told him everything she knew about the Rembrandt.

"I imagine part of it's revenge on Stuart," she continued, while Adam smoked in silence and she again swirled her brandy without drinking. "Somehow Stuart found out about Papa's hobby and threatened exposure the night I broke our engagement. Papa told me not to worry, that Stuart wasn't in a position to make waves. At the time I had no idea about the Rembrandt business."

She was opening up to him, no questions, no hesitation. He was going to probe, God help him, he hadn't a choice. "Do you have any idea where he might've hidden it?"

"No, but I haven't looked." When she looked at him, she wasn't the exotic princess. She was only a daughter concerned about an adored father. "He's a good man, Adam. No one knows that better than I. I know there's a reason for what he's done, and for the time being, I have to accept that. I don't expect you to share my loyalty, just my confidence." He didn't speak, and she took his silence for agreement. "My main concern now is that Papa's underestimating Stuart's ruthlessness."

"He won't when you tell him about the scene in the library."

"I'm not going to tell him. Because," she continued before Adam could argue, "I have no way of predicting his reaction. You may have noticed, Papa's a very volatile man." Tilting her glass, she met his gaze with a quick change of mood. "I don't want you to worry about all this, Adam. Talk to Papa about it if you like. Have a chat with Harriet, too. Personally, I find it helpful to tuck the whole business away from time to time and let it hibernate. Like a grizzly bear."

"Grizzly bear."

She laughed and rose. "Let me get you some more brandy."

He stopped her with a hand on her wrist. "Have you told me everything?"

With a frown, she brushed at a speck of lint on the bedspread. "Did I mention the Van Gogh?"

"Oh, God." He pressed his fingers to his eyes. Somehow he'd hoped there'd be an end without really believing it. "What Van Gogh?"

Kirby pursed her lips. "Not exactly a Van Gogh."

"Your father?"

"His latest. He's sold it to Victor Alvarez, a coffee baron in South America." She smiled as Adam said nothing and stared straight ahead. "The working conditions on his farm are deplorable. Of course, there's nothing we can do to remedy that, but Papa's already allocated the purchase price for a school somewhere in the area. It's his last for several years, Adam," she added as he sat with his fingers pressed against his eyes. "And really, I think he'll be pleased that you know all about everything. He'd love to show this painting to you. He's particularly pleased with it."

Adam rubbed his hands over his face. It didn't surprise him to hear himself laughing. "I suppose I should be grateful he hasn't decided to do the ceiling in the Sistine Chapel."

"Only after he retires," Kirby put in cheerfully. "And that's years off yet."

Not certain whether she was joking or not, he let it pass. "I've got to give all this a little time to settle."

"Fair enough."

He wasn't going back to his room to report to McIntyre, he decided as he set his brandy aside. He wasn't ready for that yet, so soon after Kirby shared it all with him without questions, without limitations. It wasn't possible to think about his job, or remember outside obligations, when she looked at him with all her trust. No, he'd find a way, somehow, to justify what he chose to do in the end. Right and wrong weren't so well defined now.

Looking at her, he needed to give, to soothe, to show her she'd been right to give him that most precious of gifts—unqualified trust. Perhaps he didn't deserve it, but he needed it. He needed her.

Without a word, he pulled her into his arms and crushed his mouth to hers, no patience, no requests. Before either of them could think, he drew down the zipper at the back of her dress.

She wanted to give to him—anything, everything he wanted. She didn't want to question him but to forget all the reasons why they shouldn't be together. It would be so easy to drown in the flood of feeling that was so new and so unique. And yet, anything real, anything strong, was never easy. She'd been taught from an early age that the things that mattered most were the hardest to obtain. Drawing back, she determined to put things back on a level she could deal with.

"You surprise me," she said with a smile she had to work at.

He pulled her back. She wouldn't slip away from him this time. "Good."

"You know, most women expect a seduction, no matter how perfunctory."

The amusement might be in her eyes, but he could feel the thunder of her heart against his. "Most women aren't Kirby Fairchild." If she wanted to play it lightly, he'd do his damnedest to oblige her—as long as the result was the same. "Why don't we call this my next spontaneous act?" he suggested, and slipped her dress down her shoulders. "I wouldn't want to bore you with a conventional pursuit."

How could she resist him? The hands light on her skin, the mouth that smiled and tempted? She'd never hesitated about taking what she wanted . . . until now. Perhaps the time had come for the chess game to stop at a stalemate, with neither winning all and neither losing anything.

Slowly she smiled and let her dress whisper almost soundlessly to the floor.

He found her a treasure of cool satin and warm flesh. She was as seductive, as alluring, as he'd known she'd be. Once she'd decided to give, there were no restrictions. In a simple gesture she opened her arms to him and they came together.

Soft sighs, low murmurs, skin against skin. Moonlight and the rose tint from the lamp competed, then merged, as the mattress yielded under their weight. Her mouth was hot and open, her arms were strong. As she moved under him, inviting, taunting, he forgot how small she was.

Everything. All. Now. Needs drove them both to take without patience, and yet. Somehow, beneath the passion, under the heat, was a tenderness neither had expected from the other.

He touched. She trembled. She tasted. He throbbed. They wanted until the air seemed to spark with it. With each second both of them found more of what they'd needed, but the findings brought more greed. Take, she seemed to say, then give and give and give.

She had no time to float, only to throb. For him. From him. Her body craved—*yearn* was too soft a word. She required him, something unique for her. And he, with a kiss, with a touch of his hand, could raise her up to planes she'd only dreamed existed. Here was the completion, here was the delight, she'd hoped for without truly believing in. This was what she'd wanted so desperately in her life but had never found. Here and now. Him. There was and needed to be nothing else.

He edged toward madness. She held him, hard and tight, as they swung toward the edge together. Together was all she could think. Together.

Quiet. It was so quiet there might never have been such a thing as sound. Her hair brushed against his cheek. Her hand, balled into a loose fist, lay over his heart. Adam lay in the silence and hurt as he'd never expected to hurt.

How had he let it happen? Control? What had made him think he had control when it came to Kirby? Somehow she'd wrapped herself around him, body and mind, while he'd been pretending he'd known exactly what he'd been doing.

He'd come to do a job, he reminded himself. He still had to do it, no matter what had passed between them. Could he go on with what he'd come to do, and protect her? Was it possible to split himself in two when his road had always been so straight? He wasn't certain of anything now, but the tug-of-war he'd lose whichever way the game ended. He had to think, create the distance he needed to do so. Better for both of them if he started now.

But when he shifted away, she held him tighter. Kirby lifted her head so that moonlight caught in her eyes and mesmerized him. "Don't go," she murmured. "Stay and sleep with me. I don't want it to end yet."

He couldn't resist her now. Perhaps he never would.

Saying nothing, Adam drew her close again and closed his
eyes. For a little while he could pretend tomorrow would
take care of itself.

*　*　*

Sunlight woke her, but Kirby tried to ignore it by piling pillows on top of her head. It didn't work for long. Resigned,
she tossed them on the floor and lay quietly, alone.

She hadn't heard Adam leave, nor had she expected him
to stay until morning. As it was, she was grateful to have woken alone. Now she could think.

How was it she'd given her complete trust to a man she
hardly knew? No answer. Why hadn't she evaded his questions, skirted her way around certain facts as she was well
capable of doing? No answer.

It wasn't true. Kirby closed her eyes a moment, knowing
she'd been more honest with Adam than she was being with
herself. She knew the answer.

She'd given him more than she'd ever given to any man.
It had been more than a physical alliance, more than a few
hours of pleasure in the night. The essence of self had been
shared with him. There was no taking it back now, even if
both of them would have preferred it.

Unknowingly, he'd taken her innocence. Emotional virginity was just as real, just as vital, as the physical. And it
was just as impossible to reclaim. She, thinking of the night,
knew that she had no desire to go back. Now they would both
move forward to whatever waited for them.

Rising, she prepared to face the day.

*　*　*

Upstairs in Fairchild's studio, Adam studied the rural landscape. He could feel the agitation and drama. The serene scene leaped with frantic life. Vivid, real, disturbing.

Its creator stood beside him, not the Vincent van Gogh who Adam would've sworn had wielded the brush and pallette, but Philip Fairchild.

"It's magnificent," Adam murmured. The compliment was out before he could stop it.

"Thank you, Adam. I'm fond of it." Fairchild spoke as a man who'd long before accepted his own superiority and the responsibility that came with it.

"Mr. Fairchild—"

"Philip," Fairchild interrupted genially. "No reason for formality between us."

Somehow Adam felt even the casual intimacy could complicate an already hopelessly tangled situation. "Philip," he began again, "this is fraud. Your motives might be sterling, but the result remains fraud."

"Absolutely." Fairchild bobbed his head in agreement. "Fraud, misrepresentation, a bald-faced lie without a doubt." He lifted his arms and let them fall. "I'm stripped of defenses."

Like hell, Adam thought grimly. Unless he was very much mistaken, he was about to be treated to the biggest bag of pure, classic bull on record.

"Adam . . ." Fairchild drew out the name and steepled his hands. "You're an astute man, a rational man. I pride myself on being a good judge of character." As if he were very old and frail, Fairchild lowered himself into a chair. "Then, again, you're imaginative and open-minded—that shows in your work."

Adam reached for the coffee Cards had brought up. "So?"

"Your help with our little problem last night—and your skill in turning my own plot against me—leads me to believe you have the ability to adapt to what some might term the unusual."

"Some might."

"Now." Accepting the cup Adam handed him, Fairchild leaned back. "You tell me Kirby filled you in on everything.

Odd, but we'll leave that for now." He'd already drawn his
own conclusions there and found them to his liking. He
wasn't about to lose on other points. "After what you've been
told, can you find one iota of selfishness in my enterprise? Can
you see my motive as anything but humanitarian?" On a roll,
Fairchild set down his cup and let his hands fall between his
bony knees. "Small, sick children, and those less fortunate
than ourselves, have benefited from my hobby. Not one dollar have I kept, not a dollar, a franc, a sou. Never, never have
I asked for credit or honor that, naturally, society would be
anxious to bestow on me."

"You haven't asked for the jail sentence they'd bestow on
you, either."

Fairchild tilted his head in acknowledgment but didn't
miss a beat. "It's my gift to mankind, Adam. My payment
for the talent awarded to me by a higher power. These
hands . . ." He held them up, narrow, gaunt and oddly beautiful. "These hands hold a skill I'm obliged to pay for in
my own way. This I've done." Bowing his head, Fairchild
dropped them into his lap. "However, if you must condemn
me, I understand."

Fairchild looked, Adam mused, like a stalwart Christian
faced by pagan lions: firm in his belief, resigned to his fate.
"One day," Adam murmured, "your halo's going to slip and
strangle you."

"A possibility." Grinning, he lifted his head again. "But in
the meantime, we enjoy what we can. Let's have one of those
Danishes, my boy."

Wordlessly, Adam handed him the tray. "Have you considered the repercussions to Kirby if your . . . hobby is discovered?"

"Ah." Fairchild swallowed pastry. "A straight shot to my
Achilles' heel. Naturally both of us know that Kirby can meet
any obstacle and find a way over, around or through it." He
bit off more Danish, enjoying the tang of raspberry. "Still,

merely by being, Kirby demands emotion of one kind or another. You'd agree?"

Adam thought of the night, and what it had changed in him. "Yes."

The brief, concise answer was exactly what Fairchild had expected. "I'm taking a hiatus from this business for various reasons, the first of which is Kirby's position."

"And her position as concerns the Merrick Rembrandt?"

"A different kettle of fish." Fairchild dusted his fingers on a napkin and considered another pastry. "I'd like to share the ins and outs of that business with you, Adam, but I'm not free to just yet." He smiled and gazed over Adam's head. "One could say I've involved Kirby figuratively, but until things are resolved, she's a minor player in the game."

"Are you casting as well as directing this performance, Papa?" Kirby walked into the room and picked up the Danish Fairchild had been eyeing. "Did you sleep well, darling?"

"Like a rock, brat," he muttered, remembering the confusion of waking up on the sofa under her cape. He didn't care to be outwitted, but was a man who acknowledged a quick mind. "I'm told your evening activities went well."

"The deed's done." She glanced at Adam before resting her hands on her father's shoulders. The bond was there, unbreakable. "Maybe I should leave the two of you alone for a while. Adam has a way of digging out information. You might tell him what you won't tell me."

"All in good time." He patted her hands. "I'm devoting the morning to my hawk." Rising, he went to uncover his clay, an obvious dismissal. "You might give Harriet a call and tell her all's well before you two amuse yourselves."

Kirby held out her hand. "Have you any amusements in mind, Adam?"

"As a matter of fact . . ." He went with the impulse and kissed her as her father watched and speculated. "I had a session of oils and canvas in mind. You'll have to change."

"If that's the best you can do. Two hours only," she warned as they walked from the room. "Otherwise my rates go up. I have my own work, you know."

"Three."

"Two and a half." She paused at the second-floor landing.

"You looked like a child this morning," he murmured, and touched her cheek. "I couldn't bring myself to wake you." He left his hand there only a moment, then moved away. "I'll meet you upstairs."

Kirby went to her room and tossed the red dress on the bed. While she undressed with one hand, she dialed the phone with the other.

"Harriet, it's Kirby to set your mind at rest."

"Clever child. Was there any trouble?"

"No." She wiggled out of her jeans. "We managed."

"We? Did Philip go with you?"

"Papa was snoozing on the couch after Adam switched drinks."

"Oh, dear." Amused, Harriet settled back. "Was he very angry?"

"Papa or Adam?" Kirby countered, then shrugged. "No matter, in the end they were both very reasonable. Adam was a great help."

"The test isn't for a half hour. Give me the details."

Struggling in and out of clothes, Kirby told her everything.

"Marvelous!" Pleased with the drama, Harriet beamed at the phone. "I wish I'd done it. I'll have to get to know your Adam better and find some spectacular way of showing him my gratitude. Do you think he'd like the crocodile teeth?"

"Nothing would please him more."

"Kirby, you know how grateful I am to you." Harriet's voice was abruptly serious and maternal. "The situation's awkward to say the least."

"The contract's binding?"

"Yes." She let out a sigh at the thought of losing the Titian.

"My fault. I should've explained to Stuart that the painting wasn't to be sold. Philip must be furious with me."

"You can handle him. You always do."

"Yes, yes. Lord knows what I'd do without you, though. Poor Melly just can't understand me as you do."

"She's just made differently." Kirby stared down at the floor and tried not to think about the Rembrandt and the guilt it brought her. "Come to dinner tonight, Harriet, you and Melanie."

"Oh, I'd love to, darling, but I've a meeting. Tomorrow?"

"Fine. Shall I call Melly, or will you speak with her?"

"I'll see her this afternoon. Take care and do thank Adam for me. Damn shame I'm too old to give him anything but crocodile teeth."

With a laugh, Kirby hung up.

* * *

The sun swept over her dress, shooting it with flames or darkening it to blood. It glinted from the rings at her ears, the bracelets on her arms. Knowing the light was as perfect as it would ever be, Adam worked feverishly.

He was an artist of subtle details, one who used light and shadow for mood. In his portraits he strove for an inner reality, the truth beneath the surface of the model. In Kirby he saw the essence of woman—power and frailty and that elusive, mystical quality of sex. Aloof, alluring. She was both. Now, more than ever, he understood it.

Hours passed without him giving them a thought. His model, however, had a different frame of mind.

"Adam, if you'll consult your watch, you'll see I've given you more than the allotted time already."

He ignored her and continued to paint.

"I can't stand here another moment." She let her arms drop from their posed position, then wiggled them from the shoulders down. "As it is, I'll probably never pole-vault again."

"I can work on the background awhile," he muttered. "I need another three hours in the morning. The light's best then."

Kirby bit off a retort. Rudeness was something to be expected when an artist was taken over by his art. Stretching her muscles, she went to look over his shoulder.

"You've a good hand with light," she decided as she studied the emerging painting. "It's very flattering, certainly, rather fiery and defiant with the colors you've chosen." She looked carefully at the vague lines of her face, the tints and hues he was using to create her on canvas. "Still, there's a fragility here I don't quite understand."

"Maybe I know you better than you know yourself." He never looked at her, but continued to paint. In not looking, he didn't see the stunned expression or the gradual acceptance.

Linking her hands together, Kirby wandered away. She'd have to do it quickly, she decided. It needed to be done, to be said. "Adam . . ."

An inarticulate mutter. His back remained to her.

Kirby took a deep breath. "I love you."

"Umm-hmm."

Some women might've been crushed. Others would've been furious. Kirby laughed and tossed back her hair. Life was never what you expected. "Adam, I'd like just a moment of your attention." Though she continued to smile, her knuckles turned white. "I'm in love with you."

It got through on the second try. His brush, tipped in coral, stopped in midair. Very slowly, he set it down and turned. She was looking at him, the half smile on her face, her hands linked together so tightly they hurt. She hadn't expected a response, nor would she demand one.

"I don't tell you that to put pressure on you, or to embarrass you." Nerves showed only briefly as she moistened her lips. "It's just that I think you have a right to know." Her words began to spill out quickly. "We haven't known each

other for long, I know, but I suppose it just happens this way
sometimes. I couldn't do anything about it. I don't expect anything from you, permanently or temporarily." When he still
didn't speak, she felt a jolt of panic she didn't know how to
deal with. Had she ruined it? Now the smile didn't reach her
eyes. "I've got to change," she said lightly. "You've made me
miss lunch as it is."

She was nearly to the door before he stopped her. As he
took her shoulders, he felt her tense. And as he felt it, he understood she'd given him everything that was in her heart.
Something he knew instinctively had never been given to any
other man.

"Kirby, you're the most exceptional woman I've ever
known."

"Yes, someone's always pointing that out." She had to get
through the door and quickly. "Are you coming down, or
shall I have a tray sent up?"

He lowered his head to the top of hers and wondered how
things had happened so quickly, so finally. "How many people could make such a simple and unselfish declaration of
love, then walk away without asking for anything? From the
beginning you haven't done one thing I'd've expected." He
brushed his lips over her hair, lightly, so that she hardly felt
it. "Don't I get a chance to say anything?"

"It's not necessary."

"Yes, it is." Turning her, he framed her face with his hands.
"And I'd rather have my hands on you when I tell you I love
you."

She stood very straight and spoke very calmly. "Don't feel
sorry for me, Adam. I couldn't bear it."

He started to say all the sweet, romantic things a woman
wanted to hear when love was declared. All the traditional,
normal words a man offered when he offered himself. They
weren't for Kirby. Instead he lifted a brow. "If you hadn't
counted on being loved back, you'll have to adjust."

She waited a moment because she had to be certain. She'd

take the risk, take any risk, if she was certain. As she looked into his eyes, she began to smile. The tension in her shoulders vanished. "You've brought it on yourself."

"Yeah. I guess I have to live with it."

The smile faded as she pressed against him. "Oh, God, Adam, I need you. You've no idea how much."

He held her just as tightly, just as desperately. "Yes, I do."

CHAPTER 9

To love and to be loved in return. It was bewildering to Kirby, frightening, exhilarating. She wanted time to experience it, absorb it. Understanding it didn't matter, not now, in the first rush of emotion. She only knew that although she'd always been happy in her life, she was being offered more. She was being offered laughter at midnight, soft words at dawn, a hand to hold and a life to share. The price would be a portion of her independence and the loyalty that had belonged only to her father.

To Kirby, love meant sharing, and sharing had no restrictions. Whatever she had, whatever she felt, belonged to Adam as much as to herself. Whatever happened between them now, she'd never be able to change that. No longer able to work, she went down from her studio to find him.

The house was quiet in the early-evening lull with the staff downstairs making the dinner preparations and gossiping. Kirby had always liked this time of day—after a long, productive session in her studio, before the evening meal. These were the hours to sit in front of a roaring fire, or walk along the cliffs. Now there was someone she needed to share those hours with. Stopping in front of Adam's door, she raised a hand to knock.

The murmur of voices stopped her. If Adam had her father

in another discussion, he might learn something more about the Rembrandt that would put her mind at ease. While she hesitated, the thumping of the front door knocker vibrated throughout the house. With a shrug, she turned away to answer.

Inside his room, Adam shifted the transmitter to his other hand. "This is the first chance I've had to call in. Besides, there's nothing new."

"You're supposed to check in every night." Annoyed, McIntyre barked into the receiver. "Damn it, Adam, I was beginning to think something had happened to you."

"If you knew these people, you'd realize how ridiculous that is."

"They don't suspect anything?"

"No." Adam swore at the existence of this job.

"Tell me about Mrs. Merrick and Hiller."

"Harriet's charming and flamboyant." He wouldn't say harmless. Though he thought of what he and Kirby had done the night before, he left it alone. Adam had already rationalized the entire business as having nothing to do with his job. Not specifically. That was enough to justify his keeping it from McIntyre. Instead, Adam would tell him what Adam felt applied and nothing more. "Hiller's very smooth and a complete phony. I walked in on him and Kirby in time to keep him from shoving her around."

"What was his reason?"

"The Rembrandt. He doesn't believe her father's keeping her in the dark about it. He's the kind of man who thinks you can always get what you want by knocking the other person around—if they're smaller."

"Sounds like a gem." But he'd heard the change in tone. If Adam was getting involved with the Fairchild woman . . . No. McIntyre let it go. That they didn't need. "I've got a line on Victor Alvarez."

"Drop it." Adam kept his voice casual, knowing full well

just how perceptive Mac could be. "It's a wild-goose chase. I've already dug it up and it doesn't have anything to do with the Rembrandt."

"You know best."

"Yeah." McIntyre, he knew, would never understand Fairchild's hobby. "Since we agree about that, I've got a stipulation."

"Stipulation?"

"When I find the Rembrandt, I handle the rest my own way."

"What do you mean your own way? Listen, Adam—"

"My way," Adam cut him off. "Or you find someone else. I'll get it back for you, Mac, but after I do, the Fairchilds are kept out of it."

"Kept out?" McIntyre exploded so that the receiver crackled with static. "How the hell do you expect me to keep them out?"

"That's your problem. Just do it."

"The place is full of crazies," McIntyre muttered. "Must be contagious."

"Yeah. I'll get back to you." With a grin, Adam switched off the transmitter.

Downstairs, Kirby opened the door and looked into the myopic, dark-framed eyes of Rick Potts. Knowing his hand would be damp with nerves, she held hers out. "Hello, Rick. Papa told me you were coming to visit."

"Kirby." He swallowed and squeezed her hand. Just the sight of her played havoc with his glands. "You look mar-marvelous." He thrust drooping carnations into her face.

"Thank you." Kirby took the flowers Rick had partially strangled and smiled. "Come, let me fix you a drink. You've had a long drive, haven't you? Cards, see to Mr. Potts's luggage, please," she continued without giving Rick a chance to speak. He'd need a little time, she knew, to draw words together. "Papa should be down soon." She found a club soda and poured it over ice. "He's been giving a lot of time to his new project; I'm sure he'll want to discuss it with you." After handing him his drink, she gestured to a chair. "So, how've you been?"

He drank first, to separate his tongue from the roof of his mouth. "Fine. That is, I had a bit of a cold last week, but I'm much better now. I'd never come to see you if I had any germs."

She turned in time to hide a grin and poured herself a glass of Perrier. "That's very considerate of you, Rick."

"Have you—have you been working?"

"Yes, I've nearly done enough for my spring showing."

"It'll be wonderful," he told her with blind loyalty. Though he recognized the quality of her work, the more powerful pieces intimidated him. "You'll be staying in New York?"

"Yes." She walked over to sit beside him. "For a week."

"Then maybe—that is, I'd love to, if you had the time, of course, I'd like to take you to dinner." He gulped down club soda. "If you had an evening free."

"That's very sweet of you."

Astonished, he gaped, pupils dilating. From the doorway, Adam watched the puppylike adulation of the lanky, somewhat untidy man. In another ten seconds, Adam estimated, Kirby would have him at her feet whether she wanted him there or not.

Kirby glanced up, and her expression changed so subtly Adam wouldn't have noticed if he hadn't been so completely tuned in to her. "Adam." If there'd been relief in her eyes, her voice was casual. "I was hoping you'd come down. Rick, this is Adam Haines. Adam, I think Papa mentioned Rick Potts to you the other day."

The message came across loud and clear. Be kind. With an easy smile, Adam accepted the damp handshake. "Yes,

Philip said you were coming for a few days. Kirby tells me you work in watercolors."

"She did?" Nearly undone by the fact that Kirby would speak of him at all, Rick simply stood there a moment.

"We'll have to have a long discussion after dinner." Rising, Kirby began to lead Rick gently toward the door. "I'm sure you'd like to rest a bit after your drive. You can find the way to your room, can't you?"

"Yes, yes, of course."

Kirby watched him wander down the hall before she turned back. She walked back to Adam and wrapped her arms around him. "I hate to repeat myself, but I love you."

He framed her face with his hands and kissed her softly, lightly, with the promise of more. "Repeat yourself as often as you like." He stared down at her, suddenly and completely aroused by no more than her smile. He pressed his mouth into her palm with a restraint that left her weak. "You take my breath away," he murmured. "It's no wonder you turn Rick Potts to jelly."

"I'd rather turn you to jelly."

She did. It wasn't an easy thing to admit. With a half smile, Adam drew her away. "Are you really going to tell him I'm a jealous lover with a stiletto?"

"It's for his own good." Kirby picked up her glass of Perrier. "He's always so embarrassed after he loses control. Did you learn any more from Papa?"

"No." Puzzled, he frowned. "Why?"

"I was coming to see you right before Rick arrived. I heard you talking."

She slipped a hand into his and he fought to keep the tension from being noticeable. "I don't want to press things now." That much was the truth, he thought fiercely. That much wasn't a lie.

"No, you're probably right about that. Papa tends to get

obstinate easily. Let's sit in front of the fire for a little while," she said as she drew him over to it. "And do nothing."

He sat beside her, holding her close, and wished things were as simple as they seemed.

* * *

Hours went by before they sat in the parlor again, but they were no longer alone. After an enormous meal, Fairchild and Rick settled down with them to continue the ongoing discussion of art and technique. Assisted by two glasses of wine and half a glass of brandy, Rick began to heap praise on Kirby's work. Adam recognized the warning signals of battle—Fairchild's pink ears and Kirby's guileless eyes.

"Thank you, Rick." With a smile, Kirby lifted her brandy. "I'm sure you'd like to see Papa's latest work. It's an attempt in clay. A bird or something, isn't it, Papa?"

"A bird? A bird?" In a quick circle, he danced around the table. "It's a hawk, you horrid girl. A bird of prey, a creature of cunning."

A veteran, Rick tried to soothe. "I'd love to see it, Mr. Fairchild."

"And so you will." In one dramatic gulp, Fairchild finished off his drink. "I intend to donate it to the Metropolitan."

Whether Kirby's snort was involuntary or contrived, it produced results.

"Do you mock your father?" Fairchild demanded. "Have you no faith in these hands?" He held them out, fingers spread. "The same hands that held you fresh from your mother's womb?"

"Your hands are the eighth wonder of the world," Kirby told him. "However . . ." She set down her glass, sat back and crossed her legs. Meticulously she brought her fingers together and looked over them. "From my observations, you have difficulty with your structure. Perhaps with a few years of practice, you'll develop the knack of construction."

"Structure?" he sputtered. "Construction?" His eyes narrowed, his jaw clenched. "Cards!" Kirby sent him an easy smile and picked up her glass again. "Cards!"

"Yes, Mr. Fairchild."

"Cards," Fairchild repeated, glaring at the dignified butler, who stood waiting in the doorway.

"Yes, Mr. Fairchild."

"Cards!" He bellowed and pranced.

"I believe Papa wants a deck of cards—Cards," Kirby explained. "Playing cards."

"Yes, miss." With a slight bow, Cards went to get some.

"What's the matter with that man?" Fairchild muttered. In hurried motions, he began to clear off a small table. Exquisite Wedgwood and delicate Venetian glass were dumped unceremoniously on the floor. "You'd think I didn't make myself clear."

"It's so hard to get good help these days," Adam said into his glass.

"Your cards, Mr. Fairchild." The butler placed two sealed decks on the table before gliding from the room.

"Now I'll show you about construction." Fairchild pulled up a chair and wrapped his skinny legs around its legs. Breaking the seal on the first deck, he poured the cards on the table. With meticulous care, he leaned one card against another and formed an arch. "A steady hand and a discerning eye," Fairchild mumbled as he began slowly, and with total intensity, to build a house of cards.

"That should keep him out of trouble for a while," Kirby declared. Sending Adam a wink, she turned to Rick and drew him into a discussion on mutual friends.

An hour drifted by over brandy and quiet conversation. Occasionally there was a mutter or a grumble from the architect in the corner. The fire crackled. When Montique entered and jumped into Adam's lap, Rick paled and sprang up.

"You shouldn't do that. She'll be here any second." He set

down his glass with a clatter. "Kirby, I think I'll go up. I want to start work early."

"Of course." She watched his retreat before turning to Adam. "He's terrified of Isabelle. Montique got into his room when he was sleeping and curled on his pillow. Isabelle woke Rick with some rather rude comments while she stood on his chest. I'd better go up and make sure everything's in order." She rose, then bent over and kissed him lightly.

"That's not enough."

"No?" The slow smile curved her lips. "Perhaps we'll fix that later. Come on, Montique, let's go find your wretched keeper."

"Kirby . . ." Adam waited until both she and the puppy were at the doorway. "Just how much rent does Isabelle pay?"

"Ten mice a month," she told him soberly. "But I'm going to raise it to fifteen in November. Maybe she'll be out by Christmas." Pleased with the thought, she led Montique away.

"A fascinating creature, my Kirby," Fairchild commented.

Adam crossed the room and stared down at the huge, erratic card structure Fairchild continued to construct. "Fascinating."

"She's a woman with much below the surface. Kirby can be cruel when she feels justified. I've seen her squash a six-foot man like a bug." He held a card between the index fingers of both hands, then slowly lowered it into place. "You'll notice, however, that her attitude toward Rick is invariably kind."

Though Fairchild continued to give his full attention to his cards, Adam knew it was more than idle conversation. "Obviously she doesn't want to hurt him."

"Exactly." Fairchild began to patiently build another wing. Unless Adam was very much mistaken, the cards were slowly taking on the lines of the house they were in. "She'll take great care not to because she knows his devotion to her is sincere. Kirby's a strong, independent woman. Where her heart's involved, however, she's a marshmallow. There are a handful of people on this earth she'd sacrifice anything she could for. Rick's one of them—Melanie and Harriet are others. And myself." He held a card on the tops of his fingers as if weighing it. "Yes, myself," he repeated softly. "Because of this, the circumstances of the Rembrandt are very difficult for her. She's torn between separate loyalties. Her father, and the woman who's been her mother most of her life."

"You do nothing to change it," Adam accused. Irrationally he wanted to sweep the cards aside, flatten the meticulously formed construction. He pushed his hands into his pockets, where they balled into fists. Just how much could he berate Fairchild, when he was deceiving Kirby in nearly the same way? "Why don't you give her some explanation? Something she could understand?"

"Ignorance is bliss," Fairchild stated calmly. "In this case, the less Kirby knows, the simpler things are for her."

"You've a hell of a nerve, Philip."

"Yes, yes, that's quite true." He balanced more cards, then went back to the subject foremost in his mind. "There've been dozens of men in Kirby's life. She could choose and discard them as other women do clothing. Yet, in her own way, she was always cautious. I think Kirby believed she wasn't capable of loving a man and had decided to settle for much, much less by agreeing to marry Stuart. Nonsense, of course." Fairchild picked up his drink and studied his rambling card house. "Kirby has a great capacity for love. When she loves a man, she'll love with unswerving devotion and loyalty. And when she does, she'll be vulnerable. She loves intensely, Adam."

For the first time, he raised his eyes and met Adam's. "When her mother died, she was devastated. I wouldn't want to live to see her go through anything like that again."

What could he say? Less than he wanted to, but still only the truth. "I don't want to hurt Kirby. I'll do everything I can to keep from hurting her."

Fairchild studied him a moment with the pale blue eyes that saw deep and saw much. "I believe you, and hope you

find a way to avoid it. Still, if you love her, you'll find a way
to mend whatever damage is done. The game's on, Adam, the
rules set. They can't be altered now, can they?"

Adam stared down at the round face. "You know why I'm
here, don't you?"

With a cackle, Fairchild turned back to his cards. Yes, indeed, Adam Haines was sharp, he thought, pleased. Kirby
had called it from the beginning. "Let's just say for now that
you're here to paint and to . . . observe. Yes, to observe." He
placed another card. "Go up to her now, you've my blessing
if you feel the need for it. The game's nearly over, Adam.
Soon enough we'll have to pick up the pieces. Love's tenuous
when it's new, my boy. If you want to keep her, be as stubborn as she is. That's my advice."

* * *

In long, methodical strokes, Kirby pulled the brush through
her hair. She'd turned the radio on low so that the hot jazz
was hardly more than a pulse beat. At the sound of a knock,
she sighed. "Rick, you really must go to bed. You'll hate yourself in the morning."

Adam pushed open the door. He took a long look at the
woman in front of the mirror, dressed in wisps of beige silk
and ivory lace. Without a word, he closed and latched the door
behind him.

"Oh, my." Setting the brush on her dresser, Kirby turned
around with a little shudder. "A woman simply isn't safe these
days. Have you come to have your way with me—I hope?"

Adam crossed to her. Letting his hands slide along the
silk, he wrapped his arms around her. "I was just passing
through." When she smiled, he lowered his mouth to hers.
"I love you, Kirby. More than anyone, more than anything."
Suddenly his mouth was fierce, his arms were tight. "Don't
ever forget it."

"I won't." But her words were muffled against his mouth.

"Just don't stop reminding me. Now . . ." She drew away, inches only, and slowly began to loosen his tie. "Maybe I should remind you."

He watched his tie slip to the floor just before she began to ease his jacket from his shoulders. "It might be a good idea."

"You've been working hard," she told him as she tossed his jacket in the general direction of a chair. "I think you should be pampered a bit."

"Pampered?"

"Mmm." Nudging him onto the bed, she knelt to take off his shoes. Carelessly she let them drop, followed by his socks, before she began to massage his feet. "Pampering's good for you in small doses."

He felt the pleasure spread through him at the touch that could almost be described as motherly. Her hands were soft, with that ridge of callus that proved they weren't idle. They were strong and clever, belonging both to artist and to woman. Slowly she slid them up his legs, then down— teasing, promising, until he wasn't certain whether to lay back and enjoy, or to grab and take. Before he could do either, Kirby stood and began to unbutton his shirt.

"I like everything about you," she murmured as she tugged the shirt from the waistband of his slacks. "Have I mentioned that?"

"No." He let her loosen the cuffs and slip the shirt from him. Taking her time, Kirby ran her hands up his rib cage to his shoulders. "The way you look." Softly she pressed a kiss to his cheek. "The way you feel." Then the other. "The way you think." Her lips brushed over his chin. "The way you taste." Unhooking his slacks, she drew them off, inch by slow inch. "There's nothing about you I'd change."

She straddled him and began to trace long, lingering kisses over his face and neck. "Once when I wondered about falling in love, I decided there simply wasn't a man I'd like well enough to make it possible." Her mouth paused just above his. "I was wrong."

Soft, warm and exquisitely tender, her lips met his. Pampering . . . the word drifted through his mind as she gave him more than any man could expect and only a few might dream of. The strength of her body and her mind, the delicacy of both. They were his, and he didn't have to ask. They'd be his as long as his arms could hold her and open wide enough to give her room.

Knowing only that she loved, Kirby gave. His body heated beneath hers, lean and hard. Disciplined. Somehow the word excited her. He knew who he was and what he wanted. He'd work for both. And he wouldn't demand that she lose any part of what she was to suit that.

His shoulders were firm. Not so broad they would overwhelm her, but wide enough to offer security when she needed it. She brushed her lips over them. There were muscles in his arms, but subtle, not something he'd flex to show her his superiority, but there to protect if she chose to be protected. She ran her fingers over them. His hands were clever, elegantly masculine. They wouldn't hold her back from the places she had to go, but they would be there, held out, when she returned. She pressed her mouth to one, then the other.

No one had ever loved him just like this—patiently, devotedly. He wanted nothing more than to go on feeling those long, slow strokes of her fingers, those moist, lingering traces of her lips. He felt each in every pore. A total experience. He could see the glossy black fall of her hair as it tumbled over his skin and hear the murmur of her approval as she touched him.

The house was quiet again, but for the low, simmering sound of the music. The quilt was soft under his back. The light was dim and gentle—the best light for lovers. And while he lay, she loved him until he was buried under layer upon layer of pleasure. This he would give back to her.

He could touch the silk, and her flesh, knowing that both were exquisite. He could taste her lips and know that he'd never go hungry as long as she was there. When he heard her sigh, he knew he'd be content with no other sound. The need for him was in her eyes, clouding them, so that he knew he could live with little else as long as he could see her face.

Patience began to fade in each of them. He could feel her body spring to frantic life wherever he touched. He could feel his own strain from the need only she brought to him. Desperate, urgent, exclusive. If he'd had only a day left to live, he'd have spent every moment of it there, with Kirby in his arms.

She smelled of wood smoke and musky flowers, of woman and of sex, ripe and ready. If he'd had the power, he'd have frozen time just then, as she loomed above him in the moonlight, eyes dark with need, skin flashing against silk.

Then he drew the silk up and over her head so that he could see her as he swore no man would ever see her again. Her hair tumbled down, streaking night against her flesh. Naked and eager, she was every primitive fantasy, every midnight dream. Everything.

Her lips were parted as the breath hurried between them. Passion swamped her so that she shuddered and rushed to take what she needed from him—for him. Everything. Everything and more. With a low sound of triumph, Kirby took him inside her and led the way. Fast, furious.

Her body urged her on relentlessly while her mind exploded with images. Such color, such sound. Such frenzy. Arched back, she moved like lightning, hardly aware of how tightly his hands gripped her hips. But she heard him say her name. She felt him fill her.

The first crest swamped her, shocking her system then thrusting her along to more, and more and more. There was nothing she couldn't have and nothing she wouldn't give. Senseless, she let herself go.

With his hands on her, with the taste of her still on his lips, Adam felt his system shudder on the edge of release. For a moment, only a moment, he held back. He could see her above him, poised like a goddess, flesh damp and glowing, hair streaming back as she lifted her hands to it in ecstasy. This he would remember always.

* * *

The moon was no longer full, but its light was soft and white. They were still on top of the quilt, tangled close as their breathing settled. As she lay over him, Adam thought of everything Fairchild had said. And everything he could and couldn't do about it.

Slowly their systems settled, but he could find none of the answers he needed so badly. What answers would there be based on lies and half-truths?

Time. Perhaps time was all he had now. But how much or how little was no longer up to him. With a sigh, he shifted and ran a hand down her back.

Kirby rose on an elbow. Her eyes were no longer clouded, but saucy and clear. She smiled, touched a fingertip to her own lips and then to his. "Next time you're in town, cowboy," she drawled as she tossed her hair over her shoulder, "don't forget to ask for Lulu."

She'd expected him to grin, but he grabbed her hair and held her just as she was. There was no humor in his eyes, but the intensity she'd seen when he held a paintbrush. His muscles had tensed, she could feel it.

"Adam?"

"No, don't." He forced his hand to relax, then stroked her cheek. It wouldn't be spoiled by the wrong word, the wrong move. "I want to remember you just like this. Fresh from loving, with moonlight on your hair."

He was afraid, unreasonably, that he'd never see her like that again—with that half smile inches away from his face. He'd never feel the warmth of her flesh spread over his with nothing, nothing to separate them.

The panic came fast and was very real. Unable to stop it, Adam pulled her against him and held her as if he'd never let her go.

CHAPTER 10

After thirty minutes of posing, Kirby ordered herself not to be impatient. She'd agreed to give Adam two hours, and a bargain was a bargain. She didn't want to think about the time she had left to stand idle, so instead tried to concentrate on her plans for sculpting once her obligation was over. Her *Anger* was nearly finished.

But the sun seemed too warm and too bright. Every so often her mind would go oddly blank until she pulled herself back just to remember where she was.

"Kirby." Adam called her name for the third time and watched as she blinked and focused on him. "Could you wait until the session's over before you take a nap?"

"Sorry." With an effort, she cleared her head and smiled at him. "I was thinking of something else."

"Don't think at all if it puts you to sleep," he muttered, and slashed scarlet across the canvas. It was right, so right. Nothing he'd ever done had been as right as this painting. The need to finish it was becoming obsessive. "Tilt your head to the right again. You keep breaking the pose."

"Slave driver." But she obeyed and tried to concentrate.

"Cracking the whip's the only way to work with you." With care, he began to perfect the folds in the skirt of her dress. He wanted them soft, flowing, but clearly defined. "You'd better get used to posing for me. I've already several other studies in mind that I'll start after we're married."

Giddiness washed over her. She felt it in waves—physical, emotional—she couldn't tell one from the other. Without thinking, she dropped her arms.

"Damn it, Kirby." He started to swear at her again when he saw how wide and dark her eyes were. "What is it?"

"I hadn't thought . . . I didn't realize that you . . ." Lifting a hand to her spinning head, she walked around the room. The bracelets slid down to her elbow with a musical jingle. "I need a minute," she murmured. Should she feel as though someone had cut off her air? As if her head was three feet above her shoulders?

Adam watched her for a moment. She didn't seem quite steady, he realized. And there was an unnaturally high color in her cheeks. Standing, he took her hand and held her still. "Are you ill?"

"No." She shook her head. She was never ill, Kirby reminded herself. Just a bit tired—and, perhaps for the first time in her life, completely overwhelmed. She took a deep breath, telling herself she'd be all right in a moment. "I didn't know you wanted to marry me, Adam."

Was that it? he wondered as he ran the back of his hand over her cheek. Shouldn't she have known? And yet, he remembered, everything had happened so fast. "I love you." It was simple for him. Love led to marriage and marriage to family. But how could he have forgotten Kirby wasn't an ordinary woman and was anything but simple? "You accused me of being conventional," he reminded her, and ran his hands down her hair to her shoulders. "Marriage is a very conventional institution." And one she might not be ready for, he thought with a quick twinge of panic. He'd have to give her room if he wanted to keep her. But how much room did she need, and how much could he give?

"I want to spend my life with you." Adam waited until her gaze had lifted to his again. She looked stunned by his words—a woman like her, Adam thought. Beautiful, sensuous, strong. How was it a woman like Kirby would be surprised to be wanted? Perhaps he'd moved too quickly, and too clumsily. "Any way you choose, Kirby. Maybe I should've chosen a better time, a better place, to ask rather than assume."

"It's not that." Shaky, she lifted a hand to his face. It was so solid, so strong. "I don't need that." His face blurred a moment, and, shaking her head, she moved away again until she stood where she'd been posing. "I've had marriage proposals before—and a good many less binding requests." She managed a smile. He wanted her, not just for today, but for the tomorrows, as well. He wanted her just as she was. She felt the tears well up, of love, of gratitude, but blinked them back. When wishes came true it was no time for tears. "This is the one I've been waiting for all of my life, I just didn't expect to be so flustered."

Relieved, he started to cross to her. "I'll take that as a good sign. Still, I wouldn't mind a simple yes."

"I hate to do anything simple."

She felt the room lurch and fade, then his hands on her shoulders.

"Kirby—Good God, there's gas leaking!" As he stood holding her up, the strong, sweet odor rushed over him. "Get out! Get some air! It must be the heater." Giving her a shove toward the door, he bent over the antiquated unit.

She stumbled across the room. The door seemed miles away, so that when she finally reached it she had only the strength to lean against the heavy wood and catch her breath. The air was cleaner there. Gulping it in, Kirby willed herself to reach for the knob. She tugged, but it held firm.

"Damn it, I told you to get out!" He was already choking on the fumes when he reached her. "The gas is pouring out of that thing!"

"I can't open the door!" Furious with herself, Kirby pulled again. Adam pushed her hands away and yanked himself. "Is it jammed?" she murmured, leaning against him. "Cards will see to it."

Locked, he realized. From the outside. "Stay here." After propping her against the door, Adam picked up a chair and smashed it against the window. The glass cracked, but held. Again, he rammed the chair, and again, until with a final heave, the glass shattered. Moving quickly, he went back for Kirby and held her head near the jagged opening.

"Breathe," he ordered.

For the moment she could do nothing else but gulp fresh air into her lungs and cough it out again. "Someone's locked us in, haven't they?"

He'd known it wouldn't take her long once her head had cleared. Just as he knew better than to try to evade. "Yes."

"We could shout for hours." She closed her eyes and concentrated. "No one would hear us, we're too isolated up here." With her legs unsteady, she leaned against the wall. "We'll have to wait until someone comes to look for us."

"Where's the main valve for that heater?"

"Main valve?" She pressed her fingers to her eyes and forced herself to think. "I just turn the thing on when it's cold up here. . . . Wait. Tanks—there are tanks out in back of the kitchen." She turned back to the broken window again, telling herself she couldn't be sick. "One for each tower and for each floor."

Adam glanced at the small, old-fashioned heater again. It wouldn't take much longer, even with the broken window. "We're getting out of here."

"How?" If she could just lie down—just for a minute . . . "The door's locked. I don't think we'd survive a jump into Jamie's zinnias," she added, looking down to where the chair had landed. But he wasn't listening to her. When Kirby turned, she saw Adam running his hand over the ornate trim. The panel yawned open. "How'd you find that one?"

He grabbed her by the elbow and pulled her forward. "Let's go."

"I can't." With the last of her strength, Kirby braced her hands against the wall. Fear and nausea doubled at the thought of going into the dark, dank hole in the wall. "I can't go in there."

"Don't be ridiculous."

When he would've pulled her through, Kirby jerked away and backed up. "No, you go. I'll wait for you to come around and open the door."

"Listen to me." Fighting the fumes, he grabbed her shoulders. "I don't know how long it'd take me to find my way through that maze in the dark."

"I'll be patient."

"You could be dead," he countered between his teeth. "That heater's unstable—if there's a short this whole room would go up! You've already taken in too much of the gas."

"I won't go in!" Hysteria bubbled, and she didn't have the strength or the wit to combat it. Her voice rose as she stumbled back from him. "I can't go in, don't you understand?"

"I hope you understand this," he muttered, and clipped her cleanly on the jaw. Without a sound, she collapsed into his arms. Adam didn't hesitate. He tossed her unceremoniously over his shoulder and plunged into the passageway.

With the panel closed to cut off the flow of gas, the passage was in total darkness. With one arm holding Kirby in place, Adam inched along the wall. He had to reach the stairs, and the first mechanism. Groping, testing each step, he hugged the wall, knowing what would happen to both of them if he rushed and plunged them headlong down the steep stone stairway.

He heard the skitter of rodents and brushed spiderwebs out of his face. Perhaps it was best that Kirby was unconscious, he decided. He'd get her through a lot easier carrying her than he would dragging her.

Five minutes, then ten, then at last his foot met empty space.

Cautiously, he shifted Kirby on his shoulder, pressed the

other to the wall, and started down. The steps were stone, and treacherous enough with a light. In the dark, with no rail for balance, they were deadly. Fighting the need to rush, Adam checked himself on each step before going on to the next. When he reached the bottom, he went no faster, but began to trace his hand along the wall, feeling for a switch.

The first one stuck. He had to concentrate just to breathe. Kirby swayed on his shoulder as he maneuvered the sharp turn in the passage. Swearing, Adam moved forward blindly until his fingers brushed over a second lever. The panel groaned open just enough for him to squeeze himself and his burden through. Blinking at the sunlight, he dashed around dust-covered furniture and out into the hall.

When he reached the second floor and passed Cards, he didn't break stride. "Turn off the gas to Kirby's studio from the main valve," he ordered, coughing as he moved by. "And keep everyone away from there."

"Yes, Mr. Haines." Cards continued to walk toward the main stairway, carrying his pile of fresh linens.

When Adam reached her room, he laid Kirby on the bed, then opened the windows. He stood there a moment, just breathing, letting the air rush over his face and soothe his eyes. His stomach heaved. Forcing himself to take slow, measured breaths, he leaned out. When the nausea passed, he went back to her.

The high color had faded. Now she was as pale as the quilt. She didn't move. Hadn't moved, he remembered, since he'd hit her. With a tremor, he pressed his fingers to her throat and felt a slow, steady pulse. Quickly he went into the bathroom and soaked a cloth with cold water. As he ran it over her face, he said her name.

She coughed first, violently. Nothing could've relieved him more. When her eyes opened, she stared at him dully.

"You're in your room," he told her. "You're all right now."

"You hit me."

He grinned because there was indignation in her voice.

"I thought you'd take a punch better with a chin like that. I barely tapped you."

"So you say." Gingerly she sat up and touched her chin. Her head whirled once, but she closed her eyes and waited for it to pass. "I suppose I had it coming. Sorry I got neurotic on you."

He let his forehead rest against hers. "You scared the hell out of me. I guess you're the only woman who's received a marriage proposal and a right jab within minutes of each other."

"I hate to do the ordinary." Because she needed another minute, she lay back against the pillows. "Have you turned off the gas?"

"Cards is seeing to it."

"Of course." She said this calmly enough, then began to pluck at the quilt with her fingers. "As far as I know, no one's tried to kill me before."

It made it easier, he thought, that she understood and accepted that straight off. With a nod, he touched a hand to her cheek. "First we call a doctor. Then we call the police."

"I don't need a doctor. I'm just a little queasy now, it'll pass." She took both his hands and held them firmly. "And we can't call the police."

He saw something in her eyes that nearly snapped his temper. Stubbornness. "It's the usual procedure after attempted murder, Kirby."

She didn't wince. "They'll ask annoying questions and skulk all over the house. It's in all the movies."

"This isn't a game." His hands tightened on hers. "You could've been killed—would've been if you'd been in there alone. I'm not giving him another shot at you."

"You think it was Stuart." She let out a long breath. Be objective, she told herself. Then you can make Adam be objective. "Yes, I suppose it was, though I wouldn't have thought him ingenious enough. There's no one else who'd want to hurt me. Still, we can't prove a thing."

"That has yet to be seen." His eyes flashed a moment as he thought of the satisfaction he'd get from beating a confession out of Hiller. She saw it. She understood it.

"You're more primitive than I'd imagined." Touched, she traced her finger down his jaw. "I didn't know how nice it would be to have someone want to vanquish dragons for me. Who needs a bunch of silly police when I have you?"

"Don't try to outmaneuver me."

"I'm not." The smile left her eyes and her lips. "We're not in the position to call the police. I couldn't answer the questions they'd ask, don't you see? Papa has to resolve the business of the Rembrandt, Adam. If everything came out now, he'd be hopelessly compromised. He might go to prison. Not for anything," she said softly. "Not for anything would I risk that."

"He won't," Adam said shortly. No matter what strings he'd have to pull, what dance he'd have to perform, he'd see to it that Fairchild stayed clear. "Kirby, do you think your father would continue with whatever he's plotting once he knew of this?"

"I couldn't predict his reaction." Weary, she let out a long breath and tried to make him understand. "He might destroy the Rembrandt in a blind rage. He could go after Stuart single-handed. He's capable of it. What good would any of that do, Adam?" The queasiness was passing, but it had left her weak. Though she didn't know it, the vulnerability was her best weapon. "We have to let it lie for a while longer."

"What do you mean, let it lie?"

"I'll speak to Papa—tell him what happened in my own way, so that he doesn't overreact. Harriet and Melanie are coming to dinner tonight. It has to wait until tomorrow."

"How can he sit down and have dinner with Harriet when he has stolen something from her?" Adam demanded. "How can he do something like this to a friend?"

Pain shot into her eyes. Deliberately she lowered them, but he'd already seen it. "I don't know."

"I'm sorry."

She shook her head. "No, you have no reason to be. You've been wonderful through all of this."

"No, I haven't." He pressed the heels of his hands to his eyes.

"Let me be the judge of that. And give me one more day." She touched his wrists and waited until he lowered his hands. "Just one more day, then I'll talk to Papa. Maybe we'll get everything straightened out."

"That much, Kirby. No more." He had some thinking of his own to do. Perhaps one more night would give him some answers. "Tomorrow you tell Philip everything, no glossing over the details. If he doesn't agree to resolve the Rembrandt business then, I'm taking over."

She hesitated a minute. She'd said she trusted him. It was true. "All right."

"And I'll deal with Hiller."

"You're not going to fight with him."

Amused, he lifted a brow. "No?"

"Adam, I won't have you bruised and bloodied. That's it."

"Your confidence in me is overwhelming."

With a laugh, she sat up again and threw her arms around him. "My hero. He'd never lay a hand on you."

"I beg your pardon, Miss Fairchild."

"Yes, Cards." Shifting her head, Kirby acknowledged the butler in the doorway.

"It seems a chair has somehow found its way through your studio window. Unfortunately, it landed in Jamie's bed of zinnias."

"Yes, I know. I suppose he's quite annoyed."

"Indeed, miss."

"I'll apologize, Cards. Perhaps a new lawn mower . . . You'll see to having the window repaired?"

"Yes, miss."

"And have that heater replaced by something from the twentieth-century," Adam added. He watched as Cards glanced at him then back at Kirby.

"As soon as possible, please, Cards."

With a nod, the butler backed out of the doorway.

"He takes his orders from you, doesn't he?" Adam commented as the quiet footsteps receded. "I've seen the subtle nods and looks between the two of you."

She brushed a smudge of dirt on the shoulder of his shirt. "I've no idea what you mean."

"A century ago, Cards would've been known as the queen's man." When she laughed at the term, he eased her back on the pillows. "Rest," he ordered.

"Adam, I'm fine."

"Want me to get tough again?" Before she could answer, he covered her mouth with his, lingering. "Turn the batteries down awhile," he murmured. "I might have to call the doctor after all."

"Blackmail." She brought his mouth back to hers again. "But maybe if you rested with me."

"Rest isn't what would happen then." He drew away as she grumbled a protest.

"A half hour."

"Fine. I'll be back."

She smiled and let her eyes close. "I'll be waiting."

* * *

It was too soon for stars, too late for sunbeams. From a window in the parlor, Adam watched the sunset hold off twilight just a few moments longer.

After reporting the attempt on Kirby's life to McIntyre, he'd found himself suddenly weary. Half lies, half truths. It had to end. It would end, he decided, tomorrow. Fairchild would have to see reason, and Kirby would be told everything. The hell with McIntyre, the job and anything else. She deserved honesty along with everything else he wanted to give her. Everything else, he realized, would mean nothing to Kirby without it.

The sun lowered further and the horizon exploded with rose-gold light. He thought of the Titian woman. She'd understand, he told himself. She had to understand. He'd make her understand. Thinking to check on her again, Adam turned from the window.

When he reached her room, he heard the sound of running water. The simple, natural sound of her humming along with her bath dissolved his tension. He thought about joining her, then remembered how pale and tired she'd looked. Another time, he promised both of them as he shut the door to her room again. Another time he'd have the pleasure of lounging in the big marble tub with her.

"Where's that wretched girl?" Fairchild demanded from behind him. "She's been hiding out all day."

"Having a bath," Adam told him.

"She'd better have a damn good explanation, that's all I have to say." Looking grim, Fairchild reached for the doorknob. Adam blocked the door automatically.

"For what?"

Fairchild glared at him. "My shoes."

Adam looked down at Fairchild's small stockinged feet. "I don't think she has them."

"A man tugs himself into a restraining suit, chokes himself with a ridiculous tie, then has no shoes." Fairchild pulled at the knot around his neck. "Is that justice?"

"No. Have you tried Cards?"

"Cards couldn't get his big British feet in my shoes." Then he frowned and pursed his lips. "Then again, he did have my suit."

"I rest my case."

"The man's a kleptomaniac," Fairchild grumbled as he wandered down the hall. "I'd check my shorts if I were you.

No telling what he'll pick up next. Cocktails in a half hour, Adam. Hustle along."

Deciding a quiet drink was an excellent idea after the day they'd put in, Adam went to change. He was adjusting the knot in his own tie when Kirby knocked. She opened it without waiting for his answer, then stood a moment, deliberately posed in the doorway—head thrown back, one arm raised high on the jamb, the other at her hip. The slinky jumpsuit clung to every curve, falling in folds from her neck and dispensing with a back altogether. At her ears, emeralds the size of quarters picked up the vivid green shade. Five twisted, gold chains hung past her waist.

"Hello, neighbor." Glittering and gleaming, she crossed to him. Adam put a finger under her chin and studied her face. As an artist, she knew how to make use of the colors of a makeup palette. Her cheeks were tinted with a touch of bronze, her lips just a bit darker. "Well?"

"You look better," he decided.

"That's a poor excuse for a compliment."

"How do you feel?"

"I'd feel a lot better if you'd stop examining me as though I had a rare terminal disease and kiss me as you're supposed to." She twisted her arms around his neck and let her lashes lower.

It was them he kissed first, softly, with a tenderness that had her sighing. Then his lips skimmed down, over her cheeks, gently over her jawline.

"Adam . . ." His name was only a breath on the air as his mouth touched hers. She wanted it all now. Instantly. She wanted the fire and flash, the pleasure and the passion. She wanted that calm, spreading contentment that only he could give to her. "I love you," she murmured. "I love you until there's nothing else but that."

"There is nothing else but that," he said, almost fiercely. "We've a lifetime for it." He drew her away so he could bring both of her hands to his lips. "A lifetime, Kirby, and it isn't long enough."

"Then we'll have to start soon." She felt the giddiness again, the light-headedness, but she wouldn't run from it. "Very soon," she added. "But we have to wait at least until after dinner. Harriet and Melanie should be here any minute."

"If I had my choice, I'd stay with you alone in this room and make love until sunrise."

"Don't tempt me to tarnish your reputation." Because she knew she had to, she stepped back and finished adjusting his tie herself. It was a brisk, womanly gesture he found himself enjoying. "Ever since I told Harriet about your help with the Titian, she's decided you're the greatest thing since peanut butter. I wouldn't want to mess that up by making you late for dinner."

"Then we'd better go now. Five more minutes alone with you and we'd be a lot more than late." When she laughed, he linked her arm through his and led her from the room. "By the way, your father's shoes were stolen."

* * *

To the casual observer, the group in the parlor would have seemed a handful of elegant, cosmopolitan people. Secure, friendly, casually wealthy. Looking beyond the sparkle and glitter, a more discerning eye might have seen the pallor of Kirby's skin that her careful application of makeup disguised. Someone looking closely might have noticed that her friendly nonsense covered a discomfort that came from battling loyalties.

To someone from the outside, the group might have taken on a different aspect if the canvas were stretched. Rick's stuttering nerves were hardly noticed by those in the parlor. As was Melanie's subtle disdain for him. Both were the expected. Fairchild's wolfish grins and Harriet's jolting laughter covered the rest.

Everyone seemed relaxed, except Adam. The longer it went on, the more he wished he'd insisted that Kirby post-pone the dinner party. She looked frail. The more energy she poured out, the more fragile she seemed to him. And touch-ingly valiant. Her devotion to Harriet hadn't been lip service. Adam could see it, hear it. When she loved, as Fairchild had said, she loved completely. Even the thought of the Rem-brandt would be tearing her in two. Tomorrow. By the next day, it would be over.

"Adam." Harriet took his arm as Kirby poured after-dinner drinks. "I'd love to see Kirby's portrait."

"As soon as it's finished you'll have a private viewing." And until the repairs in the tower were complete, he thought, he was keeping all outsiders away.

"I'll have to be content with that, I suppose." She pouted a moment, then forgave him. "Sit beside me," Harriet com-manded and spread the flowing vermilion of her skirt on the sofa. "Kirby said I could flirt with you."

Adam noticed that Melanie turned a delicate pink at her mother's flamboyance. Unable to resist, he lifted Harriet's hand to his lips. "Do I need permission to flirt with you?"

"Guard your heart, Harriet," Kirby warned as she set out drinks.

"Mind your own business," Harriet tossed back. "By the way, Adam, I'd like you to have my necklace of crocodile teeth as a token of my appreciation."

"Good heavens, Mother." Melanie sipped at her blackberry brandy. "Why would Adam want that hideous thing?"

"Sentiment," she returned without blinking an eye. "Ad-am's agreed to let me exhibit Kirby's portrait, and I want to repay him."

The old girl's quick, Adam decided as she sent him a guile-less smile, and Melanie's been kept completely in the dark about the hobby her mother shares with Fairchild. Studying

Melanie's cool beauty, Adam decided her mother knew best. She'd never react as Kirby did. Melanie could have their love and affection, but secrets were kept within the triangle. No, he realized, oddly pleased. It was now a rectangle.

"He doesn't have to wear it," Harriet went on, breaking into his thoughts.

"I should hope not," Melanie put in, rolling her eyes at Kirby.

"It's for good luck." Harriet sent Kirby a glance, then squeezed Adam's arm. "But perhaps you have all the luck you need."

"Perhaps my luck's just beginning."

"How quaintly they speak in riddles." Kirby sat on the arm of Melanie's chair. "Why don't we ignore them?"

"Your hawk's coming along nicely, Mr. Fairchild," Rich hazarded.

"Aha!" It was all Fairchild needed. Bursting with good feelings, he treated Rick to an in-depth lecture on the use of calipers.

"Rick's done it now," Kirby whispered to Melanie. "Papa has no mercy on a captive audience."

"I didn't know Uncle Philip was sculpting."

"Don't mention it," Kirby said quickly. "You'll never escape." Pursing her lips, she looked down at Melanie's elegant dark rose dress. The lines flowed fluidly with the flash of a studded buckle at the waist. "Melly, I wonder if you'd have time to design a dress for me."

Surprised, Melanie glanced up. "Oh course, I'd love to. But I've been trying to talk you into it for years and you've always refused to go through the fittings."

Kirby shrugged. A wedding dress was a different matter, she mused. Still, she didn't mention her plans with Adam. Her father would know first. "I usually buy on impulse, whatever appeals at the time."

"From Goodwill to Rive Gauche," Melanie murmured. "So this must be special."

"I'm taking a page from your book," Kirby evaded. "You know I've always admired your talent, I just knew I wouldn't have the patience for all the preliminaries." She laughed. "Do you think you can design a dress that'd make me look demure?"

"Demure?" Harriet cut in, pouncing on the word. "Poor Melanie would have to be a sorceress to pull that off. Even as a child in that sweet little muslin you looked capable of battling a tribe of Comanches. Philip, you must let me borrow that painting of Kirby for the gallery."

"We'll see." His eyes twinkled. "You'll have to soften me up a bit first. I've always had a deep affection for that painting." With a hefty sigh, he leaned back with his drink. "Its value goes below the surface."

"He still begrudges me my sitting fee." Kirby sent her father a sweet smile. "He forgets I never collected for any of the others."

"You never posed for the others," Fairchild reminded her.

"I never signed a release for them, either."

"Melly posed for me out of the goodness of her heart."

"Melly's nicer than I am," Kirby said simply. "I like being selfish."

"Heartless creature," Harriet put in mildly. "It's so selfish of you to teach sculpture in the summer to those handicapped children."

Catching Adam's surprised glance, Kirby shifted uncomfortably. "Harriet, think of my reputation."

"She's sensitive about her good deeds," Harriet told Adam with a squeeze for his knee.

"I simply had nothing else to do." With a shrug, Kirby turned away. "Are you going to Saint Moritz this year, Melly?"

Fraud, Adam thought as he watched her guide the subject away from herself. A beautiful, sensitive fraud. And finding her so, he loved her more.

By the time Harriet and Melanie rose to leave, Kirby was fighting off a raging headache. Too much strain, she knew, but she wouldn't admit it. She could tell herself she needed only a good night's sleep, and nearly believe it.

"Kirby." Harriet swirled her six-foot shawl over her shoulder before she took Kirby's chin in her hand. "You look tired, and a bit pale. I haven't seen you look pale since you were thirteen and had the flu. I remember you swore you'd never be ill again."

"After that disgusting medicine you poured down my throat, I couldn't afford to. I'm fine." But she threw her arms around Harriet's neck and held on. "I'm fine, really."

"Mmm." Over her head, Harriet frowned at Fairchild. "You might think about Australia. We'll put some color in your cheeks."

"I will. I love you."

"Go to sleep, child," Harriet murmured.

The moment the door was closed, Adam took Kirby's arm. Ignoring her father and Rick, he began to pull her up the stairs. "You belong in bed."

"Shouldn't you be dragging me by the hair instead of the arm?"

"Some other time, when my intentions are less peaceful." He stopped outside her door. "You're going to sleep."

"Tired of me already?"

The words were hardly out of her mouth when his covered it. Holding her close, he let himself go for a moment, releasing the needs, the desires, the love. He could feel her heart thud, her bones melt. "Can't you see how tired I am of you?" He kissed her again with his hands framing her face. "You must see how you bore me."

"Anything I can do?" she murmured, slipping her hands under his jacket.

"Get some rest." He took her by the shoulders. "This is your last opportunity to sleep alone."

"Am I sleeping alone?"

It wasn't easy for him. He wanted to devour her, he wanted to delight her. He wanted, more than anything else, to have a clean slate between them before they made love again. If she hadn't looked so weary, so worn, he'd have told her everything then and there. "This may come as a shock to you," he said lightly. "But you're not Wonder Woman."

"Really?"

"You're going to get a good night's sleep. Tomorrow." He took her hands and the look, the sudden intenseness, confused her. "Tomorrow, Kirby, we have to talk."

"About what?"

"Tomorrow," he repeated before he could change his mind. "Rest now." He gave her a nudge inside. "If you're not feeling any better tomorrow, you're going to stay in bed and be pampered."

She managed one last wicked grin. "Promise?"

CHAPTER 11

It was clear after Kirby had tossed in bed and fluffed up her pillow for more than an hour that she wasn't going to get the rest everyone seemed to want for her. Her body was dragging, but her mind refused to give in to it.

She tried. For twenty minutes she recited dull poetry. Closing her eyes, she counted five hundred and twenty-seven camels. She turned on her bedside radio and found chamber music. She was, after all of it, wide awake.

It wasn't fear. If Stuart had indeed tried to kill her, he'd failed. She had her own wits, and she had Adam. No, it wasn't fear.

The Rembrandt. She couldn't think of anything else after seeing Harriet laughing, after remembering how Harriet had nursed her through the flu and had given her a sweet and totally unnecessary woman-to-woman talk when she'd been a girl.

Kirby had grieved for her own mother, and though she'd died when Kirby had been a child, the memory remained perfectly clear. Harriet hadn't been a substitute. Harriet had simply been Harriet. Kirby loved her for that alone.

How could she sleep?

Annoyed, Kirby rolled over on her back and stared at the ceiling. Maybe, just maybe, she could make use of the insomnia and sort it all out and make some sense out of it.

Her father, she was certain, would do nothing to hurt Harriet without cause. Was revenge on Stuart cause enough? After a moment, she decided it didn't follow.

Harriet had gone to Africa—that was first. It had been nearly two weeks after that when Kirby had broken her engagement with Stuart. Afterward she had told her father of Stuart's blackmail threats and he'd been unconcerned. He'd said, Kirby remembered, that Stuart wasn't in any position to make waves.

Then it made sense to assume they'd already begun plans to switch the paintings. Revenge was out.

Then why?

Not for money, Kirby thought. Not for the desire to own the painting himself. That wasn't his way—she knew better than anyone how he felt about greed. But then, stealing from a friend wasn't his way, either.

If she couldn't find the reason, perhaps she could find the painting itself.

Still staring at the ceiling, she began to go over everything her father had said. So many ambiguous comments, she mused. But then, that was typical of him. In the house—that much was certain. In the house, hidden with appropriate affection and respect. Just how many hundreds of possibilities could she sort through in one night?

She blew out a disgusted breath and rolled over again. With a last thump for her pillow, she closed her eyes. The yawn, she felt, was a hopeful sign. As she snuggled deeper, a tiny memory probed.

She'd think about it tomorrow. . . . No, now, she thought, and rolled over again. She'd think about it now. What was it her father had been saying to Adam when she'd walked into his studio the night after the Titian switch? Something . . . Something . . . about involving her figuratively.

"Root rot," she muttered, and squeezed her eyes shut in concentration. "What the devil was that supposed to mean?" Just as she was about to give up, the idea seeped in. Her eyes sprang open as she sprang up. "It'd be just like him!"

Grabbing a robe, she dashed from the room.

For a moment in the hall she hesitated. Perhaps she should wake Adam and tell him of her theory. Then again, it was no more than that, and he hadn't had the easiest day of it, either. If she produced results, then she'd wake him. And if she was wrong, her father would kill her.

She made a quick trip to her father's studio, then went down to the dining room.

On neither trip did she bother with lights. She wanted no one to pop out of their room and ask what she was up to. Carrying a rag, a bottle and a stack of newspapers, she went silently through the dark. Once she'd reached the dining room, she turned on the lights. No one would investigate downstairs except Cards. He'd never question her. She worked quickly.

Kirby spread the newspapers in thick pads on the dining room table. Setting the bottle and the rag on them, she turned to her own portrait.

"You're too clever for your own good, Papa," she murmured as she studied the painting. "I'd never be able to tell if this was a duplicate. There's only one way."

Once she'd taken the portrait from the wall, Kirby laid it on the newspaper. "Its value goes below the surface," she murmured. Isn't that what he'd said to Harriet? And he'd been smug. He'd been smug right from the start. Kirby opened the bottle and tipped the liquid onto the rag. "Forgive me, Papa," she said quietly.

With the lightest touch—an expert's touch—she began to remove layers of paint in the lower corner. Minutes passed. If she was wrong, she wanted the damage to be minimal. If she was right, she had something priceless in her hands. Either way, she couldn't rush.

She dampened the rag and wiped again. Her father's bold signature disappeared, then the bright summer grass beneath it, and the primer.

And there, beneath where there should have been only canvas, was a dark, somber brown. One letter, then another, appeared. It was all that was necessary.

"Great buckets of blood," she murmured. "I was right."

Beneath the feet of the girl she'd been was Rembrandt's signature. She'd go no further. As carefully as she'd unstopped it, Kirby secured the lid of the bottle.

"So, Papa, you put Rembrandt to sleep under a copy of my portrait. Only you would've thought to copy yourself to pull it off."

"Very clever."

Whirling, Kirby looked behind her into the dark outside the dining room. She knew the voice; it didn't frighten her. As her heart pounded, the shadows moved. What now? she asked herself quickly. Just how would she explain it?

"Cleverness runs in the family, doesn't it, Kirby?"

"So I'm told." She tried to smile. "I'd like to explain. You'd better come in out of the dark and sit down. It could take—" She stopped as the first part of the invitation was accepted. She stared at the barrel of a small polished revolver. Lifting her gaze from it, she stared into clear, delicate blue eyes. "Melly, what's going on?"

"You look surprised. I'm glad." With a satisfied smile, Melanie aimed the gun at Kirby's head. "Maybe you're not so clever after all."

"Don't point that at me."

"I intend to point it at you." She lowered the gun to chest level. "And I'll do more than point it if you move."

"Melly." She wasn't afraid, not yet. She was confused, even annoyed, but she wasn't afraid of the woman she'd grown up with. "Put that thing away and sit down. What're you doing here this time of night?"

"Two reasons. First, to see if I could find any trace of the painting you've so conveniently found for me. Second, to finish the job that was unsuccessful this morning."

"This morning?" Kirby took a step forward then froze

when she heard the quick, deadly click. Good God, could it actually be loaded? "Melly . . ."

"I suppose I must have miscalculated a bit or you'd be dead already." The elegant rose silk whispered as she shrugged. "I know the passages very well. Remember, you used to drag me around in them when we were children—before you went in with a faulty flashlight. I'd changed the batteries in it, you see. I'd never told you about that, had I?" She laughed as Kirby remained silent. "I used the passages this morning. Once I was sure you and Adam were settled in, I went out and turned on the gas by the main valve—I'd already broken the switch on the unit."

"You can't be serious." Kirby dragged a hand through her hair.

"Deadly serious, Kirby."

"Why?"

"Primarily for money, of course."

"Money?" She would've laughed, but her throat was closing. "But you don't need money."

"You're so smug." The venom came through. Kirby wondered that she'd never heard it before. "Yes, I need money."

"You wouldn't take a settlement from your ex-husband."

"He wouldn't give me a dime," Melanie corrected. "He cut me off, and as he had me cold on adultery, I wasn't in a position to take him to court. He let me get a quiet, discreet divorce so that our reputations wouldn't suffer. And except for one incident, I'd been very discreet. Stuart and I were always very careful."

"Stuart?" Kirby lifted a hand to rub at her temple. "You and Stuart?"

"We've been lovers for over three years. Questions are just buzzing around in your head, aren't they?" Enjoying herself, Melanie stepped closer. The whiff of Chanel followed her. "It was more practical for us if we pretended to be just acquaintances. I convinced Stuart to ask you to marry him. My inheritance has dwindled to next to nothing. Your money would have met Stuart's and my tastes very nicely. And we'd have got close to Uncle Philip."

She ignored the rest and homed in on the most important. "What do you want from my father?"

"I found out about the little game he and Mother indulged in years ago. Not all the details, but enough to know I could use it if I had to. I thought it was time to use your father's talent for my own benefit."

"You made plans to steal from your own mother."

"Don't be so self-righteous." Her voice chilled. The gun was steady. "Your father betrayed her without a murmur, then double-crossed us in the bargain. Now you've solved that little problem for me." With her free hand, she gestured to the painting. "I should be grateful I failed this morning. I'd still be looking for the painting."

Somehow, some way, she'd deal with this. Kirby started with the basics. "Melly, how could you hurt me? We've been friends all our lives."

"Friends?" The word sounded like an obscenity. "I've hated you for as long as I can remember."

"No—"

"Hated," Melanie repeated, coldly this time and with the ring of truth. "It was always you people flocked around, always you men preferred. My own mother preferred you."

"That's not true." Did it go so deep? Kirby thought with a flood of guilt. Should she have seen it before? "Melly—" But as she started forward, Melanie gestured with the gun.

"'Melanie, don't be so stiff and formal. . . . Melanie, where's your sense of humor?'" Her eyes narrowed into slits. "She never came right out and said I should be more like you, but that's what she wanted."

"Harriet loves you—"

"Love?" Melanie cut Kirby off with a laugh. "I don't give a damn for love. It won't buy what I need. You may have taken my mother, but that was a minor offense. The men you snatched from under my nose time and time again is a bigger one."

"I never took a man from you. I've never shown an interest in anyone you were serious about."

"There have been dozens," Melanie corrected. Her voice was as brittle as glass. "You'd smile and say something stupid and I'd be forgotten. You never had my looks, but you'd use that so-called charm and lure them away, or you'd freeze up and do the same thing."

"I might've been friendly to someone you cared for," Kirby said quickly. "If I froze, it was to discourage them. Good God, Melly, I'd never have done anything to hurt you. I love you."

"I've no use for your love any longer. It served its purpose well enough." She smiled slowly as tears swam in Kirby's eyes. "My only regret is that you didn't fall for Stuart. I wanted to see you fawn over him, knowing he preferred me—married you only because I wanted it. When you came to see him that night, I nearly came out of the bedroom just for the pleasure of seeing your face. But . . ." She shrugged. "We had long-range plans."

"You used me," Kirby said quietly when she could no longer deny it. "You had Stuart use me."

"Of course. Still, it wasn't wise of me to come back from New York for the weekend to be with him."

"Why, Melanie? Why have you pretended all these years?"

"You were useful. Even as a child I knew that. Later, in Paris, you opened doors for me, then again in New York. It was even due to you that I spent a year of luxury with Carlyse. You wouldn't sleep with him and you wouldn't marry him. I did both."

"And that's all?" Kirby murmured. "That's all?"

"That's all. You're not useful any longer, Kirby. In fact, you're an inconvenience. I'd planned your death as a warning to Uncle Philip, now it's just a necessity."

She wanted to turn away, but she needed to face it. "How could I have known you all my life and not seen it? How could you have hated me and not shown it?"

"You let emotions rule your life, I don't. Pick up the

painting, Kirby." With the gun, she gestured. "And be careful with it. Stuart and I have been offered a healthy sum for it. If you call out," she added, "I'll shoot you now and be in the passage with the painting before anyone comes down."

"What are you going to do?"

"We're going into the passage. You're going to have a nasty spill, Kirby, and break your neck. I'm going to take the painting home and wait for the call to tell me of your accident."

She'd stall. If only she'd woken Adam . . . No, if she'd woken him, he, too, would have a gun pointed at him. "Everyone knows how I feel about the passages."

"It'll be a mystery. When they find the empty space on the wall, they'll know the Rembrandt was responsible. Stuart should be the first target, but he's out of town and has been for three days. I'll be devastated by the death of my oldest and dearest friend. It'll take months in Europe to recover from the grief."

"You've thought this out carefully." Kirby rested against the table. "But are you capable of murder, Melly?" Slowly she closed her fingers around the bottle, working off the top with her thumb. "Face-to-face murder, not remote-control like this morning."

"Oh, yes." Melanie smiled beautifully. "I prefer it. I feel better with you knowing who's going to kill you. Now pick up the painting, Kirby. It's time."

With a jerk of her arm, Kirby tossed the turpentine mixture, splattering it on Melanie's neck and dress. When Melanie tossed up her hand in protection, Kirby lunged. Together they fell in a rolling heap onto the floor, the gun pressed between them.

* * *

What do you mean Hiller's been in New York since yesterday?" Adam demanded. "What happened this morning wasn't an accident. He had to have done it."

"No way." In a few words McIntyre broke Adam's theory. "I have a good man on him. I can give you the name of Hiller's hotel. I can give you the name of the restaurant where he had lunch and what he ate while you were throwing chairs through windows. He's got his alibi cold, Adam, but it doesn't mean he didn't arrange it."

"Damn." Adam lowered the transmitter while he rearranged his thinking. "It gives me a bad feeling, Mac. Dealing with Hiller's one thing, but it's a whole new story if he has a partner or he's hired a pro to do his dirty work. Kirby needs protection, official protection. I want her out."

"I'll work on it. The Rembrandt—"

"I don't give a damn about the Rembrandt," Adam tossed back. "But it'll be in my hands tomorrow if I have to hang Fairchild up by his thumbs."

McIntyre let out a sigh of relief. "That's better. You were making me nervous thinking you were hung up on the Fairchild woman."

"I am hung up on the Fairchild woman," Adam returned mildly. "So you'd better arrange for—" He heard the shot. One, sharp and clean. It echoed and echoed through his head. *"Kirby!"* He thought of nothing else as he dropped the open transmitter on the floor and ran.

He called her name again as he raced downstairs. But his only answer was silence. He called as he rushed like a madman through the maze of rooms downstairs, but she didn't call back. Nearly blind with terror, his own voice echoing back to mock him, he ran on, slamming on lights as he went until the house was lit up like a celebration. Racing headlong into the dining room, he nearly fell over the two figures on the floor.

"Oh, my God!"

"I've killed her! Oh, God, Adam, help me! I think I've killed her!" With tears streaming down her face, Kirby pressed a blood-soaked linen napkin against Melanie's side. The stain spread over the rose silk of the dress and onto Kirby's hand.

"Keep the pressure firm." He didn't ask questions, but grabbed a handful of linen from the buffet behind him. Nudging Kirby aside, he felt for a pulse. "She's alive." He pressed more linen to Melanie's side. "Kirby—"

Before he could speak again, there was chaos. The rest of the household poured into the dining room from every direction. Polly let out one squeal that never ended.

"Call an ambulance," Adam ordered Cards, even as the butler turned to do so. "Shut her up, or get her out," he told Rick, nodding to Polly.

Recovering quickly, Fairchild knelt beside his daughter and the daughter of his closest friend. "Kirby, what happened here?"

"I tried to take the gun from her." She struggled to breathe as she looked down at the blood on her hands. "We fell. I don't—Papa, I don't even know which one of us pulled the trigger. Oh, God, I don't even know."

"Melanie had a gun?" Steady as a rock, Fairchild took Kirby's shoulders and turned her to face him. "Why?"

"She hates me." Her voice shook, then leveled as she stared into her father's face. "She's always hated me, I never knew. It was the Rembrandt, Papa. She'd planned it all."

"Melanie?" Fairchild glanced beyond Kirby to the unconscious figure on the floor. "She was behind it." He fell silent, only a moment. "How bad, Adam?"

"I don't know, damn it. I'm an artist, not a doctor." There was fury in his eyes and blood on his hands. "It might've been Kirby."

"Yes, you're right." Fairchild's fingers tightened on his daughter's shoulder. "You're right."

"I found the Rembrandt," Kirby murmured. If it was shock that was making her light-headed, she wouldn't give in to it. She forced herself to think and to speak clearly.

Fairchild looked at the empty space on the wall, then at the table where the painting lay. "So you did."

With a cluck of her tongue, Tulip pushed Fairchild aside

and took Kirby by the arm. Ignoring everyone else, she pulled Kirby to her feet. "Come with me, lovie. Come along with me now, that's a girl."

Feeling helpless, Adam watched Kirby being led away while he fought to stop the bleeding. "You'd better have a damn good explanation," he said between his teeth as his gaze swept over Fairchild.

"Explanations don't seem to be enough at this point," he murmured. Very slowly he rose. The sound of sirens cut through the quiet. "I'll phone Harriet."

Almost an hour had passed before Adam could wash the blood from his hands. Unconscious still, Melanie was speeding on her way to the hospital. His only thought was for Kirby now, and he left his room to find her. When he reached the bottom landing, he came upon an argument in full gear. Though the shouting was all one-sided, the noise vibrated through the hall.

"I want to see Adam Haines and I want to see him immediately!"

"Gate-crashing, Mac?" Adam moved forward to stand beside Cards.

"Adam, thank God." The small, husky man with the squared-off face and disarming eyes ran a hand through his disheveled mat of hair. "I didn't know what'd happened to you. Tell this wall to move aside, will you?"

"It's all right, Cards." He drew an expressionless stare. "He's not a reporter. I know him."

"Very well, sir."

"What the hell's going on?" McIntyre demanded when Cards walked back down the hall. "Who just got carted out of here in an ambulance? Damn it, Adam, I thought it might be you. Last thing I know, you're shouting and breaking transmission."

"It's been a rough night." Putting a hand on his shoulder, Adam led him into the parlor. "I need a drink." Going directly to the bar, Adam poured, drank and poured again.

"Drink up, Mac," he invited. "This has to be better than the stuff you've been buying in that little motel down the road. Philip," he continued as Fairchild walked into the room, "I imagine you could use one of these."

"Yes." With a nod of acknowledgment for McIntyre, and no questions, Fairchild accepted the glass Adam offered.

"We'd better sit down. Philip Fairchild," Adam went on as Fairchild settled himself, "Henry McIntyre, investigator for the Commonwealth Insurance company."

"Ah, Mr. McIntyre." Fairchild drank half his Scotch in one gulp. "We have quite a bit to discuss. But first, Adam, satisfy my curiosity. How did you become involved with the investigation?"

"It's not the first time I've worked for Mac, but it's the last." He sent McIntyre a quiet look that was lined in steel. "There's a matter of our being cousins," he added. "Second cousins."

"Relatives." Fairchild smiled knowingly, then gave McIntyre a charming smile.

"You knew why I was here," Adam said. "How?"

"Well, Adam, my boy, it's nothing to do with your cleverness." Fairchild tossed off the rest of the Scotch, then rose to fill his glass again. "I was expecting someone to come along. You were the only one who did." He sat back down with a sigh. "Simple as that."

"Expecting?"

"Would someone tell me who was in that ambulance?" McIntyre cut in.

"Melanie Burgess." Fairchild looked into his Scotch. "Melly." It would hurt, he knew, for a long time. For himself, for Harriet and for Kirby. It was best to begin to deal with it. "She was shot when Kirby tried to take her gun away— the gun she was pointing at my daughter."

"Melanie Burgess," McIntyre mused. "It fits with the information I got today. Information," he added to Adam, "I was about to give you when you broke transmission. I'd like it from the beginning, Mr. Fairchild. I assume the police are on their way."

"Yes, no way around that." Fairchild sipped at his Scotch and deliberated on just how to handle things. Then he saw he no longer had McIntyre's attention. He was staring at the doorway.

Dressed in jeans and a white blouse, Kirby stood just inside the room. She was pale, but her eyes were dark. She was beautiful. It was the first thing McIntyre thought. The second was that she was a woman who could empty a man's mind the way a thirsty man empties a bottle.

"Kirby." Adam was up and across the room. He had his hands on hers. Hers were cold, but steady. "Are you all right?"

"Yes. Melanie?"

"The paramedics handled everything. I got the impression the wound wasn't as bad as it looked. Go lie down," he murmured. "Forget it for a while."

"No." She shook her head and managed a weak smile. "I'm fine, really. I've been washed and patted and plied with liquor, though I wouldn't mind another. The police will want to question me." Her gaze drifted to McIntyre. She didn't ask, but simply assumed he was with the police. "Do you need to talk to me?"

It wasn't until then he realized he'd been staring. Clearing his throat, McIntyre rose. "I'd like to hear your father's story first, Miss Fairchild."

"Wouldn't we all?" Struggling to find some balance, she walked to her father's chair. "Are you going to come clean, Papa, or should I hire a shady lawyer?"

"Unnecessary, my sweet." He took her hand and held it. "The beginning," he continued with a smile for McIntyre. "It started, I suppose, a few days before Harriet flew off to Africa. She's an absentminded woman. She had to return to the gallery one night to pick up some papers she'd forgotten. When she saw the light in Stuart's office, she started to go in and scold him for working late. Instead she eavesdropped on his phone conversation and learned of his plans to steal the Rembrandt. Absentminded but shrewd, Harriet left and let Stuart think his plans were undetected." He grinned and squeezed Kirby's hand. "An intelligent woman, she came directly to a friend known for his loyalty and his sharp mind."

"Papa." With a laugh of relief, she bent over and kissed his head. "You were working together, I should've known."

"We developed a plan. Perhaps unwisely, we decided not to bring Kirby into it." He looked up at her. "Should I apologize?"

"Never."

But the fingers brushing over her hand said it for him. "Kirby's relationship with Stuart helped us along in that decision. And her occasional shortsightedness. That is, when she doesn't agree with my point of view."

"I might take the apology after all."

"In any case." Rising, Fairchild began to wander around the room, hands clasped behind his back. His version of Sherlock Holmes, Kirby decided, and settled back for the show. "Harriet and I both knew Stuart wasn't capable of constructing and carrying through on a theft like this alone. Harriet hadn't any idea whom he'd been talking to on the phone, but my name had been mentioned. Stuart had said he'd, ah, 'feel me out on the subject of producing a copy of the painting.'" His face fell easily into annoyed lines. "I've no idea why he should've thought a man like me would do something so base, so dishonest."

"Incredible," Adam murmured, and earned a blinding smile from father and daughter.

"We decided I'd agree, after some fee haggling. I'd then have the original in my possession while palming the copy off on Stuart. Sooner or later, his accomplice would be forced into the open to try to recover it. Meanwhile, Harriet reported the theft, but refused to file a claim. Instead she demanded that the insurance company act with discretion. Reluctantly she told them of her suspicion that I was involved, thereby ensuring that the investigation would be centered around me, and by association, Stuart and his accomplice. I concealed the Rembrandt behind a copy of a painting of my daughter, the original of which is tucked away in my room. I'm sentimental."

"Why didn't Mrs. Merrick just tell the police and the insurance company the truth?" McIntyre demanded after he'd worked his way through the explanation.

"They might have been hasty. No offense," Fairchild added indulgently. "Stuart might've been caught, but his accomplice would probably have gotten away. And, I confess, it was the intrigue that appealed to both of us. It was irresistible. You'll want to corroborate my story, of course."

"Of course," McIntyre agreed, and wondered if he could deal with another loony.

"We'd have done things differently if we'd had any idea that Melanie was involved. It's going to be difficult for Harriet." Pausing, he aimed a long look at McIntyre that was abruptly no-nonsense. "Be careful with her. Very careful. You might find our methods unorthodox, but she's a mother who's had two unspeakable shocks tonight: her daughter's betrayal and the possibility of losing her only child." He ran a hand over Kirby's hair as he stopped by her. "No matter how deep the hurt, the love remains, doesn't it, Kirby?"

"All I feel is the void," she murmured. "She hated me, and I think, I really think, she wanted me dead more than she wanted the painting. I wonder . . . I wonder just how much I'm to blame for that."

"You can't blame yourself for being, Kirby." Fairchild cupped her chin. "You can't blame a tree for reaching for the sun or another for rotting from within. We make our own choices and we're each responsible for them. Blame and credit belong to the individual. You haven't the right to claim either from someone else."

"You won't let me cover the hurt with guilt." After a long breath she rose and kissed his cheek. "I'll have to deal with it." Without thinking, she held out a hand for Adam before she turned to McIntyre. "Do you need a statement from me?"

"No, the shooting's not my jurisdiction, Miss Fairchild. Just the Rembrandt." Finishing off the rest of his Scotch he rose. "I'll have to take it with me, Mr. Fairchild."

All graciousness, Fairchild spread his arms wide. "Perfectly understandable."

"I appreciate your cooperation." If he could call it that. With a weary smile, he turned to Adam. "Don't worry, I haven't forgotten your terms. If everything's as he says, I should be able to keep them out of it officially, as we agreed the other day. Your part of the job's over, and all in all you handled it well. So, I'll be sorry if you're serious about not working for me anymore. You got the Rembrandt back, Adam. Now I've got to get started on untangling the red tape."

"Job?" Going cold, Kirby turned. Her hand was still linked in Adam's, but she felt it go numb as she drew it slowly away. "Job?" she repeated, pressing the hand to her stomach as if to ward off a blow.

Not now, he thought in frustration, and searched for the words he'd have used only a few hours later. "Kirby—"

With all the strength she had left, all the bitterness she'd felt, she brought her hand across his face. "Bastard," she whispered. She fled at a dead run.

"Damn you, Mac." Adam raced after her.

CHAPTER 12

Adam caught up to her just as Kirby started to slam her bedroom door. Shoving it open, he pushed his way inside. For a moment, they only stared at each other.

"Kirby, let me explain."

"No." The wounded look had been replaced by glacial anger. "Just get out. All the way out, Adam—of my house and my life."

"I can't." He took her by the shoulders, but her head snapped up, and the look was so cold, so hard, he dropped his hands again. It was too late to explain the way he'd planned. Too late to prevent the hurt. Now he had to find the way around it. "Kirby, I know what you must be thinking. I want—"

"Do you?" It took all of her effort to keep her voice from rising. Instead it was cool and calm. "I'm going to tell you anyway so we can leave everything neat and tidy." She faced him because she refused to turn her back on the pain or on the betrayal. "I'm thinking that I've never detested anyone more than I detest you at this moment. I'm thinking Stuart and Melanie could take lessons on using people from you. I'm thinking how naive I was, how stupid, to have believed there was something special about you, something stable and honest. And I wonder how I could've made love with you and never seen it. Then again, I didn't see it in Melanie, either. I loved and trusted her." Tears burned behind her eyes but she ignored them. "I loved and trusted you."

"Kirby . . ."

"Don't touch me." She backed away, but it was the tremor in her voice, not the movement, that stopped him from going to her. "I don't ever want to feel your hands on me again." Because she wanted to weep, she laughed, and the sound was as sharp as a knife. "I've always admired a really good liar, Adam, but you're the best. Every time you touched me, you lied. You prostituted yourself in that bed." She gestured toward it and wanted to scream. She wanted to fling herself on it and weep until she was empty. She stood, straight as an arrow. "You lay beside me and said all the things I wanted to hear. Do you get extra points for that, Adam? Surely that was above and beyond the call of duty."

"Don't." He'd had enough. Enough of her cold, clear look, her cold, clear words. "You know there was no dishonesty there. What happened between us had nothing to do with the rest."

"It has everything to do with it."

"No." He'd take everything else she could fling at him, but not that. She'd changed his life with hardly more than a look. She had to know it. "I should never have put my hands on you, but I couldn't stop myself. I wanted you. I needed you. You have to believe that."

"I'll tell you what I believe," she said quietly, because every word he spoke was another slice into her heart. She'd finished with being used. "You came here for the Rembrandt, and you meant to find it no matter who or what you had to go through. My father and I were means to an end. Nothing more, nothing less."

He had to take it, had to let her say it, but there'd be no lies between them any longer. "I came for the Rembrandt. When I walked through the door, I only had one priority, to find it. But I didn't know you when I walked through the door. I wasn't in love with you then."

"Is this the part where you say everything changed?" she demanded, falling back on fury. "Shall we wait for the violins?" She was weakening. She turned away and leaned on the post of the bed. "Do better, Adam."

She could be cruel. He remembered her father's warning. He only wished he believed he had a defense. "I can't do better than the truth."

"Truth? What the hell do you know about truth?" She whirled back around, eyes damp now and shimmering with heat. "I stood here in this room and told you everything, everything I knew about my father. I trusted you with his welfare, the most important thing in my life. Where was your truth then?"

"I had a commitment. Do you think it was easy for me to sit here and listen, knowing I couldn't give you what you were giving me?"

"Yes." Her tone was dead calm, but her eyes were fierce. "Yes, I think it was a matter of routine for you. If you'd told me that night, the next day or the next, I might've believed you. If I'd heard it from you, I might've forgiven you."

Timing. Hadn't she told him how vital timing could be? Now he felt her slipping away from him, but he had nothing but excuses to give her. "I was going to tell you everything, start to finish, tomorrow."

"Tomorrow?" Slowly she nodded. "Tomorrows are very convenient. A pity for us all how rarely they come."

All the warmth, all the fire, that had drawn him to her was gone. He'd only seen this look on her face once before—when Stuart had backed her into a corner and she'd had no escape. Stuart had used physical dominance, but it was no prettier than the emotional pressure Adam knew he used. "I'm sorry, Kirby. If I'd taken the risk and told you this morning, it would've been different for all of us."

"I don't want your apology!" The tears beat her and poured out. She'd sacrificed everything else, now her pride was gone, as well. "I thought I'd found the man I could share my life

with. I fell in love with you in the flash of an instant. No questions, no doubts. I believed everything you said to me. I gave
you everything I had. In all my life no one's been allowed to
know me as you did. I entrusted you with everything I am
and you used me." Turning, she pressed her face into the
bedpost.

He had, he couldn't deny it even to himself. He'd used her,
as Stuart had used her. As Melanie had used her. Loving her
made no difference, yet he had to hope it made all the difference. "Kirby." It took all the strength he had not to go to
her, to comfort her, but he'd only be comforting himself if
he put his arms around her now. "There's nothing you can
say to me I haven't said to myself. I came here to do a job,
but I fell in love with you. There wasn't any warning for me,
either. I know I've hurt you. There's nothing I can do to turn
back the clock."

"Do you expect me to fall into your arms? Do you expect me to say nothing else matters but us?" She turned, and
though her cheeks were still damp, her eyes were dry. "It all
matters," she said flatly. "Your job's finished here, Adam.
You've recovered your Rembrandt. Take it, you earned it."

"You're not going to cut me out of your life."

"You've done that for me."

"No." The fury and frustration took over so that he grabbed
her arm and jerked her against him. "No, you'll have to adjust to the way things are, because I'm coming back." He ran
his hands down her hair, and they weren't steady. "You can
make me suffer. By God, you can do it. I'll give you that,
Kirby, but I'll be back."

Before his anger could push him too far, he whirled around
and left her alone.

Fairchild was waiting for him, sitting calmly in the parlor
by the fire. "I thought you'd need this." Without getting up,
he gestured to the glass of Scotch on the table beside him.
He waited until Adam had tossed it back. He didn't need to
be told what had passed between them. "I'm sorry. She's

hurt. Perhaps in time the wounds will close and she'll be able to listen."

Adam's knuckles whitened on the glass. "That's what I told her, but I didn't believe it. I betrayed her." His glance lowered and settled on the older man. "And you."

"You did what you had to do. You had a part to play." Fairchild spread his hands on his knees and stared at them, thinking of his own part. "She would've dealt with it, Adam. She's strong enough. But even Kirby has a breaking point. Melanie . . . It was too soon after Melanie."

"She won't let me comfort her." It was that anguish that had him turning to stare out of the window. "She looks so wounded, and my being here only makes it harder for her." Steadying himself, he stared out at nothing. "I'll be out as soon as I can pack." He turned, his head only, and looked at the small, balding man in front of the fire. "I love her, Philip."

In silence Fairchild watched Adam walk away. For the first time in his six decades he felt old. Old and tired. With a deep, deep sigh he rose and went to his daughter.

He found her curled on her bed, her head cradled by her knees and arms. She sat silent and unmoving and, he knew, utterly, utterly beaten. When he sat beside her, her head jerked up. Slowly, with his hand stroking her hair, her muscles relaxed.

"Do we ever stop making fools of ourselves, Papa?"

"You've never been a fool."

"Oh, yes, yes, it seems I have." Settling her chin on her knees, she stared straight ahead. "I lost our bet. I guess you'll be breaking open that box of cigars you've been saving."

"I think we can consider the extenuating circumstances."

"How generous of you." She tried to smile and failed. "Aren't you going to the hospital to be with Harriet?"

"Yes, of course."

"You'd better go then. She needs you."

His thin, bony hand continued to stroke her hair. "Don't you?"

"Oh, Papa." Tears came in a flood as she turned into his arms.

* * *

Kirby followed Cards downstairs as he carried her bags. In the week since the discovery of the Rembrandt she'd found it impossible to settle. She found no comfort in her art, no comfort in her home. Everything here held memories she could no longer deal with. She slept little and ate less. She knew she was losing touch with the person she was, and so she'd made plans to force herself back.

She opened the door for Cards and stared out at the bright, cheery morning. It made her want to weep.

"I don't know why a sensible person would get up at this ridiculous hour to drive to the wilderness."

Kirby forced back the gloom and turned to watch her father stride down the stairs in a ratty bathrobe and bare feet. What hair he had left was standing on end. "The early bird gathers no moss," she told him. "I want to get to the lodge and settle in. Want some coffee?"

"Not while I'm sleeping," he muttered as she nuzzled his cheek. "I don't know what's wrong with you, going off to that shack in the Himalayas."

"It's Harriet's very comfortable cabin in the Adirondacks, twenty miles from Lake Placid."

"Don't nitpick. You'll be alone."

"I've been alone before," she reminded him. "You're annoyed because you won't have anyone but Cards to shout at for a few weeks."

"He never shouts back." But even as he grumbled, Fairchild was studying Kirby's face. The shadows were still under her eyes and the loss of weight was much too apparent. "Tulip should go with you. Someone has to make you eat."

"I'm going to do that. Mountain air should make me ravenous." When he continued to frown at her, she touched his cheek. "Don't worry, Papa."

"I am worried." Taking her shoulders, he held her at arm's length. "For the first time in your life, you're causing me genuine concern."

"A few pounds, Papa."

"Kirby." He cupped her face in his strong, thin hand. "You have to talk to Adam."

"No!" The word came out violently. With an effort, she drew a steadying breath. "I've said all I want to say to Adam. I need time and some solitude, that's all."

"Running away, Kirby?"

"As fast as I can. Papa, Rick proposed to me again before he left."

"What the hell does that have to do with anything?" he demanded. "He always proposes to you before he leaves."

"I nearly said yes." She lifted her hands to his, willing him to understand. "I nearly said yes because it seemed an easy way out. I'd have ruined his life."

"What about yours?"

"I have to glue the pieces back together. Papa, I'll be fine. It's Harriet who needs you now."

He thought of his friend, his oldest and closest friend. He thought of the grief. "Melanie's going to Europe when she's fully recovered."

"I know." Kirby tried not to remember the gun, or the hate. "Harriet told me. She'll need both of us when Melly's gone. If I can't help myself, how can I help Harriet?"

"Melanie won't see Harriet. The girl's destroying herself with hate." He looked at his own daughter, his pride, his treasure. "The sooner Melanie's out of the hospital and thousands of miles away, the better it'll be for everyone."

She knew what he'd done, how he'd fought against his feelings about Melanie to keep from causing either her or

Harriet more grief. He'd comforted them both without releasing his own fury. She held him tightly a moment, saying nothing. Needing to say nothing.

"We all need some time," she murmured. When she drew away, she was smiling. She wouldn't leave him with tears in her eyes. "I'll cloister myself in the wilderness and sculpt while you pound on your hawk."

"Such a wicked tongue in such a pretty face."

"Papa . . ." Absently she checked the contents of her purse. "Whatever painting you do will be done under your own name?" When he didn't answer, she glanced up, narrowing her eyes. "Papa?"

"All my paintings will be Fairchilds. Haven't I given you my word?" He sniffed and looked injured. Kirby began to feel alarmed.

"This obsession with sculpting," she began, eyeing him carefully. "You don't have it in your head to attempt an emulation of a Rodin or Cellini?"

"You ask too many questions," he complained as he nudged her toward the door. "The day's wasting away, better get started. Don't forget to write."

Kirby paused on the porch and turned back to him. "It'll take you years," she decided. "If you ever acquire the talent. Go ahead and play with your hawk." She kissed his forehead. "I love you, Papa."

He watched her dart down the steps and into her car. "One should never interfere in the life of one's child," he murmured. Smiling broadly, he waved goodbye. When she was out of sight, he went directly to the phone.

*　*　*

The forest had always appealed to her. In mid-autumn, it shouted with life. The burst of colors were a last swirling fling before the trees went into the final cycle. It was an order

Kirby accepted—birth, growth, decay, rebirth. Still, after three days alone, she hadn't found her serenity.

The stream she walked past rushed and hissed. The air was brisk and tangy. She was miserable.

She'd nearly come to terms with her feelings about Melanie. Her childhood friend was ill, had been ill for a long, long time and might never fully recover. It hadn't been a betrayal any more than cancer was a betrayal. But it was a malignancy Kirby knew she had to cut out of her life. She'd nearly accepted it, for Melanie's sake and her own.

She could come to terms with Melanie, but she had yet to deal with Adam. He'd had no illness, nor a lifetime of resentments to feed it. He'd simply had a job to do. And that was too cold for her to accept.

With her hands in her pockets, she sat down on a log and scowled into the water. Her life, she admitted, was a mess. She was a mess. And she was damn sick of it.

She tried to tell herself she'd put Adam out of her life. She hadn't. Yes, she'd refused to listen to him. She'd made no attempt to contact him. It wasn't enough. It wasn't enough, Kirby decided, because it left things unfinished. Now she'd never know if he'd had any real feelings for her. She'd never know if, even briefly, he'd belonged to her.

Perhaps it was best that way.

Standing, she began to walk again, scuffing the leaves that danced around her feet. She was tired of herself. Another first. It wasn't going to go on, she determined. Whatever the cost, she was going to whip Kirby Fairchild back into shape. Starting now. At a brisk pace, she started back to the cabin.

She liked the way it looked, set deep in the trees by itself. The roof was pitched high and the glass sparkled. Today, she thought as she went in through the back door, she'd work. After she'd worked, she'd eat until she couldn't move.

Peeling off her coat as she went, she walked directly to the worktable she'd set up in the corner of the living room.

Without looking around, she tossed the coat aside and looked at her equipment. She hadn't touched it in days. Now she sat and picked up a formless piece of wood. This was to be her *Passion*. Perhaps now more than ever, she needed to put that emotion into form.

There was silence as she explored the feel and life of the wood in her hands. She thought of Adam, of the nights, the touches, the tastes. It hurt. Passion could. Using it, she began to work.

*   *   *

An hour slipped by. She only noticed when her fingers cramped. With a sigh, she set the wood down and stretched them. The healing had begun. She could be certain of it now. "A start," she murmured to herself. "It's a start."

"It's *Passion*. I can already see it."

The knife slipped out of her hand and clattered on the table as she whirled. Across the room, calmly sitting in a faded wing-back chair, was Adam. She'd nearly sprung out of the chair to go to him before she stopped herself. He looked the same, just the same. But nothing was. That she had to remember.

"How did you get in here?"

He heard the ice in her voice. But he'd seen her eyes. In that one instant, she'd told him everything he'd ached for. Still, he knew she couldn't be rushed. "The front door wasn't locked." He rose and crossed to her. "I came inside to wait for you, but when you came in, you looked so intense; then you started right in. I didn't want to disturb your work." When she said nothing, he picked up the wood and turned it over in his hand. He thought it smoldered. "Amazing," he murmured. "Amazing what power you have." Just holding it made him want her more, made him want what she'd put into the wood. Carefully he set it down again, but his eyes were just as intense when he studied her. "What the hell've you been doing? Starving yourself?"

"Don't be ridiculous." She stood and walked away from him, but she didn't know where to go.

"Am I to blame for that, too?"

His voice was quiet, serious. She'd never be able to resist that tone. Gathering her strength, she turned back to him. "Did Tulip send you to check up on me?"

She was too thin. Damn it. Had the pounds melted off her? She was so small. How could she be so small and look so arrogant? He wanted to go to her. Beg. He was nearly certain she'd listen now. Yet she wouldn't want it that way. Instead, he tucked his hands in his pockets and rocked back on his heels. "This is a cozy little place. I wandered around a bit while you were out."

"Glad you made yourself at home."

"It's everything Harriet said it would be." He looked at her again and smiled. "Isolated, cozy, charming."

She lifted a brow. It was easiest with the distance between them. "You've spoken to Harriet?"

"I took your portrait to the gallery."

Emotion came and went again in her eyes. Picking up a small brass pelican, she caressed it absently. "My portrait?"

"I promised her she could exhibit it when I'd finished." He watched her nervous fingers run over the brass. "It wasn't difficult to finish without you. I saw you everywhere I looked."

Quickly she turned to walk to the front wall. It was all glass, open to the woods. No one could feel trapped with that view. Kirby clung to it. "Harriet's having a difficult time."

"The strain shows a bit." In her, he thought, and in you. "I think it's better for her that Melanie won't see her at this point. With Stuart out of the way, the gallery's keeping Harriet busy." He stared at her back, trying to imagine what expression he'd find on her face. "Why aren't you pressing charges, Kirby?"

"For what purpose?" she countered. She set the piece of brass down. A crutch was a crutch, and she was through with them. "Both Stuart and Melanie are disgraced, banished from the elite that means so much to them. The publicity's been horrid. They have no money, no reputation. Isn't that punishment enough?"

"Melanie tried to kill you. Twice." Suddenly furious at the calm, even tone, he went to her and spun her around. "Damn it, Kirby, she wanted you dead!"

"It was she who nearly died." Her voice was still even, but she took a step back, from him. "The police have to accept my story that the gun went off accidentally, even if others don't. I could have sent Melly to jail. Wouldn't I feel avenged watching Harriet suffer?"

Adam forced back the impatience and stared through the glass. "She's worried about you."

"Harriet?" Kirby shrugged. "There's no need. When you see her, tell her I'm well."

"You can tell her yourself when we get back."

"We?" The lightest hint of temper entered her voice. Nothing could have relieved him more. "I'm going to be here for some time yet."

"Fine. I've nothing better to do."

"That wasn't an invitation."

"Harriet already gave me one," he told her easily. He gave the room another sweeping glance while Kirby smoldered. "The place looks big enough for two."

"That's where you're wrong, but don't let me spoil your plans." She spun on her heel and headed for the stairs. Before she'd gotten five feet, his fingers curled around her arm and held her still. When she whirled, he saw that his fiery lover was back.

"You don't really think I'd let you leave? Kirby, you disappoint me."

"You don't *let* me do anything, Adam. Nor do you prevent me from doing anything."

"Only when it's necessary." While she stood rigid, he put his hands on her shoulders. "You're going to listen to me this time. And you're going to start listening in just a minute."

He pressed his mouth to hers as he'd needed to for weeks. She didn't resist. Nor did she respond. He could feel her fighting the need to do both. He could press her, he knew, and she'd give in to him. Then he might never really have her. Slowly their gazes locked; he straightened.

"You're nearly through making me suffer," he murmured. "I've paid, Kirby, in every moment I haven't been with you. Through every night you haven't been beside me. When are you going to stop punishing me?"

"I don't want to punish you." It was true. She'd already forgiven him. Yet, her confidence, that strong, thin shield she'd always had, had suffered an enormous blow. This time when she stepped back, he didn't try to stop her. "I know we parted badly. Maybe it'd be best if we just admitted we'd both made a mistake and left it at that. I realize you did what you had to do. I've always done the same. It's time I got on with my life and you with yours."

He felt a quick jiggle of panic. She was too calm, much too calm. He wanted emotion from her, any kind she'd give. "What sort of life would either of us have without the other?"

None. But she shook her head. "I said we made a mistake—"

"And now you're going to tell me you don't love me?"

She looked straight at him and opened her mouth. Weakening, she shifted her gaze to just over his shoulder. "No, I don't love you, Adam. I'm sorry."

She'd nearly cut him off at the knees. If she hadn't looked away at the last instant, it would've been over for him. "I'd've thought you could lie better than that." In one move he closed the distance between them. His arms were around her, firm, secure. The same, she thought. Nothing had changed after all. "I've given you two weeks, Kirby. Maybe I should give you more time, but I can't." He buried his face in her hair while she squeezed her eyes shut. She'd been wrong, she remembered. She'd been wrong about so many things. Could this be right?

"Adam, please . . ."

"No, no more. I love you." He drew away, barely resisting the need to shake her. "I love you and you'll have to get used to it. It isn't going to change."

She curled her hand into a fist before she could stroke his cheek. "I think you're getting pompous again."

"Then you'll have to get used to that, too. Kirby." He framed her face with his hands. "How many ways would you like me to apologize?"

"No." Shaking her head she moved away again. She should be able to think, she warned herself. She had to think. "I don't need apologies, Adam."

"You wouldn't," he murmured. Forgiveness would come as easily to her as every other emotion. "Your father and I had a long talk before I drove up here."

"Did you?" She gave her attention to a bowl of dried flowers. "How nice."

"He's given me his word he'll no longer . . . emulate paintings."

With her back to him, she smiled. The pain vanished without her realizing it, and with it, the doubts. They loved. There was so little else in life. Still smiling, Kirby decided she wouldn't tell Adam of her father's ambition with sculpting. Not just yet. "I'm glad you convinced him," she said with her tongue in her cheek.

"He decided to concede the point to me, since I'm going to be a member of the family."

With a flutter of her lashes, she turned. "How lovely. Is Papa adopting you?"

"That wasn't precisely the relationship we discussed." Crossing to her, he took her into his arms again. This time he felt the give and the strength. "Tell me again that you don't love me."

"I don't love you," she murmured, and pulled his mouth to hers. "I don't want you to hold me." Her arms wound around his neck. "I don't want you to kiss me again. Now." Her lips clung to his, opening, giving. As the heat built, he groaned and drew her in.

"Obstinate, aren't you?" he muttered.

"Invariably."

"But are you going to marry me?"

"On my terms."

When her head tilted back, he ran kisses up the length of her throat. "Which are?"

"I may come easy, but I don't come free."

"What do you want, a marriage settlement?" On a half laugh, he drew away. She was his, whoever, whatever she was. He'd never let her go again. "Can't you think of anything but money?"

"I'm fond of money—and we still have to discuss my sitting fee. However . . ." She drew a deep breath. "My terms for marriage are four children."

"Four?" Even knowing Kirby, he'd been caught off guard. "Four children?"

She moistened her lips but her voice was strong. "I'm firm on that number, Adam. The point's non-negotiable." Then her eyes were young and full of needs. "I want children. Your children."

Every time he thought he loved her completely, he found he could love her more. Still more. "Four," he repeated with a slow nod. "Any preference to gender?"

The breath she'd been holding came out on a laugh. No, she hadn't been wrong. They loved. There was very little else. "I'm flexible, though a mix of some sort would be nice." She tossed her head back and smiled up at him. "What do you think?"

He swept her into his arms then headed for the stairs. "I think we'd better get started."

Risky Business

CHAPTER 1

W atch your step, please. Please, watch your step. Thank you." Liz took a ticket from a sunburned man with palm trees on his shirt, then waited patiently for a woman with two bulging straw baskets to dig out another one.

"I hope you haven't lost it, Mabel. I told you to let me hold it."

"I haven't lost it," the woman said testily before she pulled out the little piece of blue cardboard.

"Thank you. Please take your seats." It was several more minutes before everyone was settled and she could take her own. "Welcome aboard the *Fantasy,* ladies and gentlemen."

With her mind on a half dozen other things, Liz began her opening monologue. She gave an absent-minded nod to the man on the dock who cast off the ropes before she started the engine. Her voice was pleasant and easy as she took another look at her watch. They were already fifteen minutes behind schedule. She gave one last scan of the beach, skimming by lounge chairs, over bodies already stretched and oiled slick, like offerings to the sun. She couldn't hold the tour any longer.

The boat swayed a bit as she backed it from the dock and took an eastern course. Though her thoughts were scattered, she made the turn from the coast expertly. She could have navigated the boat with her eyes closed. The air that ruffled

around her face was soft and already warming, though the
hour was early. Harmless and powder-puff white, clouds dot-
ted the horizon. The water, churned by the engine, was as
blue as the guide-books promised. Even after ten years, Liz
took none of it for granted—especially her livelihood. Part
of that depended on an atmosphere that made muscles relax
and problems disappear.

Behind her in the long, bullet-shaped craft were eighteen
people seated on padded benches. They were already murmuring about the fish and formations they saw through the
glass bottom. She doubted if any of them thought of the wor-
ries they'd left behind at home.

"We'll be passing Paraiso Reef North," Liz began in a low,
flowing voice. "Diving depths range from thirty to fifty feet.
Visibility is excellent, so you'll be able to see star and brain
corals, sea fans and sponges, as well as schools of sergeant
majors, groupers and parrot fish. The grouper isn't one of your
prettier fish, but it's versatile. They're all born female and pro-
duce eggs before they change sex and become functioning
males."

Liz set her course and kept the speed steady. She went on
to describe the elegantly colored angelfish, the shy, silvery
smallmouth grunts, and the intriguing and dangerous sea urchin. Her clients would find the information useful when she
stopped for two hours of snorkeling at Palancar Reef.

She'd made the run before, too many times to count. It
might have become routine, but it was never monotonous. She
felt now, as she always did, the freedom of open water, blue
sky and the hum of engine with her at the controls. The boat
was hers, as were three others, and the little concrete block
dive shop close to shore. She'd worked for all of it, sweating
through months when the bills were steep and the cash flow
slight. She'd made it. Ten years of struggle had been a small
price to pay for having something of her own. Turning her
back on her country, leaving behind the familiar, had been a
small price to pay for peace of mind.

The tiny, rustic island of Cozumel in the Mexican Caribbean promoted peace of mind. It was her home now, the only one that mattered. She was accepted there, respected. No one on the island knew of the humiliation and pain she'd gone through before she'd fled to Mexico. Liz rarely thought of it, though she had a vivid reminder.

Faith. Just the thought of her daughter made her smile. Faith was small and bright and precious, and so far away. Just six weeks, Liz thought, and she'd be home from school for the summer.

Sending her to Houston to her grandparents had been for the best, Liz reminded herself whenever the ache of loneliness became acute. Faith's education was more important than a mother's needs. Liz had worked, gambled, struggled so that Faith could have everything she was entitled to, everything she would have had if her father . . .

Determined, Liz set her mind on other things. She'd promised herself a decade before that she would cut Faith's father from her mind, just as he had cut her from his life. It had been a mistake, one made in naïveté and passion, one that had changed the course of her life forever. But she'd won something precious from it: Faith.

"Below, you see the wreck of a forty-passenger Convair airliner lying upside down." She slowed the boat so that her passengers could examine the wreck and the divers out for early explorations. Bubbles rose from air tanks like small silver disks. "The wreck's no tragedy," she continued. "It was sunk for a scene in a movie and provides divers with easy entertainment."

Her job was to do the same for her passengers, she reminded herself. It was simple enough when she had a mate on board. Alone, she had to captain the boat, keep up the light, informative banter, deal with snorkel equipment, serve lunch and count heads. It just hadn't been possible to wait any longer for Jerry.

She muttered to herself a bit as she increased speed. It

wasn't so much that she minded the extra work, but she felt her paying customers were entitled to the best she could offer. She should have known better than to depend on him. She could have easily arranged for someone else to come along. As it was, she had two men on the dive boat and two more in the shop. Because her second dive boat was due to launch at noon, no one could be spared to mate the glass bottom on a day trip. And Jerry had come through before, she reminded herself. With him on board, the women passengers were so charmed that Liz didn't think they even noticed the watery world the boat passed over.

Who could blame them? she thought with a half smile. If she hadn't been immune to men in general, Jerry might have had her falling over her own feet. Most women had a difficult time resisting dark, cocky looks, a cleft chin and smoky gray eyes. Add to that a lean, muscular build and a glib tongue, and no female was safe.

But that hadn't been why Liz had agreed to rent him a room, or give him a part-time job. She'd needed the extra income, as well as the extra help, and she was shrewd enough to recognize an operator when she saw one. Previous experience had taught her that it made good business sense to have an operator on your side. She told herself he'd better have a good excuse for leaving her without a crew, then forgot him.

The ride, the sun, the breeze relaxed her. Liz continued to speak of the sea life below, twining facts she'd learned while studying marine biology in college with facts she'd learned firsthand in the waters of the Mexican Caribbean. Occasionally one of her passengers would ask a question or call out in excitement over something that skimmed beneath them. She answered, commented and instructed while keeping the flow light. Because three of her passengers were Mexican, she repeated all her information in Spanish. Because there were several children on board, she made certain the facts were fun.

If things had been different, she would have been a teacher.

Liz had long since pushed that early dream from her mind, telling herself she was more suited to the business world. Her business world. She glanced over where the clouds floated lazily over the horizon. The sun danced white and sharp on the surface of blue water. Below, coral rose like castles or waved like fans. Yes, she'd chosen her world and had no regrets.

When a woman screamed behind her, Liz let off the throttle. Before she could turn, the scream was joined by another. Her first thought was that perhaps they'd seen one of the sharks that occasionally visited the reefs. Set to calm and soothe, Liz let the boat drift in the current. A woman was weeping in her husband's arms, another held her child's face protectively against her shoulder. The rest were staring down through the clear glass. Liz took off her sunglasses as she walked down the two steps into the cabin.

"Please try to stay calm. I promise you, there's nothing down there that can hurt you in here."

A man with a Nikon around his neck and an orange sun visor over a balding dome gave her a steady look.

"Miss, you'd better radio the police."

Liz looked down through the clear glass, through the crystal blue water. Her heart rose to her throat. She saw now why Jerry had stood her up. He was lying on the white sandy bottom with an anchor chain wrapped around his chest.

* * *

The moment the plane finished its taxi, Jonas gathered his garment bag and waited impatiently for the door to be opened. When it did, there was a whoosh of hot air and the drone of engines. With a quick nod to the flight attendant he strode down the steep metal stairs. He didn't have the time or the inclination to appreciate the palm trees, the bursts of flowers or the dreamy blue sky. He walked purposefully, eyes straight ahead and narrowed against the sun. In his dark suit and trim tie he could have been a businessman, one who'd come to Cozumel to work, not to play. Whatever grief, whatever anger he felt were carefully masked by a calm, unapproachable expression.

The terminal was small and noisy. Americans on vacation stood in groups laughing or wandered in confusion. Though he knew no Spanish, Jonas passed quickly through customs then into a small, hot alcove where men waited at podiums to rent cars and Jeeps. Fifteen minutes after landing, Jonas was backing a compact out of a parking space and heading toward town with a map stuck in the sun visor. The heat baked right through the windshield.

Twenty-four hours before, Jonas had been sitting in his large, elegantly furnished, air-conditioned office. He'd just won a long, tough case that had taken all his skill and mountains of research. His client was a free man, acquitted of a felony charge that carried a minimum sentence of ten years. He'd accepted his fee, accepted the gratitude and avoided as much publicity as possible.

Jonas had been preparing to take his first vacation in eighteen months. He'd felt satisfied, vaguely tired and optimistic. Two weeks in Paris seemed like the perfect reward for so many months of ten-hour days. Paris, with its ageless sophistication and cool parks, its stunning museums and incomparable food was precisely what suited Jonas Sharpe.

When the call had come through from Mexico, it had taken him several moments to understand. When he'd answered that he did indeed have a brother Jeremiah, Jonas's predominant thought had been that Jerry had gotten himself into trouble again, and he was going to have to bail him out.

By the time he'd hung up the phone, Jonas couldn't think at all. Numb, he'd given his secretary instructions to cancel his Paris arrangements and to make new ones for a flight to Cozumel the next day. Then Jonas had picked up the phone to call his parents and tell them their son was dead.

He'd come to Mexico to identify the body and take his brother home to bury. With a fresh wave of grief, Jonas experienced a sense of inevitability. Jerry had always lived on the edge of disaster. This time he'd stepped over. Since childhood Jerry had courted trouble—charmingly. He'd once joked that Jonas had taken to law so he could find the most efficient way to get his brother out of jams. Perhaps in a sense it had been true.

Jerry had been a dreamer. Jonas was a realist. Jerry had been unapologetically lazy, Jonas a workaholic. They were—had been—two sides of a coin. As Jonas drew up to the police station in San Miguel it was with the knowledge that part of himself had been erased.

The scene at port should have been painted. There were small fishing boats pulled up on the grass. Huge gray ships sat complacently at dock while tourists in flowered shirts or skimpy shorts strolled along the sea wall. Water lapped and scented the air.

Jonas got out of the car and walked to the police station to begin to wade through the morass of paperwork that accompanied a violent death.

Captain Moralas was a brisk, no-nonsense man who had been born on the island and was passionately dedicated to protecting it. He was approaching forty and awaiting the birth of his fifth child. He was proud of his position, his education and his family, though the order often varied. Basically, he was a quiet man who enjoyed classical music and a movie on Saturday nights.

Because San Miguel was a port, and ships brought sailors on leave, tourists on holiday, Moralas was no stranger to trouble or the darker side of human nature. He did, however, pride himself on the low percentage of violent crime on his island. The murder of the American bothered him in the way a pesky fly bothered a man sitting contentedly on his porch swing. A cop didn't have to work in a big city to recognize a professional hit. There was no room for organized crime on Cozumel.

But he was also a family man. He understood love, and

he understood grief, just as he understood certain men were compelled to conceal both. In the cool, flat air of the morgue, he waited beside Jonas. The American stood a head taller, rigid and pale.

"This is your brother, Mr. Sharpe?" Though he didn't have to ask.

Jonas looked down at the other side of the coin. "Yes."

In silence, he backed away to give Jonas the time he needed.

It didn't seem possible. Jonas knew he could have stood for hours staring down at his brother's face and it would never seem possible. Jerry had always looked for the easy way, the biggest deal, and he hadn't always been an admirable man. But he'd always been so full of life. Slowly, Jonas laid his hand on his brother's. There was no life there now, and nothing he could do; no amount of maneuvering or pulling of strings would bring it back. Just as slowly he removed his hand. It didn't seem possible, but it was.

Moralas nodded to the attendant. "I'm sorry."

Jonas shook his head. Pain was like a dull-edged knife through the base of his skull. He coated it with ice. "Who killed my brother, Captain?"

"I don't know. We're investigating."

"You have leads?"

Moralas gestured and started down the corridor. "Your brother had been in Cozumel only three weeks, Mr. Sharpe. At the moment, we are interviewing everyone who had contact with him during that time." He opened a door and stepped out into the air, breathing deeply of the fresh air and the flowers. The man beside him didn't seem to notice the change. "I promise you, we will do everything possible to find your brother's killer."

The rage Jonas had controlled for so many hours bubbled toward the surface. "I don't know you." With a steady hand he drew out a cigarette, watching the captain with narrowed eyes as he lit it. "You didn't know Jerry."

"This is my island." Moralas's gaze remained locked with Jonas's. "If there's a murderer on it, I'll find him."

"A professional." Jonas blew out smoke that hung in the air with no breeze to brush it away. "We both know that, don't we?"

Moralas said nothing for a moment. He was still waiting to receive information on Jeremiah Sharpe. "Your brother was shot, Mr. Sharpe, so we're investigating to find out why, how and who. You could help me by giving me some information."

Jonas stared at the door a moment—the door that led down the stairs, down the corridor and to his brother's body. "I've got to walk," he murmured.

Moralas waited until they'd crossed the grass, then the road. For a moment, they walked near the sea wall in silence. "Why did your brother come to Cozumel?"

"I don't know." Jonas drew deeply on the cigarette until it burned into the filter. "Jerry liked palm trees."

"His business? His work?"

With a half laugh Jonas ground the smoldering filter underfoot. Sunlight danced in diamonds on the water. "Jerry liked to call himself a freelancer. He was a drifter." And he'd brought complications to Jonas's life as often as he'd brought pleasure. Jonas stared hard at the water, remembering shared lives, diverse opinions. "For Jerry, it was always the next town and the next deal. The last I heard—two weeks ago—he was giving diving lessons to tourists."

"The Black Coral Dive Shop," Moralas confirmed. "Elizabeth Palmer hired him on a part-time basis."

"Palmer." Jonas's attention shifted away from the water. "That's the woman he was living with."

"Miss Palmer rented your brother a room," Moralas corrected, abruptly proper. "She was also among the group to discover your brother's body. She's given my department her complete cooperation."

Jonas's mouth thinned. How had Jerry described this Liz

Palmer in their brief phone conversation weeks before? A sexy little number who made great tortillas. She sounded like another one of Jerry's tough ladies on the lookout for a good time and the main chance. "I'll need her address." At the captain's quiet look he only raised a brow. "I assume my brother's things are still there."

"They are. I have some of your brother's personal effects, those that he had on him, in my office. You're welcome to collect them and what remains at Miss Palmer's. We've already been through them."

Jonas felt the rage build again and smothered it. "When can I take my brother home?"

"I'll do my best to complete the paperwork today. I'll need you to make a statement. Of course, there are forms." He looked at Jonas's set profile and felt a new tug of pity. "Again, I'm sorry."

He only nodded. "Let's get it done."

* * *

Liz let herself into the house. While the door slammed behind her, she flicked switches, sending two ceiling fans whirling. The sound, for the moment, was company enough. The headache she'd lived with for over twenty-four hours was a dull, nagging thud just under her right temple. Going into the bathroom, she washed down two aspirin before turning on the shower.

She'd taken the glass bottom out again. Though it was off season, she'd had to turn a dozen people away. It wasn't every day a body was found off the coast, and the curious had come in force. Morbid, she thought, then stripped and stepped under the cold spray of the shower. How long would it take, she wondered, before she stopped seeing Jerry on the sand beneath the water?

True, she'd barely known him, but he'd been fun and interesting and good company. He'd slept in her daughter's bed and eaten in her kitchen. Closing her eyes, she let the water sluice over her, willing the headache away. She'd be better, she thought, when the police finished the investigation. It had been hard, very hard, when they'd come to her house and searched through Jerry's things. And the questions.

How much had she known about Jerry Sharpe? He'd been American, an operator, a womanizer. She'd been able to use all three to her benefit when he'd given diving lessons or acted as mate on one of her boats. She'd thought him harmless—sexy, attractive and basically lazy. He'd boasted of making it big, of wheeling a deal that would set him up in style. Liz had considered it so much hot air. As far as she was concerned, nothing set you up in style but years of hard work—or inherited wealth.

But Jerry's eyes had lit up when he'd talked of it, and his grin had been appealing. If she'd been a woman who allowed herself dreams, she would have believed him. But dreams were for the young and foolish. With a little tug of regret, she realized Jerry Sharpe had been both.

Now he was gone, and what he had left was still scattered in her daughter's room. She'd have to box it up, Liz decided as she turned off the taps. It was something, at least. She'd box up Jerry's things and ask that Captain Moralas what to do about them. Certainly his family would want whatever he'd left behind. Jerry had spoken of a brother, whom he'd affectionately referred to as "the stuffed shirt." Jerry Sharpe had been anything but stuffy.

As she walked to the bedroom, Liz wrapped her hair in the towel. She remembered the way Jerry had tried to talk his way between her sheets a few days after he'd moved in. Smooth talk, smooth hands. Though he'd had her backed into the doorway, kissing her before she'd evaded it, Liz had easily brushed him off. He'd taken her refusal good-naturedly, she recalled, and they'd remained on comfortable terms. Liz pulled on an oversized shirt that skimmed her thighs.

The truth was, Jerry Sharpe had been a good-natured,

comfortable man with big dreams. She wondered, not for the first time, if his dreams had had something to do with his death.

She couldn't go on thinking about it. The best thing to do was to pack what had belonged to Jerry back into his suitcase and take it to the police.

It made her feel gruesome. She discovered that after only five minutes. Privacy, for a time, had been all but her only possession. To invade someone else's made her uneasy. Liz folded a faded brown T-shirt that boasted the wearer had hiked the Grand Canyon and tried not to think at all. But she kept seeing him there, joking about sleeping with one of Faith's collection of dolls. He'd fixed the window that had stuck and had cooked paella to celebrate his first paycheck.

Without warning, Liz felt the first tears flow. He'd been so alive, so young, so full of that cocky sense of confidence. She'd hardly had time to consider him a friend, but he'd slept in her daughter's bed and left clothes in her closet.

She wished now she'd listened to him more, been friendlier, more approachable. He'd asked her to have drinks with him and she'd brushed him off because she'd had paperwork to do. It seemed petty now, cold. If she'd given him an hour of her life, she might have learned who he was, where he'd come from, why he'd died.

When the knock at the door sounded, she pressed her hands against her cheeks. Silly to cry, she told herself, when tears never solved anything. Jerry Sharpe was gone, and it had nothing to do with her.

She brushed away the tears as she walked to the door. The headache was easing. Liz decided it would be best if she called Moralas right away and arranged to have the clothes picked up. She was telling herself she really wasn't involved at all when she opened the door.

For a moment she could only stare. The T-shirt she hadn't been aware of still holding slipped from her fingers. She took one stumbling step back as she felt a rushing sound fill her head. Because her vision dimmed, she blinked to clear it. The man in the doorway stared back at her accusingly.

"Jer-Jerry," she managed and nearly screamed when he took a step forward.

"Elizabeth Palmer?"

She shook her head, numb and terrified. She had no superstitions. She believed in action and reaction on a purely practical level. When someone died, they couldn't come back. And yet she stood in her living room with the fans whirling and watched Jerry Sharpe step over her threshold. She heard him speak to her again.

"Are you Liz Palmer?"

"I saw you." She heard her own voice rise with nerves but couldn't take her eyes from his face. The cocky good looks, the cleft chin, the smoky eyes under thick dark brows. It was a face that appealed to a woman's need to risk, or to her dreams of risking. "Who are you?"

"Jonas Sharpe. Jerry was my brother. My twin brother."

When she discovered her knees were shaking, she sat down quickly. No, not Jerry, she told herself as her heartbeat leveled. The hair was just as dark, just as full, but it lacked Jerry's unkempt shagginess. The face was just as attractive, just as ruggedly hewn, but she'd never seen Jerry's eyes so hard, so cold. And this man wore a suit as though he'd been born in one. His stance was one of restrained passion and impatience. It took her a moment, only a moment, before anger struck.

"You did that on purpose." Because her palms were damp she rubbed them against her knees. "It was a hideous thing to do. You knew what I'd think when I opened the door."

"I needed a reaction."

She sat back and took a deep, steadying breath. "You're a bastard, Mr. Sharpe."

For the first time in hours, his mouth curved . . . only slightly. "May I sit down?"

She gestured to a chair. "What do you want?"

"I came to get Jerry's things. And to talk to you."

As he sat, Jonas took a long look around. His was not the polite, casual glance a stranger indulges himself in when he walks into someone else's home, but a sharp-eyed, intense study of what belonged to Liz Palmer. It was a small living area, hardly bigger than his office. While he preferred muted colors and clean lines, Liz chose bright, contrasting shades and odd knickknacks. Several Mayan masks hung on the walls, and rugs of different sizes and hues were scattered over the floor. The sunlight, fading now, came in slats through red window blinds. There was a big blue pottery vase on a woven mat on the table, but the butter-yellow flowers in it were losing their petals. The table itself didn't gleam with polish, but was covered with a thin layer of dust.

The shock that had had her stomach muscles jumping had eased. She said nothing as he looked around the room because she was looking at him. A mirror image of Jerry, she thought. And weren't mirror images something like negatives? She didn't think he'd be fun to have around. She had a frantic need to order him out, to pitch him out quickly and finally. Ridiculous, she told herself. He was just a man, and nothing to her. And he had lost his brother.

"I'm sorry, Mr. Sharpe. This is a very difficult time for you."

His gaze locked on hers so quickly that she tensed again. She'd barely been aware of his inch-by-inch study of her room, but she couldn't remain unmoved by his study of her.

She wasn't what he'd expected. Her face was all angles— wide cheekbones, a long narrow nose and a chin that came to a suggestion of a point. She wasn't beautiful, but stunning in an almost uncomfortable way. It might have been the eyes, a deep haunted brown, that rose a bit at the outer edge. It might have been the mouth, full and vulnerable. The shirt overwhelmed her body with its yards of material, leaving only long, tanned legs bare. Her hands, resting on the arms of her chair, were small, narrow and ringless. Jonas had thought he knew his brother's taste as well as his own. Liz Palmer didn't suit Jerry's penchant for the loud and flamboyant, or his own for the discreet sophisticate.

Still, Jerry had lived with her. Jonas thought grimly that she was taking the murder of her lover very well. "And a difficult time for you."

His long study had left her shaken. It had gone beyond natural curiosity and made her feel like a specimen, filed and labeled for further research. She tried to remember that grief took different forms in different people. "Jerry was a nice man. It isn't easy to—"

"How did you meet him?"

Words of sympathy cut off, Liz straightened in her chair. She never extended friendliness where it wasn't likely to be accepted. If he wanted facts only, she'd give him facts. "He came by my shop a few weeks ago. He was interested in diving."

Jonas's brow lifted as in polite interest but his eyes remained cold. "In diving."

"I own a dive shop on the beach—rent equipment, boat rides, lessons, day trips. Jerry was looking for work. Since he knew what he was doing, I gave it to him. He crewed on the dive boat, gave some of the tourists lessons, that sort of thing."

Showing tourists how to use a regulator didn't fit with Jonas's last conversation with his brother. Jerry had talked about cooking up a big deal. Big money, big time. "He didn't buy in as your partner?"

Something came into her face—pride, disdain, amusement. Jonas couldn't be sure. "I don't take partners, Mr. Sharpe. Jerry worked for me, that's all."

"All?" The brow came up again. "He was living here."

She caught the meaning, had dealt with it from the police. Liz decided she'd answered all the questions she cared to and that she'd given Jonas Sharpe more than enough of her time. "Jerry's things are in here." Rising, she walked out of the room. Liz waited at the doorway to her daughter's room until Jonas joined her. "I was just beginning to pack his clothes. You'd probably prefer to do that yourself. Take as much time as you need."

When she started to turn away, Jonas took her arm. He wasn't looking at her, but into the room with the shelves of dolls, the pink walls and lacy curtains. And at his brother's clothes tossed negligently over the back of a painted white chair and onto a flowered spread. It hurt, Jonas discovered, all over again.

"Is this all?" It seemed so little.

"I haven't been through the drawers or the closet yet. The police have." Suddenly weary, she pulled the towel from her head. Dark blond hair, still damp, tumbled around her face and shoulders. Somehow her face seemed even more vulnerable. "I don't know anything about Jerry's personal life, his personal belongings. This is my daughter's room." She turned her head until their eyes met. "She's away at school. This is where Jerry slept." She left him alone.

Twenty minutes was all he needed. His brother had traveled light. Leaving the suitcase in the living room, Jonas walked through the house. It wasn't large. The next bedroom was dim in the early evening light, but he could see a splash of orange over a rattan bed and a desk cluttered with files and papers. It smelled lightly of spice and talcum powder. Turning away, he walked toward the back and found the kitchen. And Liz.

It was when he smelled the coffee that Jonas remembered he hadn't eaten since morning. Without turning around, Liz poured a second cup. She didn't need him to speak to know he was there. She doubted he was a man who ever had to announce his presence. "Cream?"

Jonas ran a hand through his hair. He felt as though he were walking through someone else's dream. "No, black."

When Liz turned to offer the cup, he saw the quick jolt.

"I'm sorry," she murmured, taking up her own cup. "You look so much like him."

"Does that bother you?"

"It unnerves me."

He sipped the coffee, finding it cleared some of the mists of unreality. "You weren't in love with Jerry."

Liz sent him a look of mild surprise. She realized he'd thought she'd been his brother's lover, but she hadn't thought he'd have taken the next step. "I only knew him a few weeks." Then she laughed, remembering another time, another life. "No, I wasn't in love with him. We had a business relationship, but I liked him. He was cocky and well aware of his own charms. I had a lot of repeat female customers over the past couple of weeks. Jerry was quite an operator," she murmured, then looked up, horrified. "I'm sorry."

"No." Interested, Jonas stepped closer. She was a tall woman, so their eyes stayed level easily. She smelled of the talcum powder and wore no cosmetics. Not Jerry's type, he thought again. But there was something about the eyes. "That's what he was, only most people never caught on."

"I've known others." And her voice was flat. "Not so harmless, not so kind. Your brother was a nice man, Mr. Sharpe. And I hope whoever . . . I hope they're found."

She watched the gray eyes ice over. The little tremor in her stomach reminded her that cold was often more dangerous than heat. "They will be. I may need to talk with you again."

It seemed a simple enough request, but she backed away from it. She didn't want to talk to him again, she didn't want to be involved in any way. "There's nothing else I can tell you."

"Jerry was living in your house, working for you."

"I don't know anything." Her voice rose as she spun away to stare out the window. She was tired of the questions, tired of people pointing her out on the beach as the woman who'd found the body. She was tired of having her life turned upside down by the death of a man she had hardly known. And she was nervous, she admitted, because Jonas Sharpe struck her as a man who could keep her life turned upside down as long as it suited him. "I've talked to the police again and again. He worked for me. I saw him a few hours out of the day. I don't know where he went at night, who he saw, what he did. It wasn't my business as long as he paid for the room and showed up to work." When she looked back, her face was set. "I'm sorry for your brother, I'm sorry for you. But it's not my business."

He saw the nerves as her hands unclenched but interpreted them in his own way. "We disagree, Mrs. Palmer."

"Miss Palmer," she said deliberately, and watched his slow, acknowledging nod. "I can't help you."

"You don't know that until we talk."

"All right. I won't help you."

He inclined his head and reached for his wallet. "Did Jerry owe you anything on the room?"

She felt the insult like a slap. Her eyes, usually soft, usually sad, blazed. "He owed me nothing, and neither do you. If you've finished your coffee . . ."

Jonas set the cup on the table. "I've finished. For now." He gave her a final study. Not Jerry's type, he thought again, or his. But she had to know something. If he had to use her to find out, he would. "Good night."

Liz stayed where she was until the sound of the front door closing echoed back at her. Then she shut her eyes. None of her business, she reminded herself. But she could still see Jerry under her boat. And now, she could see Jonas Sharpe with grief hard in his eyes.

CHAPTER 2

L iz considered working in the dive shop the next thing to taking a day off. Taking a day off, actually staying away from the shop and the boats, was a luxury she allowed herself rarely, and only when Faith was home on holiday. Today, she'd indulged herself by sending the boats out without her so that she could manage the shop alone. Be alone. By noon, all the serious divers had already rented their tanks so that business at the shop would be sporadic. It gave Liz a chance to spend a few hours checking equipment and listing inventory.

The shop was a basic cinder-block unit. Now and again, she toyed with the idea of having the outside painted, but could never justify the extra expense. There was a cubbyhole she wryly referred to as an office, where she'd crammed an old gray steel desk and one swivel chair. The rest of the room was crowded with equipment that lined the floor, was stacked on shelves or hung from hooks. Her desk had a dent in it the size of a man's foot, but her equipment was top grade and flawless.

Masks, flippers, tanks, snorkels could be rented individually or in any number of combinations. Liz had learned that the wider the choice, the easier it was to move items out and draw the customer back. The equipment was the backbone of her business. Prominent next to the wide square opening that was only closed at night with a heavy wooden shutter was a list, in English and Spanish, of her equipment, her services and the price.

When she'd started eight years before, Liz had stocked enough tanks and gear to outfit twelve divers. It had taken every penny she'd saved—every penny Marcus had given a young, dewy-eyed girl pregnant with his child. The girl had become a woman quickly, and that woman now had a business that could accommodate fifty divers from the skin out, dozens of snorkelers, underwater photographers, tourists who wanted an easy day on the water or gung-ho deep-sea fishermen.

The first boat she'd gambled on, a dive boat, had been christened *Faith,* for her daughter. She'd made a vow when she'd been eighteen, alone and frightened, that the child she carried would have the best. Ten years later, Liz could look around her shop and know she'd kept her promise.

More, the island she'd fled to for escape had become home. She was settled there, respected, depended on. She no longer looked over the expanses of white sand, blue water, longing for Houston or a pretty house with a flowing green lawn. She no longer looked back at the education she'd barely begun, or what she might have been. She'd stopped pining for a man who didn't want her or the child they'd made. She'd never go back. But Faith could. Faith could learn how to speak French, wear silk dresses and discuss wine and music. One day Faith would go back and mingle unknowingly with her cousins on their own level.

That was her dream, Liz thought as she carefully filled tanks. To see her daughter accepted as easily as she herself had been rejected. Not for revenge, Liz mused, but for justice.

"Howdy there, missy."

Crouched near the back wall, Liz turned and squinted against the sun. She saw a portly figure stuffed into a black-and-red wet suit, topped by a chubby face with a fat cigar stuck in the mouth.

"Mr. Ambuckle. I didn't know you were still on the island."

"Scooted over to Cancun for a few days. Diving's better here."

With a smile, she rose to go to her side of the opening. Ambuckle was a steady client who came to Cozumel two or three times a year and always rented plenty of tanks. "I could've told you that. See any of the ruins?"

"Wife dragged me to Tulum." He shrugged and grinned at her with popping blue eyes. "Rather be thirty feet down than climbing over rocks all day. Did get some snorkeling in. But a man doesn't fly all the way from Dallas just to paddle around. Thought I'd do some night diving."

Her smile came easily, adding something soft and approachable to eyes that were usually wary. "Fix you right up. How much longer are you staying?" she asked as she checked an underwater flash.

"Two more weeks. Man's got to get away from his desk."

"Absolutely." Liz had often been grateful so many people from Texas, Louisiana and Florida felt the need to get away.

"Heard you had some excitement while we were on the other side."

Liz supposed she should be used to the comment by now, but a shiver ran up her spine. The smile faded, leaving her face remote. "You mean the American who was murdered?"

"Put the wife in a spin. Almost couldn't talk her into coming back over. Did you know him?"

No, she thought, not as well as she should have. To keep her hands busy, she reached for a rental form and began to fill it out. "As a matter of fact, he worked here a little while."

"You don't say?" Ambuckle's small blue eyes sparkled a bit. But Liz supposed she should be used to that, as well.

"You might remember him. He crewed the dive boat the last time you and your wife went out."

"No kidding?" Ambuckle's brow creased as he chewed on the cigar. "Not that good-looking young man—Johnny, Jerry," he remembered. "Had the wife in stitches."

"Yes, that was him."

"Shame," Ambuckle murmured, but looked rather pleased to have known the victim. "Had a lot of zip."

"Yes, I thought so, too." Liz lugged the tanks through the door and set them on the stoop. "That should take care of it, Mr. Ambuckle."

"Add a camera on, missy. Want to get me a picture of one of those squids. Ugly things."

Amazed, Liz plucked one from the shelf and added it to the list on a printed form. She checked her watch, noted down the time and turned the form for Ambuckle's signature. After signing, he handed her bills for the deposit. She appreciated the fact that Ambuckle always paid in cash, American. "Thanks. Glad to see you back, Mr. Ambuckle."

"Can't keep me away, missy." With a whoosh and a grunt, he hefted the tanks on his shoulders. Liz watched him cross to the walkway before she filed the receipt. Unlocking her cash box, she stored the money.

"Business is good."

She jolted at the voice and looking up again stared at Jonas Sharpe.

She'd never again mistake him for Jerry, though his eyes were almost hidden this time with tinted glasses, and he wore shorts and an open shirt in lieu of a suit. There was a long gold chain around his neck with a small coin dangling. She recalled Jerry had worn one. But something in the way Jonas stood, something in the set of his mouth made him look taller and tougher than the man she'd known.

Because she didn't believe in polite fencing, Liz finished relocking the cash box and began to check the straps and fasteners on a shelf of masks. No faulty equipment went out of her shop. "I didn't expect to see you again."

"You should have." Jonas watched her move down the shelf. She seemed stronger, less vulnerable than she had when he'd seen her a week ago. Her eyes were cool, her voice remote.

It made it easier to do what he'd come for. "You have quite a reputation on the island."

She paused long enough to look over her shoulder. "Really?"

"I checked," he said easily. "You've lived here for ten years. Built this place from the first brick and have one of the most successful businesses on the island."

She examined the mask in her hand meticulously. "Are you interested in renting some equipment, Mr. Sharpe? I can recommend the snorkeling right off this reef."

"Maybe. But I think I'd prefer to scuba."

"Fine. I can give you whatever you need." She set the mask down and chose another. "It isn't necessary to be certified to dive in Mexico; however, I'd recommend a few basic lessons before you go down. We offer two different courses—individual or group."

He smiled at her for the first time, a slow, appealing curving of lips that softened the toughness around his mouth. "I might take you up on that. Meantime, when do you close?"

"When I'm ready to." The smile made a difference, she realized, and she couldn't let it. In defense, she shifted her weight on one hip and sent him a look of mild insolence. "This is Cozumel, Mr. Sharpe. We don't run nine to five here. Unless you want to rent some equipment or sign up for a tour, you'll have to excuse me."

He reached in to close his hand over hers. "I didn't come back to tour. Have dinner with me tonight. We can talk."

She didn't attempt to free her hand but stared at him. Running a business had taught her to be scrupulously polite in any circumstances. "No, thank you."

"Drinks, then."

"No."

"Miss Palmer . . ." Normally, Jonas was known for his deadly, interminable patience. It was a weapon, he'd learned, in the courtroom and out of it. With Liz, he found it difficult to wield it. "I don't have a great deal to go on at this point, and the police haven't made any progress at all. I need your help."

This time Liz did pull away. She wouldn't be sucked in, that she promised herself, not by quiet words or intense eyes. She had her life to lead, a business to run and, most important, a daughter coming home in a matter of weeks. "I won't get involved. I'm sorry, even if I wanted to, there'd be nothing I could do to help."

"Then it won't hurt to talk to me."

"Mr. Sharpe." Liz wasn't known for her patience. "I have very little free time. Running this business isn't a whim or a lark, but a great deal of work. If I have a couple of hours to myself in the evening, I'm not going to spend them being grilled by you. Now—"

She started to brush him off again when a young boy came running up to the window. He was dressed in a bathing suit and slick with suntan lotion. With a twenty-dollar bill crumpled in his hand, he babbled a request for snorkeling equipment for himself and his brother. He spoke in quick, excited Spanish as Liz checked out the equipment, asking if she thought they'd see a shark.

She answered him in all seriousness as she exchanged money for equipment. "Sharks don't live in the reef, but they do visit now and again." She saw the light of adventure in his eyes. "You'll see parrot fish." She held her hands apart to show him how big. "And if you take some bread crumbs or crackers, the sergeant majors will follow you, lots of them, close enough to touch."

"Will they bite?"

She grinned. "Only the bread crumbs. Adios."

He dashed away, kicking up sand.

"You speak Spanish like a native," Jonas observed, and thought it might come in handy. He'd also noticed the pleasure that had come into her eyes when she'd talked with the boy. There'd been nothing remote then, nothing sad or haunted. Strange, he mused, he'd never noticed just how much a barometer of feeling the eyes could be.

"I live here," she said simply. "Now, Mr. Sharpe—"

"How many boats?"

"What?"

"How many do you have?"

She sucked in a deep breath and decided she could humor him for another five minutes. "I have four. The glass bottom, two dive boats and one for deep-sea fishing."

"Deep-sea fishing." That was the one, Jonas decided. A fishing boat would be private and isolated. "I haven't done any in five or six years. Tomorrow." He reached in his wallet. "How much?"

"It's fifty dollars a person a day, but I don't take the boat out for one man, Mr. Sharpe." She gave him an easy smile. "It doesn't make good business sense."

"What's your minimum?"

"Three. And I'm afraid I don't have anyone else lined up. So—"

He set four fifty-dollar bills on the counter. "The extra fifty's to make sure you're driving the boat." Liz looked down at the money. An extra two hundred would help buy the aqua bikes she'd been thinking about. Several of the other dive shops already had them and she kept a constant eye on competition. Aqua biking and wind surfing were becoming increasingly popular, and if she wanted to keep up . . . She looked back at Jonas Sharpe's dark, determined eyes and decided it wasn't worth it.

"My schedule for tomorrow's already set. I'm afraid I—"

"It doesn't make good business sense to turn down a profit, Miss Palmer." When she only moved her shoulders, he smiled again, but this time it wasn't so pleasant. "I'd hate to mention at the hotel that I couldn't get satisfaction at The Black Coral. It's funny how word of mouth can help or damage a small business."

Liz picked up the money, one bill at a time. "What business are you in, Mr. Sharpe?"

"Law."

She made a sound that might have been a laugh as she pulled out a form. "I should've guessed. I knew someone studying law once." She thought of Marcus with his glib, calculating tongue. "He always got what he wanted, too. Sign here. We leave at eight," she said briskly. "The price includes a lunch on board. If you want beer or liquor, you bring your own. The sun's pretty intense on the water, so you'd better buy some sunscreen." She glanced beyond him. "One of my dive boats is coming back. You'll have to excuse me."

"Miss Palmer . . ." He wasn't sure what he wanted to say to her, or why he was uncomfortable having completed a successful maneuver. In the end, he pocketed his receipt. "If you change your mind about dinner—"

"I won't."

"I'm at the El Presidente."

"An excellent choice." She walked through the doorway and onto the dock to wait for her crew and clients.

*   *   *

By seven-fifteen, the sun was up and already burning off a low ground mist. What clouds there were, were thin and shaggy and good-natured.

"Damn!" Liz kicked the starter on her motorbike and turned in a little U toward the street. She'd been hoping for rain.

He was going to try to get her involved. Even now, Liz could imagine those dark, patient gray eyes staring into hers, hear the quietly insistent voice. Jonas Sharpe was the kind of man who took no for an answer but was dogged enough to wait however long it took for the yes. Under other circumstances, she'd have admired that. Being stubborn had helped her start and succeed in a business when so many people had shaken their heads and warned her against it. But she couldn't afford to admire Jonas Sharpe. Budgeting her feelings was every bit as important as budgeting her accounts.

She couldn't help him, Liz thought again, as the soft air began to play around her face. Everything she'd known about Jerry had been said at least twice. Of course she was sorry, and had grieved a bit herself for a man she'd hardly known, but murder was a police matter. Jonas Sharpe was out of his element.

She was in hers, Liz thought as her muscles began to relax with the ride. The street was bumpy, patched in a good many places. She knew when to weave and sway. There were houses along the street with deep green grass and trailing vines. Already clothes were waving out on lines. She could hear an early newscast buzzing through someone's open window and the sound of children finishing chores or breakfast before school. She turned a corner and kept her speed steady.

There were a few shops here, closed up tight. At the door of a market, Señor Pessado fumbled with his keys. Liz tooted her horn and exchanged waves. A cab passed her, speeding down the road to the airport to wait for the early arrivals. In a matter of moments, Liz caught the first scent of the sea. It was always fresh. As she took the last turn, she glanced idly in her rearview mirror. Odd, she thought—hadn't she seen that little blue car yesterday? But when she swung into the hotel's parking lot, it chugged past.

Liz's arrangement with the hotel had been of mutual benefit. Her shop bordered the hotel's beach and encouraged business on both sides. Still, whenever she went inside, as she did today to collect the lunch for the fishing trip, she always remembered the two years she'd spent scrubbing floors and making beds.

"*Buenos días,* Margarita."

The young woman with a bucket and mop started to smile. "*Buenos días,* Liz. *¿Cómo està?*"

"*Bien.* How's Ricardo?"

"Growing out of his pants." Margarita pushed the button of the service elevator as they spoke of her son. "Faith comes home soon. He'll be glad."

"So will I." They parted, but Liz remembered the months they'd worked together, changing linen, hauling towels, washing floors. Margarita had been a friend, like so many others she'd met on the island who'd shown kindness to a young woman who'd carried a child but had no wedding ring.

She could have lied. Even at eighteen Liz had been aware she could have bought a ten-dollar gold band and had an easy story of divorce or widowhood. She'd been too stubborn. The baby that had been growing inside her belonged to her. Only to her. She'd feel no shame and tell no lies.

By seven forty-five, she was crossing the beach to her shop, lugging a large cooler packed with two lunches and a smaller one filled with bait. She could already see a few tubes bobbing on the water's surface. The water would be warm and clear and uncrowded. She'd like to have had an hour for snorkeling herself.

"Liz!" The trim, small-statured man who walked toward her was shaking his head. There was a faint, pencil-thin mustache above his lip and a smile in his dark eyes. "You're too skinny to carry that thing."

She caught her breath and studied him up and down. He wore nothing but a skimpy pair of snug trunks. She knew he enjoyed the frank or surreptitious stares of women on the beach. "So're you, Luis. But don't let me stop you."

"So you take the fishing boat today?" He hefted the larger cooler and walked with her toward the shop. "I changed the schedule for you. Thirteen signed up for the glass bottom for the morning. We got both dive boats going out, so I told my cousin Miguel to help fill in today. Okay?"

"Terrific." Luis was young, fickle with women and fond of his tequila, but he could be counted on in a pinch. "I guess I'm going to have to hire someone on, at least part-time."

Luis looked at her, then at the ground. He'd worked closest with Jerry. "Miguel, he's not dependable. Here one day, gone the next. I got a nephew, a good boy. But he can't work until he's out of school."

"I'll keep that in mind," Liz said absently. "Let's just put this right on the boat. I want to check the gear."

On board, Liz went through a routine check on the tackle and line. As she looked over the big reels and massive rods, she wondered, with a little smirk, if the lawyer had ever done any big-game fishing. Probably wouldn't know a tuna if it jumped up and bit his toe, she decided.

The decks were clean, the equipment organized, as she insisted. Luis had been with her the longest, but anyone who worked for Liz understood the hard and fast rule about giving the clients the efficiency they paid for.

The boat was small by serious sport fishing standards, but her clients rarely went away dissatisfied. She knew the waters all along the Yucatan Peninsula and the habits of the game that teemed below the surface. Her boat might not have sonar and fish finders and complicated equipment, but she determined to give Jonas Sharpe the ride of his life. She'd keep him so busy, strapped in a fighting chair, that he wouldn't have time to bother her. By the time they docked again, his arms would ache, his back would hurt and the only thing he'd be interested in would be a hot bath and bed. And if he wasn't a complete fool, she'd see to it that he had a trophy to take back to wherever he'd come from.

Just where was that? she wondered as she checked the gauges on the bridge. She'd never thought to ask Jerry. It hadn't seemed important. Yet now she found herself wondering where Jonas came from, what kind of life he led there. Was he the type who frequented elegant restaurants with an equally elegant woman on his arm? Did he watch foreign films and play bridge? Or did he prefer noisy clubs and hot jazz? She hadn't been able to find his slot as easily as she did with most people she met, so she wondered, perhaps too much. Not my business, she reminded herself and turned to call to Luis.

"I'll take care of everything here. Go ahead and open the shop. The glass bottom should be ready to leave in half an hour."

But he wasn't listening. Standing on the deck, he stared back at the narrow dock. She saw him raise a shaky hand to cross himself. *"Madre de Dios."*

"Luis?" She came down the short flight of stairs to join him. "What—"

Then she saw Jonas, a straw hat covering his head, sunglasses shading his eyes. He hadn't bothered to shave, so that the light growth of beard gave him a lazy, vagrant look accented by a faded T-shirt and brief black trunks. He didn't, she realized, look like a man who'd play bridge. Knowing what was going through Luis's mind, Liz shook his arm and spoke quickly.

"It's his brother, Luis. I told you they were twins."

"Back from the dead," Luis whispered.

"Don't be ridiculous." She shook off the shudder his words brought her. "His name is Jonas and he's nothing like Jerry at all, really. You'll see when you talk to him. You're prompt, Mr. Sharpe," she called out, hoping to jolt Luis out of his shock. "Need help coming aboard?"

"I can manage." Hefting a small cooler, Jonas stepped lightly on deck. "The *Expatriate*." He referred to the careful lettering on the side of the boat. "Is that what you are?"

"Apparently." It was something she was neither proud nor ashamed of. "This is Luis—he works for me. You gave him a jolt just now."

"Sorry." Jonas glanced at the slim man hovering by Liz's side. There was sweat beading on his lip. "You knew my brother?"

"We worked together," Luis answered in his slow, precise English. "With the divers. Jerry, he liked best to take out the dive boat. I'll cast off." Giving Jonas a wide berth, Luis jumped onto the dock.

"I seem to affect everyone the same way," Jonas observed. "How about you?" He turned dark, direct eyes to her. Though he no longer made her think of Jerry, he unnerved her just the same. "Still want to keep me at arm's length?"

"We pride ourselves in being friendly to all our clients. You've hired the *Expatriate* for the day, Mr. Sharpe. Make yourself comfortable." She gestured toward a deck chair before climbing the steps to the bridge and calling out to Luis. "Tell Miguel he gets paid only if he finishes out the day." With a final wave to Luis, she started the engine, then cruised sedately toward the open sea.

The wind was calm, barely stirring the water. Liz could see the dark patches that meant reefs and kept the speed easy. Once they were in deeper water, she'd open it up a bit. By midday the sun would be stunningly hot. She wanted Jonas strapped in his chair and fighting two hundred pounds of fish by then.

"You handle a wheel as smoothly as you do a customer."

A shadow of annoyance moved in her eyes, but she kept them straight ahead. "It's my business. You'd be more comfortable on the deck in a chair, Mr. Sharpe."

"Jonas. And I'm perfectly comfortable here." He gave her a casual study as he stood beside her. She wore a fielder's cap over her hair with white lettering promoting her shop. On her T-shirt, the same lettering was faded from the sun and frequent washings. He wondered, idly, what she wore under it. "How long have you had this boat?"

"Almost eight years. She's sound." Liz pushed the throttle forward. "The waters are warm, so you'll find tuna, marlin, swordfish. Once we're out you can start chumming."

"Chumming?"

She sent him a quick look. So she'd been right—he didn't know a line from a pole. "Bait the water," she began. "I'll keep the speed slow and you bait the water, attract the fish."

"Seems like taking unfair advantage. Isn't fishing supposed to be luck and skill?"

"For some people it's a matter of whether they'll eat or
not." She turned the wheel a fraction, scanning the water for
unwary snorkelers. "For others, it's a matter of another trophy for the wall."

"I'm not interested in trophies."

She shifted to face him. No, he wouldn't be, she decided,
not in trophies or in anything else without a purpose. "What
are you interested in?"

"At the moment, you." He put his hand over hers and let
off the throttle. "I'm in no hurry."

"You paid to fish." She flexed her hand under his.

"I paid for your time," he corrected.

He was close enough that she could see his eyes beyond
the tinted lenses. They were steady, always steady, as if he
knew he could afford to wait. The hand still over hers wasn't
smooth as she'd expected, but hard and worked. No, he
wouldn't play bridge, she thought again. Tennis, perhaps, or
hand ball, or something else that took sweat and effort. For the
first time in years she felt a quick thrill race through her—a
thrill she'd been certain she was immune to. The wind tossed
the hair back from her face as she studied him.

"Then you wasted your money."

Her hand moved under his again. Strong, he thought,
though her looks were fragile. Stubborn. He could judge that
by the way the slightly pointed chin stayed up. But there was
a look in her eyes that said *I've been hurt, I won't be hurt
again*. That alone was intriguing, but added to it was a quietly simmering sexuality that left him wondering how it was
his brother hadn't been her lover. Not, Jonas was sure, for lack
of trying.

"If I've wasted my money, it won't be the first time. But
somehow I don't think I have."

"There's nothing I can tell you." Her hand jerked and
pushed the throttle up again.

"Maybe not. Or maybe there's something you know without realizing it. I've dealt in criminal law for over ten years. You'd be surprised how important small bits of information can be. Talk to me." His hand tightened briefly on hers. "Please."

She thought she'd hardened her heart, but she could feel herself weakening. Why was it she could haggle for hours over the price of scuba gear and could never refuse a softly spoken request? He was going to cause her nothing but trouble. Because she already knew it, she sighed.

"We'll talk." She cut the throttle so the boat would drift. "While you fish." She managed to smile a bit as she stepped away. "No chum."

With easy efficiency, Liz secured the butt of a rod into the socket attached to a chair. "For now, you sit and relax," she told him. "Sometimes a fish is hot enough to take the hook without bait. If you get one, you strap yourself in and work."

Jonas settled himself in the chair and tipped back his hat. "And you?"

"I go back to the wheel and keep the speed steady so we tire him out without losing him." She gathered her hair in one hand and tossed it back. "There're better spots than this, but I'm not wasting my gas when you don't care whether you catch a fish or not."

His lips twitched as he leaned back in the chair. "Sensible. I thought you would be."

"Have to be."

"Why did you come to Cozumel?" Jonas ignored the rod in front of him and took out a cigarette.

"You've been here for a few days," she countered. "You shouldn't have to ask."

"Parts of your own country are beautiful. If you've been here ten years, you'd have been a child when you left the States."

"No, I wasn't a child." Something in the way she said it had him watching her again, looking for the secret she held just beyond her eyes. "I came because it seemed like the right thing to do. It was the right thing. When I was a girl, my parents would come here almost every year. They love to dive."

"You moved here with your parents?"

"No, I came alone." This time her voice was flat. "You didn't pay two hundred dollars to talk about me, Mr. Sharpe."

"It helps to have some background. You said you had a daughter. Where is she?"

"She goes to school in Houston—that's where my parents live."

Toss a child, and the responsibility, onto grandparents and live on a tropical island. It might leave a bad taste in his mouth, but it wasn't something that would surprise him. Jonas took a deep drag as he studied Liz's profile. It just didn't fit. "You miss her."

"Horribly," Liz murmured. "She'll be home in a few weeks, and we'll spend the summer together. September always comes too soon." Her gaze drifted off as she spoke, almost to herself. "It's for the best. My parents take wonderful care of her and she's getting an excellent education—taking piano lessons and ballet. They sent me pictures from a recital, and . . ." Her eyes filled with tears so quickly that she hadn't any warning. She shifted into the wind and fought them back, but he'd seen them. He sat smoking silently to give her time to recover.

"Ever get back to the States?"

"No." Liz swallowed and called herself a fool. It had been the pictures, she told herself, the pictures that had come in yesterday's mail of her little girl wearing a pink dress.

"Hiding from something?"

She whirled back, tears replaced with fury. Her body was arched like a bow ready to launch. Jonas held up a hand.

"Sorry. I have a habit of poking into secrets."

She forced herself to relax, to strap back passion as she'd taught herself so long ago. "It's a good way to lose your fingers, Mr. Sharpe."

He chuckled. "That's a possibility. I've always considered it worth the risk. They call you Liz, don't they?"

Her brow lifted under the fringe that blew around her brow. "My friends do."

"It suits you, except when you try to be aloof. Then it should be Elizabeth."

She sent him a smoldering look, certain he was trying to annoy her. "No one calls me Elizabeth."

He merely grinned at her. "Why weren't you sleeping with Jerry?"

"I beg your pardon?"

"Yes, definitely Elizabeth. You're a beautiful woman in an odd sort of way." He tossed out the compliment as casually as he tossed the cigarette into the water. "Jerry had a . . . fondness for beautiful women. I can't figure out why you weren't lovers."

For a moment, only a moment, it occurred to her that no one had called her beautiful in a very long time. She'd needed words like that once. Then she leaned back on the rail, planted her hands and aimed a killing look. She didn't need them now.

"I didn't choose to sleep with him. It might be difficult for you to accept, as you share the same face, but I didn't find Jerry irresistible."

"No?" As relaxed as she was tensed, Jonas reached into the cooler, offering her a beer. When she shook her head, he popped the top on one for himself. "What did you find him?"

"He was a drifter, and he happened to drift into my life. I gave him a job because he had a quick mind and a strong back. The truth was, I never expected him to last over a month. Men like him don't."

Though he hadn't moved a muscle, Jonas had come to attention. "Men like him?"

"Men who look for the quickest way to easy street. He worked because he liked to eat, but he was always looking for the big strike—one he wouldn't have to sweat for."

"So you did know him," Jonas murmured. "What was he looking for here?"

"I tell you I don't know! For all I know he was looking for a good time and a little sun." Frustration poured out of her as she tossed a hand in the air. "I let him have a room because he seemed harmless and I could use the money. I wasn't intimate with him on any level. The closest he came to talking about what he was up to was bragging about diving for big bucks."

"Diving? Where?"

Fighting for control, she dragged a hand through her hair. "I wish you'd leave me alone."

"You're a realistic woman, aren't you, Elizabeth?"

Her chin was set when she looked back at him. "Yes."

"Then you know I won't. Where was he going to dive?"

"I don't know. I barely listened to him when he got started on how rich he was going to be."

"What did he say?" This time Jonas's voice was quiet, persuading. "Just try to think back and remember what he told you."

"He said something about making a fortune diving, and I joked about sunken treasure. And he said . . ." She strained to remember the conversation. It had been late in the evening, and she'd been busy, preoccupied. "I was working at home," Liz remembered. "I always seem to handle the books better at night. He'd been out, partying I thought, because he was a little unsteady when he came in. He pulled me out of the chair. I remember I started to swear at him but he looked so damn happy, I let it go. Really, I hardly listened because I was picking up all the papers he'd scattered, but he was saying something about the big time and buying champagne to celebrate. I told him he'd better stick to beer on his salary. That's when he talked about deals coming through and diving for big bucks. Then I made some comment about sunken treasure . . ."

"And what did he say?"

"Sometimes you make more putting stuff in than taking it out." With a line between her brows, she remembered how he'd laughed when she'd told him to go sleep it off. "He made a pass neither one of us took seriously, and then . . . I think he made a phone call. I went back to work."

"When was this?"

"A week, maybe one week after I took him on."

"That must have been when he called me." Jonas looked out to sea. And he hadn't paid much attention, either, he reminded himself. Jerry had talked about coming home in style. But then he had always been talking about coming home in style. And the call, as usual, had been collect.

"Did you ever see him with anyone? Talking, arguing?"

"I never saw him argue with anyone. He flirted with the women on the beach, made small talk with the clients and got along just fine with everyone he worked with. I assumed he spent most of his free time in San Miguel. I think he cruised a few bars with Luis and some of the others."

"What bars?"

"You'll have to ask them, though I'm sure the police already have." She took a deep breath. It was bringing it all back again, too close. "Mr. Sharpe, why don't you let the police handle this? You're running after shadows."

"He was my brother." And more, what he couldn't explain, his twin. Part of himself had been murdered. If he were ever to feel whole again, he had to know why. "Haven't you wondered why Jerry was murdered?"

"Of course." She looked down at her hands. They were empty and she felt helpless. "I thought he must've gotten into a fight, or maybe he bragged to the wrong person. He had a bad habit of tossing what money he had around."

"It wasn't robbery or a mugging, Elizabeth. It was professional. It was business."

Her heart began a slow, painful thud. "I don't understand."

"Jerry was murdered by a pro, and I'm going to find out why."

Because her throat was suddenly dry, she swallowed. "If you're right, then that's all the more reason to leave it to the police."

He drew out his cigarettes again, but stared ahead to where the sky met the water. "Police don't want revenge. I do." In his voice, she heard the calm patience and felt a shiver.

Staring, she shook her head. "Even if you found the person who did it, what could you do?"

He took a long pull from his beer. "As a lawyer, I suppose I'd be obliged to see they had their day in court. As a brother . . ." He trailed off and drank again. "We'll have to see."

"I don't think you're a very nice man, Mr. Sharpe."

"I'm not." He turned his head until his eyes locked on hers. "And I'm not harmless. Remember, if I make a pass, we'll both take it seriously."

She started to speak, then saw his line go taut. "You've got a fish, Mr. Sharpe," she said dryly. "You'd better strap in or he'll pull you overboard."

Turning on her heel, she went back to the bridge, leaving Jonas to fend for himself.

CHAPTER 3

It was sundown when Liz parked her bike under the lean-to beside her house. She was still laughing. However much trouble Jonas had caused her, however much he had annoyed her in three brief meetings, she had his two hundred dollars. And he had a thirty-pound marlin—whether he wanted it or not. *We deliver,* she thought as she jingled her keys.

Oh, it had been worth it, just to see his face when he'd found himself on the other end of the wire from a big, bad-tempered fish. Liz believed he'd have let it go if she hadn't taken the time for one last smirk. Stubborn, she thought again. Yes, any other time she'd have admired it, and him.

Though she'd been wrong about his not being able to handle a rod, he'd looked so utterly perplexed with the fish lying at his feet on the deck that she'd nearly felt sorry for him. But his luck, or the lack of it, had helped her make an easy exit once they'd docked. With all the people crowding around to get a look at his catch and congratulate him, Jonas hadn't been able to detain her.

Now she was ready for an early evening, she thought. And a rainy one if the clouds moving in from the east delivered. Liz let herself into the house, propping the door open to bring in the breeze that already tasted of rain. After the fans were whirling, she turned on the radio automatically. Hurricane season might be a few months off, but the quick tropical storms were unpredictable. She'd been through enough of them not to take them lightly.

In the bedroom she prepared to strip for the shower that would wash the day's sweat and salt from her skin. Because it was twilight, she was already reaching for the light switch when a stray thought stopped her. Hadn't she left the blinds up that morning? Liz stared at them, tugged snugly over the windowsill. Odd, she was sure she'd left them up, and why wasn't the cord wrapped around its little hook? She was fanatical about that kind of detail, she supposed because ropes on a boat were always secured.

She hesitated, even after light spilled into the room. Then she shrugged. She must have been more distracted that morning than she'd realized. Jonas Sharpe, she decided, was taking up too much of her time, and too many of her thoughts. A man like him was bound to do so, even under different circumstances. But she'd long since passed the point in her life where a man could dominate it. He only worried her because he was interfering in her time, and her time was a precious commodity. Now that he'd had his way, and his talk, there should be no more visits. She remembered, uncomfortably, the way he'd smiled at her. It would be best, she decided, if he went back to where he'd come from and she got on with her own routine.

To satisfy herself, Liz walked over to the first shade and secured the cord. From the other room, the radio announced an evening shower before music kicked in. Humming along with it, she decided to toss together a chicken salad before she logged the day's accounts.

As she straightened, the breath was knocked out of her by an arm closing tightly around her neck. The dying sun caught a flash of silver. Before she could react, she felt the quick prick of a knife blade at her throat.

"Where is it?"

The voice that hissed in her ear was Spanish. In reflex, she brought her hands to the arm around her neck. As her nails dug in, she felt hard flesh and a thin metal band. She gasped for air, but stopped struggling when the knife poked threateningly at her throat.

"What do you want?" In terror her mind skimmed forward. She had less than fifty dollars cash and no jewelry of value except a single strand of pearls left by her grandmother. "My purse is in on the table. You can take it."

The vicious yank on her hair had her gasping in pain. "Where did he put it?"

"Who? I don't know what you want."

"Sharpe. Deal's off, lady. If you want to live, you tell me where he put the money."

"I don't know." The knife point pricked the vulnerable skin at her throat. She felt something warm trickle down her skin. Hysteria bubbled up behind it. "I never saw any money. You can look—there's nothing here."

"I've already looked." He tightened his hold until her vision grayed from lack of air. "Sharpe died fast. You won't be so lucky. Tell me where it is and nothing happens."

He was going to kill her. The thought ran in her head. She was going to die for something she knew nothing about. Money . . . he wanted money and she only had fifty dollars. Faith. As she felt herself on the verge of unconsciousness, she thought of her daughter. Who would take care of her? Liz bit down on her lip until the pain cleared her mind. She couldn't die.

"Please . . ." She let herself go limp in his arms. "I can't tell you anything. I can't breathe."

His hold loosened just slightly. Liz slumped against him and when he shifted, she brought her elbow back with all her strength. She didn't bother to turn around but ran blindly. A rug slid under her feet, but she stumbled ahead, too terrified to look back. She was already calling for help when she hit the front door.

Her closest neighbor was a hundred yards away. She vaulted the little fence that separated the yards and sprinted toward the house. She stumbled up the steps, sobbing. Even as the door opened, she heard the sound of a car squealing tires on the rough gravel road behind her.

"He tried to kill me," she managed, then fainted.

* * *

There is no further information I can give you, Mr. Sharpe." Moralas sat in his neat office facing the waterfront. The file on his desk wasn't as thick as he would have liked. Nothing in his investigation had turned up a reason for Jerry Sharpe's murder. The man who sat across from him stared straight ahead. Moralas had a photo of the victim in the file, and a mirror image a few feet away. "I wonder, Mr. Sharpe, if your brother's death was a result of something that happened before his coming to Cozumel."

"Jerry wasn't running when he came here."

Moralas tidied his papers. "Still, we have asked for the cooperation of the New Orleans authorities. That was your brother's last known address."

"He never had an address," Jonas murmured. Or a conventional job, a steady woman. Jerry had been a comet, always refusing to burn itself out. "I've told you what Miss Palmer said. Jerry was cooking up a deal, and he was cooking it up in Cozumel."

"Yes, having to do with diving." Always patient, Moralas drew out a thin cigar. "Though we've already spoken with Miss Palmer, I appreciate your bringing me the information."

"But you don't know what the hell to do with it."

Moralas flicked on his lighter, smiling at Jonas over the flame. "You're blunt. I'll be blunt, as well. If there was a trail to follow to your brother's murder, it's cold. Every day it grows colder. There were no fingerprints, no murder weapon, no witnesses." He picked up the file, gesturing with it. "That doesn't mean I intend to toss this in a drawer and forget about it. If there is a murderer on my island, I intend to find him.

At the moment, I believe the murderer is miles away, perhaps in your own country. Procedure now is to backtrack on your brother's activities until we find something. To be frank, Mr. Sharpe, you're not doing yourself or me any good by being here."

"I'm not leaving."

"That is, of course, your privilege—unless you interfere with police procedure." At the sound of the buzzer on his desk, Moralas tipped his ash and picked up the phone.

"Moralas." There was a pause. Jonas saw the captain's thick, dark brows draw together. "Yes, put her on. Miss Palmer, this is Captain Moralas."

Jonas stopped in the act of lighting a cigarette and waited. Liz Palmer was the key, he thought again. He had only to find what lock she fit.

"When? Are you injured? No, please stay where you are, I'll come to you." Moralas was rising as he hung up the phone. "Miss Palmer has been attacked."

Jonas was at the door first. "I'm coming with you."

His muscles ached with tension as the police car raced out of town toward the shore. He asked no questions. In his mind, Jonas could see Liz as she'd been on the bridge hours before—tanned, slim, a bit defiant. He remembered the self-satisfied smirk she'd given him when he'd found himself in a tug-of-war with a thirty-pound fish. And how neatly she'd skipped out on him the moment they'd docked.

She'd been attacked. Why? Was it because she knew more than she'd been willing to tell him? He wondered if she were a liar, an opportunist or a coward. Then he wondered how badly she'd been hurt.

As they pulled down the narrow drive, Jonas glanced toward Liz's house. The door was open, the shades drawn. She lived there alone, he thought, vulnerable and unprotected. Then he turned his attention to the little stucco building next door. A woman in a cotton dress and apron came onto the porch. She carried a baseball bat.

"You are the police." She nodded, satisfied, when Mora-las showed his identification. "I am Señora Alderez. She's in-side. I thank the Virgin we were home when she came to us."

"Thank you."

Jonas stepped inside with Moralas and saw her. She was sitting on a patched sofa, huddled forward with a glass of wine in both hands. Jonas saw the liquid shiver back and forth as her hands trembled. She looked up slowly when they came in, her gaze passing over Moralas to lock on Jonas. She stared, with no expression in those deep, dark eyes. Just as slowly, she looked back at her glass.

"Miss Palmer." With his voice very gentle, Moralas sat down beside her. "Can you tell me what happened?"

She took the smallest of drinks, pressed her lips together briefly, then began as though she were reciting. "I came home at sunset. I didn't close the front door or lock it. I went straight into the bedroom. The shades were down, and I thought I'd left them up that morning. The cord wasn't secured, so I went over and fixed it. That's when he grabbed me—from behind. He had his arm around my neck and a knife. He cut me a lit-tle." In reflex, she reached up to touch the inch-long scratch her neighbor had already cleaned and fussed over. "I didn't fight because he had the knife at my throat and I thought he would kill me. He was going to kill me." She brought her head up to look directly into Moralas's eyes. "I could hear it in his voice."

"What did he say to you, Miss Palmer?"

"He said, 'Where is it?' I didn't know what he wanted. I told him he could take my purse. He was choking me and he said, 'Where did he put it?' He said Sharpe." This time she looked at Jonas. When she lifted her head, he saw that bruises were already forming on her throat. "He said the deal was off and he wanted the money. If I didn't tell him where it was, he'd kill me, and I wouldn't die quickly, the way Jerry had. He didn't believe me when I said I didn't know anything." She spoke directly to Jonas. As she stared at him he felt the guilt rise.

Patient, Moralas touched her arm to bring her attention back to him. "He let you go?"

"No, he was going to kill me." She said it dully, without fear, without passion. "I knew he would whether I told him anything or not, and my daughter—she needs me. I slumped as if I'd fainted, then I hit him. I think I hit him in the throat with my elbow. And I ran."

"Can you identify the man?"

"I never saw him. I never looked."

"His voice."

"He spoke Spanish. I think he was short because his voice was right in my ear. I don't know anything else. I don't know anything about money or Jerry or anything else." She looked back into her glass, abruptly terrified she would cry. "I want to go home."

"As soon as my men make certain it's safe. You'll have police protection, Miss Palmer. Rest here. I'll come back for you and take you home."

She didn't know if it had been minutes or hours since she'd fled through the front door. When Moralas took her back, it was dark with the moon just rising. An officer would remain outside in her driveway and all her doors and windows had been checked. Without a word, she went through the house into the kitchen.

"She was lucky." Moralas gave the living room another quick check. "Whoever attacked her was careless enough to be caught off guard."

"Did the neighbors see anything?" Jonas righted a table that had been overturned in flight. There was a conch shell on the floor that had cracked.

"A few people noticed a blue compact outside the house late this afternoon. Señora Alderez saw it drive off when she opened the door to Miss Palmer, but she couldn't identify the make or the plates. We will, of course, keep Miss Palmer under surveillance while we try to track it down."

"It doesn't appear my brother's killer's left the island."

Moralas met Jonas's gaze blandly. "Apparently whatever deal your brother was working on cost him his life. I don't intend for it to cost Miss Palmer hers. I'll drive you back to town."

"No. I'm staying." Jonas examined the pale pink shell with the crack spreading down its length. He thought of the mark on Liz's throat. "My brother involved her." Carefully, he set the damaged shell down. "I can't leave her alone."

"As you wish." Moralas turned to go when Jonas stopped him.

"Captain, you don't still think the murderer's hundreds of miles away."

Moralas touched the gun that hung at his side. "No, Mr. Sharpe, I don't. *Buenas noches.*"

Jonas locked her door himself, then rechecked the windows before he went back to the kitchen. Liz was pouring her second cup of coffee. "That'll keep you up."

Liz drank half a cup, staring at him. She felt nothing at the moment, no anger, no fear. "I thought you'd gone."

"No." Without invitation, he found a mug and poured coffee for himself.

"Why are you here?"

He took a step closer, to run a fingertip gently down the mark on her throat. "Stupid question," he murmured.

She backed up, fighting to maintain the calm she'd clung to. If she lost control, it wouldn't be in front of him, in front of anyone. "I want to be alone."

He saw her hands tremble before she locked them tighter on the cup. "You can't always have what you want. I'll bunk in your daughter's room."

"No!" After slamming the cup down, she folded her arms across her chest. "I don't want you here."

With studied calm, he set his mug next to hers. When he

took her shoulders, his hands were firm, not gentle. When he spoke, his voice was brisk, not soothing. "I'm not leaving you alone. Not now, not until they find Jerry's killer. You're involved whether you like it or not. And so, damn it, am I."

Her breath came quickly, too quickly, though she fought to steady it. "I wasn't involved until you came back and started hounding me."

He'd already wrestled with his conscience over that. Neither one of them could know if it were true. At the moment, he told himself it didn't matter. "However you're involved, you are. Whoever killed Jerry thinks you know something. You'll have an easier time convincing me you don't than you will them. It's time you started thinking about cooperating with me."

"How do I know you didn't send him here to frighten me?"

His eyes stayed on hers, cool and unwavering. "You don't. I could tell you that I don't hire men to kill women, but you wouldn't have to believe it. I could tell you I'm sorry." For the first time, his tone gentled. He lifted a hand to brush the hair back from her face and his thumb slid lightly over her cheekbone. Like the conch shell, she seemed delicate, lovely and damaged. "And that I wish I could walk away, leave you alone, let both of us go back to the way things were a few weeks ago. But I can't. We can't. So we might as well help each other."

"I don't want your help."

"I know. Sit down. I'll fix you something to eat."

She tried to back away. "You can't stay here."

"I am staying here. Tomorrow, I'm moving my things from the hotel."

"I said—"

"I'll rent the room," he interrupted, turning away to rummage through the cupboards. "Your throat's probably raw. This chicken soup should be the best thing."

She snatched the can from his hand. "I can fix my own dinner, and you're not renting a room."

"I appreciate your generosity." He took the can back from her. "But I'd rather keep it on a business level. Twenty dollars a week seems fair. You'd better take it, Liz," he added before she could speak. "Because I'm staying, one way or the other. Sit down," he said again and looked for a pot.

She wanted to be angry. It would help keep everything else bottled up. She wanted to shout at him, to throw him bodily out of her house. Instead she sat because her knees were too weak to hold her any longer.

What had happened to her control? For ten years she'd been running her own life, making every decision by herself, for herself. For ten years, she hadn't asked advice, she hadn't asked for help. Now something had taken control and decisions out of her hands, something she knew nothing about. Her life was part of a game, and she didn't know any of the rules.

She looked down and saw the tear drop on the back of her hand. Quickly, she reached up and brushed others from her cheeks. But she couldn't stop them. One more decision had been taken from her.

"Can you eat some toast?" Jonas asked her as he dumped the contents of the soup in a pan. When she didn't answer, he turned to see her sitting stiff and pale at the table, tears running unheeded down her face. He swore and turned away again. There was nothing he could do for her, he told himself. Nothing he could offer. Then, saying nothing, he came to the table, pulled a chair up beside her and waited.

"I thought he'd kill me." Her voice broke as she pressed a hand to her face. "I felt the knife against my throat and thought I was going to die. I'm so scared. Oh God, I'm so scared."

He drew her against him and let her sob out the fear. He wasn't used to comforting women. Those he knew well were too chic to shed more than a delicate drop or two. But he held her close during a storm of weeping that shook her body and left her gasping.

Her skin was icy, as if to prove the fact that fear made the blood run cold. She couldn't summon the pride to draw herself away, to seek a private spot as she'd always done in a crisis. He didn't speak to tell her everything would be fine; he didn't murmur quiet words of comfort. He was simply there. When she was drained, he still held her. The rain began slowly, patting the glass of the windows and pinging on the roof. He still held her.

When she shifted away, he rose and went back to the stove. Without a word, he turned on the burner. Minutes later he set a bowl in front of her then went back to ladle some for himself. Too tired to be ashamed, Liz began to eat. There was no sound in the kitchen but the slow monotonous plop of rain on wood, tin and glass.

She hadn't realized she could be hungry, but the bowl was empty almost before she realized it. With a little sigh, she pushed it away. He was tipped back in his chair, smoking in silence.

"Thank you."

"Okay." Her eyes were swollen, accentuating the vulnerability that always haunted them. It tugged at him, making him uneasy. Her skin, with its ripe, warm honey glow was pale, making her seem delicate and defenseless. She was a woman, he realized, that a man had to keep an emotional distance from. Get too close and you'd be sucked right in. It wouldn't do to care about her too much when he needed to use her to help both of them. From this point on, he'd have to hold the controls.

"I suppose I was more upset than I realized."

"You're entitled."

She nodded, grateful he was making it easy for her to skim over what she considered an embarrassing display of weakness. "There's no reason for you to stay here."

"I'll stay anyway."

She curled her hand into a fist, then uncurled it slowly. It wasn't possible for her to admit she wanted him to, or that for the first time in years she was frightened of being alone. Since she had to cave in, it was better to think of the arrangement on a practical level.

"All right, the room's twenty a week, first week in advance."

He grinned as he reached for his wallet. "All business?"

"I can't afford anything else." After putting the twenty on the counter, she stacked the bowls. "You'll have to see to your own food. The twenty doesn't include meals."

He watched her take the bowls to the sink and wash them. "I'll manage."

"I'll give you a key in the morning." She took a towel and meticulously dried the bowls. "Do you think he'll be back?" She tried to make her voice casual, and failed.

"I don't know." He crossed to her to lay a hand on her shoulder. "You won't be alone if he does."

When she looked at him, her eyes were steady again. Something inside him unknotted. "Are you protecting me, Jonas, or just looking for your revenge?"

"I do one, maybe I'll get the other." He twined the ends of her hair around his finger, watching the dark gold spread over his skin. "You said yourself I'm not a nice man."

"What are you?" she whispered.

"Just a man." When his gaze lifted to hers, she didn't believe him. He wasn't just a man, but a man with patience, with power and with violence. "I've wondered the same about you. You've got secrets, Elizabeth."

She was breathless. In defense, she lifted her hand to his. "They've got nothing to do with you."

"Maybe they don't. Maybe you do."

It happened very slowly, so slowly she could have stopped it. Yet she seemed unable to move. His arms slipped around her, drawing her close with an arrogant sort of laziness that should have been his undoing. Instead, Liz watched, fascinated, as his mouth lowered to hers.

She'd just thought of him as a violent man, but his lips were soft, easy, persuading. It had been so long since she'd allowed herself to be persuaded. With barely any pressure, with only the slightest hint of power, he sapped the will she'd always relied on. Her mind raced with questions, then clouded over to a fine, smoky mist. She wasn't aware of how sweetly, how hesitantly her mouth answered his.

Whatever impulse had driven him to kiss her was lost in the reality of mouth against mouth. He'd expected her to resist, or to answer with fire and passion. To find her so soft, yielding, unsteady, had his own desire building in a way he'd never experienced. It was as though she'd never been kissed before, never been held close to explore what man and woman have for each other. Yet she had a daughter, he reminded himself. She'd had a child, she was young, beautiful. Other men had held her like this. Yet he felt like the first and had no choice but to treat her with care.

The more she gave, the more he wanted. He'd known needs before. The longer he held her, the longer he wanted to. He understood passions. But a part of himself he couldn't understand held back, demanded restraint. She wanted him—he could feel it. But even as his blood began to swim, his hands, as if under their own power, eased her away.

Needs, so long unstirred, churned in her. As she stared back at him, Liz felt them spring to life, with all their demands and risks. It wouldn't happen to her again. But even as she renewed the vow she felt the soft, fluttering longings waltz through her. It couldn't happen again. But the eyes that were wide and on his reflected confusion and hurt and hope. It was a combination that left Jonas shaken.

"You should get some sleep," he told her, and took care not to touch her again.

So that was all, Liz thought as the flicker of hope died. It was foolish to believe, even for a moment, anything could change. She brought her chin up and straightened her shoulders. Perhaps she'd lost control of many things, but she could still control her heart. "I'll give you a receipt for the rent and the key in the morning. I get up at six." She took the twenty-dollar bill she'd left on the counter and walked out.

CHAPTER 4

The jury was staring at him. Twelve still faces with blank eyes were lined behind the rail. Jonas stood before them in a small, harshly lit courtroom that echoed with his own voice. He carried stacks of law books, thick, dusty and heavy enough to make his arms ache. But he knew he couldn't put them down. Sweat rolled down his temples, down his back as he gave an impassioned closing plea for his client's acquittal. It was life and death, and his voice vibrated with both. The jury remained unmoved, disinterested. Though he struggled to hold them, the books began to slip from his grasp. He heard the verdict rebound, bouncing off the courtroom walls.

Guilty. Guilty. Guilty.

Defeated, empty-handed, he turned to the defendant. The man stood, lifting his head so that they stared, eye to eye, twin images. Himself? Jerry. Desperate, Jonas walked to the bench. In black robes, Liz sat above him, aloof with distance. But her eyes were sad as she slowly shook her head. "I can't help you."

Slowly, she began to fade. He reached up to grab her hand, but his fingers passed through hers. All he could see were her dark, sad eyes. Then she was gone, his brother was gone, and he was left facing a jury—twelve cold faces who smiled smugly back at him.

Jonas lay still, breathing quickly. He found himself staring back at the cluster of gaily dressed dolls on the shelf beside
the bed. A flamenco dancer raised her castanets. A princess
held a glass slipper. A spiffily dressed Barbie relaxed in a
pink convertible, one hand raised in a wave.

Letting out a long breath, Jonas ran a hand over his face
and sat up. It was like trying to sleep in the middle of a party,
he decided. No wonder he'd had odd dreams. On the opposing wall was a collection of stuffed animals ranging from the
dependable bear to something that looked like a blue dust rag
with eyes.

Coffee, Jonas thought, closing his own. He needed coffee. Trying to ignore the dozens of smiling faces surrounding him, he dressed. He wasn't sure how or where
to begin. The coin on his chain dangled before he pulled a
shirt over his chest. Outside, birds were sending up a clatter. At home there would have been the sound of traffic as
Philadelphia awoke for the day. He could see a bush close
to the window where purple flowers seemed to crowd each
other for room. There were no sturdy elms, no tidy ever-
green hedges or chain-link fences. No law books would
help him with what he had to do. There was nothing familiar, no precedents to follow. Each step he took would
be taken blindly, but he had to take them. He smelled the
coffee the moment he left the room.

Liz was in the kitchen dressed in a T-shirt and what appeared to be the bottoms of a skimpy bikini. Jonas wasn't a
man who normally awoke with all batteries charged, but he
didn't miss a pair of long, honey-toned legs. Liz finished but-
tering a piece of toast.

"Coffee's on the stove," she said without turning around.
"There're some eggs in the refrigerator. I don't stock cereal
when Faith's away."

"Eggs are fine," he mumbled, but headed for the coffee.

"Use what you want, as long as you replace it." She turned
up the radio to listen to the weather forecast. "I leave in a

half hour, so if you want a ride to your hotel, you'll have to be ready."

Jonas let the first hot taste of coffee seep into his system. "My car's in San Miguel."

Liz sat down at the table to go over that day's schedule. "I can drop you by the El Presidente or one of the other hotels on the beach. You'll have to take a cab from there."

Jonas took another sip of coffee and focused on her fully. She was still pale, he realized, so that the marks on her neck stood out in dark relief. The smudges under her eyes made him decide she'd slept no better than he had. He tossed off his first cup of coffee and poured another.

"Ever consider taking a day off?"

She looked at him for the first time. "No," she said simply and lowered her gaze to her list again.

So they were back to business, all business, and don't cross the line. "Don't you believe in giving yourself a break, Liz?"

"I've got work to do. You'd better fix those eggs if you want to have time to eat them. The frying pan's in the cupboard next to the stove."

He studied her for another minute, then with a restless movement of his shoulders prepared to cook his breakfast. Liz waited until she was sure his back was to her before she looked up again.

She'd made a fool of herself the night before. She could almost accept the fact that she'd broken down in front of him because he'd taken it so matter-of-factly. But when she added the moments she'd stood in his arms, submissive, willing, hoping, she couldn't forgive herself. Or him.

He'd made her feel something she hadn't felt in a decade. Arousal. He'd made her want what she'd been convinced she didn't want from a man. Affection. She hadn't backed away or brushed him aside as she'd done with any other man who'd approached her. She hadn't even tried. He'd made her feel soft again, then he'd shrugged her away.

So it would be business, she told herself. Straight, imper-sonal business as long as he determined to stay. She'd put the rent money aside until she could manage the down payment on the aqua bikes. Jonas sat at the table with a plate of eggs that sent steam rising toward the ceiling.

"Your key." Liz slid it over to him. "And your receipt for the first week's rent."

Without looking at it, Jonas tucked the paper in his pocket. "Do you usually take in boarders?"

"No, but I need some new equipment." She rose to pour another cup of coffee and wash her plate. The radio an-nounced the time before she switched it off. She was ten minutes ahead of schedule, but as long as she continued to get up early enough, they wouldn't have to eat together. "Do you usually rent a room in a stranger's house rather than a hotel suite?"

He tasted the eggs and found himself vaguely dissatisfied with his own cooking. "No, but we're not strangers anymore."

Liz watched him over the rim of her cup. He looked a little rough around the edges this morning, she decided. It added a bit too much sexuality to smooth good looks. She debated offering him a razor, then rejected the notion. Too personal. "Yes, we are."

He continued to eat his eggs so that she thought he'd taken her at her word. "I studied law at Notre Dame, apprenticed with Neiram and Barker in Boston, then opened my own practice five years ago in Philadelphia." He added some salt, hoping it would jazz up his cooking. "I specialize in crimi-nal law. I'm not married, and live alone. In an apartment," he added. "On weekends I'm remodeling an old Victorian house I bought in Chadd's Ford."

She wanted to ask him about the house—was it big, did it have those wonderful high ceilings and rich wooden floors? Were the windows tall and mullioned? Was there a garden where roses climbed on trellises? Instead she turned to rinse out her cup. "That doesn't change the fact that we're strangers."

"Whether we know each other or not, we have the same problem."

The cup rattled in the sink as it slipped from her hand. Silently, Liz picked it up again, rinsed it off and set it in the drainer. She'd chipped it, but that was a small matter at the moment. "You've got ten minutes," she said, but he took her arm before she could skirt around him.

"We do have the same problem, Elizabeth." His voice was quiet, steady. She could have hated him for that alone.

"No, we don't. You're trying to avenge your brother's death. I'm just trying to make a living."

"Do you think everything would settle down quietly if I were back in Philadelphia?"

She tugged her arm uselessly. "Yes!" Because she knew she lied, her eyes heated.

"One of the first impressions I had of you was your intelligence. I don't know why you're hiding on your pretty little island, Liz, but you've got a brain, a good one. We both know that what happened to you last night would have happened with or without me."

"All right." She relaxed her arm. "What happened wasn't because of you, but because of Jerry. That hardly makes any difference to my position, does it?"

He stood up slowly, but didn't release her arm. "As long as someone thinks you knew what Jerry was into, you're the focus. As long as you're the focus, I'm standing right beside you, because directly or indirectly, you're going to lead me to Jerry's killer."

Liz waited a moment until she was sure she could speak calmly. "Is that all people are to you, Jonas? Tools? Means to an end?" She searched his face and found it set and remote. "Men like you never look beyond their own interests."

Angry without knowing why, he cupped her face in his hand. "You've never known a man like me."

"I think I have," she said softly. "You're not unique, Jonas. You were raised with money and expectations, you went to the best schools and associated with the best people. You had your goal set and if you had to step on or over a few people on the way to it, it wasn't personal. That's the worst of it," she said on a long breath. "It's never personal." Lifting her chin, she pushed his hand from her face. "What do you want me to do?"

Never in his life had anyone made him feel so vile. With a few words she'd tried and condemned him. He remembered the dream, and the blank, staring eyes of the jury. He swore at her and turned to pace to the window. He couldn't back away now, no matter how she made him feel because he was right—whether he was here or in Philadelphia, she was still the key.

There was a hammock outside, bright blue and yellow strings stretched between two palms. He wondered if she ever gave herself enough time to use it. He found himself wishing he could take her hand, walk across the yard and lie with her on the hammock with nothing more important to worry about than swatting at flies.

"I need to talk to Luis," he began. "I want to know the places he went with Jerry, the people he may have seen Jerry talk to."

"I'll talk to Luis." When Jonas started to object, Liz shook her head. "You saw his reaction yesterday. He wouldn't be able to talk to you because you make him too nervous. I'll get you a list."

"All right." Jonas fished for his cigarettes and found with some annoyance that he'd left them in the bedroom. "I'll need you to go with me, starting tonight, to the places Luis gives you."

A feeling of stepping into quicksand came strongly. "Why?"

He wasn't sure of the answer. "Because I have to start somewhere."

"Why do you need me?"

And even less sure of this one. "I don't know how long it'll take, and I'm not leaving you alone."

She lifted a brow. "I have police protection."

"Not good enough. In any case, you know the language, the customs. I don't. I need you." He tucked his thumbs in his pockets. "It's as simple as that."

Liz walked over to turn off the coffee and move the pot to a back burner. "Nothing's simple," she corrected. "But I'll get your list, and I'll go along with you under one condition."

"Which is?"

She folded her hands. Jonas was already certain by her stance alone that she wasn't set to bargain but to lay down the rules. "That no matter what happens, what you find out or don't find out, you're out of this house and out of my life when my daughter comes home. I'll give you four weeks, Jonas—that's all."

"It'll have to be enough."

She nodded and started out of the room. "Wash your dishes. I'll meet you out front."

The police car still sat in the driveway when Jonas walked out the front door. A group of children stood on the verge of the road and discussed it in undertones. He heard Liz call one of them by name before she took out a handful of coins. Jonas didn't have to speak Spanish to recognize a business transaction. Moments later, coins in hand, the boy raced back to his friends.

"What was that about?"

Liz smiled after them. Faith would play with those same children throughout the summer. "I told them they were detectives. If they see anyone but you or the police around the house, they're to run right home and call Captain Moralas. It's the best way to keep them out of trouble."

Jonas watched the boy in charge pass out the coins. "How much did you give them?"

"Twenty pesos apiece."

He thought of the current rate of exchange and shook his head. "No kid in Philadelphia would give you the time of day for that."

"This is Cozumel," she said simply and wheeled out her bike.

Jonas looked at it, then at her. The bike would have sent a young teenager into ecstasies. "You drive this thing?"

Something in his tone made her want to smile. Instead, she kept her voice cool. "This thing is an excellent mode of transportation."

"A BMW's an excellent mode of transportation."

She laughed. He hadn't heard her laugh so easily since he'd met her. When she looked back at him, her eyes were warm and friendly. Jonas felt the ground shift dangerously under his feet. "Try to take your BMW on some of the back roads to the coast or into the interior." She swung a leg over the seat. "Hop on, Jonas, unless you want to hike back to the hotel."

Though he had his doubts, Jonas sat behind her. "Where do I put my feet?"

She glanced down and didn't bother to hide the grin. "Well, if I were you, I'd keep them off the ground." With this she started the engine then swung the bike around in the driveway. After adjusting for the added weight, Liz kept the speed steady. Jonas kept his hands lightly at her hips as the bike swayed around ruts and potholes.

"Are there roads worse than this?"

Liz sped over a bump. "What's wrong with this?"

"Just asking."

"If you want sophistication, try Cancun. It's only a few minutes by air."

"Ever get there?"

"Now and again. Last year Faith and I took the *Expatriate* over and spent a couple of days seeing the ruins. We have some shrines here. They're not well restored, but you shouldn't miss them. Still, I wanted her to see the pyramids and walled cities around Cancun."

"I don't know much about archaeology."

"You don't have to. All you need's an imagination."

She tooted the horn. Jonas saw an old, bent man straighten

from the door of a shop and wave. "Señor Pessado," she said. "He gives Faith candy they both think I don't know about."

Jonas started to ask her about her daughter, then decided to wait for a better time. As long as she was being expansive, it was best to keep things less personal. "Do you know a lot of people on the island?"

"It's like a small town, I suppose. You don't necessarily have to know someone to recognize their face. I don't know a lot of people in San Miguel or on the east coast. I know a few people from the interior because we worked at the hotel."

"I didn't realize your shop was affiliated with the hotel."

"It's not." She paused at a stop sign. "I used to work in the hotel. As a maid." Liz gunned the engine and zipped across the intersection.

He looked at her hands, lean and delicate on the handle-bars. He studied her slender shoulders, thought of the slight hips he was even now holding. It was difficult to imagine her lugging buckets and pails. "I'd have thought you more suited to the front desk or the concierge."

"I was lucky to find work at all, especially during the off season." She slowed the bike a bit as she started down the long drive to El Presidente. She'd indulge herself for a moment by enjoying the tall elegant palms that lined the road and the smell of blooming flowers. She was taking one of the dive boats out today, with five beginners who'd need instruction and constant supervision, but she wondered about the people inside the hotel who came to such a place to relax and to play.

"Is it still gorgeous inside?" she asked before she could stop herself.

Jonas glanced ahead to the large stately building. "Lots of glass," he told her. "Marble. The balcony of my room looks out over the water." She steered the bike to the curb. "Why don't you come in? See for yourself."

She was tempted. Liz had an affection for pretty things, elegant things. It was a weakness she couldn't allow herself. "I have to get to work."

Jonas stepped onto the curb, but put his hand over hers before she could drive away. "I'll meet you at the house. We'll go into town together."

She only nodded before turning the bike back toward the road. Jonas watched her until the sound of the motor died away. Just who was Elizabeth Palmer? he wondered. And why was it becoming more and more important that he find out?

* * *

By evening she was tired. Liz was used to working long hours, lugging equipment, diving, surfacing. But after a fairly easy day, she was tired. It should have made her feel secure to have had the young policeman identify himself to her and join her customers on the dive boat. It should have eased her mind that Captain Moralas was keeping his word about protection. It made her feel caged.

All during the drive home, she'd been aware of the police cruiser keeping a discreet distance. She'd wanted to run into her house, lock the door and fall into a dreamless, private sleep. But Jonas was waiting. She found him on the phone in her living room, a legal pad on his lap and a scowl on his face. Obviously a complication at his office had put him in a nasty mood. Ignoring him, Liz went to shower and change.

Because her wardrobe ran for the most part to beachwear, she didn't waste time studying her closet. Without enthusiasm, she pulled out a full cotton skirt in peacock blue and matched it with an oversized red shirt. More to prolong her time alone than for any other reason, she fiddled with her little cache of makeup. She was stalling, brushing out her braided hair, when Jonas knocked on her door. He didn't give her time to answer before he pushed it open.

"Did you get the list?"

Liz picked up a piece of notepaper. She could, of course, snap at him for coming in, but the end result wouldn't change. "I told you I would."

He took the paper from her to study it. He'd shaved, she noticed, and wore a casually chic jacket over bone-colored slacks. But the smoothness and gloss didn't mesh with the toughness around his mouth and in his eyes. "Do you know these places?"

"I've been to a couple of them. I don't really have a lot of time for bar- or club-hopping."

He glanced up and his curt answer slipped away. The shades behind her were up as she preferred them, but the light coming through the windows was pink with early evening. Though she'd buttoned the shirt high over her throat, her hair was brushed back, away from her face. She'd dawdled over the makeup, but her hand was always conservative. Her lashes were darkened, the lids lightly touched with shadow. She'd brushed some color over her cheeks but not her lips.

"You should be careful what you do to your eyes," Jonas murmured, absently running his thumb along the top curve of her cheek. "They're a problem."

She felt the quick, involuntary tug but stood still. "A problem?"

"My problem." Uneasy, he tucked the paper in his pocket and glanced around the room. "Are you ready?"

"I need my shoes."

He didn't leave her as she'd expected, instead wandering around her room. It was, as was the rest of the house, furnished simply but with jarring color. The spicy scent he'd noticed before came from a wide green bowl filled with potpourri. On the wall were two colored sketches, one of a sunset very much like the quietly brilliant one outside the window, and another of a storm-tossed beach. One was all serenity, the other all violence. He wondered how much of each were inside Elizabeth Palmer. Prominent next to the bed was a framed photograph of a young girl.

She was all smiles in a flowered blouse tucked at the shoulders. Her hair came to a curve at her jawline, black and shiny.

A tooth was missing, adding charm to an oval, tanned face.
If it hadn't been for the eyes, Jonas would never have con-
nected the child with Liz. They were richly, deeply brown,
slightly tilted. Still, they laughed out of the photo, open and
trusting, holding none of the secrets of her mother's.

"This is your daughter."

"Yes." Liz slipped on the second shoe before taking the
photo out of Jonas's hand and setting it down again.

"How old is she?"

"Ten. Can we get started? I don't want to be out late."

"Ten?" A bit stunned, Jonas stopped her with a look. He'd
assumed Faith was half that age, a product of a relationship
Liz had fallen into while on the island. "You can't have a ten-
year-old child."

Liz glanced down at the picture of her daughter. "I do have
a ten-year-old child."

"You'd have been a child yourself."

"No. No, I wasn't." She started to leave again, and again
he stopped her.

"Was she born before you came here?"

Liz gave him a long, neutral look. "She was born six
months after I moved to Cozumel. If you want my help, Jonas, we go now. Answering questions about Faith isn't part
of our arrangement."

But he didn't let go of her hand. As it could become
so unexpectedly, his voice was gentle. "He was a bastard,
wasn't he?"

She met his eyes without wavering. Her lips curved, but
not with humor. "Yes. Oh yes, he was."

Without knowing why he was compelled to, Jonas bent and
just brushed her lips with his. "Your daughter's lovely, Elizabeth. She has your eyes."

She felt herself softening again, too much, too quickly.
There was understanding in his voice without pity. Nothing could weaken her more. In defense she took a step back.

"Thank you. Now we have to go. I have to be up early tomorrow."

* * *

The first club they hit was noisy and crowded with a high percentage of American clientele. In a corner booth, a man in a tight white T-shirt spun records on a turntable and announced each selection with a display of colored lights. They ordered a quick meal in addition to drinks while Jonas hoped someone would have a reaction to his face.

"Luis said they came in here a lot because Jerry liked hearing American music." Liz nibbled on hot nachos as she looked around. It wasn't the sort of place she normally chose to spend an evening. Tables were elbow to elbow, and the music was pitched to a scream. Still, the crowd seemed good-natured enough, shouting along with the music or just shouting to each other. At the table beside them a group of people experimented with a bottle of tequila and a bowl of lemon wedges. Since they were a group of young gringos, she assumed they'd be very sick in the morning.

It was definitely Jerry's milieu, Jonas decided. Loud, just this side of wild and crammed to the breaking point. "Did Luis say if he spoke with anyone in particular?"

"Women." Liz smiled a bit as she sampled a tortilla. "Luis was very impressed with Jerry's ability to . . . interest the ladies."

"Any particular lady?"

"Luis said there was one, but Jerry just called her baby."

"An old trick," Jonas said absently.

"Trick?"

"If you call them all baby, you don't mix up names and complicate the situation."

"I see." She sipped her wine and found it had a delicate taste.

"Could Luis describe her?"

"Only that she was a knockout—a Mexican knockout, if that helps. She had lots of hair and lots of hip. Luis's words," Liz added when Jonas gave her a mild look. "He also said there were a couple of men Jerry talked to a few times, but he always went over to them, so Luis didn't know what they spoke about. One was American, one was Mexican. Since Luis was more interested in the ladies, he didn't pay any attention. But he did say Jerry would cruise the bars until he met up with them, then he'd usually call it a night."

"Did he meet them here?"

"Luis said it never seemed to be in the same place twice."

"Okay, finish up. We'll cruise around ourselves."

By the fourth stop, Liz was fed up. She noticed that Jonas no more than toyed with a drink at each bar, but she was tired of the smell of liquor. Some places were quiet, and on the edge of seamy. Others were raucous and lit with flashing lights. Faces began to blur together. There were young people, not so young people. There were Americans out for exciting nightlife, natives celebrating a night on the town. Some courted on dance floors or over tabletops. She saw those who seemed to have nothing but time and money, and others who sat alone nursing a bottle and a black mood.

"This is the last one," Liz told him as Jonas found a table at a club with a crowded dance floor and recorded music.

Jonas glanced at his watch. It was barely eleven. Action rarely heated up before midnight. "All right," he said easily, and decided to distract her. "Let's dance."

Before she could refuse, he was pulling her into the crowd. "There's no room," she began, but his arms came around her.

"We'll make some." He had her close, his hand trailing up her back. "See?"

"I haven't danced in years," she muttered, and he laughed.

"There's no room anyway." Locked together, jostled by the crowd, they did no more than sway.

"What's the purpose in all this?" she demanded.

"I don't know until I find it. Meantime, don't you ever relax?" He rubbed his palm up her back again, finding the muscles taut.

"No."

"Let's try it this way." His gaze skimmed the crowd as he spoke. "What do you do when you're not working?"

"I think about working."

"Liz."

"All right, I read—books on marine life mostly."

"Busman's holiday?"

"It's what interests me."

Her body shifted intimately against his. Jonas forgot to keep his attention on the crowd and looked down at her. "*All* that interests you?"

He was too close. Liz tried to ease away and found his arms very solid. In spite of her determination to remain unmoved, her heart began to thud lightly in her head. "I don't have time for anything else."

She wore no perfume, he noted, but carried the scent of powder and spice. He wondered if her body would look as delicate as it felt against his. "It sounds as though you limit yourself."

"I have a business to run," she murmured. Would it be the same if he kissed her again? Sweet, overpowering. His lips were so close to hers, closer still when he ran his hand through her hair and drew her head back. She could almost taste him.

"Is making money so important?"

"It has to be," she managed, but could barely remember why. "I need to buy some aqua bikes."

Her eyes were soft, drowsy. They made him feel invulnerable. "Aqua bikes?"

"If I don't keep up with the competition . . ." He pressed a kiss to the corner of her mouth.

"The competition?" he prompted.

"I . . . the customers will go someplace else. So I . . ." The kiss teased the other corner.

"So?"

"I have to buy the bikes before the summer season."

"Of course. But that's weeks away. I could make love with you dozens of times before then. Dozens," he repeated as she stared at him. Then he closed his mouth over hers.

He felt her jolt—surprise, resistance, passion—he couldn't be sure. He only knew that holding her had led to wanting her and wanting to needing. By nature, he was a man who preferred his passion in private, quiet spots of his own choosing. Now he forgot the crowded club, loud music and flashing lights. They no longer swayed, but were hemmed into a corner of the dance floor, surrounded, pressed close. Oblivious.

She felt her head go light, heard the music fade. The heat from his body seeped into hers and flavored the kiss. Hot, molten, searing. Though they stood perfectly still, Liz had visions of racing. The breath backed up in her lungs until she released it with a shuddering sigh. Her body, coiled like a spring, went lax on a wave of confused pleasure. She strained closer, reaching up to touch his face. Abruptly the music changed from moody to rowdy. Jonas shifted her away from flailing arms.

"Poor timing," he murmured.

She needed a minute. "Yes." But she meant it in a more general way. It wasn't a matter of time and place, but a matter of impossibility. She started to move away when Jonas's grip tightened on her. "What is it?" she began, but only had to look at his face.

Cautiously, she turned to see what he stared at. A woman in a skimpy red dress stared back at him. Liz recognized the shock in her eyes before the woman turned and fled, leaving her dance partner gaping.

"Come on." Without waiting for her, Jonas sprinted through

the crowd. Dodging, weaving and shoving when she had to, Liz dashed after him.

The woman had barely gotten out to the street when Jonas caught up to her. "What are you running away from?" he demanded. His fingers dug into her arms as he held her back against a wall.

"Por favor, no comprendo," she murmured and shook like a leaf.

"Oh yes, I think you do." With his fingers bruising her arms, Jonas towered over her until she nearly squeaked in fear. "What do you know about my brother?"

"Jonas." Appalled, Liz stepped between them. "If this is the way you intend to behave, you'll do without my help." She turned away from him and touched the woman's shoulder. *"Lo siento mucho,"* she began, apologizing for Jonas. "He's lost his brother. His brother, Jerry Sharpe. Did you know him?"

She looked at Liz and whispered. "He has Jerry's face. But he's dead—I saw in the papers."

"This is Jerry's brother, Jonas. We'd like to talk to you."

As Liz had, the woman had already sensed the difference between Jonas and the man she'd known. She'd never have cowered away from Jerry for the simple reason that she'd known herself to be stronger and more clever. The man looming over her now was a different matter.

"I don't know anything."

"Por favor. Just a few minutes."

"Tell her I'll make it worth her while," Jonas added before she could refuse again. Without waiting for Liz to translate, he reached for his wallet and took out a bill. He saw fear change to speculation.

"A few minutes," she agreed, but pointed to an outdoor café. "There."

Jonas ordered two coffees and a glass of wine. "Ask her her name," he told Liz.

"I speak English." The woman took out a long, slim

cigarette and tapped it on the tabletop. "I'm Erika. Jerry and I were friends." More relaxed, she smiled at Jonas. "You know, good friends."

"Yes, I know."

"He was very good-looking," she added, then caught her bottom lip between her teeth. "Lots of fun."

"How long did you know him?"

"A couple of weeks. I was sorry when I heard he was dead."

"Murdered," Jonas stated.

Erika took a deep drink of wine. "Do you think it was because of the money?"

Every muscle in his body tensed. Quickly, he shot Liz a warning look before she could speak. "I don't know—it looks that way. How much did he tell you about it?"

"Oh, just enough to intrigue me. You know." She smiled again and held out her cigarette for a light. "Jerry was very charming. And generous." She remembered the little gold bracelet he'd bought for her and the earrings with the pretty blue stones. "I thought he was very rich, but he said he would soon be much richer. I like charming men, but I especially like rich men. Jerry said when he had the money, we could take a trip." She blew out smoke again before giving a philosophical little shrug. "Then he was dead."

Jonas studied her as he drank coffee. She was, as Luis had said, a knockout. And she wasn't stupid. He was also certain her mind was focusing on one point, and one point alone. "Do you know when he was supposed to have the money?"

"Sure, I had to take off work if we were going away. He called me—it was Sunday. He was so excited. 'Erika,' he said, 'I hit the jackpot.' I was a little mad because he hadn't shown up Saturday night. He told me he'd done some quick business in Acapulco and how would I like to spend a few weeks in Monte Carlo?" She gave Jonas a lash-fluttering smile. "I decided to forgive him. I was packed," she added, blowing smoke past Jonas's shoulder. "We were supposed to leave

Tuesday afternoon. I saw in the papers Monday night that he was dead. The papers said nothing about the money."

"Do you know who he had business with?"

"No. Sometimes he would talk to another American, a skinny man with pale hair. Other times he would see a Mexican. I didn't like him—he had *mal ojo*."

"Evil eye," Liz interpreted. "Can you describe him?"

"Not pretty," she said offhandedly. "His face was pitted. His hair was long in the back, over his collar and he was very thin and short." She glanced at Jonas again with a sultry smile that heated the air. "I like tall men."

"Do you know his name?"

"No. But he dressed very nicely. Nice suits, good shoes. And he wore a silver band on his wrist, a thin one that crossed at the ends. It was very pretty. Do you think he knows about the money? Jerry said it was lots of money."

Jonas merely reached for his wallet. "I'd like to find out his name," he told her and set a fifty on the table. His hand closed over hers as she reached for it. "His name, and the name of the American. Don't hold out on me, Erika."

With a toss of her head, she palmed the fifty. "I'll find out the names. When I tell you, it's another fifty."

"When you tell me." He scrawled Liz's number on the back of a business card. "Call this number when you have something."

"Okay." She slipped the fifty into her purse as she stood up. "You know, you don't look as much like Jerry as I thought." With the click of high heels, she crossed the pavement and went back into the club.

"It's a beginning," Jonas murmured as he pushed his coffee aside. When he looked over, he saw Liz studying him. "Problem?"

"I don't like the way you work."

He dropped another bill on the table before he rose. "I don't have time to waste on amenities."

"What would you have done if I hadn't calmed her down? Dragged her off to the nearest alley and beaten it out of her?"

He drew out a cigarette, struggling with temper. "Let's go home, Liz."

"I wonder if you're any different from the men you're looking for." She pushed back from the table. "Just as a matter of interest, the man who broke into my house and attacked me wore a thin band at his wrist. I felt it when he held the knife to my throat."

She watched as his gaze lifted from the flame at the end of the cigarette and came to hers. "I think you two might recognize each other when the time comes."

CHAPTER 5

A lways check your gauges," Liz instructed, carefully in-dicating each one on her own equipment as she spoke. "Each one of these gauges is vital to your safety when you dive. That's true if it's your first dive or your fiftieth. It's very easy to become so fascinated not only by the fish and coral, but the sensation of diving itself, that you can forget you're dependent on your air tank. Always be certain you start your ascent while you have five or ten minutes of air left."

She'd covered everything, she decided, in the hour lesson. If she lectured any more, her students would be too impatient to listen. It was time to give them a taste of what they were paying for.

"We'll dive as a group. Some of you may want to explore on your own, but remember, always swim in pairs. As a final precaution, check the gear of the diver next to you."

Liz strapped on her own weight belt as her group of nov-ices followed instructions. So many of them, she knew, looked on scuba diving as an adventure. That was fine, as long as they remembered safety. Whenever she instructed, she stressed the what ifs just as thoroughly as the how tos. Any-one who went down under her supervision would know what steps to take under any circumstances. Diving accidents were most often the result of carelessness. Liz was never careless with herself or with her students. Most of them were talking excitedly as they strapped on tanks.

"This group." Luis hefted his tank. "Very green."

"Yeah." Liz helped him with the straps. As she did with all her employees, Liz supplied Luis's gear. It was checked just as thoroughly as any paying customer's. "Keep an eye on the honeymoon couple, Luis. They're more interested in each other than their regulators."

"No problem." He assisted Liz with her tank, then stepped back while she cinched the straps. "You look tired, kid."

"No, I'm fine."

When she turned, he glanced at the marks on her neck. The story had already made the rounds. "You sure? You don't look so fine."

She lifted a brow as she hooked on her diving knife. "Sweet of you."

"Well, I mean it. You got me worried about you."

"No need to worry." As Liz pulled on her mask, she glanced over at the roly-poly fatherly type who was struggling with his flippers. He was her bodyguard for the day. "The police have everything under control," she said, and hoped it was true. She wasn't nearly as sure about Jonas.

He hadn't shocked her the night before. She'd sensed that dangerously waiting violence in him from the first. But seeing his face as he'd grabbed Erika, hearing his voice, had left her with a cold, flat feeling in her stomach. She didn't know him well enough to be certain if he would choose to control the violence or let it free. More, how could she know he was capable of leashing it? Revenge, she thought, was never pretty. And that's what he wanted. Remembering the look in his eyes, Liz was very much afraid he'd get it.

The boat listed, bringing her back to the moment. She couldn't think about Jonas now, she told herself. She had a business to run and customers to satisfy.

"Miss Palmer." A young American with a thin chest and

a winning smile maneuvered over to her. "Would you mind giving me a check?"

"Sure." In her brisk, efficient way, Liz began to check gauges and hoses.

"I'm a little nervous," he confessed. "I've never done this sort of thing before."

"It doesn't hurt to be a little nervous. You'll be more careful. Here, pull your mask down. Make sure it's comfortable but snug."

He obeyed, and his eyes looked wide and pale through the glass. "If you don't mind, I think I'll stick close to you down there."

She smiled at him. "That's what I'm here for. The depth here is thirty feet," she told the group in general. "Remember to make your adjustments for pressure and gravity as you descend. Please keep the group in sight at all times." With innate fluidity, she sat on the deck and rolled into the water. With Luis on deck, and Liz treading a few feet away, they waited until each student made his dive. With a final adjustment to her mask, Liz went under.

She'd always loved it. The sensation of weightlessness, the fantasy of being unimpeded, invulnerable. From near the surface, the sea floor was a spread of white. She loitered there a moment, enjoying the cathedral-like view. Then, with an easy kick, she moved down with her students.

The newlyweds were holding hands and having the time of their lives. Liz reminded herself to keep them in sight. The policeman assigned to her was plodding along like a sleepy sea turtle. He'd keep her in sight. Most of the others remained in a tight group, fascinated but cautious. The thin American gave her a wide-eyed look that was a combination of pleasure and nerves and stuck close by her side. To help him relax, Liz touched his shoulder and pointed up. In an easy motion, she turned on her back so that she faced the surface. Sunlight streaked thinly through the water. The hull of the dive boat was plainly visible. He nodded and followed her down.

Fish streamed by, some in waves, some on their own. Though the sand was white, the water clear, there was a montage of color. Brain coral rose up in sturdy mounds, the color of saffron. Sea fans, as delicate as lace, waved pink and purple in the current. She signaled to her companion and watched a school of coral sweepers, shivering with metallic tints, turn as a unit and skim through staghorn coral.

It was a world she understood as well as, perhaps better, than the one on the surface. Here, in the silence, Liz often found the peace of mind that eluded her from day to day. The scientific names of the fish and formations they passed were no strangers to her. Once she'd studied them diligently, with dreams of solving mysteries and bringing the beauty of the world of the sea to others. That had been another life. Now she coached tourists and gave them, for hourly rates, something memorable to take home after a vacation. It was enough.

Amused, she watched an angelfish busy itself by swallowing the bubbles rising toward the surface. To entertain her students, she poked at a small damselfish. The pugnacious male clung to his territory and nipped at her. To the right, she saw sand kick up and cloud the water. Signaling for caution, Liz pointed out the plate-like ray that skimmed away, annoyed by the intrusion.

The new husband showed off a bit, turning slow somersaults for his wife. As divers gained confidence, they spread out a little farther. Only her bodyguard and the nervous American stayed within an arm span at all times. Throughout the thirty-minute dive, Liz circled the group, watching individual divers. By the time the lesson was over, she was satisfied that her customers had gotten their money's worth. This was verified when they surfaced.

"Great!" A British businessman on his first trip to Mexico clambered back onto the deck. His face was reddened by the sun but he didn't seem to mind. "When can we go down again?"

With a laugh, Liz helped other passengers on board. "You have to balance your down time with your surface time. But we'll go down again."

"What was that feathery-looking stuff?" someone else asked. "It grows like a bush."

"It's a gorgonian, from the Gorgons of mythology." She slipped off her tanks and flexed her muscles. "If you remember, the Gorgons had snakes for hair. The whip gorgonian has a resilient skeletal structure and undulates like a snake with the current."

More questions were tossed out, more answers supplied. Liz noticed the American who'd stayed with her, sitting by himself, smiling a little. Liz moved around gear then dropped down beside him.

"You did very well."

"Yeah?" He looked a little dazed as he shrugged his shoulders. "I liked it, but I gotta admit, I felt better knowing you were right there. You sure know what you're doing."

"I've been at it a long time."

He sat back, unzipping his wet suit to his waist. "I don't mean to be nosy, but I wondered about you. You're American, aren't you?"

It had been asked before. Liz combed her fingers through her wet hair. "That's right."

"From?"

"Houston."

"No kidding." His eyes lit up. "Hell, I went to school in Texas. Texas A and M."

"Really?" The little tug she felt rarely came and went. "So did I, briefly."

"Small world," he said, pleased with himself. "I like Texas. Got a few friends in Houston. I don't suppose you know the Dresscots?"

"No."

"Well, Houston isn't exactly small-town U.S.A." He stretched out long, skinny legs that were shades paler than his arms but starting to tan. "So you went to Texas A and M."

"That's right."

"What'd you study?"

She smiled and looked out to sea. "Marine biology."

"Guess that fits."

"And you?"

"Accounting." He flashed his grin again. "Pretty dry stuff. That's why I always take a long breather after tax time."

"Well, you chose a great place to take it. Ready to go down again?"

He took a long breath as if to steady himself. "Yeah. Hey, listen, how about a drink after we get back in?"

He was attractive in a mild sort of way, pleasant enough. She gave him an apologetic smile as she rose. "It sounds nice, but I'm tied up."

"I'll be around for a couple of weeks. Some other time?"

"Maybe. Let's check your gear."

By the time the dive boat chugged into shore, the afternoon was waning. Her customers, most of them pleased with themselves, wandered off to change for dinner or spread out on the beach. Only a few loitered near the boat, including her bodyguard and the accountant from America. It occurred to Liz that she might have been a bit brisk with him.

"I hope you enjoyed yourself, Mr . . ."

"Trydent. But it's Scott, and I did. I might just try it again."

Liz smiled at him as she helped Luis and another of her employees unload the boat. "That's what we're here for."

"You, ah, ever give private lessons?"

Liz caught the look. Perhaps she hadn't been brisk enough. "On occasion."

"Then maybe we could—"

"Hey, there, missy."

Liz shaded her eyes. "Mr. Ambuckle."

He stood on the little walkway, his legs bulging out of

the short wet suit. What hair he had was sleeked wetly back. Beside him, his wife stood wearily in a bathing suit designed to slim down wide hips. "Just got back in!" he shouted. "Had a full day of it."

He seemed enormously pleased with himself. His wife looked at Liz and rolled her eyes. "Maybe I should take you out as crew, Mr. Ambuckle."

He laughed, slapping his side. "Guess I'd rather dive than anything." He glanced at his wife and patted her shoulder. "Almost anything. Gotta trade in these tanks, honey, and get me some fresh ones."

"Going out again?"

"Tonight. Can't talk the missus into it."

"I'm crawling into bed with a good book," she told Liz. "The only water I want to see is in the tub."

With a laugh, Liz jumped down to the walkway. "At the moment, I feel the same way. Oh, Mr. and Mrs. Ambuckle, this is Scott Trydent. He just took his first dive."

"Well now." Expansive, Ambuckle slapped him on the back. "How'd you like it?"

"Well, I—"

"Nothing like it, is there? You want to try it at night, boy. Whole different ball game at night."

"I'm sure, but—"

"Gotta trade in these tanks." After slapping Scott's back again, Ambuckle hefted his tanks and waddled off toward the shop.

"Obsessed," Mrs. Ambuckle said, casting her eyes to the sky. "Don't let him get started on you, Mr. Trydent. You'll never get any peace."

"No, I won't. Nice meeting you, Mrs. Ambuckle." Obviously bemused, Scott watched her wander back toward the hotel. "Quite a pair."

"That they are." Liz lifted her own tanks. She stored them separately from her rental equipment. "Goodbye, Mr. Trydent."

"Scott," he said again. "About that drink—"

"Thanks anyway," Liz said pleasantly and left him standing on the walkway. "Everything in?" she asked Luis as she stepped into the shop.

"Checking it off now. One of the regulators is acting up."

"Set it aside for Jose to look at." As a matter of habit, she moved into the back to fill her tanks before storage. "All the boats are in, Luis. We shouldn't have too much more business now. You and the rest can go on as soon as everything's checked in. I'll close up."

"I don't mind staying."

"You closed up last night," she reminded him. "What do you want?" She tossed a grin over her shoulder. "Overtime? Go on home, Luis. You can't tell me you don't have a date."

He ran a fingertip over his mustache. "As a matter of fact . . ."

"A hot date?" Liz lifted a brow as air hissed into her tank.

"Is there any other kind?"

Chuckling, Liz straightened. She noticed Ambuckle trudging across the sand with his fresh tanks. Her other employees talked among themselves as the last of the gear was stored. "Well, go make yourself beautiful then. The only thing I have a date with is the account books."

"You work too much," Luis mumbled.

Surprised, Liz turned back to him. "Since when?"

"Since always. It gets worse every time you send Faith back to school. Better off if she was here."

That her voice cooled only slightly was a mark of her affection for Luis. "No, she's happy in Houston with my parents. If I thought she wasn't, she wouldn't be there."

"She's happy, sure. What about you?"

Her brows drew together as she picked her keys from a drawer. "Do I look unhappy?"

"No." Tentatively, he touched her shoulder. He'd known Liz for years, and understood there were boundaries she wouldn't let anyone cross. "But you don't look happy either.

How come you don't give one of these rich American tourists a spin? That one on the boat—his eyes popped out every time he looked at you."

The exaggeration made her laugh, so she patted his cheek. "So you think a rich American tourist is the road to happiness?"

"Maybe a handsome Mexican."

"I'll think about it—after the summer season. Go home," she ordered.

"I'm going." Luis pulled a T-shirt over his chest. "You look out for that Jonas Sharpe," he added. "He's got a different kind of look in his eyes."

Liz waved him off. *"Hasta luego."*

When the shop was empty, Liz stood, jingling her keys and looking out onto the beach. People traveled in couples, she noted, from the comfortably married duo stretched out on lounge chairs, to the young man and woman curled together on a beach towel. Was it an easy feeling, she wondered, to be half of a set? Or did you automatically lose part of yourself when you joined with another?

She'd always thought of her parents as separate people, yet when she thought of one, the other came quickly to mind. Would it be a comfort to know you could reach out your hand and someone else's would curl around it?

She held out her own and remembered how hard, how strong, Jonas's had been. No, he wouldn't make a relationship a comfortable affair. Being joined with him would be demanding, even frightening. A woman would have to be strong enough to keep herself intact, and soft enough to allow herself to merge. A relationship with a man like Jonas would be a risk that would never ease.

For a moment, she found herself dreaming of it, dreaming of what it had been like to be held close and kissed as though nothing and no one else existed. To be kissed like that always, to be held like that whenever the need moved you—it might be worth taking chances for.

Stupid, she thought quickly, shaking herself out of it. Jonas wasn't looking for a partner, and she wasn't looking for a dream. Circumstances had tossed them together temporarily. Both of them had to deal with their own realities. But she felt a sense of regret and a stirring of wishes.

Because the feeling remained, just beyond her grasp, Liz concentrated hard on the little details that needed attending to before she could close up. The paperwork and the contents of the cash box were transferred to a canvas portfolio. She'd have to swing out of her way to make a night deposit, but she no longer felt safe taking the cash or the checks home. She spent an extra few minutes meticulously filling out a deposit slip.

It wasn't until she'd picked up her keys again that she remembered her tanks. Tucking the portfolio under the counter, she turned to deal with her own gear.

It was perhaps her only luxury. She'd spent more on her personal equipment than she had on all the contents of her closet and dresser. To Liz, the wet suit was more exciting than any French silks. All her gear was kept separate from the shop's inventory. Unlocking the door to the closet, Liz hung up her wet suit, stored her mask, weight belt, regulator. Her knife was sheathed and set on a shelf. After setting her tanks side by side, she shut the door and prepared to lock it again. After she'd taken two steps away she looked down at the keys again. Without knowing precisely why, she moved each one over the ring and identified it.

The shop door, the shop window, her bike, the lock for the chain, the cash box, the front and back doors of her house, her storage room. Eight keys for eight locks. But there was one more on her ring, a small silver key that meant nothing to her at all.

Puzzled, she counted off the keys again, and again found one extra. Why should there be a key on her ring that didn't belong to her? Closing her fingers over it, she tried to think if anyone had given her the key to hold. No, it didn't make sense. Brows drawn together, she studied the key again. Too small for a car or door key, she decided. It looked like the key to a locker, or a box or . . . Ridiculous, she decided on a long breath. It wasn't her key but it was on her ring. Why?

Because someone put it there, she realized, and opened her hand again. Her keys were often tossed in the drawer at the shop for easy access for Luis or one of the other men. They needed to open the cash box. And Jerry had often worked in the shop alone.

With a feeling of dread, Liz slipped the keys into her pocket. Jonas's words echoed in her head. *"You're involved, whether you want to be or not."*

Liz closed the shop early.

* * *

Jonas stepped into the dim bar to the scent of garlic and the wail of a squeaky jukebox. In Spanish, someone sang of endless love. He stood for a moment, letting his eyes adjust, then skimmed his gaze over the narrow booths. As agreed, Erika sat all the way in the back, in the corner.

"You're late." She waved an unlit cigarette idly as he joined her.

"I passed it the first time. This place isn't exactly on the tourist route."

She closed her lips over the filter as Jonas lit her cigarette. "I wanted privacy."

Jonas glanced around. There were two men at the bar, each deep in separate bottles. Another couple squeezed themselves together on one side of a booth. The rest of the bar was deserted. "You've got it."

"But I don't have a drink."

Jonas slid out from the booth and bought two drinks at the bar. He set tequila and lime in front of Erika and settled for club soda. "You said you had something for me."

Erica twined a string of colored beads around her finger. "You said you would pay fifty for a name."

In silence, Jonas took out his wallet. He set fifty on the table, but laid his hand over it. "You have the name."

Erika smiled and sipped at her drink. "Maybe. Maybe you want it bad enough to pay another fifty."

Jonas studied her coolly. This was the type his brother had always been attracted to. The kind of woman whose hard edge was just a bit obvious. He could give her another fifty, Jonas mused, but he didn't care to be taken for a sucker. Without a word, he picked up the bill and tucked it into his pocket. He was halfway out of the booth when Erika grabbed his arm.

"Okay, don't get mad. Fifty." She sent him an easy smile as he settled back again. Erika had been around too long to let an opportunity slip away. "A girl has to make a living, *sí?* The name is Pablo Manchez—he's the one with the face."

"Where can I find him?"

"I don't know. You got the name."

With a nod, Jonas took the bill out and passed it to her. Erika folded it neatly into her purse. "I'll tell you something else, because Jerry was a sweet guy." Her gaze skimmed the bar again as she leaned closer to Jonas. "This Manchez, he's bad. People got nervous when I asked about him. I heard he was mixed up in a couple of murders in Acapulco last year. He's paid, you know, to . . ." She made a gun out of her hand and pushed down her thumb. "When I hear that, I stop asking questions."

"What about the other one, the American?"

"Nothing. Nobody knows him. But if he hangs out with Manchez, he's not a Boy Scout." Erika tipped back her drink. "Jerry got himself in some bad business."

"Yeah."

"I'm sorry." She touched the bracelet on her wrist. "He gave me this. We had some good times."

The air in the bar was stifling him. Jonas rose and hesitated only a moment before he took out another bill and set it next to her drink. "Thanks."

Erika folded the bill as carefully as the first. *"De nada."*

* * *

She'd wanted him to be home. When Liz found the house empty, she made a fist over the keys in her hand and swore in frustration. She couldn't sit still; her nerves had been building all during the drive home. Outside, Moralas's evening shift was taking over.

For how long? she wondered. How long would the police sit patiently outside her house and follow her through her daily routine? In her bedroom, Liz closed the canvas bag of papers and cash in her desk. She regretted not having a lock for it, as well. Sooner or later, she thought, Moralas would back off on the protection. Then where would she be? Liz looked down at the key again. She'd be alone, she told herself bluntly. She had to do something.

On impulse, she started into her daughter's room. Perhaps Jerry had left a case, a box of some kind that the police had overlooked. Systematically she searched Faith's closet. When she found the little teddy bear with the worn ear, she brought it down from the shelf. She'd bought it for Faith before she'd been born. It was a vivid shade of purple, or had been so many years before. Now it was faded a bit, a little loose at the seams. The ear had been worn down to a nub because Faith had always carried him by it. They'd never named it, Liz recalled. Faith had merely called it *mine* and been satisfied.

On a wave of loneliness that rocked her, Liz buried her face against the faded purple pile. "Oh, I miss you, baby," she murmured. "I don't know if I can stand it."

"Liz?"

On a gasp of surprise, Liz stumbled back against the closet

door. When she saw Jonas, she put the bear behind her back. "I didn't hear you come in," she said, feeling foolish.

"You were busy." He came toward her to gently pry the bear from her fingers. "He looks well loved."

"He's old." She cleared her throat and took the toy back again. But she found it impossible to stick it back on the top shelf. "I keep meaning to sew up the seams before the stuffing falls out." She set the bear down on Faith's dresser. "You've been out."

"Yes." He'd debated telling her of his meeting with Erika, and had decided to keep what he'd learned to himself, at least for now. "You're home early."

"I found something." Liz reached in her pocket and drew out her keys. "This isn't mine."

Jonas frowned at the key she indicated. "I don't know what you mean."

"I mean this isn't my key, and I don't know how it got on my ring."

"You just found it today?"

"I found it today, but it could have been put on anytime. I don't think I would've noticed." With the vain hope of distancing herself, Liz unhooked it from the others and handed it to Jonas. "I keep these in a drawer at the shop when I'm there. At home, I usually toss them on the kitchen counter. I can't think of any reason for someone to put it with mine unless they wanted to hide it."

Jonas examined the key. "'The Purloined Letter,'" he murmured.

"What?"

"It was one of Jerry's favorite stories when we were kids. I remember when he tested out the theory by putting a book he'd bought for my father for Christmas on the shelf in the library."

"So do you think it was his?"

"I think it would be just his style."

Liz picked up the bear again, finding it comforted her. "It

doesn't do much good to have a key when you don't have the lock."

"It shouldn't be hard to find it." He held the key up by the stem. "Do you know what it is?"

"A key." Liz sat on Faith's bed. No, she hadn't distanced herself. The quicksand was bubbling again.

"To a safe-deposit box." Jonas turned it over to read the numbers etched into the metal.

"Do you think Captain Moralas can trace it?"

"Eventually," Jonas murmured. The key was warm in his hand. It was the next step, he thought. It had to be. "But I'm not telling him about it."

"Why?"

"Because he'd want it, and I don't intend to give it to him until I open the lock myself."

She recognized the look easily enough now. It was still revenge. Leaving the bear on her daughter's bed, Liz rose. "What are you going to do, go from bank to bank and ask if you can try the key out? You won't have to call the police, they will."

"I've got some connections—and I've got the serial number." Jonas pocketed the key. "With luck, I'll have the name of the bank by tomorrow afternoon. You may have to take a couple of days off."

"I can't take a couple of days off, and if I could, why should I need to?"

"We're going to Acapulco."

She started to make some caustic comment, then stopped. "Because Jerry told Erika he'd had business there?"

"If Jerry was mixed up in something, and he had something important or valuable, he'd tuck it away. A safe-deposit box in Acapulco makes sense."

"Fine. If that's what you believe, have a nice trip." She started to brush past him. Jonas only had to shift his body to bar the door.

"We go together."

The word "together" brought back her thoughts on couples and comfort. And it made her remember her conclusion about Jonas. "Look, Jonas, I can't drop everything and follow you on some wild-goose chase. Acapulco is very cosmopolitan. You won't need an interpreter."

"The key was on your ring. The knife was at your throat. I want you where I can see you."

"Concerned?" Her face hardened, muscle by muscle. "You're not concerned with me, Jonas. And you're certainly not concerned *about* me. The only thing you care about is your revenge. I don't want any part of it, or you."

He took her by the shoulders until she was backed against the door. "We both know that's not true. We've started something." His gaze skimmed down, lingered on her lips. "And it's not going to stop until we're both finished with it."

"I don't know what you're talking about."

"Yes, you do." He pressed closer so that their bodies met and strained, one against the other. He pressed closer to prove something, perhaps only to himself. "Yes, you do," he repeated. "I came here to do something, and I intend to do it. I don't give a damn if you call it revenge."

Her heart was beating lightly at her throat. She wouldn't call it fear. But his eyes were cold and close. "What else?"

"Justice."

She felt an uncomfortable twinge, remembering her own feelings on justice. "You're not using your law books, Jonas."

"Law doesn't always equal justice. I'm going to find out what happened to my brother and why." He skimmed his hand over her face and tangled his fingers in her hair. He didn't find silk and satin, but a woman of strength. "But there's more now. I look at you and I want you." He reached out, taking her face in his hand so that she had no choice but to look directly at him. "I hold you and I forget what I have to do. Damn it, you're in my way."

At the end of the words, his mouth was crushed hard on hers. He hadn't meant to. He hadn't had a choice. Before he'd been gentle with her because the look in her eyes requested it. Now he was rough, desperate, because the power of his own needs demanded it.

He frightened her. She'd never known fear could be a source of exhilaration. As her heart pounded in her throat, she let him pull her closer, still closer to the edge. He dared her to jump off, to let herself tumble down into the unknown. To risk.

His mouth drew desperately from hers, seeking passion, seeking submission, seeking strength. He wanted it all. He wanted it mindlessly from her. His hands were reaching for her as if they'd always done so. When he found her, she stiffened, resisted, then melted so quickly that it was nearly impossible to tell one mood from the next. She smelled of the sea and tasted of innocence, a combination of mystery and sweetness that drove him mad.

Forgetting everything but her, he drew her toward the bed and fulfillment.

"No." Liz pushed against him, fighting to bring herself back. They were in her daughter's room. "Jonas, this is wrong."

He took her by the shoulders. "Damn it, it may be the only thing that's right."

She shook her head, and though unsteady, backed away. His eyes weren't cold now. A woman might dream of having a man look at her with such fire and need. A woman might toss all caution aside if only to have a man want her with such turbulent desire. She couldn't.

"Not for me. I don't want this, Jonas." She reached up to push back her hair. "I don't want to feel like this."

He took her hand before she could back away. His head was swimming. There had been no other time, no other place, no other woman that had come together to make him ache. "Why?"

"I don't make the same mistake twice."

"This is now, Liz."

"And it's my life." She took a long, cleansing breath and found she could face him squarely. "I'll go with you to Acapulco because the sooner you have what you want, the sooner you'll go." She gripped her hands together tightly, the only outward sign that she was fighting herself. "You know Moralas will have us followed."

He had his own battles to fight. "I'll deal with that."

Liz nodded because she was sure he would. "Do what you have to do. I'll make arrangements for Luis to take over the shop for a day or two."

When she left him alone, Jonas closed his hands over the key again. It would open a lock, he thought. But there was another lock that mystified and frustrated him. Idly, he picked up the bear Liz had left on the bed. He looked from it to the key in his hand. Somehow he'd have to find a way to bring them together.

CHAPTER 6

Acapulco wasn't the Mexico Liz understood and loved. It wasn't the Mexico she'd fled to a decade before, nor where she'd made her home. It was sophisticated and ultra modern with spiraling high-rise hotels crowded together and gleaming in tropical sunlight. It was swimming pools and trendy shops. Perhaps it was the oldest resort in Mexico, and boasted countless restaurants and nightclubs, but Liz preferred the quietly rural atmosphere of her own island.

Still she had to admit there was something awesome about the city, cupped in the mountains and kissed by a magnificent bay. She'd lived all her life in flat land, from Houston to Cozumel. The mountains made everything else seem smaller, and somehow protected. Over the water, colorful parachutes floated, allowing the adventurous a bird's-eye view and a stunning ride. She wondered fleetingly if skimming through the sky would be as liberating as skimming through the water.

The streets were crowded and noisy, exciting in their own way. It occurred to her that she'd seen more people in the hour since they'd landed at the airport than she might in a week on Cozumel. Liz stepped out of the cab and wondered if she'd have time to check out any of the dive shops.

Jonas had chosen the hotel methodically. It was luxuriously

expensive—just Jerry's style. The villas overlooked the Pacific and were built directly into the mountainside. Jonas took a suite, pocketed the key and left the luggage to the bellman.

"We'll go to the bank now." It had taken him two days to match the key with a name. He wasn't going to waste any more time.

Liz followed him out onto the street. True, she hadn't come to enjoy herself, but a look at their rooms and a bite of lunch didn't seem so much to ask. Jonas was already climbing into a cab. "I don't suppose you'd considered making that a request."

He gave her a brief look as she slammed the cab door. "No." After giving the driver their direction, Jonas settled back. He could understand Jerry drifting to Acapulco, with its jet-set flavor, frantic nightlife and touches of luxury. When Jerry landed in a place for more than a day, it was a city that had the atmosphere of New York, London, Chicago. Jerry had never been interested in the rustic, serene atmosphere of a spot like Cozumel. So since he'd gone there, stayed there, he'd had a purpose. In Acapulco, Jonas would find out what it was.

As to the woman beside him, he didn't have a clue. Was she caught up in the circumstances formed before they'd ever met, or was he dragging her in deeper than he had a right to? She sat beside him, silent and a little sulky. Probably thinking about her shop, Jonas decided, and wished he could send her safely back to it. He wished he could turn around, go back to the villa and make love with her until they were both sated.

She shouldn't have appealed to him at all. She wasn't witty, flawlessly polished or classically beautiful. But she did appeal to him, so much so that he was spending his nights awake and restless, and his days on the edge of frustration. He wanted her, wanted to fully explore the tastes of passion she'd given him. He wanted to arouse her until she couldn't think of accounts or customers or schedules. Perhaps it was a matter of wielding power—he could no longer be sure. But mostly, inexplicably, he wanted to erase the memory of how she'd looked when he'd walked into her daughter's room and found her clutching a stuffed bear.

When the cab rolled up in front of the bank, Liz stepped out on the curb without a word. There were shops across the streets, boutiques where she could see bright, wonderful dresses on cleverly posed mannequins. Even with the distance, she caught the gleam and glimmer of jewelry. A limousine rolled by, with smoked glass windows and quiet engine. Liz looked beyond the tall, glossy buildings to the mountains, and space.

"I suppose this is the sort of place that appeals to you."

He'd watched her survey. She didn't have to speak for him to understand that she'd compared Acapulco with her corner of Mexico and found Acapulco lacking. "Under certain circumstances." Taking her arm, Jonas led her inside.

The bank was, as banks should be, quiet and sedate. Clerks wore neat suits and polite smiles. What conversation there was, was carried on in murmurs. Jerry, he thought, had always preferred the ultraconservative in storing his money, just as he'd preferred the wild in spending it. Without hesitation, Jonas strolled over to the most attractive teller. "Good afternoon."

She glanced up. It only took a second for her polite smile to brighten. "Mr. Sharpe, *buenos días*. It's nice to see you again."

Beside him, Liz stiffened. He's been here before, she thought. Why hadn't he told her? She sent a long, probing look his way. Just what game was he playing?

"It's nice to see you." He leaned against the counter, urbane and, she noted, flirtatious. The little tug of jealousy was as unexpected as it was unwanted. "I wondered if you'd remember me."

The teller blushed before she glanced cautiously toward her supervisor. "Of course. How can I help you today?"

Jonas took the key out of his pocket. "I'd like to get into my box." He simply turned and stopped Liz with a look when she started to speak.

"I'll arrange that for you right away." The teller took a form, dated it and passed it to Jonas. "If you'll just sign here."

Jonas took her pen and casually dashed off a signature. Liz read: *Jeremiah C. Sharpe.* Though she looked up quickly, Jonas was smiling at the teller. Because her supervisor was hovering nearby, the teller stuck to procedure and checked the signature against the card in the files. They matched perfectly.

"This way, Mr. Sharpe."

"Isn't that illegal?" Liz murmured as the teller led them from the main lobby.

"Yes." Jonas gestured for her to precede him through the doorway.

"And does it make me an accessory?"

He smiled at her, waiting while the teller drew the long metal box from its slot. "Yes. If there's any trouble, I'll recommend a good lawyer."

"Great. All I need's another lawyer."

"You can use this booth, Mr. Sharpe. Just ring when you're finished."

"Thanks." Jonas nudged Liz inside, shut, then locked, the door.

"How did you know?"

"Know what?" Jonas set the box on a table.

"To go to that clerk? When she first spoke to you, I thought you'd been here before."

"There were three men and two women. The other woman was into her fifties. As far as Jerry would've been concerned, there would have been only one clerk there."

That line of thinking was clear enough, but his actions weren't. "You signed his name perfectly."

Key in hand, Jonas looked at her. "He was part of me. If we were in the same room, I could have told you what he was thinking. Writing his name is as easy as writing my own."

"And was it the same for him?"

It could still hurt, quickly and unexpectedly. "Yes, it was the same for him."

But Liz remembered Jerry's good-natured description of his brother as a stuffed shirt. The man Liz was beginning to know didn't fit. "I wonder if you understood each other as well as both of you thought." She looked down at the box again. None of her business, she thought, and wished it were true as she'd once believed. "I guess you'd better open it."

He slipped the key into the lock, then turned it soundlessly. When he drew back the lid, Liz could only stare. She'd never seen so much money in her life. It sat in neat stacks, tidily banded, crisply American. Unable to resist, Liz reached out to touch.

"God, it looks like thousands." She swallowed. "Hundreds of thousands."

His face expressionless, Jonas flipped through the stacks. The booth became as quiet as a tomb. "Roughly three hundred thousand, in twenties and fifties."

"Do you think he stole it?" she murmured, too overwhelmed to notice Jonas's hands tighten on the money. "This must be the money the man who broke into my house wanted."

"I'm sure it is." Jonas set down a stack of bills and picked up a small bag. "But he didn't steal it." He forced his emotions to freeze. "I'm afraid he earned it."

"How?" she demanded. "No one earns this kind of money in a matter of days, and I'd swear Jerry was nearly broke when I hired him. I know Luis lent him ten thousand pesos before his first paycheck."

"I'm sure he was." He didn't bother to add that he'd wired his brother two hundred before Jerry had left New Orleans. Carefully, Jonas reached under the stack of money and pulled out a small plastic bag, dipped in a finger and tasted. But he'd already known.

"What is that?"

His face expressionless, Jonas sealed the bag. He couldn't allow himself any more grief. "Cocaine."

Horrified, Liz stared at the bag. "I don't understand. He lived in my house. I'd have known if he were using drugs."

Jonas wondered if she realized just how innocent she was of the darker side of humanity. Until that moment, he hadn't fully realized just how intimate he was with it. "Maybe, maybe not. In any case, Jerry wasn't into this sort of thing. At least not for himself."

Liz sat down slowly. "You mean he sold it?"

"Dealt drugs?" Jonas nearly smiled. "No, that wouldn't have been exciting enough." In the corner of the box was a small black address book. Jonas took it out to leaf through it. "But smuggling," he murmured. "Jerry could have justified smuggling. Action, intrigue and fast money."

Her mind was whirling as she tried to focus back on the man she'd known so briefly. Liz had thought she'd understood him, categorized him, but he was more of a stranger now than when he'd been alive. It didn't seem to matter anymore who or what Jerry Sharpe had been. But the man in front of her mattered. "And you?" she asked. "Can you justify it?"

He glanced down at her, over the book in his hands. His eyes were cold, so cold that she could read nothing in them at all. Without answering, Jonas went back to the book.

"He'd listed initials, dates, times and some numbers. It looks as though he made five thousand a drop. Ten drops."

Liz glanced over at the money again. It no longer seemed crisp and neat but ugly and ill used. "That only makes fifty thousand. You said there was three hundred."

"That's right." Plus a bag of uncut cocaine with a hefty street value. Jonas took out his own book and copied down the pages from his brother's.

"What are we going to do with this?"

"Nothing."

"Nothing?" Liz rose again, certain she'd stepped into a

dream. "Do you mean just leave it here? Just leave it here in this box and walk away?"

With the last of the numbers copied, Jonas replaced his brother's book. "Exactly."

"Why did we come if we're not going to do anything with it?"

He slipped his own book into his jacket. "To find it."

"Jonas." Before he could close the lid she had her hand on his wrist. "You have to take it to the police. To Captain Moralas."

In a deliberate gesture, he removed her hand, then picked up the bag of coke. She understood rejection and braced herself against it. But it wasn't rejection she saw in his face; it was fury. "You want to take this on the plane, Liz? Any idea on what the penalty is in Mexico for carrying controlled substances?"

"No."

"And you don't want to." He closed the lid, locked it. "For now, just forget you saw anything. I'll handle this in my own way."

"No."

His emotions were raw and tangled, his patience thin. "Don't push me, Liz."

"Push you?" Infuriated, she grabbed his shirtfront and planted her feet. "You've pushed me for days. Pushed me right into the middle of something that's so opposed to the way I've lived I can't even take it all in. Now that I'm over my head in drug smuggling and something like a quarter of a million dollars, you tell me to forget it. What do you expect me to do, go quietly back and rent tanks? Maybe you've finished using me now, Jonas, but I'm not ready to be brushed aside. There's a murderer out there who thinks I know where the money is." She stopped as her skin iced over. "And now I do."

"That's just it," Jonas said quietly. For the second time,

he removed her hands, but this time he held on to her wrists. Frightened, he thought. He was sure her pulse beat with fear as well as anger. "Now you do. The best thing for you to do now is stay out of it, let them focus on me."

"Just how am I supposed to do that?"

The anger was bubbling closer, the anger he'd wanted to lock in the box with what had caused it. "Go to Houston, visit your daughter."

"How can I?" she demanded in a whisper that vibrated in the little room. "They might follow me." She looked down at the long, shiny box. "They would follow me. I won't risk my daughter's safety."

She was right, and because he knew it, Jonas wanted to rage. He was boxed in, trapped between love and loyalty and right and wrong. Justice and the law. "We'll talk to Moralas when we get back." He picked up the box again, hating it.

"Where are we going now?"

Jonas unlocked the door. "To get a drink."

* * *

Rather than going with Jonas to the lounge, Liz took some time for herself. Because she felt he owed her, she went into the hotel's boutique, found a simple one-piece bathing suit and charged it to the room. She hadn't packed anything but a change of clothes and toiletries. If she was stuck in Acapulco for the rest of the evening, she was going to enjoy the private pool each villa boasted.

The first time she walked into the suite, she was dumbfounded. Her parents had been reasonably successful, and she'd been raised in a quietly middle-class atmosphere. Nothing had prepared her for the sumptuousness of the two-bedroom suite overlooking the Pacific. Her feet sank cozily into the carpet. Softly colored paintings were spaced along ivory-papered walls. The sofa, done in grays and greens and blues, was big enough for two to sprawl on for a lazy after-noon nap.

She found a phone in the bathroom next to a tub so wide and deep that she was almost tempted to take her dip there. The sink was a seashell done in the palest of pinks.

So this is how the rich play, she mused as she wandered to the bedroom where her overnight bag was set at the end of a bed big enough for three. The drapes of her balcony were open so that she could see the tempestuous surf of the Pacific hurl up and spray. She pulled the glass doors open, wanting the noise.

This was the sort of world Marcus had told her of so many years before. He'd made it seem like a fairy tale with gossamer edges. Liz had never seen his home, had never been permitted to, but he'd described it to her. The white pillars, the white balconies, the staircase that curved up and up. There were servants to bring you tea in the afternoons, a stable where grooms waited to saddle glossy horses. Champagne was drunk from French crystal. It had been a fairy tale, and she hadn't wanted it for herself. She had only wanted him.

A young girl's foolishness, Liz thought now. In her naive way, she'd made a prince out of a man who was weak and selfish and spoiled. But over the years she had thought of the house he'd talked of and pictured her daughter on those wide, curving stairs. That had been her sense of justice.

The image wasn't as clear now, not now that she'd seen wealth in a long metal box and understood where it had come from. Not when she'd seen Jonas's eyes when he'd spoken of his kind of justice. That hadn't been a fairy tale with gos-samer edges, but grimly real. She had some thinking to do. But before she could plan for the rest of her life, and for her daughter's, she had to get through the moment.

Jonas. She was bound to him through no choice of her own. And perhaps he was bound to her in the same way. Was that the reason she was drawn to him? Because they were trapped in the same puzzle? If she could only explain it away, maybe she could stop the needs that kept swimming through her. If she could only explain it away, maybe she would be in control again.

But how could she explain the feelings she'd experienced on the silent cab ride back to the hotel? She had had to fight the desire to put her arms around him, to offer comfort when nothing in his manner had indicated he needed or wanted it. There were no easy answers—no answers at all to the fact that she was slowly, inevitably falling in love with him.

It was time to admit that, she decided, because you could never face anything until it was admitted. You could never solve anything until it was faced. She'd lived by that rule years before during the biggest crisis of her life. It still held true.

So she loved him, or very nearly loved him. She was no longer naive enough to believe that love was the beginning of any answer. He would hurt her. There were no ifs about that. He'd steal from her the one thing she'd managed to hold fast to for ten years. And once he'd taken her heart, what would it mean to him? She shook her head. No more than such things ever mean to those who take them.

Jonas Sharpe was a man on a mission, and she was no more to him than a map. He was ruthless in his own patient way. When he had finished what he'd come to do, he would turn away from her, go back to his life in Philadelphia and never think of her again.

Some women, Liz thought, were doomed to pick the men who could hurt them the most. Making her mind a blank, Liz stripped and changed to her bathing suit. But Jonas, thoughts of Jonas, kept slipping through the barriers.

Maybe if she talked to Faith—if she could touch her greatest link with normality, things would snap back into focus. On impulse, Liz picked up the phone beside her bed and began the process of placing the call. Faith would just be home from school, Liz calculated, growing more excited as she heard the clinks and buzzes on the receiver. When the phone began to ring, she sat on the bed. She was already smiling.

"Hello?"

"Mom?" Liz felt the twin surges of pleasure and guilt as she heard her mother's voice. "It's Liz."

"Liz!" Rose Palmer felt identical surges. "We didn't expect to hear from you. Your last letter just came this morning. Nothing's wrong, is it?"

"No, no, nothing's wrong." Everything's wrong. "I just wanted to talk to Faith."

"Oh, Liz, I'm so sorry. Faith's not here. She has her piano lesson today."

The letdown came, but she braced herself against it. "I forgot." Tears threatened, but she forced them back. "She likes the lessons, doesn't she?"

"She loves them. You should hear her play. Remember when you were taking them?"

"I had ten thumbs." She managed to smile. "I wanted to thank you for sending the pictures. She looks so grown up. Momma, is she . . . looking forward to coming back?"

Rose heard the need, felt the ache. She wished, not for the first time, that her daughter was close enough to hold. "She's marking off the days on her calendar. She bought you a present."

Liz had to swallow. "She did?"

"It's supposed to be a surprise, so don't tell her I told you."

"I won't." She dashed tears away, grateful she could keep her voice even. It hurt, but was also a comfort to be able to speak to someone who knew and understood Faith as she did. "I miss her. The last few weeks always seem the hardest."

Her voice wasn't as steady as she thought—and a mother hears what others don't. "Liz, why don't you come home? Spend the rest of the month here while she's in school?"

"No, I can't. How's Dad?"

Rose fretted impatiently at the change of subject, then

subsided. She'd never known anyone as thoroughly stubborn as her daughter. Unless it was her granddaughter. "He's fine. Looking forward to coming down and doing some diving."

"We'll take one of the boats out—just the four of us. Tell Faith I . . . tell her I called," she finished lamely.

"Of course I will. Why don't I have her call you back when she gets home? The car pool drops her off at five."

"No. No, I'm not home. I'm in Acapulco—on business." Liz let out a long breath to steady herself. "Just tell her I miss her and I'll be waiting at the airport. You know I appreciate everything you're doing. I just—"

"Liz." Rose interrupted gently. "We love Faith. And we love you."

"I know." Liz pressed her fingers to her eyes. She did know, but was never quite sure what to do about it. "I love you, too. It's just that sometimes things get so mixed up."

"Are you all right?"

She dropped her hand again, and her eyes were dry. "I will be when you get there. Tell Faith I'm marking off the days, too."

"I will."

"Bye, Momma."

She hung up and sat until the churning emptiness had run its course. If she'd had more confidence in her parents' support, more trust in their love, would she have fled the States and started a new life on her own? Liz dragged a hand through her hair. She'd never be sure of that, nor could she dwell on it. She'd burned her own bridges. The only thing that was important was Faith, and her happiness.

*   *   *

An hour later, Jonas found her at the pool. She swam laps in long, smooth strokes, her body limber. She seemed tireless, and oddly suited to the private luxury. Her suit was a flashy red, but the cut so simple that it relied strictly on the form it covered for style.

He counted twenty laps before she stopped, and wondered how many she'd completed before he'd come down. It seemed to him as if she swam to drain herself of some tension or sorrow, and that with each lap she'd come closer to succeeding. Waiting, he watched her tip her head back in the water so that her hair slicked back. The marks on her neck had faded. As she stood, water skimmed her thigh.

"I've never seen you relaxed," Jonas commented. But even as he said the words, he could see her muscles tense again. She turned away from her contemplation of the mountains and looked at him.

He was tired, she realized, and wondered if she should have seen it before. There was a weariness around his eyes that hadn't been there that morning. He hadn't changed his clothes, and had his hands tucked into the pockets of bone-colored slacks. She wondered if he'd been up to the suite at all.

"I didn't bring a suit with me." Liz pushed against the side of the pool and hitched herself out. Water rained from her. "I charged this one to the room."

The thighs were cut nearly to the waist. Jonas caught himself wondering just how the skin would feel there. "It's nice."

Liz picked up her towel. "It was expensive."

He only lifted a brow. "I could deduct it from the rent."

Her lips curved a little as she rubbed her hair dry. "No, you can't. But since you're a lawyer, I imagine you can find a way to deduct it from something else. I saved the receipt."

He hadn't thought he could laugh. "I appreciate it. You know, I get the impression you don't think much of lawyers."

Something came and went in her eyes. "I try not to think of them at all."

Taking the towel from her, he gently dried her face. "Faith's father's a lawyer?"

Without moving, she seemed to shift away from him. "Leave it alone, Jonas."

"You don't."

"Actually I do, most of the time. Maybe it's been on my mind the past few weeks, but that's my concern."

He draped the towel around her shoulders and, holding the ends, drew her closer. "I'd like you to tell me about it."

It was his voice, she thought, so calm, so persuasive, that nearly had her opening both mind and heart. She could almost believe as she looked at him that he really wanted to know, to understand. The part of her that was already in love with him needed to believe he might care. "Why?"

"I don't know. Maybe it's that look that comes into your eyes. It makes a man want to stroke it away."

Her chin came up a fraction. "There's no need to feel sorry for me."

"I don't think sympathy's the right word." Abruptly weary, he dropped his forehead to hers. He was tired of fighting demons, of trying to find answers. "Damn."

Uncertain, she stood very still. "Are you all right?"

"No. No, I'm not." He moved away from her to walk to the end of the path where a plot of tiny orange flowers poked up through white gravel. "A lot of things you said today were true. A lot of things you've said all along are true. I can't do anything about them."

"I don't know what you want me to say now."

"Nothing." Hideously tired, he ran both hands over his face. "I'm trying to live with the fact that my brother's dead, and that he was murdered because he decided to make some easy money drug-trafficking. He had a good brain, but he always chose to use it in the wrong way. Every time I look in the mirror, I wonder why."

Liz was beside him before she could cut off her feelings. He hurt. It was the first time she'd seen below the surface to the pain. She knew what it was like to live with pain. "He was different, Jonas. I don't think he was bad, just weak. Mourning him is one thing—blaming yourself for what he did, or for what happened to him, is another."

He hadn't known he needed comfort, but her hand resting on him had something inside him slowly uncurling. "I was the only one who could reach him, keep him on some kind of level. There came a point where I just got tired of running both our lives."

"Do you really believe you could have prevented him from doing what he did?"

"Maybe. That's something else I have to live with."

"Just a minute." She took his shirtfront in much the same way she had that afternoon. There was no sympathy now, but annoyance on her face. He hadn't known he needed that, as well. "You were brothers, twins, but you were separate people. Jerry wasn't a child to be guided and supervised. He was a grown man who made his decisions."

"That's the trouble. Jerry never grew up."

"And you did," she tossed back. "Are you going to punish yourself for it?"

He'd been doing just that, Jonas realized. He'd gone home, buried his brother, comforted his parents and blamed himself for not preventing something he knew in his heart had been inevitable. "I have to find out who killed him, Liz. I can't set the rest aside until I do."

"We'll find them." On impulse, she pressed her cheek to his. Sometimes the slightest human contact could wash away acres of pain. "Then it'll be over."

He wasn't sure he wanted it to be, not all of it. He ran a hand down her arm, needing the touch of her skin. He found it chilled. "The sun's gone down." He wrapped the towel around her in a gesture that would have been mere politeness with another woman. With Liz, it was for protection. "You'd better get out of that wet suit. We'll have dinner."

"Here?"

"Sure. The restaurant's supposed to be one of the best."

Liz thought of the elegance of their suite and the contents of her overnight bag. "I didn't bring anything to wear."

He laughed and swung an arm around her. It was the first purely frivolous thing he'd heard her say. "Charge something else."

"But—"

"Don't worry, I've got the best crooked accountant in Philadelphia."

CHAPTER 7

B ecause she'd been certain she would never sleep away from home, in a hotel bed, Liz was surprised to wake to full sunlight. Not only had she slept, she realized, she'd slept like a rock for eight hours and was rested and ready to go. True, it was just a little past six, and she had no business to run, but her body was tuned to wake at that hour. A trip to Acapulco didn't change that.

It had changed other things, she reminded herself as she stretched out in the too-big bed. Because of it, she'd become inescapably tangled in murder and smuggling. Putting the words together made her shake her head. In a movie, she might have enjoyed watching the melodrama. In a book, she'd have turned the page to read more. But in her own life, she preferred the more mundane. Liz was too practical to delude herself into believing she could distance herself from any part of the puzzle any longer. For better or worse, she was personally involved in this melodrama. That included Jonas Sharpe. The only question now was which course of action to take.

She couldn't run. That had never been a choice. Liz had already concluded she couldn't hide behind Moralas and his men forever. Sooner or later the man with the knife would come back, or another man more determined or more desperate. She wouldn't escape a second time. The moment she'd looked into the safe-deposit box, she'd become a full-fledged player in the game. Which brought her back full circle to Jonas. She had no choice but to put her trust in him now. If he were to give up on his brother's murder and return to Philadelphia she would be that much more alone. However much she might wish it otherwise, Liz needed him just as much as he needed her.

Other things had changed, she thought. Her feelings for him were even more undefined and confusing than they had started out to be. Seeing him as she had the evening before, hurt and vulnerable, had touched off more than impersonal sympathy or physical attraction. It had made her feel a kinship, and the kinship urged her to help him, not only for her own welfare, but for his. He suffered, for his brother's loss, but also for what his brother had done. She'd loved once, and had suffered, not only because of loss but because of disillusionment.

A lifetime ago? Liz wondered. Did we ever really escape from one lifetime to another? It seemed years could pass, circumstances could change, but we carried our baggage with us through each phase. If anything, with each phase we had to carry a bit more. There was little use in thinking, she told herself as she climbed from the bed. From this point on, she had little choice but to act.

Jonas heard her the moment she got up. He'd been awake since five, restless and prowling. For over an hour he'd been racking his brain and searching his conscience for a way to ease Liz out of a situation his brother, and he himself had locked her into. He'd already thought of several ways to draw attention away from her to himself, but that wouldn't guarantee Liz's safety. She wouldn't go to Houston, and he understood her feelings about endangering her daughter in any way.

As the days passed, he felt he was coming to understand her better and better. She was a loner, but only because she saw it as the safest route. She was a businesswoman, but only because she looked to her daughter's welfare first. Inside, he thought, she was a woman with dreams on hold and love held in bondage. She had steered both toward her child and denied herself. And, Jonas added, she'd convinced herself she was content.

That was something else he understood, because until a few weeks before he had also convinced himself he was content. It was only now, after he'd had the opportunity to look at his life from a distance, that he realized he had merely been drifting. Perhaps, when the outward trimmings were stripped away, he hadn't been so different from his brother. For both of them, success had been the main target, they had simply aimed for it differently. Though Jonas had a steady job, a home of his own, there had never been an important woman. He'd put his career first. Jonas wasn't certain he'd be able to do so again. It had taken the loss of his brother to make him realize he needed something more, something solid. Exploring the law was only a job. Winning cases was only a transitory satisfaction. Perhaps he'd known it for some time. After all, he'd bought the old house in Chadd's Ford to give himself something permanent. When had he started thinking about sharing it?

Still, thinking about his own life didn't solve the problem of Liz Palmer and what he was going to do with her. She couldn't go to Houston, he thought again, but there were other places she could go until he could assure her that her life could settle back the way she wanted it. His parents were his first thought, and the quiet country home they'd retired to in Lancaster. If he could find a way to slip her out of Mexico, she would be safe there. It would even be possible to have her daughter join her. Then his conscience would ease. Jonas had no doubt that his parents would accept them both, then dote on them.

Once he'd done what he'd come to do, he could go to Lancaster himself. He'd like to see Liz there, in surroundings he was used to. He wanted time to talk with her about simple things. He wanted to hear her laugh again, as she had only once in all the days he'd known her. Once they were there, away from the ugliness, he might understand his feelings better. Perhaps by then he'd be able to analyze what had happened inside him when she'd pressed her cheek against his and had offered unconditional support.

He'd wanted to hold on to her, to just hold on and the hell with the world. There was something about her that made him think of lazy evenings on cool porches and long Sunday afternoon walks. He couldn't say why. In Philadelphia he rarely took time for such things. Even socializing had become business. And he'd seen for himself that she never gave herself an idle hour. Why should he, a man dedicated to his work, think of lazing days away with a woman obsessed by hers?

She remained a mystery to him, and perhaps that was an answer in itself. If he thought of her too often, too deeply, it was only because while his understanding was growing, he still knew so little. If it sometimes seemed that discovering Liz Palmer was just as important as discovering his brother's killer, it was only because they were tied together. How could he take his mind off one without taking his mind off the other? Yet when he thought of her now, he thought of her stretched out on his mother's porch swing, safe, content and waiting for him.

Annoyed with himself, Jonas checked his watch. It was after nine on the East Coast. He'd call his office, he thought. A few legal problems might clear his mind. He'd no more than picked up the receiver when Liz came out from her bedroom.

"I didn't know you were up," she said, and fiddled nervously with her belt. Odd, she felt entirely different about sharing the plush little villa with him than she did her home. After all, she reasoned, at home he was paying rent.

"I thought you'd sleep longer." He replaced the receiver again. The office could wait.

"I never sleep much past six." Feeling awkward, she wandered to the wide picture window. "Terrific view."

"Yes, it is."

"I haven't stayed in a hotel in . . . in years," she finished. "When I came to Cozumel, I worked in the same hotel where I'd stayed with my parents. It was an odd feeling. So's this."

"No urge to change the linen or stack the towels?"

When she chuckled, some of the awkwardness slipped away. "No, not even a twinge."

"Liz, when we're finished with all this, when it's behind us, will you talk to me about that part of your life?"

She turned to him, away from the window, but they both felt the distance. "When we're finished with this, there won't be any reason to."

He rose and came to her. In a gesture that took her completely by surprise, he took both of her hands. He lifted one, then the other, to his lips and watched her eyes cloud. "I can't be sure of that," he murmured. "Can you?"

She couldn't be sure of anything when his voice was quiet, his hands gentle. For a moment, she simply absorbed the feeling of being a woman cared for by a man. Then she stepped back, as she knew she had to. "Jonas, you told me once we had the same problem. I didn't want to believe it then, but it was true. It is true. Once that problem is solved, there really isn't anything else between us. Your life and mine are separated by a lot more than miles."

He thought of his house and his sudden need to share it. "They don't have to be."

"There was a time I might have believed that."

"You're living in the past." He took her shoulders, but this time his hands weren't as gentle. "You're fighting ghosts."

"I may have my ghosts, but I don't live in the past. I can't afford to." She put her hands to his wrists, but let them lie there only a moment before she let go. "I can't afford to pretend to myself about you."

He wanted to demand, he wanted to pull her with him to the sofa and prove to her that she was wrong. He resisted. It wasn't the first time he'd used courtroom skill, courtroom tactics, to win on a personal level. "We'll leave it your way for now," he said easily. "But the case isn't closed. Are you hungry?"

Unsure whether she should be uneasy or relieved, Liz nodded. "A little."

"Let's have breakfast. We've got plenty of time before the plane leaves."

*   *   *

She didn't trust him. Though Jonas kept the conversation light and passionless throughout breakfast, Liz kept herself braced for a countermove. He was a clever man, she knew. He was a man, she was certain, who made sure he got his own way no matter how long it took. Liz considered herself a woman strong enough to keep promises made, even when they were to herself. No man, not even Jonas, was going to make her change the course she'd set ten years before. There was only room enough for two loves in her life. Faith and her work.

"I can't get used to eating something at this hour of the morning that's going to singe my stomach lining."

Liz swallowed the mixture of peppers, onions and eggs. "Mine's flame resistant. You should try my chili."

"Does that mean you're offering to cook for me?"

When Liz glanced up, she wished he hadn't been smiling at her in just that way. "I suppose I could make enough for two as easily as enough for one. But you don't seem to have any trouble in the kitchen."

"Oh, I can cook. It's just that once I've finished, it never seems worth the bother." He leaned forward to run a finger down her hand from wrist to knuckle. "Tell you what—I'll buy the supplies and even clean up the mess if you handle the chili."

Though she smiled, Liz drew her hand away. "The question is, can you handle the chili? It might burn right through a soft lawyer's stomach."

Appreciating the challenge, he took her hand again. "Why don't we find out? Tonight."

"All right." She flexed her fingers, but he merely linked his with them. "I can't eat if you have my hand."

He glanced down. "You have another one."

He made her laugh when she'd been set to insist. "I'm entitled to two."

"I'll give it back. Later."

"Hey, Jerry!"

The easy smile on Jonas's face froze. Only his eyes changed, locking on to Liz's, warning and demanding. His hand remained on hers, but the grip tightened. The message was very clear—she was to do nothing, say nothing until he'd tallied the odds. He turned, flashing a new smile. Liz's stomach trembled. It was Jerry's smile, she realized. Not Jonas's.

"Why didn't you tell me you were back in town?" A tall, tanned man with sandy blond hair and a trim beard dropped a hand on Jonas's shoulder. Liz caught the glint of a diamond on his finger. He was young, she thought, determined to store everything she could, barely into his thirties, and dressed with slick, trendy casualness.

"Quick trip," Jonas said as, like Liz, he took in every detail. "Little business . . ." He cast a meaningful glance toward Liz. "Little pleasure."

The man turned and stared appreciatively at Liz. "Is there any other way?"

Thinking fast, Liz offered her hand. "Hello. Since Jerry's too rude to introduce us, we'll have to do it ourselves. I'm Liz Palmer."

"David Merriworth." He took her hand between both of his. They were smooth and uncallused. "Jerry might have trouble with manners, but he's got great taste."

She smiled, hoping she did it properly. "Thank you."

"Pull up a chair, Merriworth." Jonas took out a cigarette. "As long as you keep your hands off my lady." He said it in the good-natured, only-kidding tone Jerry had inevitably used, but his eyes were Jonas's, warning her to tread carefully.

"Wouldn't mind a quick cup of coffee." David pulled over a chair after he checked his watch. "Got a breakfast meeting in a few minutes. So how are things on Cozumel?" He inclined his head ever so slightly. "Getting in plenty of diving?"

Jonas allowed his lips to curve and kept his eyes steady. "Enough."

"Glad to hear it. I was going to check in with you myself, but I've been in the States for a couple weeks. Just got back in last night." He used two sugars after the waiter set a fresh cup of coffee beside him. "Business is good, buddy. Real good."

"What business are you in, Mr. Merriworth?"

He gave Liz a big grin before he winked at Jonas. "Sales, sweetheart. Imports, you might say."

"Really." Because her throat was dry she drank more coffee. "It must be fascinating."

"It has its moments." He turned in his chair so that he could study her face. "So where did Jerry find you?"

"On Cozumel." She sent Jonas a steady look. "We're partners."

David lowered his cup. "That so?"

They were in too deep, Jonas thought, for him to contradict her. "That's so," he agreed.

David picked up his cup again with a shrug. "If it's okay with the boss, it doesn't bother me."

"I do things my way," Jonas drawled. "Or I don't do them."

Amused, and perhaps admiring, David broke into a smile. "That never changes. Look, I've been out of touch for a few weeks. The drops still going smooth?"

With those words, Jonas's last hopes died. What he'd found in the safe-deposit box had been real, and it had been Jerry's. He buttered a roll as though he had all the time in the world. Beneath the table, Liz touched his leg once, hoping he'd take it as comfort. He never looked at her. "Why shouldn't they?"

"It's the classiest operation I've ever come across," David commented, taking a cautious glance around to other tables. "Wouldn't like to see anything screw it up."

"You worry too much."

"You're the one who should worry," David pointed out. "I don't have to deal with Manchez. You weren't around last year when he took care of those two Colombians. I was. You deal with supplies, I stick with sales. I sleep better."

"I just dive," Jonas said, and tapped out his cigarette. "And I sleep fine."

"He's something, isn't he?" David sent Liz another grin. "I knew Jerry here was just the man the boss was looking for. You keep diving, kid." He tipped his cup at Jonas. "It makes me look good."

"Sounds like you two have known each other for a while," Liz said with a smile. Under the table, she twisted the napkin in her lap.

"Go way back, don't we, Jer?"

"Yeah. We go back."

"First time we hooked up was six, no, seven years ago. We were working a pigeon drop in L.A. We'd have had that twenty thousand out of that old lady if her daughter hadn't caught on." He took out a slim cigarette case. "Your brother got you out of that one, didn't he? The East Coast lawyer."

"Yeah." Jonas remembered posting the bond and pulling the strings.

"Now I've been working out of here for almost five. A real businessman." He slapped Jonas's arm. "Hell of a lot better than the pigeon drop, huh, Jerry?"

"Pays better."

David let out a roar of laughter. "Why don't I show you two around Acapulco tonight?"

"Gotta get back." Jonas signaled for the check. "Business."

"Yeah, I know what you mean." He nodded toward the restaurant's entrance. "Here's my customer now. Next time you drop down, give a call."

"Sure."

"And give my best to old Clancy." With another laugh, David gave them each a quick salute. They watched him stride across the room and shake hands with a dark-suited man.

"Don't say anything here," Jonas murmured as he signed the breakfast check. "Let's go."

Liz's crumpled napkin slid to the floor as she rose to walk out with him. He didn't speak again until they had the door of the villa closed behind them.

"You had no business telling him we were partners."

Because she'd been ready for the attack, she shrugged it off. "He said more once I did."

"He'd have said just as much if you'd made an excuse and left the table."

She folded her arms. "We have the same problem, remember?"

He didn't care to have his own words tossed back at him. "The least you could have done was to give him another name."

"Why? They know who I am. Sooner or later he's going to talk to whoever's in charge and get the whole story."

She was right. He didn't care for that either. "Are you packed?"

"Yes."

"Then let's check out. We'll go to the airport."

"And then?"

"And then we go straight to Moralas."

*　*　*

You've been very busy." Moralas held on to his temper as he rocked back in his chair. "Two of my men wasted their valuable time looking for you in Acapulco. You might have told me, Mr. Sharpe, that you planned to take Miss Palmer on a trip."

"I thought a police tail in Acapulco might be inconvenient."

"And now that you have finished your own investigation, you bring me this." He held up the key and examined it. "This which Miss Palmer discovered several days ago. As a lawyer, you must understand the phrase 'withholding evidence.'"

"Of course." Jonas nodded coolly. "But neither Miss Palmer nor myself could know the key was evidence. We speculated, naturally, that it might have belonged to my brother. Withholding a speculation is hardly a crime."

"Perhaps not, but it is poor judgment. Poor judgment often translates into an offense."

Jonas leaned back in his chair. If Moralas wanted to argue law, they'd argue law. "If the key belonged to my brother, as executor of his estate, it became mine. In any case, once it was proved to me that the key did indeed belong to Jerry, and that the contents of the safe-deposit box were evidence, I brought both the key and a description of the contents to you."

"Indeed. And do you also speculate as to how your brother came to possess those particular items?"

"Yes."

Moralas waited a beat, then turned to Liz. "And you, Miss Palmer—you also have your speculations?"

She had her hands gripped tightly in her lap, but her voice was matter-of-fact and reasonable. "I know that whoever attacked me wanted money, obviously a great deal of money. We found a great deal."

"And a bag of what Mr. Sharpe . . . speculates is cocaine." Moralas folded his hands on the desk with the key under them. "Miss Palmer, did you at any time see Mr. Jeremiah Sharpe in possession of cocaine?"

"No."

"Did he at any time speak to you of cocaine or drug-trafficking?"

"No, of course not. I would have told you."

"As you told me about the key?" When Jonas started to protest, Moralas waved him off. "I will need a list of your customers for the past six weeks, Miss Palmer. Names and, wherever possible, addresses."

"My customers? Why?"

"It's more than possible that Mr. Sharpe used your shop for his contacts."

"My shop." Outraged, she stood up. "My boats? Do you think he could have passed drugs under my nose without me being aware?"

Moralas took out a cigar and studied it. "I very much hope you were unaware, Miss Palmer. You will bring me the list of clients by the end of the week." He glanced at Jonas. "Of course, you are within your rights to demand a warrant. It will simply slow down the process. And I, of course, am within my rights to hold Miss Palmer as a material witness."

Jonas watched the pale blue smoke circle toward the ceiling. It was tempting to call Moralas's bluff simply as an exercise in testing two ends of the law. And in doing so, he and the captain could play tug-of-war with Liz for hours. "There are times, Captain, when it's wiser not to employ certain rights. I think I'm safe in saying that the three of us in this room want basically the same thing." He rose and flicked his lighter at the end of Moralas's cigar. "You'll have your list, Captain. And more."

Moralas lifted his gaze and waited.

"Pablo Manchez," Jonas said, and was gratified to see Moralas's eyes narrow.

"What of Manchez?"

"He's on Cozumel. Or was," Jonas stated. "My brother met with him several times in local bars and clubs. You may also be interested in David Merriworth, an American working out of Acapulco. Apparently he's the one who put my brother onto his contacts in Cozumel. If you contact the authorities in the States, you'll find that Merriworth has an impressive rap sheet."

In his precise handwriting, Moralas noted down the names, though he wasn't likely to forget them. "I appreciate the information. However, in the future, Mr. Sharpe, I would appreciate it more if you stayed out of my way. *Buenas tardes,* Miss Palmer."

Moments later, Liz strode out to the street. "I don't like being threatened. That's what he was doing, wasn't it?" she demanded. "He was threatening to put me in jail."

Very calm, even a bit amused, Jonas lit a cigarette. "He was pointing out his options, and ours."

"He didn't threaten to put you in jail," Liz muttered.

"He doesn't worry as much about me as he does about you."

"Worry?" She stopped with her hand gripping the handle of Jonas's rented car.

"He's a good cop. You're one of his people."

She looked back toward the police station with a scowl. "He has a funny way of showing it." A scruffy little boy scooted up to the car and gallantly opened the door for her. Even as he prepared to hold out a hand, Liz was digging for a coin.

"Gracias."

He checked the coin, grinned at the amount and nodded approval. *"Buenas tardes, señorita."* Just as gallantly he closed the door for her while the coin disappeared into a pocket.

"It's a good thing you don't come into town often," Jonas commented.

"Why?"

"You'd be broke in a week."

Liz found a clip in her purse and pulled back her hair. "Because I gave a little boy twenty-five pesos?"

"How much did you give the other kid before we went into Moralas?"

"I bought something from him."

"Yeah." Jonas swung away from the curb. "You look like a woman who can't go a day without a box of Chiclets."

"You're changing the subject."

"That's right. Now tell me where I can find the best place for buying ingredients for chili."

"You want me to cook for you tonight?"

"It'll keep your mind off the rest. We've done everything we can do for the moment," he added. "Tonight we're going to relax."

She would have liked to believe he was right. Between nerves and anger, she was wound tight. "Cooking's supposed to relax me?"

"Eating is going to relax you. It's just an unavoidable circumstance that you have to cook it first."

It sounded so absurd that she subsided. "Turn left at the next corner. I tell you what to buy, you buy it, then you stay out of my way."

"Agreed."

"And you clean up."

"Absolutely."

"Pull over here," she directed. "And remember, you asked for it."

* * *

Liz never skimped when she cooked, even taking into account that authentic Mexican spices had more zing than the sort sold in the average American supermarket. She'd developed a taste for Mexican food and Yucatán specialties when she'd been a child, exploring the peninsula with her parents. She wasn't an elaborate cook, and when alone would often make do with a sandwich, but when her heart was in it, she could make a meal that would more than satisfy.

Perhaps, in a way, she wanted to impress him. Liz found she was able to admit it while she prepared a Mayan salad for chilling. It was probably very natural and harmless to want to impress someone with your cooking. After peeling and slicing an avocado, she found, oddly enough, she was relaxing.

So much of what she'd done in the past few days had been difficult or strange. It was a relief to make a decision no more vital than the proper way to slice her fruits and vegetables. In the end, she fussed with the arrangement a bit more, pleased with the contrasting colors of greens and oranges and cherry tomatoes. It was, she recalled, the only salad she could get Faith to eat because it was the only one Faith considered pretty enough. Liz didn't realize she was smiling as she began to sauté onions and peppers. She added a healthy dose of garlic and let it all simmer.

"It already smells good," Jonas commented as he strode through the doorway.

She only glanced over her shoulder. "You're supposed to stay out of my way."

"You cook, I take care of the table."

Liz only shrugged and turned back to the stove. She measured, stirred and spiced until the kitchen was filled with a riot of scent. The sauce, chunky with meat and vegetables, simmered and thickened on low heat. Pleased with herself, she wiped her hands on a cloth and turned around. Jonas was sitting comfortably at the table watching her.

"You look good," he told her. "Very good."

It seemed so natural, their being together in the kitchen with a pot simmering and a breeze easing its way through the screen. It made her remember how hard it was not to want such simple things in your life. Liz set the cloth down and found she didn't know what to do with her hands. "Some men think a woman looks best in front of a stove."

"I don't know. It's a toss-up with the way you looked at the wheel of a boat. How long does that have to cook?"

"About a half hour."

"Good." He rose and went to the counter where he'd left two bottles. "We have time for some wine."

A little warning signal jangled in her brain. Liz decided she needed a lid for the chili. "I don't have the right glasses."

"I already thought of that." From a bag beside the bottle, he pulled out two thin-stemmed wineglasses.

"You've been busy," she murmured.

"You didn't like me hovering over you in the market. I had to do something." He drew out the cork, then let the wine breathe.

"These candles aren't mine."

He turned to see Liz fiddling with the fringe of one of the woven mats he'd set on the table. In the center were two deep blue tapers that picked up the color in the border of her dishes.

"They're ours," Jonas told her.

She twisted the fringe around one finger, let it go, then twisted it again. The last time she'd burned candles had been during a power failure. These didn't look sturdy, but slender and frivolous. "There wasn't any need to go to all this trouble. I don't—"

"Do candles and wine make you uneasy?"

Dropping the fringe, she let her hands fall to her sides. "No, of course not."

"Good." He poured rich red wine into both glasses. Walking to her, he offered one. "Because I find them relaxing. We did agree to relax."

She sipped, and though she wanted to back away, held her ground. "I'm afraid you may be looking for more than I can give."

"No." He touched his glass to hers. "I'm looking for exactly what you can give."

Recognizing when she was out of her depth, Liz turned toward the refrigerator. "We can start on the salad."

He lit the candles and dimmed the lights. She told herself it didn't matter. Atmosphere was nothing more than a pleasant addition to a meal.

"Very pretty," Jonas told her when she'd mixed the dressing and arranged avocado slices. "What's it called?"

"It's a Mayan salad." Liz took the first nibble and was satisfied. "I learned the recipe when I worked at the hotel. Actually, that's where most of my cooking comes from."

"Wonderful," Jonas decided after the first bite. "It makes me wish I'd talked you into cooking before."

"A one time only." She relaxed enough to smile. "Meals aren't—"

"Included in the rent," Jonas finished. "We might negotiate."

This time she laughed at him and chose a section of grapefruit. "I don't think so. How do you manage in Philadelphia?"

"I have a housekeeper who'll toss together a casserole on Wednesdays." He took another bite, enjoying the contrast of crisp greens and spicy dressing. "And I eat out a lot."

"And parties? I suppose you go to a lot of parties."

"Some business, some pleasure." He'd almost forgotten what it was like to sit in a kitchen and enjoy a simple meal. "To be honest, it wears a bit. The cruising."

"Cruising?"

"When Jerry and I were teenagers, we might hop in the car on a Friday night and cruise. The idea was to see what teenage girls had hopped in their cars to cruise. The party circuit's just adult cruising."

She frowned a bit because it didn't seem as glamorous as she'd imagined. "It seems rather aimless."

"Doesn't seem. Is."

"You don't appear to be a man who does anything without a purpose."

"I've had my share of aimless nights," he murmured. "You come to a point where you realize you don't want too many more." That was just it, he realized. It wasn't the work, the hours spent closeted with law books or in a courtroom. It was the nights without meaning that left him wanting more. He lifted the wine to top off her glass, but his eyes stayed on hers. "I came to that realization very recently."

Her blood began to stir. Deliberately, Liz pushed her wine aside and rose to go to the stove. "We all make decisions at certain points in our lives, realign our priorities."

"I have the feeling you did that a long time ago."

"I did. I've never regretted it."

That much was true, he thought. She wasn't a woman for regrets. "You wouldn't change it, would you?"

Liz continued to spoon chili into bowls. "Change what?"

"If you could go back eleven years and take a different path, you wouldn't do it."

She stopped. From across the room he could see the flicker of candlelight in her eyes as she turned to him. More, he could see the strength that softness and shadows couldn't disguise. "That would mean I'd have to give up Faith. No, I wouldn't do it."

When she set the bowls on the table, Jonas took her hand. "I admire you."

Flustered, she stared down at him. "What for?"

"For being exactly what you are."

CHAPTER 8

No smooth phrases, no romantic words could have affected her more deeply. She wasn't used to flattery, but flattery, Liz was sure, could be brushed easily aside by a woman who understood herself. Sincere and simple approval was a different matter. Perhaps it was the candlelight, the wine, the intimacy of the small kitchen in the empty house, but she felt close to him, comfortable with him. Without being aware of it happening, Liz dropped her guard.

"I couldn't be anything else."

"Yes, you could. I'm glad you're not."

"What are you?" she wondered as she sat beside him.

"A thirty-five-year-old lawyer who's just realizing he's wasted some time." He lifted his glass and touched it to hers. "To making the best of whatever there is."

Though she wasn't certain she understood him, Liz drank, then waited for him to eat.

"You could fuel an engine with this stuff." Jonas dipped his spoon into the chili again and tasted. Hot spice danced on his tongue. "It's great."

"Not too hot for your Yankee stomach?"

"My Yankee stomach can handle it. You know, I'm surprised you haven't opened a restaurant, since you can cook like this."

She wouldn't have been human if the compliment hadn't pleased her. "I like the water more than I like the kitchen."

"I can't argue with that. So you picked this up in the kitchen when you worked at the hotel?"

"That's right. We'd take a meal there. The cook would show me how much of this and how much of that. He was very kind," Liz remembered. "A lot of people were kind."

He wanted to know everything—the small details, the feelings, the memories. Because he did, he knew he had to probe with care. "How long did you work there?"

"Two years. I lost count of how many beds I made."

"Then you started your own business?"

"Then I started the dive shop." She took a thin cracker and broke it in two. "It was a gamble, but it was the right one."

"How did you handle it?" He waited until she looked over at him. "With your daughter?"

She withdrew. He could hear it in her voice. "I don't know what you mean."

"I wonder about you." He kept the tone light, knowing she'd never respond to pressure. "Not many women could have managed all you've managed. You were alone, pregnant, making a living."

"Does that seem so unusual?" It made her smile to think of it. "There are only so many choices, aren't there?"

"A great many people would have made a different one."

With a nod, she accepted. "A different one wouldn't have been right for me." She sipped her wine as she let her mind drift back. "I was frightened. Quite a bit at first, but less and less as time when on. People were very good to me. It might have been different if I hadn't been lucky. I went into labor when I was cleaning room 328." Her eyes warmed as if she'd just seen something lovely. "I remember holding this stack of towels in my hand and thinking, 'Oh God, this is it, and I've only done half my rooms.'" She laughed and went back to her meal. Jonas's bowl sat cooling.

"You worked the day your baby was born?"

"Of course. I was healthy."

"I know men who take the day off if they need a tooth filled."

She laughed again and passed him the crackers. "Maybe women take things more in stride."

Only some women, he thought. Only a few exceptional women. "And afterward?"

"Afterward I was lucky again. A woman I worked with knew Señora Alderez. When Faith was born, her youngest had just turned five. She took care of Faith during the day, so I was able to go right back to work."

The cracker crumbled in his hand. "It must have been difficult for you."

"The only hard part was leaving my baby every morning, but the señora was wonderful to Faith and to me. That's how I found this house. Anyway, one thing led to another. I started the dive shop."

He wondered if she realized that the more simply she described it, the more poignant it sounded. "You said the dive shop was a gamble."

"Everything's a gamble. If I'd stayed at the hotel, I never would have been able to give Faith what I wanted to give her. And I suppose I'd have felt cheated myself. Would you like some more?"

"No." He rose to take the bowls himself while he thought out how to approach her. If he said the wrong thing, she'd pull away again. The more she told him, the more he found he needed to know. "Where did you learn to dive?"

"Right here in Cozumel, when I was just a little older than Faith." As a matter of habit she began to store the leftovers while Jonas ran water in the sink. "My parents brought me. I took to it right away. It was like, I don't know, learning to fly I suppose."

"Is that why you came back?"

"I came back because I'd always felt peaceful here. I needed to feel peaceful."

"But you must have still been in school in the States."

"I was in college." Crouching, Liz shifted things in the refrigerator to make room. "My first year. I was going to be a marine biologist, a teacher who'd enlighten class after class on the mysteries of the sea. A scientist who'd find all the answers. It was such a big dream. It overwhelmed everything else to the point where I studied constantly and rarely went out. Then I—" She caught herself. Straightening slowly, she closed the refrigerator. "You'll want the lights on to do those dishes."

"Then what?" Jonas demanded, taking her shoulder as she hit the switch.

She stared at him. Light poured over them without the shifting shadows of candles. "Then I met Faith's father, and that was the end of dreams."

The need to know eclipsed judgment. He forgot to be careful. "Did you love him?"

"Yes. If I hadn't, there'd have been no Faith."

It wasn't the answer he'd wanted. "Then why are you raising her alone?"

"That's obvious, isn't it?" Anger surged as she shoved his hand aside. "He didn't want me."

"Whether he did or didn't, he was responsible to you and the child."

"Don't talk to me about responsibility. Faith's my responsibility."

"The law sees things otherwise."

"Keep your law," she snapped. "He could quote it chapter and verse, and it didn't mean a thing. We weren't wanted."

"So you let pride cut you off from your rights?" Impatient with her, he stuck his hands in his pockets and strode back to the sink. "Why didn't you fight for what you were entitled to?"

"You want the details, Jonas?" Memory brought its own particular pain, its own particular shame. Liz concentrated on the anger. Going back to the table, she picked up her glass of wine and drank deeply.

"I wasn't quite eighteen. I was going to college to study exactly what I wanted to study so I could do exactly what I wanted to do. I considered myself a great deal more mature than some of my classmates who flitted around from class to class more concerned about where the action would be that night. I spent most of my evenings in the library. That's where I met him. He was in his last year and knew if he didn't pass the bar there'd be hell to pay at home. His family had been in law or politics since the Revolution. You'd understand about family honor, wouldn't you?"

The arrow hit the mark, but he only nodded.

"Then you should understand the rest. We saw each other every night in the library, so it was natural that we began to talk, then have a cup of coffee. He was smart, attractive, wonderfully mannered and funny." Almost violently, she blew out the candles. The scent carried over and hung in the room. "I fell hard. He brought me flowers and took me for long quiet drives on Saturday nights. When he told me he loved me, I believed him. I thought I had the world in the palm of my hand."

She set the wine down again, impatient to be finished. Jonas said nothing. "He told me we'd be married as soon as he established himself. We'd sit in his car and look at the stars and he'd tell me about his home in Dallas and the wonderful rooms. The parties and the servants and the chandeliers. It was like a story, a lovely happily-ever-after story. Then one day his mother came." Liz laughed, but gripped the back of her chair until her knuckles were white. She could still feel the humiliation.

"Actually, she sent her driver up to the dorm to fetch me. Marcus hadn't said a thing about her visiting, but I was thrilled that I was going to meet her. At the curb was this fabulous white Rolls, the kind you only see in movies. When the driver opened the door for me, I was floating. Then I got in and she gave me the facts of life. Her son had a certain position to maintain, a certain image to project. She was sure I was a very nice girl, but hardly suitable for a Jensann of Dallas."

Jonas's eyes narrowed at the name, but he said nothing. Restless, Liz went to the stove and began to scrub the surface. "She told me she'd already spoken with her son and he understood the relationship had to end. Then she offered me a check as compensation. I was humiliated, and worse, I was pregnant. I hadn't told anyone yet, because I'd just found out that morning. I didn't take her money. I got out of the Rolls and went straight to Marcus. I was sure he loved me enough to toss it all aside for me, and for our baby. I was wrong."

Her eyes were so dry that they hurt. Liz pressed her fingers to them a moment. "When I went to see him, he was very logical. It had been nice; now it was over. His parents held the purse strings and it was important to keep them happy. But he wanted me to know we could still see each other now and again, as long as it was on the side. When I told him about the baby, he was furious. How could I have done such a thing? *I.*"

Liz tossed the dishrag into the sink so that hot, soapy water heaved up. "It was as though I'd conceived the baby completely on my own. He wouldn't have it, he wouldn't have some silly girl who'd gotten herself pregnant messing up his life. He told me I had to get rid of it. It—as though Faith were a thing to be erased and forgotten. I was hysterical. He lost his temper. There were threats. He said he'd spread word that I was sleeping around and his friends would back him up. I'd never be able to prove the baby was his. He said my parents would be embarrassed, perhaps sued if I tried to press it. He tossed around a lot of legal phrases that I couldn't understand, but I understood he was finished with me. His family had a lot of pull at the college, and he said he'd see that I was dismissed. Because I was foolish enough to believe every-thing he said, I was terrified. He gave me a check and told me to go out of state—better, out of the country—to take care of things. That way no one would have to know.

"For a week I did nothing. I went through my classes in a daze, thinking I'd wake up and find out it had all been a bad dream. Then I faced it. I wrote my parents, telling them what I could. I sold the car they'd given me when I graduated from high school, took the check from Marcus and came to Cozumel to have my baby."

He'd wanted to know, even demanded, but now his insides were raw. "You could have gone to your parents."

"Yes, but at the time Marcus had convinced me they'd be ashamed. He told me they'd hate me and consider the baby a burden."

"Why didn't you go to his family? You were entitled to be taken care of."

"Go to them?" He'd never heard venom in her voice be-fore. "Be taken care of by them? I'd have gone to hell first."

He waited a moment, until he was sure he could speak calmly. "They don't even know, do they?"

"No. And they never will. Faith is mine."

"And what does Faith know?"

"Only what she has to know. I'd never lie to her."

"And do you know that Marcus Jensann has his sights set on the senate, and maybe higher?"

Her color drained quickly and completely. "You know him?"

"By reputation."

Panic came and went, then returned in double force. "He doesn't know Faith exists. None of them do. They can't."

Watching her steadily, he took a step closer. "What are you afraid of?"

"Power. Faith is mine, she's going to stay mine. None of them will ever touch her."

"Is that why you stay here? Are you hiding from them?"

"I'll do whatever's necessary to protect my child."

"He's still got you running scared." Furious for her, Jonas took her arms. "He's got a frightened teenager strapped inside of you who's never had the chance to stretch and feel alive. Don't you know a man like that wouldn't even remember who you are? You're still running away from a man who wouldn't recognize you on the street."

She slapped him hard enough to make his head snap back. Breathing fast, she backed away from him, appalled by a show of violence she hadn't been aware of possessing. "Don't tell me what I'm running from," she whispered. "Don't tell me what I feel." She turned and fled. Before she'd reached the front door he had her again, whirling her around, gripping her hard. He no longer knew why his anger was so fierce, only that he was past the point of controlling it.

"How much have you given up because of him?" Jonas demanded. "How much have you cut out of your life?"

"It's my life!" she shouted at him.

"And you won't share it with anyone but your daughter. What the hell are you going to do when she's grown? What the hell are you going to do in twenty years when you have nothing but your memories?"

"Don't." Tears filled her eyes too quickly to be blinked away.

He grabbed her close again, twisting until she had to look at him. "We all need someone. Even you. It's about time someone proved it to you."

"No."

She tried to turn her head but he was quick. With his mouth crushed on hers she struggled, but her arms were trapped between their bodies and his were iron-like around her. Emotions already mixed with fear and anger became more confused with passion. Liz fought not to give in to any of them as his mouth demanded both submission and response.

"You're not fighting me," he told her. His eyes were close,

searing into hers. "You're fighting yourself. You've been fighting yourself since the first time we met."

"I want you to let me go." She wanted her voice to be strong, but it trembled.

"Yes. You want me to let you go just as much as you want me not to. You've been making your own decisions for a long time, Liz. This time I'm making one for you."

Her furious protest was lost against his mouth as he pressed her down to the sofa. Trapped under him, her body began to heat, her blood began to stir. Yes, she was fighting herself. She had to fight herself before she could fight him. But she was losing.

She heard her own moan as his lips trailed down her throat, and it was a moan of pleasure. She felt the hard line of his body against hers as she arched under him, but it wasn't a movement of protest. *Want me,* she seemed to say. *Want me for what I am.*

Her pulse began to thud in parts of her body that had been quiet for so many years. Life burst through her like a torrid wind through thin glass until every line of defense was shattered. With a desperate groan, she took his face in her hands and dragged his mouth back to hers.

She could taste the passion, the life, the promises. She wanted them all. Recklessness, so long chained within, tore free and ruled. A sound bubbled in her throat she wasn't even aware was a laugh as she wrapped herself around him. She wanted. He wanted. The hell with the rest.

He wasn't sure what had driven him—anger, need, pain. All he knew now was that he had to have her, body, soul and mind. She was wild beneath him, but no longer in resistance. Every movement was a demand that he take more, give more, and nothing seemed fast enough. She was a storm set to rage, a fire desperate to consume. Whatever he'd released inside of her had whipped out and taken him prisoner.

He pulled the shirt over her head and tossed it aside. His

heartbeat thundered. She was so small, so delicate. But he had a beast inside him that had been caged too long. He took her breast in his mouth and sent them both spinning. She tasted so fresh: a cool, clear glass of water. She smelled of woman at her most unpampered and most seductive. He felt her body arch against his, taut as a bowstring, hot as a comet. The innocence that remained so integral a part of her trembled just beneath wanton passion. No man alive could have resisted it; any man alive might have wished for it. His mouth was buried at her throat when he felt the shirt rip away from his back.

She hardly knew what she was doing. Touching him sent demands to her brain that she couldn't deny. She wanted to feel him against her, flesh to flesh, to experience an intimacy she'd so long refused to allow herself. There'd been no one else. As Liz felt her skin fused to his she understood why. There was only one Jonas. She pulled his mouth back to hers to taste him again.

He drew off her slacks so that she was naked, but she didn't feel vulnerable. She felt invulnerable. Hardly able to breathe, she struggled with his. Then she gave him no choice. Desperate for that final release, she wrapped her legs around him and drew him into her until she was filled. At the shock of that first ragged peak, her eyes flew open. Inches away, he watched her face. Her mouth trembled open, but before she could catch her breath, he was driving her higher, faster. She couldn't tell how long they balanced on the edge, trapped between pleasure and fulfillment. Then his arms came around her, hers around his. Together, they broke free.

* * *

She didn't speak. Her system leveled slowly, and she was helpless to hurry it. He didn't move. He'd shifted his weight, but his arms had come around her and stayed there. She needed him to speak, to say something that would put what had happened in perspective. She'd only had one other lover and had learned not to expect.

Jonas rested his forehead against her shoulder a moment. He was wrestling with his own demons. "I'm sorry, Liz."

He could have said nothing worse. She closed her eyes and forced her emotions to drain. She nearly succeeded. Steadier, she reached for the tangle of clothes on the floor. "I don't need an apology." With her clothes in a ball in her arm, she walked quickly to the bedroom.

On a long breath, Jonas sat up. He couldn't seem to find the right buttons on Liz Palmer. Every move he made seemed to be a move in reverse. It still stunned him that he'd been so rough with her, left her so little choice in the final outcome. He'd be better off hiring her a private bodyguard and moving himself back to the hotel. It was true he didn't want to see her hurt and felt a certain responsibility for her welfare, but he didn't seem to be able to act on it properly. When she'd stood in the kitchen telling him what she'd been through, something had begun to boil in him. That it had taken the form of passion in the end wasn't something easily explained or justified. His apology had been inadequate, but he had little else.

Drawing on his pants, Jonas started for his room. It shouldn't have surprised him to find himself veering toward Liz's. She was just pulling on a robe. "It's late, Jonas."

"Did I hurt you?"

She sent him a look that made guilt turn over in his stomach. "Yes. Now I want to take a shower before I go to bed."

"Liz, there's no excuse for being so rough, and there's no making it up to you, but—"

"Your apology hurt me," she interrupted. "Now if you've said all you have to say, I'd like to be alone."

He stared at her a moment, then dragged a hand through his hair. How could he have convinced himself he understood her when she was now and always had been an enigma? "Damn it, Liz, I wasn't apologizing for making love to you, but for the lack of finesse. I practically tossed you on the ground and ripped your clothes off."

She folded her hands and tried to keep calm. "I ripped yours."

His lips twitched, then curved. "Yeah, you did."

Humor didn't come into her eyes. "And do you want an apology?"

He came to her then and rested his hands on her shoulders. Her robe was cotton and thin and whirling with bright color. "No. I guess what I'd like is for you to say you wanted me as much as I wanted you."

Her courage weakened, so she looked beyond him. "I'd have thought that was obvious."

"Liz." His hand was gentle as he turned her face back to his.

"All right. I wanted you. Now—"

"Now," he interrupted. "Will you listen?"

"There's no need to say anything."

"Yes, there is." He walked with her to the bed and drew her down to sit. Moonlight played over their hands as he took hers. "I came to Cozumel for one reason. My feelings on that haven't changed but other things have. When I first met you, I thought you knew something, were hiding something. I linked everything about you to Jerry. It didn't take long for me to see there was something else. I wanted to know about you, for myself."

"Why?"

"I don't know. It's impossible not to care about you." At her look of surprise, he smiled. "You project this image of pure self-sufficiency and still manage to look like a waif. To-night, I purposely maneuvered you into talking about Faith and what had brought you here. When you told me, I couldn't handle it."

She drew her hand from his. "That's understandable. Most people have trouble handling unwed mothers."

Anger bubbled as he grabbed her hand again. "Stop putting words in my mouth. You stood in the kitchen talking and I could see you, young, eager and trusting, being betrayed and hurt. I could see what it had done to you, how it had closed you off from things you wanted to do."

"I told you I don't have any regrets."

"I know." He lifted her hand and kissed it. "I guess for a moment I needed to have them for you."

"Jonas, do you think anyone's life turns out the way they plan it as children?"

He laughed a little as he slipped an arm around her and drew her against him. Liz sat still a moment, unsure how to react to the casual show of affection. Then she leaned her head against his shoulder and closed her eyes. "Jerry and I were going to be partners."

"In what?"

"In anything."

She touched the coin on the end of his chain. "He had one of these."

"Our grandparents gave them to us when we were kids. They're identical five-dollar gold pieces. Funny, I always wore mine heads up. Jerry wore his heads down." He closed his fingers over the coin. "He stole his first car when we were sixteen."

Her fingers crept up to his. "I'm sorry."

"The thing was he didn't need to—we had access to any car in the garage. He told me he just wanted to see if he could get away with it."

"He didn't make life easy for you."

"No, he didn't make life easy. Especially for himself. But he never did anything out of meanness. There were times I hated him, but I never stopped loving him."

Liz drew closer. "Love hurts more than hate."

He kissed the top of her head. "Liz, I don't suppose you've ever talked to a lawyer about Faith."

"Why should I?"

"Marcus has a responsibility, a financial responsibility at the least, to you and Faith."

"I took money from Marcus once. Not again."

"Child support payments could be set up very quietly. You could stop working seven days a week."

Liz took a deep breath and pulled away until she could see his face. "Faith is my child, has been my child only since the moment Marcus handed me a check. I could have had the abortion and gone back to my life as I'd planned it. I chose not to. I chose to have the baby, to raise the baby, to support the baby. She's never given me anything but pleasure from the moment she was born, and I have no intention of sharing her."

"One day she's going to ask you for his name."

Liz moistened her lips, but nodded. "Then one day I'll tell her. She'll have her own choice to make."

He wouldn't press her now, but there was no reason he couldn't have his law clerk begin to investigate child support laws and paternity cases. "Are you going to let me meet her? I know the deal is for me to be out of the house and out of your life when she gets back. I will, but I'd like the chance to meet her."

"If you're still in Mexico."

"One more question."

The smile came more easily. "One more."

"There haven't been any other men, have there?"

The smile faded. "No."

He felt twin surges of gratitude and guilt. "Then let me show you how it should be."

"There's no need—"

Gently, he brushed the hair back from her face. "Yes, there is. For both of us." He kissed her eyes closed. "I've wanted you from the first." His mouth on hers was as sweet as spring rain and just as gentle. Slowly, he slipped the robe from her shoulders, following the trail with warm lips. "Your skin's like gold," he murmured, then traced a finger over her breasts where the tone changed. "And so pale. I want to see all of you."

"Jonas—"

"All of you," he repeated, looking into her eyes until the heat kindled again. "I want to make love with all of you."

She didn't resist. Never in her life had anyone ever touched her with such reverence, looked at her with such need. When he urged her back, Liz lay on the bed, naked and waiting.

"Lovely," Jonas murmured. Her body was milk and honey in the moonlight. And her eyes were dark—dark and open and uncertain. "I want you to trust me." He began a slow journey of exploration at her ankles. "I want to know when I look at you that you're not afraid of me."

"I'm not afraid of you."

"You have been. Maybe I've even wanted you to be. No more."

His tongue slid over her skin and teased the back of her knees. The jolt of power had her rising up and gasping. "Jonas."

"Relax." He ran a hand lightly up her hip. "I want to feel your bones melt. Lie back, Liz. Let me show you how much you can have."

She obeyed, only because she hadn't the strength to resist. He murmured to her, stroking, nibbling, until she was too steeped in what he gave to give in return. But he wanted her that way, wanted to take her as though she hadn't been touched before. Not by him, not by anyone. Slowly, thoroughly and with great, great patience he seduced and pleasured. He thought as his mouth skimmed up her thigh that he could hear her skin hum.

She'd never known anything could be like this—so deep, so dark. There was a freedom here, she discovered, that she'd once only associated with diving down through silent fathoms. Her body could float, her limbs could be weightless, but she could feel every touch, every movement. Dreamlike, sensations drifted over her, so soft, so misty, each blended into the next. How long could it go on? Perhaps, after all, there were forevers.

She was lean, with muscles firm in her legs. Like a dancer's he thought, disciplined and trained. The scent from the bowl on her dresser spiced the air, but it was her fragrance, cool as a waterfall, that swam in his head. His mind emptied of everything but the need to delight her. Love, when unselfish, has incredible power.

His tongue plunged into the heat and his hands gripped hers as she arched, stunned at being flung from a floating world to a churning one. He drew from her, both patient and relentless, until she shuddered to climax and over. When her hands went limp in his, he brought them back to his body and pleasured himself.

She hadn't known passion could stretch so far or a body endure such a barrage of sensations. His hands, rough at the palm, showed her secrets she'd never had the chance to imagine. His lips, warmed from her own skin, opened mysteries and whispered the answers. He gentled her, he enticed her, he stroked with tenderness and he devoured. Gasping for air, she had no choice but to allow him whatever he wanted, and to strain for him to show her more.

When he was inside of her, she thought it was all, and more, than she could ever want. If this was love, she'd never tasted it. If this was passion, she'd only skimmed its surface. Now it was time to risk the depths. Willing, eager, she held on to him.

It was trust he felt from her, and trust that moved him unbearably. He thought he'd needed before, desired before, but never so completely. Though he knew what it was to be part of another person, he'd never expected to feel the merger again. Strong, complex, unavoidable, the emotion swamped him. He belonged to her as fully as he'd wanted her to belong to him.

He took her slowly, so that the thrill that coursed through

her seemed endless. His skin was moist when she pressed her lips to his throat. The pulse there was as quick as her own. A giddy sense of triumph moved through her, only to be whipped away with passion before it could spread.

Then he drew her up to him, and her body, liquid and limber with emotion, rose like a wave to press against his. Wrapped close, mouths fused, they moved together. Her hair fell like rain down her back. She could feel his heartbeat fast against her breast.

Still joined, they lowered again. The rhythm quickened. Desperation rose. She heard him breathe her name before the gates burst open and she was lost in the flood.

CHAPTER 9

She woke slowly, with a long, lazy stretch. Keeping her eyes closed, Liz waited for the alarm to ring. It wasn't often she felt so relaxed, even when waking, so she pampered herself and absorbed the luxury of doing nothing. In an hour, she mused, she'd be at the dive shop shifting through the day's schedule. The glass bottom, she thought, frowning a little. Was she supposed to take it out? Odd that she couldn't remember. Then with a start, it occurred to her that she didn't remember because she didn't know. She hadn't handled the schedule in two days. And last night . . .

She opened her eyes and looked into Jonas's.

"I could watch your mind wake up." He bent over and kissed her. "Fascinating."

Liz closed her fingers over the sheet and tugged it a little higher. What was she supposed to say? She'd never spent the night with a man, never awoken with one. She cleared her throat and wondered if every man awoke as sexily disheveled as Jonas Sharpe. "How did you sleep?" she managed, and felt ridiculous.

"Fine." He smiled as he brushed her hair from her cheek with a fingertip. "And you?"

"Fine." Her fingers moved restlessly on the sheet until he closed his hands over them. His eyes were warm and heavy and made her heart pound.

"It's a little late to be nervous around me, Elizabeth."

"I'm not nervous." But color rose to her cheeks when he pressed his lips to her naked shoulder.

"Still, it's rather flattering. If you're nervous . . ." He turned his head so the tip of his tongue could toy with her ear. "Then you're not unmoved. I wouldn't like to think you felt casually about being with me—yet."

Was it possible to want so much this morning what she'd sated herself with the night before? She didn't think it should be, and yet her body told her differently. She would, as she always did, listen to her intellect first. "It must be almost time to get up." One hand firmly on the sheets, she rose on her elbows to look at the clock. "That's not right." She blinked and focused again. "It can't be eight-fifteen."

"Why not?" He slipped a hand beneath the sheet and stroked her thigh.

"Because." His touch had her pulses speeding. "I always set it for six-fifteen."

Finding her a challenge, Jonas brushed light kisses over her shoulder, down her arm. "You didn't set it last night."

"I always—" She cut herself off. It was hard enough to try to think when he was touching her, but when she remembered the night before, it was nearly impossible to understand why she had to think. Her mind hadn't been on alarms and schedules and customers when her body had curled into Jonas's to sleep. Her mind, as it was now, had been filled with him.

"Always what?"

She wished he wouldn't distract her with fingertips sliding gently over her skin. She wished he could touch her everywhere at once. "I always wake up at six, whether I set it or not."

"You didn't this time." He laughed as he eased her back down. "I suppose I should be flattered again."

"Maybe I flatter you too much," she murmured and started to shift away. He simply rolled her back to him. "I have to get up."

"No, you don't."

"Jonas, I'm already late. I have to get to work."

Sunlight dappled over her face. He wanted to see it over the rest of her. "The only thing you have to do is make love with me." He kissed her fingers, then slowly drew them from the sheet. "I'll never get through the day without you."

"The boats—"

"Are already out, I'm sure." He cupped her breast, rubbing his thumb back and forth over the nipple. "Luis seems competent."

"He is. I haven't been in for two days."

"One more won't hurt."

Her body vibrated with need that slowly wound itself into her mind. Her arms came up to him, around him. "No, I guess it won't."

* * *

She hadn't stayed in bed until ten o'clock since she'd been a child. Liz felt as irresponsible as one as she started the coffee. True, Luis could handle the shop and the boats as well as she, but it wasn't his job. It was hers. Here she was, brewing coffee at ten o'clock, with her body still warm from loving. Nothing had been the same since Jonas Sharpe had arrived on her doorstep.

"It's useless to give yourself a hard time for taking a morning off," Jonas said from behind her.

Liz popped bread into the toaster. "I suppose not, since I don't even know today's schedule."

"Liz." Jonas took her by the arms and firmly turned her around. He studied her, gauging her mood before he spoke. "You know, back in Philadelphia I'm considered a workaholic. I've had friends express concern over the workload I take on and the hours I put in. Compared to you, I'm retired."

Her brows drew together as they did when she was concentrating. Or annoyed. "We each do what we have to do."

"True enough. It appears what I have to do is harass you until you relax."

She had to smile. He said it so reasonably and his eyes were laughing. "I'm sure you have a reputation for being an expert on harassment."

"I majored in it at college."

"Good for you. But I'm an expert at budgeting my own time. And there's my toast." He let her pluck it out, waited until she'd buttered it, then took a piece for himself.

"You mentioned diving lessons."

She was still frowning at him when she heard the coffee begin to simmer. She reached for one cup, then relented and took two. "What about them?"

"I'll take one. Today."

"Today?" She handed him his coffee, drinking her own standing by the stove. "I'll have to see what's scheduled. The way things have been going, both dive boats should already be out."

"Not a group lesson, a private one. You can take me out on the *Expatriate*."

"Luis usually takes care of the private lessons."

He smiled at her. "I prefer dealing with the management."

Liz dusted crumbs from her fingers. "All right then. It'll cost you."

He lifted his cup in salute. "I never doubted it."

*   *   *

Liz was laughing when Jonas pulled into a narrow parking space at the hotel. "If he'd picked your pocket, why did you defend him?"

"Everyone's entitled to representation," Jonas reminded her. "Besides, I figured if I took him on as a client, he'd leave my wallet alone."

"And did he?"

"Yeah." Jonas took her hand as they crossed the sidewalk to the sand. "He stole my watch instead."

She giggled, a foolish, girlish sound he'd never heard from her. "And did you get him off?"

"Two years probation. There, it looks like business is good."

Liz shielded her eyes from the sun and looked toward the shop. Luis was busily fitting two couples with snorkel gear. A glance to the left showed her only the *Expatriate* remained in dock. "Cozumel's becoming very popular," she murmured.

"Isn't that the idea?"

"For business?" She moved her shoulders. "I'd be a fool to complain."

"But?"

"But sometimes I think it would be nice if I could block out the changes. I don't want to see the water choked with suntan oil. *Hola,* Luis."

"Liz!" His gaze passed over Jonas briefly before he grinned at her. "We thought maybe you deserted us. How did you like Acapulco?"

"It was . . . different," she decided, and was already scooting behind the counter to find the daily schedule. "Any problems?"

"Jose took care of a couple repairs. I brought Miguel back to fill in, but I keep an eye on him. Got this—what do you call it—brochure on the aqua bikes." He pulled out a colorful pamphlet, but Liz only nodded.

"The Brinkman party's out diving. Did we take them to Palancar?"

"Two days in a row. Miguel likes them. They tip good."

"Hmm. You're handling the shop alone."

"No problem. Hey, there was a guy." He screwed up his face as he tried to remember the name. "Skinny guy, American. You know the one you took out on the beginners' trip?"

She flipped through the receipts and was satisfied. "Try-dent?"

"*Sí,* that was it. He came by a coupla times."

"Rent anything?"

"No." Luis wiggled his eyebrows at her. "He was looking for you."

Liz shrugged it off. If he hadn't rented anything, he didn't interest her. "If everything's under control here, I'm going to take Mr. Sharpe out for a diving lesson."

Luis looked quickly at Jonas, then away. The man made him uneasy, but Liz looked happier than she had in weeks. "Want me to get the gear?"

"No, I'll take care of it." She looked up and smiled at Jonas. "Write Mr. Sharpe up a rental form and give him a receipt for the gear, the lesson and the boat trip. Since it's . . ." She trailed off as she checked her watch. "Nearly eleven, give him the half-day rate."

"You're all heart," Jonas murmured as she went to the shelves to choose his equipment.

"You got the best teacher," Luis told him, but couldn't manage more than another quick look at Jonas.

"I'm sure you're right." Idly, Jonas swiveled the newspaper Luis had tossed on the counter around to face him. He missed being able to sit down with the morning paper over coffee. The Spanish headlines told him nothing. "Anything going on I should know about?" Jonas asked, indicating the paper.

Luis relaxed a bit as he wrote. Jonas's voice wasn't so much like Jerry's when you weren't looking at him. "Haven't had a chance to look at it yet. Busy morning."

Going with habit, Jonas turned the paper over. There, in a faded black-and-white picture, was Erika. Jonas's fingers tightened. He glanced back and saw that Liz was busy, her back to him. Without a word, he slid the paper over the receipt Luis was writing.

"Hey, that's the—"

"I know," Jonas said in an undertone. "What does it say?"

Luis bent over the paper to read. He straightened again very slowly, and his face was ashen. "Dead," he whispered. "She's dead."

"How?"

Luis's fingers opened and closed on the pen he held. "Stabbed."

Jonas thought of the knife held at Liz's throat. "When?"

"Last night." Luis had to swallow twice. "They found her last night."

"Jonas," Liz called from the back, "how much do you weigh?"

Keeping his eyes on Luis, Jonas turned the paper over again. "One seventy. She doesn't need to hear this now," he added under his breath. He pulled bills from his wallet and laid them on the counter. "Finish writing the receipt."

After a struggle, Luis mastered his own fear and straightened. "I don't want anything to happen to Liz."

Jonas met the look with a challenge that held for several humming seconds before he relaxed. The smaller man was terrified, but he was thinking of Liz. "Neither do I. I'm going to see nothing does."

"You brought trouble."

"I know." His gaze shifted beyond Luis to Liz. "But if I leave, the trouble doesn't."

For the first time, Luis forced himself to study Jonas's face. After a moment, he blew out a long breath. "I liked your brother, but I think it was him who brought trouble."

"It doesn't matter anymore who brought it. I'm going to look out for her."

"Then you look good," Luis warned softly. "You look real good."

"First lesson," Liz said as she unlocked her storage closet. "Each diver carries and is responsible for his own gear." She jerked her head back to where Jonas's was stacked. With a last look at Luis, he walked through the doorway to gather it up.

"Preparing for a dive is twice as much work as diving itself," she began as she hefted her tanks. "It's a good thing it's worth it. We'll be back before sundown, Luis. *Hasta luego.*"

"Liz." She stopped, turning back to where Luis hovered in the doorway. His gaze passed over Jonas, then returned to her. *"Hasta luego,"* he managed, and closed his fingers over the medal he wore around his neck.

The moment she was on board, Liz restacked her gear. As a matter of routine, she checked all the *Expatriate*'s gauges. "Can you cast off?" she asked Jonas.

He ran a hand down her hair, surprising her. She looked so competent, so in charge. He wondered if by staying close he was protecting or endangering. It was becoming vital to believe the first. "I can handle it."

She felt her stomach flutter as he continued to stare at her. "Then you'd better stop looking at me and do it."

"I like looking at you." He drew her close, just to hold her. "I could spend years looking at you."

Her arms came up, hesitated, then dropped back to her sides. It would be so easy to believe. To trust again, give again, be hurt again. She wanted to tell him of the love growing inside her, spreading and strengthening with each moment. But if she told him she'd no longer have even the illusion of control. Without control, she was defenseless.

"I clocked you on at eleven," she said, but couldn't resist breathing deeply of his scent and committing it to memory.

Because she made him smile again, he drew her back. "I'm paying the bill, I'll worry about the time."

"Diving lesson," she reminded him. "And you can't dive until you cast off."

"Aye, aye, sir." But he gave her a hard, breath-stealing kiss before he jumped back on the dock.

Liz drew air into her lungs and let it out slowly before

she turned on the engines. All she could hope was that she looked more in control than she felt. He was winning a battle, she mused, that he didn't even know he was fighting. She waited for Jonas to join her again before she eased the throttle forward.

"There are plenty of places to dive where we don't need the boat, but I thought you'd enjoy something away from the beaches. Palancar is one of the most stunning reefs in the Caribbean. It's probably the best place to start because the north end is shallow and the wall slopes rather than having a sheer vertical drop-off. There are a lot of caves and passageways, so it makes for an interesting dive."

"I'm sure, but I had something else in mind."

"Something else?"

Jonas took a small book out of his pocket and flipped through it. "What do these numbers look like to you?"

Liz recognized the book. It was the same one he'd used in Acapulco to copy down the numbers from his brother's book in the safe-deposit box. He still had his priorities, she reminded herself, then drew back on the throttle to let the boat idle.

The numbers were in precise, neat lines. Any child who'd paid attention in geography class would recognize them. "Longitude and latitude."

He nodded. "Do you have a chart?"

He'd planned this since he'd first seen the numbers, she realized. Their being lovers changed nothing else. "Of course, but I don't need it for this. I know these waters. That's just off the coast of Isla Mujeres." Liz adjusted her course and picked up speed. Perhaps, she thought, the course had already been set for both of them long before this. They had no choice but to see it through. "It's a long trip. You might as well relax."

He put his hands on her shoulders to knead. "We won't find anything, but I have to go."

"I understand."

"Would you rather I go alone?"

She shook her head violently, but said nothing.

"Liz, this had to be his drop point. By tomorrow, Moralas will have the numbers and send his own divers down. I have to see for myself."

"You're chasing shadows, Jonas. Jerry's gone. Nothing you can do is going to change that."

"I'll find out why. I'll find out who. That'll be enough."

"Will it?" With her hand gripping the wheel hard, she looked over her shoulder. His eyes were close, but they held that cool, set look again. "I don't think so—not for you." Liz turned her face back to the sea. She would take him where he wanted to go.

Isla Mujeres, Island of Women, was a small gem in the water. Surrounded by reefs and studded with untouched lagoons, it was one of the perfect retreats of the Caribbean. Party boats from the continental coast or one of the other islands cruised there daily to offer their customers snorkeling or diving at its best. It had once been known by pirates and blessed by a goddess. Liz anchored the boat off the southwest coast. Once again, she became the teacher.

"It's important to know and understand both the name and the use of every piece of equipment. It's not just a matter of stuffing in a mouthpiece and strapping on a tank. No smoking," she added as Jonas took out a cigarette. "It's ridiculous to clog up your lungs in the first place, and absurd to do it before a dive."

Jonas set the pack on the bench beside him. "How long are we going down?"

"We'll keep it under an hour. The depth here ranges to eighty feet. That means the nitrogen in your air supply will be over three times denser than what your system's accustomed to. In some people at some depths, this can cause temporary imbalances. If you begin to feel light-headed, signal to me right away. We'll descend in stages to give your body time to get used to the changes in pressure. We ascend the same way in order to give the nitrogen time to expel. If you come up too quickly, you risk decompression sickness. It can be fatal." As she spoke, she spread out the gear with the intention of explaining each piece. "Nothing is to be taken for granted in the water. It is not your milieu. You're dependent on your equipment and your own good sense. It's beautiful and it's exciting, but it's not an amusement park."

"Is this the same lecture you give on the dive boat?"

"Basically."

"You're very good."

"Thank you." She picked up a gauge. "Now—"

"Can we get started?" he asked and reached for his wet suit.

"We are getting started. You can't dive without a working knowledge of your equipment."

"That's a depth gauge." He nodded toward her hand as he stripped down to black briefs. "A very sophisticated one. I wouldn't think most dive shops would find it necessary to stock that quality."

"This is mine," she murmured. "But I keep a handful for rentals."

"I don't think I mentioned that you have the best-tended equipment I've ever seen. It isn't in the same league with your personal gear, but it's quality. Give me a hand, will you?"

Liz rose to help him into the tough, stretchy suit. "You've gone down before."

"I've been diving since I was fifteen." Jonas pulled up the zipper before bending over to check the tanks himself.

"Since you were fifteen." Liz yanked off her shirt and tossed it aside. Fuming, she pulled off her shorts until she wore nothing but a string bikini and a scowl. "Then why did you let me go on that way?"

"I liked hearing you." Jonas glanced up and felt his blood surge. "Almost as much as I like looking at you."

She wasn't in the mood to be flattered, less in the mood to be charmed. Without asking for assistance, she tugged herself into her wet suit. "You're still paying for the lesson."

Jonas grinned as he examined his flippers. "I never doubted it."

She strapped on the rest of her gear in silence. It was difficult even for her to say if she were really angry. All she knew was the day, and dive, weren't as simple as they had started out to be. Lifting the top of a bench, she reached into a compartment and took out two short metal sticks shaped like bats.

"What's this for?" Jonas asked as she handed him one.

"Insurance." She adjusted her mask. "We're going down to the caves where the sharks sleep."

"Sharks don't sleep."

"The oxygen content in the water in the cave keeps them quiescent. But don't think you can trust them."

Without another word, she swung over the side and down the ladder.

The water was as clear as glass, so she could see for more than a hundred feet. As she heard Jonas plunge in beside her, Liz turned to assure herself he did indeed know what he was doing. Catching her skeptical look, Jonas merely circled his thumb and forefinger, then pointed down.

He was tense. Liz could feel it from him, though she understood it had nothing to do with his skill underwater. His brother had dived here once—she was as certain of it as Jonas. And the reason for his dives had been the reason for his death. She no longer had to think whether she was angry. In a gesture as personal as a kiss, she reached out a hand and took his.

Grateful, Jonas curled his fingers around hers. He didn't know what he was looking for, or even why he continued to look when already he'd found more than he'd wanted to. His brother had played games with the rules and had lost. Some would say there was justice in that. But they'd shared birth. He had to go on looking, and go on hoping.

Liz saw the first of the devilfish and tugged on Jonas's hand. Such things never failed to touch her spirit. The giant manta rays cruised together, feeding on plankton and unconcerned with the human intruders. Liz kicked forward, delighted to swim among them. Their huge mouths could crush and devour crustaceans. Their wingspan of twenty feet and more was awesome. Without fear, Liz reached out to touch. Pleasure came easily, as it always did to her in the sea. Her eyes were laughing as she reached out again for Jonas.

They descended farther, and some of his tension began to dissolve. There was something different about her here, a lightness, an ease that dissolved the sadness that always seemed to linger in her eyes. She looked free, and more, as happy as he'd ever seen her. If it were possible to fall in love in a matter of moments, Jonas fell in love in those, forty feet below the surface with a mermaid who'd forgotten how to dream.

Everything she saw, everything she could touch fascinated her. He could see it in the way she moved, the way she looked at everything as though it were her first dive. If he could have found a way, he would have stayed with her there, surrounded by love and protected by fathoms.

They swam deeper, but leisurely. If something evil had been begun, or been ended there, it had left no trace. The sea was calm and silent and full of life too lovely to exist in the air.

When the shadow passed over, Liz looked up. In all her dives, she'd never seen anything so spectacular. Thousands upon thousands of silvery grunts moved together in a wave so dense that they might have been one creature. Eyes wide with the wonder of it, Liz lifted her arms and took her body up. The wave swayed as a unit, avoiding intrusion. Delighted, she signaled for Jonas to join her. The need to share the magic was natural. This was the pull of the sea that had driven her to study, urged to explore and invited her once to dream. With her fingers linked with Jonas's, she propelled them closer. The school of fish split in half so that it became two unified forms swirling on either side of them. The sea teemed with them, thick clouds of silver so tightly grouped that they seemed fused together.

For a moment she was as close to her own fantasies as she had ever been, floating free, surrounded by magic, with her lover's hand in hers. Impulsively, she wrapped her arms around Jonas and held on. The clouds of fish swarmed around them, linked into one, then swirled away.

He could feel her pulse thud when he reached for her wrist. He could see the fascinated delight in her eyes. Hampered by his human frailty in the water, he could only touch his hand to her cheek. When she lifted her own to press it closer, it was enough. Side by side they swam toward the seafloor.

The limestone caves were eerie and compelling. Once Jonas saw the head of a moray eel slide out and curve, either in curiosity or warning. An old turtle with barnacles crusting his back rose from his resting place beneath a rock and swam between them. Then at the entrance to a cave, Liz pointed and shared another mystery.

The shark moved across the sand, as a dog might on a hearth rug. His small, black eyes stared back at them as his gills slowly drew in water. While they huddled just inside the entrance, their bubbles rising up through the porous limestone and toward the surface, the shark shifted restlessly. Jonas reached for Liz's hand to draw her back, but she moved a bit closer, anxious to see.

In a quick move, the shark shot toward the entrance. Jonas was grabbing for Liz and his knife, when she merely poked at the head with her wooden bat. Without pausing, the shark swam toward the open sea and vanished.

He wanted to strangle her. He wanted to tell her how fascinating she was to watch. Since he could do neither, Jonas merely closed a hand over her throat and gave her a mock shake. Her laughter had bubbles dancing.

They swam on together, parting from time to time to explore separate interests. He decided she'd forgotten his purpose in coming, but thought it was just as well. If she could take this hour for personal freedom, he was glad of it. For him, there were demands.

The water and the life in it were undeniably beautiful, but Jonas noticed other things. They hadn't seen another diver and their down time was nearly up. The caves where the sharks slept were also a perfect place to conceal a cache of drugs. Only the very brave or the very foolish would swim in their territory at night. He thought of his brother and knew Jerry would have considered it the best kind of adventure. A man with a reason could swim into one of the caves while the sharks were out feeding, and leave or take whatever he liked.

Liz hadn't forgotten why Jonas had come. Because she thought she could understand a part of what he was feeling, she gave him room. Here, eighty feet below the surface, he was searching for something, anything, to help him accept his brother's death. And his brother's life.

It would come to an end soon, Liz reflected. The police had the name of the go-between in Acapulco. And the other name that Jonas had given them, she remembered suddenly. Where had he gotten that one? She looked toward him and realized there were things he wasn't telling her. That, too, would end soon, she promised herself. Then she found herself abruptly out of air.

She didn't panic. Liz was too well trained to panic. Immediately, she checked her gauge and saw that she had ten full minutes left. Reaching back, she ran a hand down her hose and found it unencumbered. But she couldn't draw air.

Whatever the gauge said, her life was on the line. If she swam toward the surface, her lungs would be crushed by the pressure. Forcing herself to stay calm, she swam in a diagonal toward Jonas. When she caught his ankle, she tugged sharply. The smile he turned with faded the moment he saw her eyes. Recognizing her signal, he immediately removed his regulator and passed it to her. Liz drew in air. Nodding, she handed it back to him. Their bodies brushing, her hand firm on his shoulder, they began their slow ascent.

Buddy-breathing, they rose closer to the surface, restraining themselves from rushing. What took only a matter of minutes seemed to drag on endlessly. The moment Liz's head broke water, she pushed back her mask and gulped in fresh air.

"What happened?" Jonas demanded, but when he felt her begin to shake, he only swore and pulled her with him to the ladder. "Take it easy." His hand was firm at her back as she climbed up.

"I'm all right." But she collapsed on a bench, without the energy to draw off her tanks. Her body shuddered once with relief as Jonas took the weight from her. With her head between her knees, she waited for the mists to clear. "I've never had anything like that happen," she managed. "Not at eighty feet."

He was rubbing her hands to warm them. "What did happen?"

"I ran out of air."

Enraged, he took her by the shoulders and dragged her back to a sitting position. "Ran out of air? That's unforgivably careless. How can you give lessons when you haven't the sense to watch your own gauges?"

"I watched my gauge." She drew air in and let it out slowly. "I should have had another ten minutes."

"You rent diving equipment, for God's sake! How can you be negligent with your own? You might've died."

The insult to her competence went a long way toward smothering the fear. "I'm never careless," she snapped at him. "Not with rental equipment or my own." She dragged the mask from her head and tossed it on the bench. "Look at my gauge. I should have had ten minutes left."

He looked, but it didn't relieve his anger. "Your equipment should be checked. If you go down with a faulty gauge, you're inviting an accident."

"My equipment has been checked. I check it myself after every dive, and it was fine before I stored it. I filled those tanks myself." The alternative came to her even as she finished speaking. Her face, already pale, went white. "God, Jonas, I filled them myself. I checked every piece of equipment the last time I went down."

He closed a hand over hers hard enough to make her wince. "You keep it in the shop, in that closet."

"I lock it up."

"How many keys?"

"Mine—and an extra set in the drawer. They're rarely used because I always leave mine there when I go out on the boats."

"But the extra set would have been used when we were away?"

The shaking was starting again. This time it wasn't as simple to control it. "Yes."

"And someone used the key to the closet to get in and tamper with your equipment."

She moistened her lips. "Yes."

The rage ripped inside him until he was nearly blind with it. Hadn't he just promised to watch out for her, to keep her safe? With intensely controlled movements, he pulled off his flippers and discarded his mask. "You're going back. You're going to pack, then I'm putting you on a plane. You can stay with my family until this is over."

"No."

"You're going to do exactly what I say."

"No," she said again and managed to draw the strength to stand. "I'm not going anywhere. This is the second time someone's threatened my life."

"And they're not going to have a chance to do it again."

"I'm not leaving my home."

"Don't be a fool." He rose. Knowing he couldn't touch her, he unzipped his wet suit and began to strip it off. "Your business isn't going to fall apart. You can come back when it's safe."

"I'm not leaving." She took a step toward him. "You came

here looking for revenge. When you have it, you can leave and be satisfied. Now I'm looking for answers. I can't leave because they're here."

Struggling to keep his hands gentle, he took her face between them. "I'll find them for you."

"You know better than that, don't you, Jonas? Answers don't mean anything unless you find them yourself. I want my daughter to be able to come home. Until I find those answers, until it's safe, she can't." She lifted her hands to his face so that they stood as a unit. "We both have reasons to look now."

He sat, took his pack of cigarettes and spoke flatly. "Erika's dead."

The anger that had given her the strength to stand wavered. "What?"

"Murdered." His voice was cold again, hard again. "A few days ago I met her, paid her for a name."

Liz braced herself against the rail. "The name you gave to the captain."

Jonas lit his cigarette, telling himself he was justified to put fear back into her eyes. "That's right. She asked some questions, got some answers. She told me this Pablo Manchez was bad, a professional killer. Jerry was killed by a pro. So, it appears, was Erika."

"She was shot?"

"Stabbed," Jonas corrected and watched Liz's hand reach involuntarily for her own neck. "That's right." He drew violently on the cigarette then hurled it overboard before he rose. "You're going back to the States until this is all over."

She turned her back on him a moment, needing to be certain she could be strong. "I'm not leaving, Jonas. We have the same problem."

"Liz—"

"No." When she turned back, her chin was up and her eyes were clear. "You see, I've run from problems before, and it doesn't work."

"This isn't a matter of running, it's a matter of being sensible."

"You're staying."

"I don't have a choice."

"Then neither do I."

"Liz, I don't want you hurt."

She tilted her head as she studied him. She could believe that, she realized, and take comfort in it. "Will you go?"

"I can't. You know I can't."

"Neither can I." She wrapped her arms around him, pressed her cheek to his shoulder in a first spontaneous show of need or affection. "Let's go home," she murmured. "Let's just go home."

CHAPTER 10

Every morning when Liz awoke she was certain Captain Moralas would call to tell her it was all over. Every night when she closed her eyes, she was certain it was only a matter of one more day. Time went on.

Every morning when Liz awoke she was certain Jonas would tell her he had to leave. Every night when she slept in his arms, she was certain it was the last time. He stayed.

For over ten years her life had had a certain purpose. Success. She'd started the struggle toward it in order to survive and to provide for her child. Somewhere along the way she'd learned the satisfaction of being on her own and making it work. In over ten years, Liz had gone steadily forward without detours. A detour could mean failure and the loss of independence. It had been barely a month since Jonas had walked into her house and her life. Since that time the straight road she had followed had forked. Ignoring the changes hadn't helped, fighting them hadn't worked. Now it no longer seemed she had the choice of which path to follow.

Because she had to hold on to something, she worked every day, keeping stubbornly to her old routine. It was the only aspect of her life that she could be certain she could control. Though it brought some semblance of order to her life, it didn't keep Liz's mind at rest. She found herself studying her customers with suspicion. Business thrived as the summer season drew closer. It didn't seem as important as it had even weeks before, but she kept the shop open seven days a week.

Jonas had taken the fabric of her life, plucked at a few threads and changed everything. Liz had come to the point that she could admit nothing would ever be quite the same again, but she had yet to come to the point that she knew what to do about it. When he left, as she knew he would, she would have to learn all over again how to suppress longings and black out dreams.

They would find Jerry Sharpe's killer. They would find the man with the knife. If she hadn't believed that, Liz would never have gone on day after day. But after the danger was over, after all questions were answered, her life would never be as it had been. Jonas had woven himself into it. When he went away, he'd leave a hole behind that would take all her will to mend.

Her life had been torn before. Liz could comfort herself that she had put it together again. The shape had been different, the texture had changed, but she had put it together. She could do so again. She would have to.

There were times when she lay in bed in the dark, in the early hours of the morning, restless, afraid she would have to begin those repairs before she was strong enough.

Jonas could feel her shift beside him. He'd come to understand she rarely slept peacefully. Or she no longer slept peacefully. He wished she would lean on him, but knew she never would. Her independence was too vital, and opposingly, her insecurity was too deep to allow her to admit a need for another. Even the sharing of a burden was difficult for her. He wanted to soothe. Through his adult life, Jonas had carefully chosen companions who had no problems, required no advice, no comfort, no support. A woman who required such things required an emotional attachment he had never been willing to make. He wasn't a selfish man, simply a cautious one. Throughout his youth, and through most of his adult life, he'd picked up the pieces his brother had scattered.

Consciously or unconsciously, Jonas had promised himself he'd never be put in the position of having to do so for anyone else.

Now he was drawing closer and closer to a woman who elicited pure emotion, then tried to deflect it. He was falling in love with a woman who needed him but refused to admit it. She was strong and had both the intelligence and the will to take care of herself. And she had eyes so soft, so haunted, that a man would risk anything to protect her from any more pain.

She had completely changed his life. She had altered the simple, tidy pattern he'd been weaving for himself. He *needed* to soothe, to protect, to share. There was nothing he could do to change that. Whenever he touched her, he came closer to admitting there was nothing he would do.

The bed was warm and the room smelled of the flowers that grew wild outside the open window. Their scent mixed with the bowl of potpourri on Liz's dresser. Now and then the breeze ruffled through palm fronds so that the sound whispered but didn't disturb. Beside him was a woman whose body was slim and restless. Her hair spread over her pillow and onto his, carrying no more fragrance than wind over water. The moonlight trickled in, dipping into corners, filtering over the bed so he could trace her silhouette. As she tossed in sleep, he drew her closer. Her muscles were tense, as though she were prepared to reject the gift of comfort even before it was offered. Slowly, as her breath whispered at his throat, he began to massage her shoulders. Strong shoulders, soft skin. He found the combination irresistible. She murmured, shifting toward him, but he didn't know if it was acceptance or request. It didn't matter.

She felt so good there; she felt right there. All questions, all doubts could wait for the sunrise. Before dawn they would share the need that was in both of them. In the moonlight, in the quiet hours, each would have what the other could offer. He touched his mouth lightly, ever so lightly, to hers.

She sighed, but it was only a whisper of a sound—a sigh in sleep as her body relaxed against his. If she dreamed now, she dreamed of easy things, calm water, soft grass. He trailed a hand down her back, exploring the shape of her. Long, lean, slender and strong. He felt his own body warm and pulse. Passion, still sleepy, began to stir.

She seemed to wake in stages. First her skin, then her blood, then muscle by muscle. Her body was alert and throbbing before her mind raced to join it. She found herself wrapped around Jonas, already aroused, already hungry. When his mouth came to hers again, she answered him.

There was no hesitation in her this time, no moment of doubt before desire overwhelmed reason. She wanted to give herself to him as fully as it was possible to give. It wouldn't be wise to speak her feelings out loud. It couldn't be safe to tell him with words that her heart was stripped of defenses and open for him. But she could show him, and by doing so give them both the pleasure of love without restrictions.

Her arms tightened around him as her mouth roamed madly over his. She drew his bottom lip inside the heat, inside the moistness of her mouth and nibbled, sucked until his breath came fast and erratic. She felt the abrupt tension as his body pressed against hers and realized he, too, could be seduced. He, too, could be aroused beyond reason. And she realized with a heady sort of wonder that she could be the seducer, she could arouse.

She shifted her body under his, tentatively, but with a slow rhythm that had him murmuring her name and grasping for control. Instinctively she sought out vulnerabilities, finding them one by one, learning from them, taking from them. Her tongue flicked over his throat, seeking then enjoying the subtle, distinct taste of man. His pulse was wild there, as wild as hers. She shifted again until she lay across him and his body was hers for the taking.

Her hands were inexperienced so that her stroking was

soft and hesitant. It drove him mad. No one had ever been so sweetly determined to bring him pleasure. She pressed kisses over his chest, slowly, experimentally, then rubbed her cheek over his skin so that the touch both soothed and excited.

His body was on fire, yet it seemed to float free so that he could feel the passage of air breathe cool over his flesh. She touched, and the heat spread like brushfire. She tasted and the moistness from her lips was like the whisper of a night breeze, cooling, calming.

"Tell me what you want." She looked up and her eyes were luminous in the moonlight, dark and beautiful. "Tell me what to do."

It was almost more than he could bear, the purity of the request, the willingness to give. He reached up so that his hands were lost in her hair. He could have kept her there forever, arched above him with her skin glowing gold in the thin light, her hair falling pale over her shoulders, her eyes shimmering with need. He drew her down until their lips met again. Hunger exploded between them. She didn't need to be told, she didn't need to be taught. Her body took over so that her own desire drove them both.

Jonas let reason go, let control be damned. Gripping her hips, he drew her up, then brought her to him, brought himself into her with a force that had her gasping in astonished pleasure. As she shuddered again, then again, he reached for her hands. Their fingers linked as she arched back and let her need set the pace. Frantic. Desperate. Uncontrollable. Pleasure, pain, delight, terror all whipped through her, driving her on, thrusting her higher.

He couldn't think, but he could feel. Until that moment, he wouldn't have believed it possible to feel so much so intensely. Sensations racked him, building and building and threatening to explode until the only sound he could hear was the roar of his own heart inside his head. With his eyes half open he could see her above him, naked and glorious in the moonlight.

And when she plunged him beyond sensation, beyond sight and reason, he could still see her. He always would.

*   *   *

It didn't seem possible. It didn't, Liz thought, seem reasonable that she could be managing the shop, dealing with customers, stacking equipment when her system was still soaking up every delicious sensation she'd experienced just before dawn. Yet she was there, filling out forms, giving advice, quoting prices and making change. Still it was all mechanical. She'd been wise to delegate the diving tours and remain on shore.

She greeted her customers, some old and some new, and tried not to think too deeply about the list she'd been forced to give Moralas. How many of them would come to the Black Coral for equipment or lessons if they knew that by doing only that they were under police investigation? Jerry Sharpe's murder, and her involvement in it, could endanger her business far more than a slow season or a rogue hurricane.

Over and above her compassion, her sympathy and her hopes that Jonas could put his mind and heart at rest was a desperate need to protect her own, to guard what she'd built from nothing for her daughter. No matter how she tried to bury it, she couldn't completely block out the resentment she felt for being pulled into a situation that had been none of her making.

Yet there was a tug-of-war waging inside of her. Resentment for the disruption of her life battled against the longing to have Jonas remain in it. Without the disruption, he never would have come to her. No matter how much she tried, she could never regret the weeks they'd had together. She promised herself that she never would. It was time to admit that she had a great scope of love that had been trapped inside her. Rejected once, it had refused to risk again. But Jonas had released it, or perhaps she'd released it herself. Whatever happened, however it ended, she'd been able to love again.

"You're a hard lady to pin down."

Startled out of her own thoughts, Liz looked up. It took her a moment to remember the face, and a moment still to link a name with it. "Mr. Trydent." She rose from her desk to go to the counter. "I didn't realize you were still on the island."

"I only take one vacation a year, so I like to make the most of it." He set a tall paper cup that bounced with ice on the counter. "I figured this was the only way to get you to have a drink with me."

Liz glanced at the cup and wondered if she'd been businesslike or rude. At the moment she would have liked nothing better than to be alone with her own thoughts, but a customer was a customer. "That's nice of you. I've been pretty tied up."

"No kidding." He gave her a quick smile that showed straight teeth and easy charm. "You're either out of town or out on a boat. So I thought about the mountain and Mohammed." He glanced around. "Things are pretty quiet now."

"Lunchtime," Liz told him. "Everyone who's going out is already out. Everyone else is grabbing some food or a siesta before they decide how to spend the afternoon."

"Island living."

She smiled back. "Exactly. Tried any more diving?"

He made a face. "I let myself get talked into a night dive with Mr. Ambuckle before he headed back to Texas. I'm planning on sticking to the pool for the rest of my vacation."

"Diving's not for everyone."

"You can say that again." He drank from the second cup he'd brought, then leaned on the counter. "How about dinner? Dinner's for everyone."

She lifted a brow, a little surprised, a little flattered that he seemed bent on a pursuit. "I rarely eat out."

"I like home cooking."

"Mr. Trydent—"

"Scott," he corrected.

"Scott, I appreciate the offer, but I'm . . ." How did she put it? Liz wondered. "I'm seeing someone."

He laid a hand on hers. "Serious?"

Not sure whether she was embarrassed or amused, Liz drew her hand away. "I'm a serious sort of person."

"Well." Scott lifted his cup, watching her over the rim as he drank. "I guess we'd better stick to business then. How about explaining the snorkeling equipment to me?"

With a shrug, Liz glanced over her shoulder. "If you can swim, you can snorkel."

"Let's just say I'm cautious. Mind if I come in and take a look?"

She'd been ungracious enough for one day, Liz decided. She sent him a smile. "Sure, look all you want." When he'd skirted around the counter and through the door, she walked with him to the back shelves. "The snorkel's just a hollow tube with a mouthpiece," she began as she took one down to offer it. "You put this lip between your teeth and breathe normally through your mouth. With the tube attached to a face mask, you can paddle around on the surface indefinitely."

"Okay. How about all the times I see these little tubes disappear under the water?"

"When you want to go down, you hold your breath and let out a bit of air to help you descend. The trick is to blow out and clear the tube of water when you surface. Once you get the knack, you can go down and up dozens of times without ever taking your face out of the water."

Scott turned the snorkel over in his hand. "There's a lot to see down there."

"A whole world."

He was no longer looking at the snorkel, but at her. "I guess you know a lot about the water and the reefs in this area. Know much about Isla Mujeres?"

"Excellent snorkeling and diving." Absently, Liz took down a mask to show him how to attach the snorkel. "We offer full- and half-day trips. If you're adventurous enough, there are caves to explore."

"And some are fairly remote," he said idly.

"For snorkeling you'd want to stay closer to the reefs, but an experienced diver could spend days around the caves."

"And nights." Scott passed the snorkel through his fingers as he watched her. "I imagine a diver could go down there at night and be completely undisturbed."

She wasn't certain why she felt a trickle of alarm. Automatically, she glanced over his shoulder to where her police guard half dozed in the sun. Silly, she told herself with a little shrug. She'd never been one to jump at shadows. "It's a dangerous area for night diving."

"Some people prefer danger, especially when it's profitable."

Her mouth was dry, so she swallowed as she replaced the mask on the shelf. "Perhaps. I don't."

This time his smile wasn't so charming or his eyes so friendly. "Don't you?"

"I don't know what you mean."

"I think you do." His hand closed over her arm. "I think you know exactly what I mean. What Jerry Sharpe skimmed off the top and dumped in that safe-deposit box in Acapulco was petty cash, Liz." He leaned closer as his voice lowered. "There's a lot more to be made. Didn't he tell you?"

She had a sudden, fierce memory of a knife probing against her throat. "He didn't tell me anything. I don't know anything." Before she could evade, he had her backed into a corner. "If I scream," she managed in a steady voice, "there'll be a crowd of people here before you can take a breath."

"No need to scream." He held up both hands as if to show her he meant no harm. "This is a business discussion. All I want to know is how much Jerry told you before he made the mistake of offending the wrong people."

When she discovered she was trembling, Liz forced herself to stop. He wouldn't intimidate her. What weapon could he hide in a pair of bathing trunks and an open shirt? She straightened her shoulders and looked him directly in the eye. "Jerry didn't tell me anything. I said the same thing to your friend when he had the knife at my throat. It didn't satisfy him, so he put a damaged gauge on my tanks."

"My partner doesn't understand much about finesse," Scott said easily. "I don't carry knives, and I don't know enough about your diving equipment to mess with the gauges. What I know about is you, and I know plenty. You work too hard, Liz, getting up at dawn and hustling until sundown. I'm just trying to give you some options. Business, Liz. We're just going to talk business."

It was his calm, reasonable attitude that had her temper whipping out. He could be calm, he could be reasonable, and people were dead. "I'm not Jerry and I'm not Erika, so keep that in mind. I don't know anything about the filthy business you're into, but the police do, and they'll know more. If you think you can frighten me by threatening me with a knife or damaging my equipment, you're right. But that doesn't stop me from wishing every one of you to hell. Now get out of my shop and leave me alone."

He studied her face for a long ten seconds, then backed an inch or two away. "You've got me wrong, Liz. I said this was a business discussion. With Jerry gone, an experienced diver would come in handy, especially one who knows the waters around here. I'm authorized to offer you five thousand dollars. Five thousand American dollars for doing what you do best. Diving. You go down, drop off one package and pick up another. No names, no faces. Bring the package back to me unopened and I hand you five thousand in cash. Once or twice a week, and you can build up a nice little nest egg. I'd say a woman raising a kid alone could use some extra money."

Fear had passed into fury; she clenched her hands together. "I told you to get out," she repeated. "I don't want your money."

He smiled and touched a finger to her cheek. "Give it some thought. I'll be around if you change your mind."

Liz waited for her breathing to level as she watched him walk away. With deliberate movements, she locked the shop, then walked directly to her police guard. "I'm going home," she told him as he sprang to attention. "Tell Captain Moralas to meet me there in half an hour." Without waiting for a reply, she strode across the sand.

*   *   *

Fifteen minutes later, Liz slammed into her house. The ride home hadn't calmed her. At every turn she'd been violated. At every turn, her privacy and peace had been disrupted. This last incident was the last she'd accept. She might have been able to handle another threat, another demand. But he'd offered her a job. Offered to pay her to smuggle cocaine, to take over the position of a man who'd been murdered. Jonas's brother.

A nightmare, Liz thought as she paced from window to window. She wished she could believe it was a nightmare. The cycle was drawing to a close, and she felt herself being trapped in the center. What Jerry Sharpe had started, she and Jonas would be forced to finish, no matter how painful. No matter how deadly. Finish it she would, Liz promised herself. The cycle would be broken, no matter what she had to do. She would be finished with it so her daughter could come home safely. Whatever she had to do, she would see to that.

At the sound of a car approaching, Liz went to the front window. Jonas, she thought, and felt her heart sink. Did she tell him now that she'd met face-to-face with the man who might have killed his brother? If he had the name, if he knew the man, would he race off in a rage for the revenge he'd come so far to find? And if he found his revenge, could the cycle ever be broken? Instead, she was afraid it would revolve and revolve around them, smothering everything else. She saw Jonas, a man of the law, a man of patience and compassion, shackled forever within the results of his own violence. How could she save him from that and still save herself?

Her hand was cold as she reached for the door and opened it to meet him. He knew there was something wrong before he touched her. "What are you doing home? I went by the shop and it was closed."

"Jonas." She did the only thing she knew how. She drew him against her and held on. "Moralas is on his way here."

"What happened?" A little skip of panic ran through him before he could stop it. He held her away, searching her face. "Did something happen to you? Were you hurt?"

"No, I'm not hurt. Come in and sit down."

"Liz, I want to know what happened."

She heard the sound of a second engine and looked down the street to see the unmarked car. "Moralas is here," she murmured. "Come inside, Jonas. I'd rather go through this only once."

There was really no decision to be made, Liz told herself as she moved away from the door to wait. She would give Moralas and Jonas the name of the man who had approached her. She would tell them exactly what he'd said. By doing so she would take herself one step further away from the investigation. They would have a name, a face, a location. They would have motive. It was what the police wanted, it was what she wanted. She glanced at Jonas as Moralas came up the front walk. It was what Jonas wanted. What he needed. And by giving it to him, she would take herself one step further way from him.

"Miss Palmer." Moralas took off his hat as he entered, glanced briefly at Jonas and waited.

"Captain." She stood by a chair but didn't sit. "I have some information for you. There's an American, a man named Scott Trydent. Less than an hour ago he offered me five thousand dollars to smuggle cocaine off the reef of Isla Mujeres."

Moralas's expression remained impassive. He tucked his hat under his arm. "And have you had previous dealings with this man?"

"He joined one of my diving classes. He was friendly. Today he came by the shop to talk to me. Apparently he believed that I . . ." She trailed off to look at Jonas. He stood very still and very quiet just inside the door. "He thought that Jerry had told me about the operation. He'd found out about the safe-deposit box. I don't know how. It was as though he knew every move I've made for weeks." As her nerves began to fray, she dragged a hand through her hair. "He told me that I could take over Jerry's position, make the exchange in the caves near Isla Mujeres and be rich. He knows . . ." She had to swallow to keep her voice from trembling. "He knows about my daughter."

"You would identify him?"

"Yes. I don't know if he killed Jerry Sharpe." Her gaze shifted to Jonas again and pleaded. "I don't know, but I could identify him."

Moralas watched the exchange before crossing the room. "Please sit down, Miss Palmer."

"You'll arrest him?" She wanted Jonas to say something, anything, but he continued to stand in silence. "He's part of the cocaine ring. He knows about Jerry Sharpe's murder. You have to arrest him."

"Miss Palmer." Moralas urged her down on the sofa, then sat beside her. "We have names. We have faces. The smuggling ring currently operating in the Yucatan Peninsula is under investigation by both the Mexican and the American governments. The names you and Mr. Sharpe have given me are not unfamiliar. But there is one we don't have. The person who organizes, the person who undoubtedly ordered the murder of Jerry Sharpe. This is the name we need. Without it, the arrest of couriers, of salesmen, is nothing. We need this name, Miss Palmer. And we need proof."

"I don't understand. You mean you're just going to let Trydent go? He'll just find someone else to make the drops."

"It won't be necessary for him to look elsewhere if you agree."

"No." Before Liz could take in Moralas's words, Jonas was breaking in. He said it quietly, so quietly that chills began to race up and down her spine. He took out a cigarette. His hands were rock steady. Taking his time, he flicked his lighter and drew until the tip glowed red. He blew out a stream of smoke and locked his gaze on Moralas. "You can go to hell."

"Miss Palmer has the privilege to tell me so herself."

"You're not using her. If you want someone on the inside, someone closer to the names and proof, I'll make the drop."

Moralas studied him, saw the steady nerves and untiring patience along with simmering temper. If he'd had a choice, he'd have preferred it. "It isn't you who has been asked."

"Liz isn't going down."

"Just a minute." Liz pressed both hands to her temples. "Are you saying you want me to see Trydent again, to tell him I'll take the job? That's crazy. What purpose could there be?"

"You would be a decoy." Moralas glanced down at her hands. Delicate, yes, but strong. There was nothing about Elizabeth Palmer he didn't know. "The investigation is closing in. We don't want the ring to change locations at this point. If the operation appears to go smoothly, there should be no move at this time. You've been the stumbling block, Miss Palmer, for the ring, and the investigation."

"How?" Furious, she started to stand. Moralas merely put a hand on her arm.

"Jerry Sharpe lived with you, worked for you. He had a weakness for women. Neither the police nor the smugglers have been sure exactly what part you played. Jerry Sharpe's brother is now living in your home. The key to the safe-deposit box was found by you."

"Guilty by association, Captain?" Her voice took on that ice-sharp edge Jonas had heard only once or twice before. "Have I had police protection, or have I been under surveillance?"

Moralas's tone never altered. "One serves the same purpose as the other."

"If I'm under suspicion, haven't you considered that I might simply take the money and run?"

"That's precisely what we want you to do."

"Very clever." Jonas wasn't certain how much longer he could hold on to his temper. It would have given him great satisfaction to have picked Moralas up bodily and thrown him out of the house. Out of Liz's life. "Liz double-crosses them, annoying the head of the operation. It's then necessary to eliminate her the way my brother was eliminated."

"Except that Miss Palmer will be under police protection at all times. If this one drop goes as we plan, the investigation will end, and the smugglers, along with your brother's killer, will be caught and punished. This is what you want?"

"Not if it means risking Liz. Plant your own pigeon, Moralas."

"There isn't time. With your cooperation, Miss Palmer, we can end this. Without it, it could take months."

Months? she thought. Another day would be a lifetime. "I'll do it."

Jonas was beside her in a heartbeat, pulling her off the couch. "Liz—"

"My daughter comes home in two weeks." She put her hands on his arms. "She won't come back to anything like this."

"Take her someplace else." Jonas gripped her shoulders until his fingers dug into flesh. "We'll go someplace else."

"Where?" she demanded. "Every day I tell myself I'm pulling away from this thing and every day it's a lie. I've been in it since Jerry walked in the door. We can't change that. Until it's over, really over, nothing's going to be right."

He knew she was right, had known it from the first moment. But too much had changed. There was a desperation in him now that he'd never expected to feel. It was all for her. "Come back to the States with me. It will be over."

"Will it? Will you forget your brother was murdered? Will you forget the man who killed him?" His fingers tightened, his eyes darkened, but he said nothing. Her breath came out in a sigh of acceptance. "No, it won't be over until we finish it. I've run before, Jonas. I promised myself I'd never run again."

"You could be killed."

"I've done nothing and they've nearly killed me twice." She dropped her head on his chest. "Please help me."

He couldn't force her to bend his way. Two of the things he most admired in her were her capacity to give and her will to stand firm. He could plead with her, he could argue, but he could never lie. If she ran, if they ran, they'd never be free of it. His arm came around her. Her hair smelled of summer and sea air. And before the summer ended, he promised himself, she'd be free. They'd both be free.

"I go with her." He met Moralas's eyes over her head.

"That may not be possible."

"I'll make it possible."

CHAPTER 11

She'd never been more frightened in her life. Every day she worked in the shop, waiting for Scott Trydent to approach. Every evening she locked up, went home and waited for the phone to ring. Jonas said little. She no longer knew what he did with the hours they were apart, but she was aware that he was planning his own move, in his own time. It only frightened her more.

Two days passed until her nerves were stretched thinner and tighter than she would have believed possible. On the beach, people slept or read novels, lovers walked by arm in arm. Children chattered and ran. Snorkelers splashed around the reef. She wondered why nothing seemed normal, or if it ever would again. At sundown she emptied her cash box, stacked gear and began to lock up.

"How about that drink?"

Though she'd thought she'd braced herself for the moment when it would begin, Liz jolted. Her head began to throb in a slow, steady rhythm she knew would last for hours. In the pit of her stomach she felt the twist come and go from panicked excitement. From this point on, she reminded herself, she had no room to panic. She turned and looked at Scott. "I was wondering if you'd come back."

"Told you I'd be around. I always figure people need a couple of days to mull things over."

She had a part to play, Liz reminded herself. She had to do it well. Carefully, she finished locking up, then turned back to him. She didn't smile. It was to be a business discussion, cut-and-dried. "We can get a drink over there." She pointed to the open-air thatched-roof restaurant overhanging the reef. "It's public."

"Suits me." Though he offered his hand, she ignored it and began to walk.

"You used to be friendlier."

"You used to be a customer." She sent him a sideways look. "Not a business partner."

"So . . ." She saw him glance right, then left. "You've mulled."

"You need a diver, I need money." Liz walked up the two wooden stairs and chose a chair that had her back to the water. Seconds after she sat, a man settled himself into a corner table. One of Moralas's, she thought, and ordered herself to be calm. She'd been briefed and rebriefed. She knew what to say, how to say it, and that the waiter who would serve them carried a badge and a gun. "Jerry didn't tell me a great deal," she began, and ordered an American soft drink. "Just that he made the drop and collected the money."

"He was a good diver."

Liz swallowed the little bubble of fear. "I'm better."

Scott grinned at her. "So I'm told."

A movement beside her had her glancing over, then freezing. A dark man with a pitted face took the chair beside her. Liz knew he wore a thin silver band on his wrist before she looked for it.

"Pablo Manchez, Liz Palmer. Though I think you two have met."

"*Señorita.*" Manchez's thin mouth curved as he took her hand.

"Tell your friend to keep his hands to himself." Calmly, Jonas pulled a chair up to the table. "Why don't you introduce me, Liz?" When she could do no more than stare at him, he settled back. "I'm Jonas Sharpe. Liz and I are partners." He leveled his gaze to Manchez. This was the man, he thought, whom he'd come thousands of miles to see. This was the man he'd kill. Jonas felt the hatred and the fury rise. But he knew how to strap the emotions and wait. "I believe you knew my brother."

Manchez's hand dropped from Liz's and went to his side. "Your brother was greedy and stupid."

Liz held her breath as Jonas reached in his pocket. Slowly, he pulled out his cigarettes. "I'm greedy," he said easily as he lit one. "But I'm not stupid. I've been looking for you." He leaned across the table. With a slow smile, he offered Manchez the cigarettes.

Manchez took one and broke off the filter. His hands were beautiful, with long spidery fingers and narrow palms. Liz fought back a shudder as she looked at them. "So you found me."

Jonas was still smiling as he ordered a beer. "You need a diver."

Scott sent Manchez a warning look. "We have a diver."

"What you have is a team. Liz and I work together." Jonas blew out a stream of smoke. "Isn't that right, Liz?"

He wanted them. He wasn't going to back off until he had them. And she had no choice. "That's right."

"We don't need no team." Manchez started to rise.

"You need us." Jonas took his beer as it was served. "We already know a good bit about your operation. Jerry wasn't good at keeping secrets." Jonas took a swig from the bottle. "Liz and I are more discreet. Five thousand a drop?"

Scott waited a beat, then held a hand up, signaling Manchez. "Five. If you want to work as a team, it's your business how you split it."

"Fifty-fifty." Liz spread her fingers around Jonas's beer. "One of us goes down, one stays in the dive boat."

"Tomorrow night. Eleven o'clock. You come to the shop. Go inside. You'll find a waterproof case. It'll be locked."

"So will the shop," Liz put in. "How does the case get in-side?"

Manchez blew smoke between his teeth. "I got no prob-lem getting in."

"Just take the case," Scott interrupted. "The coordinates will be attached to the handle. Take the boat out, take the case down, leave it. Then come back up and wait exactly an hour. That's when you dive again. All you have to do is take the case that's waiting for you back to the shop and leave it."

"Sounds smooth," Jonas decided. "When do we get paid?"

"After you do the job."

"Half up front." Liz took a long swallow of beer and hoped her heart would settle. "Leave twenty-five hundred with the case or I don't dive."

Scott smiled. "Not as trusting as Jerry."

She gave him a cold, bitter look. "And I intend to stay alive."

"Just follow the rules."

"Who makes them?" Jonas took the beer back from Liz. Her hand slipped down to his leg and stayed steady.

"You don't want to worry about that," Manchez advised. The cigarette was clamped between his teeth as he smiled. "He knows who you are."

"Just follow the coordinates and keep an eye on your watch." Scott dropped bills on the table as he rose. "The rest is gravy."

"Stay smart, Jerry's brother." Manchez gave them both a slow smile. *"Adios, señorita."*

Jonas calmly finished his beer as the two men walked away.

"You weren't supposed to interfere during the meeting," Liz began in a furious undertone. "Moralas said—"

"The hell with Moralas." He crushed out his cigarette, watching as the smoke plumed up. "Is that the man who put the bruises on your neck?"

Her hand moved up before she could stop it. Halfway to her throat, Liz curled her fingers into a ball and set her hand on the table. "I told you I didn't see him."

Jonas turned his head. His eyes, as they had before, reminded her of frozen smoke. "Was it the man?"

He didn't need to be told. Liz leaned closer and spoke softly. "I want it over, Jonas. And I don't need revenge. You were supposed to let me meet with Scott and set things up by myself."

In an idle move, he tilted the candle on the table toward him and lit it. "I changed my mind."

"Damn you, you could've messed everything up. I don't want to be involved but I am. The only way to get uninvolved is to finish it. How do we know they won't just back off now that you've come into it?"

"Because you're right in the middle, and you always have been." Before she could speak, he took her arm. His face was close, his voice cool and steady. "I was going to use you. From the minute I walked into your house, I was going to use you to get to Jerry's killer. If I had to walk all over you, if I had to knock you out of the way or drag you along with me, I was going to use you. Just the way Moralas is going to use you. Just the way the others are going to use you." The heat of the candle flickered between them as he drew her closer. "The way Jerry used you."

She swallowed the tremor and fought against the pain. "And now?"

He didn't speak. They were so close that he could see himself reflected in her eyes. In them, surrounding his own reflection, he saw the doubts and the defiance. His hand came to the back of her neck, held there until he could feel the rhythm of her pulse. With a simmering violence, he pulled her against him and covered her mouth with his. A flare that was passion, a glimmer that was hope—he didn't know which to reach for. So he let her go.

"No one's going to hurt you again," he murmured. "Especially not me."

* * *

It was the longest day of her life. Liz worked and waited as the hours crawled by. Moralas's men mixed with the vacationers on the beach. So obviously, it seemed to Liz, that she wondered everyone else didn't notice them as though they wore badges around their necks. Her boats went out, returned and went out again. Tanks and equipment were checked and rented. She filled out invoices and accepted credit cards as if there were some importance to daily routine. She wished for the day to end. She hoped the night would never come.

A thousand times she thought of telling Moralas she couldn't go through with it. A thousand times she called herself a coward. But as the sun went down and the beach began to clear, she realized courage wasn't something that could be willed into place. She would run, if she had the choice. But as long as she was in danger, Faith was in danger. When the sun went down, she locked the shop as if it were the end of any ordinary day. Before she'd pocketed her keys, Jonas was beside her.

"There's still time to change your mind."

"And do what? Hide?" She looked out at the beach, at the sea, at the island that was her home. And her prison. Why had she never seen it as a prison until Jonas had come to it? "You've already told me how good I am at hiding."

"Liz—"

She shook her head to stop him. "I can't talk about it. I just have to do it."

They drove home in silence. In her mind, Liz went over her instructions, every point, every word Moralas had pushed at her. She was to follow the routine, make the exchange, then turn the case with the money over to the police who'd

be waiting near the dock. She'd wait for the next move. And
while she waited, she'd never be more than ten feet away
from a cop. It sounded foolproof. It made her stomach churn.

There was a man walking a dog along the street in front
of her house. One of Moralas's men. The man whittling on
her neighbor's porch had a gun under his denim vest. Liz tried
to look at neither of them.

"You're going to have a drink, some food and a nap," Jonas ordered as he steered her inside.

"Just the nap."

"The nap first then." After securing the lock, Jonas followed her into the bedroom. He lowered the shades. "Do you
want anything?"

It was still so hard to ask. "Would you lie down with me?"

He came to her. She was already curled on her side, so he
drew her back against him and wrapped her close. "Will you
sleep?"

"I think so." In sleep she could find escape, if only temporarily. But she didn't close her eyes. "Jonas?"

"Hmm?"

"After tonight—after we've finished, will you hold me like
this again?"

He pressed his lips to her hair. He didn't think he could
love her any more. He was nearly certain if he told her she'd
pull away. "As long as you want. Just sleep."

Liz let her eyes close and her mind empty.

* * *

The case was small, the size of an executive brief-case.
It seemed too inconspicuous to be the catalyst for so
much danger. Beside it, on the counter of Liz's shop, was an
envelope. Inside was a slip of paper with longitude and latitude printed. With the slip of paper were twenty-five one-
hundred-dollar bills.

"They kept their part of the bargain," Jonas commented.

Liz merely shoved the envelope into a drawer. "I'll get my equipment."

Jonas watched her. She'd rather do this on her own, he reflected. She'd rather not think she had someone to lean on, to turn to. He took her tanks before she could heft them. She was going to learn, he reminded himself, that she had a great deal more than that. "The coordinates?"

"The same that were in Jerry's book." She found herself amazingly calm as she waited to lock the door behind him. They were being watched. She was aware that Moralas had staked men in the hotel. She was just as certain Manchez was somewhere close. She and Jonas didn't speak again until they were on the dive boat and had cast off. "This could end it." She glanced at him as she set her course.

"This could end it."

She was silent for a moment. All during the evening hours she'd thought about what she would say to him, how she would say it. "Jonas, what will you do?"

The flame of his lighter hissed, flared, then was quiet. "What I have to do."

The fear tasted like copper in her mouth, but it had nothing to do with herself and everything to do with Jonas. "If we make the exchange tonight, turn the second case over to Moralas. They'll have to come out in the open. Manchez, and the man who gives the orders."

"What are you getting at, Liz?"

"Manchez killed your brother."

Jonas looked beyond her. The sea was black. The sky was black. Only the hum of the motor broke the silence. "He was the trigger."

"Are you going to kill him?"

Slowly, he turned back to her. The question had been quiet, but her eyes weren't. They sent messages, posed argument, issued pleas. "It doesn't involve you."

That hurt deeply, sharply. With a nod, she followed the

shimmer of light on the water. "Maybe not. But if you let hate rule what you do, how you think, you'll never be free of it. Manchez will be dead, Jerry will still be dead and you . . ." She turned to look at him again. "You'll never really be alive again."

"I didn't come all this way, spend all this time, to let Manchez walk away. He kills for money and because he enjoys it. He enjoys it," Jonas repeated viciously. "You can see it in his eyes."

And she had. But she didn't give a damn about Manchez. "Do you remember telling me once that everyone was entitled to representation?"

He remembered. He remembered everything he'd once believed in. He remembered how Jerry had looked in the cold white light of the morgue. "It didn't have anything to do with this."

"I suppose you change the rules when it's personal."

"He was my brother."

"And he's dead." With a sigh she lifted her face so that the wind could cool her skin. "I'm sorry, Jonas. Jerry's dead and if you go through with what you've planned, you're going to kill something in yourself." And, though she couldn't tell him, something in her. "Don't you trust the law?"

He tossed his cigarette into the water, then leaned on the rail. "I've been playing with it for years. It's the last thing I'd trust."

She wanted to go to him but didn't know how. Still, no matter what he did, she was beside him. "Then you'll have to trust yourself. And so will I."

Slowly, he crossed to her. Taking her face in his hands, he tried to understand what she was telling him, what she was still holding back. "Will you?"

"Yes."

He leaned to press a kiss to her forehead. Inside there was a need, a fierce desire to tell her to head the boat out to sea and keep going. But that would never work, not for either of them. They stood on the boat together, and stood at the crossroads. "Then start now." He kissed her again before he turned and lifted one of the compartment seats. Liz frowned as she saw the wet suit.

"What are you doing?"

"I arranged to have Luis leave this here for me."

"Why? We can't both go down."

Jonas stripped down to his trunks. "That's right. I'm diving, you're staying with the boat."

Liz stood very straight. It wouldn't do any good to lose her temper. "The arrangements were made on all sides, Jonas. I'm diving."

"I'm changing the arrangements." He tugged the wet suit up to his waist before he looked at her. "I'm not taking any more chances with you."

"You're not taking chances with me. I am. Jonas, you don't know these waters. I do. You've never gone down here at night. I have."

"I'm about to."

"The last thing we need right now is for you to start behaving like an overprotective man."

He nearly laughed as he snapped the suit over his shoulders. "That's too bad, then, because that's just what we've got."

"I told Manchez and Trydent I was going down."

"I guess your reputation's shot when you lie to murderers and drug smugglers."

"Jonas, I'm not in the mood for jokes."

He strapped on his diver's knife, adjusted his weight belt, then reached for his mask. "Maybe not. And maybe you're not in the mood to hear this. I care about you. Too damn much." He reached out, gripping her chin. "My brother dragged you into this because he never wasted two thoughts about anyone else in his life. I pulled you in deeper because all I was thinking about was payback. Now I'm thinking about you, about us. You're not going down. If I have to tie you to the wheel, you're not going down."

"I don't want you to go." She balled her fists against his chest. "If I was down, all I'd think about was what I was doing. If I stay up here, I won't be able to stop thinking about what could happen to you."

"Time me." He lifted the tanks and held them out to her. "Help me get them on."

Hadn't she told herself weeks before that he wasn't a man who'd lose an argument? Her hands trembled a bit as she slipped the straps over his shoulders. "I don't know how to handle being protected."

He hooked the tanks as he turned back to her. "Practice."

She closed her eyes. It was too late for talk, too late for arguments. "Bear northeast as you dive. The cave's at eighty feet." She hesitated only a moment, then picked up a spear gun. "Watch out for sharks."

When he was over the side, she lowered the case to him. In seconds, he was gone and the sea was black and still. In her mind, Liz followed him fathom by fathom. The water would be dark so that he would be dependent on his gauges and the thin beam of light. Night creatures would be feeding. Squid, the moray, barracuda. Sharks. Liz closed her mind to it.

She should have forced him to let her go. How? Pacing the deck, she pushed the hair back from her face. He'd gone to protect her. He'd gone because he cared about her. Shivering, she sat down to rub her arms warm again. Was this what it was like to be cared for by a man? Did it mean you had to sit and wait? She was up again and pacing. She'd lived too much of her life doing to suddenly become passive. And yet . . . To hear him say he cared. Liz sat again and waited.

She'd checked her watch four times before she heard him at the ladder. On a shudder of relief, she dashed over to the side to help him. "I'm going down the next time," she began.

Jonas pulled off his light, then his tanks. "Forget it." Before she could protest, he dragged her against him. "We've got an hour," he murmured against her ear. "You want to spend it arguing?"

He was wet and cold. Liz wrapped herself around him. "I don't like being bossed around."

"Next time you can boss me around." He dropped onto a bench and pulled her with him. "I'd forgotten what it was like down there at night. Fabulous." And it was nearly over, he told himself. The first step had been taken, the second one had to follow. "I saw a giant squid. Scared the hell out of him with the light. I swear he was thirty feet long."

"They get bigger." She rested her head on his shoulder and tried to relax. They had an hour. "I was diving with my father once. We saw one that was nearly sixty."

"Made you nervous?"

"No. I was fascinated. I remember I swam close enough to touch the tentacles. My father gave me a twenty-minute lecture when we surfaced."

"I imagine you'd do the same thing with Faith."

"I'd be proud of her," Liz began, then laughed. "Then I'd give her a twenty-minute lecture."

For the first time that night he noticed the stars. The sky was alive with them. It made him think of his mother's porch swing and long summer nights. "Tell me about her."

"You don't want to get me started."

"Yes, I do." He slipped an arm around her shoulder. "Tell me about her."

With a half smile, Liz closed her eyes. It was good to think of Faith, to talk of Faith. A picture began to emerge for Jonas of a young girl who liked school because there was plenty to do and lots of people. He heard the love and the pride, and the wistfulness. He saw the dark, sunny-faced girl in the photo and learned she spoke two languages, liked basketball and hated vegetables.

"She's always been sweet," Liz reflected. "But she's no angel. She's very stubborn, and when she's crossed, her temper isn't pretty. Faith wants to do things herself. When she was two, she'd get very annoyed if I wanted to help her down the stairs."

"Independence seems to run in the family."

Liz moved her shoulders. "We've needed it."

"Ever thought about sharing?"

Her nerves began to hum. Though she shifted only a bit, it was away from him. "When you share, you have to give something up. I've never been able to afford to give up anything."

It was an answer he'd expected. It was an answer he intended to change. "It's time to go back down."

Liz helped him back on with his tanks. "Take the spear gun. Jonas . . ." He was already at the rail before she ran to him. "Hurry back," she murmured. "I want to go home. I want to make love with you."

"Hell of a time to bring that up." He sent her a grin, curled and fell back into the water.

Within five minutes Liz was pacing again. Why hadn't she thought to bring any coffee? She'd concentrate on that. In little more than an hour they could be huddled in her kitchen with a pot brewing. It wouldn't matter that there would be police surrounding the house. She and Jonas would be inside. Together. Perhaps she was wrong about sharing. Perhaps . . . When she heard the splash at the side of the boat, she was at the rail like a shot.

"Jonas, did something happen? Why—" She found herself looking down the barrel of a .22.

"*Señorita.*" Manchez tossed his mask and snorkel onto a bench as he climbed over the side. "*Buenas noches.*"

"What are you doing here?" She struggled to sound indignant as the blood rushed from her face. No, she wasn't brave, she realized. She wasn't brave at all. "We had a deal."

"You're an amateur," he told her. "Like Sharpe was an amateur. You think we'd just forget about the money?"

"I don't know anything about the money Jerry took." She gripped the rail. "I've told you that all along."

"The boss decided you were a loose end, pretty lady. You do us a favor and make this delivery. We do you a favor. We kill you quickly."

She didn't look at the gun again. She didn't dare. "If you keep killing your divers, you're going to be out of business."

"We're finished in Cozumel. When your friend brings up the case, I take it and go to Merida. I live in style. You don't live at all."

She wanted to sit because her knees were shaking. She stood because she thought she might never be able to again. "If you're finished in Cozumel, why did you set up this drop?"

"Clancy likes things tidy."

"Clancy?" The name David Merriworth had mentioned, Liz remembered, and strained to hear any sound from the water.

"There's a few thousand in cocaine down there, that's all. A few thousand dollars in the case coming up. The boss figures it's worth the investment to make it look like you were doing the dealing with Sharpe. Then you two have an argument and shoot each other. Case closed."

"You killed Erika, too, didn't you?"

"She asked too many questions." He lowered the gun. "You ask too many questions."

Light flooded the boat and the water so quickly that Liz's first instinct was to freeze. Before the next reaction had fully registered, she was tumbling into the water and diving blind.

How could she warn Jonas? Liz groped frantically in the water as lights played on the surface above her. She had no tanks, no mask, no protection. Any moment he'd be surfacing, unaware of any danger. He had no protection but her.

Without equipment, she'd be helpless in a matter of moments. She fought to stay down, keeping as close to the ladder as she dared. Her lungs were ready to burst when she felt the movement in the water. Liz turned toward the beam of light.

When he saw her, his heart nearly stopped. She looked like a ghost clinging to the hull of the boat. Her hair was pale and floating out in the current, her face was nearly as white as his light. Before his mind could begin to question, he was pushing his mouthpiece between her lips and giving her air. There could be no communication but emotion. He felt the fear. Jonas steadied the spear gun in his arm and surfaced.

"Mr. Sharpe." Moralas caught him in the beam of a spotlight. Liz rose up beside him. "We have everything under control." On the deck of her boat, Liz saw Manchez handcuffed and flanked by two divers. "Perhaps you will give my men and their prisoner a ride back to Cozumel."

She felt Jonas tense. The spear gun was set and aimed. Even through the mask, she could see his eyes burning, burning as only ice can. "Jonas, please." But he was already starting up the ladder. She hauled herself over the rail and tumbled onto the deck, cold and dripping. "Jonas, you can't. Jonas, it's over."

He barely heard her. All his emotion, all his concentration was on the man who stood only feet away. Their eyes were locked. It gave him no satisfaction to watch the blood drain from Manchez's face, or the knowledge leap frantically into his eyes. It was what he'd come for, what he'd promised himself. The medallion on the edge of his chain dangled and reminded him of his brother. His brother was dead. No satisfaction. Jonas lowered the gun.

Manchez tossed back his head. "I'll get out," he said quietly. The smile started to spread. "I'll get out."

The spear shot out and plowed into the deck between Manchez's feet. Liz saw the smile freeze on his face an instant before one formed on Jonas's. "I'll be waiting."

*　*　*

Could it really be over? It was all Liz could think when she awoke, warm and dry, in her own bed. She was safe, Jonas was safe and the smuggling ring on Cozumel was broken. Of course, Jonas had been furious. Manchez had been watched, they had been watched, but the police had made their presence known only after Liz had been held at gunpoint.

But he'd gotten what he'd come for, she thought. His brother's killer was behind bars. He'd face a trial and justice. She hoped it was enough for Jonas.

The morning was enough for her. The normality of it. Happy, she rolled over and pressed her body against Jonas's. He only drew her closer.

"Let's stay right here until noon."

She laughed and nuzzled against his throat. "I have—"

"A business to run," he finished.

"Exactly. And for the first time in weeks I can run it without having this urge to look over my shoulder. I'm happy." She looked at him, then tossed her arms around his neck and squeezed. "I'm so happy."

"Happy enough to marry me?"

She went still as a stone, then slowly, very slowly drew away. "What?"

"Marry me. Come home with me. Start a life with me."

She wanted to say yes. It shocked her that her heart burned to say yes. Pulling away from him was the hardest thing she'd ever done. "I can't."

He stopped her before she could scramble out of bed. It hurt, he realized, more than he could possibly have anticipated. "Why?"

"Jonas, we're two different people with two totally separate lives."

"We stopped having separate lives weeks ago." He took her hands. "They're not ever going to be separate again."

"But they will." She drew her hands away. "After you're back in Philadelphia for a few weeks, you'll barely remember what I look like."

He had her wrists handcuffed in his hands. The fury that surfaced so seldom in him seemed always on simmer when he was around her. "Why do you do that?" he demanded. "Why can't you ever take what you're given?" He swung her around until she was beneath him on the bed. "I love you."

"Don't." She closed her eyes as the wish nearly eclipsed the reason. "Don't say that to me."

Shut out. She was shutting him out. Jonas felt the panic come first, then the anger. Then the determination. "I will say it. If I say it enough, sooner or later you'll start to believe it. Do you think all these nights have been a game? Haven't you felt it? Don't you feel anything?"

"I thought I felt something once before."

"You were a child." When she started to shake her head, he gripped her tighter. "Yes, you were. In some ways you still are, but I know what goes through you when you're with me. I know. I'm not a ghost, I'm not a memory. I'm real and I want you."

"I'm afraid of you," she whispered. "I'm afraid because you make me want what I can't have. I won't marry you, Jonas, because I'm through taking chances with my life and I won't take chances with my child's life. Please let me go."

He released her, but when she stood, his arms went around her. "It isn't over for us."

She dropped her head against his chest, pressed her cheek close. "Let me have the few days we have left. Please let me have them."

He lifted her chin. Everything he needed to know was in her eyes. A man who knew and who planned to win could afford to wait. "You haven't dealt with anyone as stubborn as you are before this. And you haven't nearly finished dealing with me." Then his hand gentled as he stroked her hair. "Get dressed. I'll take you to work."

Because he acted as though nothing had been said, Liz relaxed. It was impossible, and she knew it. They'd known each other only weeks, and under circumstances that were bound to intensify any feelings. He cared. She believed that he cared, but love—the kind of love needed to build a marriage—was too much to risk.

She loved. She loved so much that she pushed him away when she wanted to pull him closer. He needed to go back to his life, back to his world. After time had passed, if he thought of her he'd think with gratitude that she had closed a door he'd opened on impulse. She would think of him. Always.

By the time Liz was walking toward the shop, she'd settled her mind. "What are you going to do today?"

"Me?" Jonas, too, had settled his mind. "I'm going to sit in the sun and do nothing."

"Nothing?" Incredulous, Liz stared at him. "All day?"

"It's known as relaxing, or taking a day off. If you do it several days running, it's called a vacation. I was supposed to have one in Paris."

Paris, she thought. It would suit him. She wondered briefly how the air smelled in Paris. "If you get bored, I'm sure one of the boats could use the extra crew."

"I've had enough diving for a few days, thanks." Jonas plopped down on a chaise in front of the shop. It was the best place to keep an eye on her.

"Miguel." Liz automatically looked around for Luis. "You're here early."

"I came with Luis. He's checking out the dive boat—got an early tour."

"Yes, I know." But she wouldn't trust Miguel to run the shop alone for long. "Why don't you help him? I'll take care of the counter."

"*Bueno*. Oh, there were a couple of guys looking at the fishing boat. Maybe they want to rent."

"I'll take a look. You go ahead." Walking back, she crouched beside Jonas. "Keep an eye on the shop for me, will you? I've got a couple of customers over by the *Expatriate*."

Jonas adjusted his sunglasses. "What do you pay per hour?"

Liz narrowed her eyes. "I might cook dinner tonight."

With a smile, he got up to go behind the counter. "Take all the time you need."

He made her laugh. Liz strolled down the walkway and to the pier, drinking up the morning. She could use a good fishing cruise. The aqua bikes had been ordered, but they still had to be paid for. Besides, she'd like the ride herself. It made her think of Jonas and his unwanted catch a few weeks before. Liz laughed again as she approached the men beside her boat.

"Buenos días," she began. "Mr. Ambuckle." Beaming a smile, Liz held out a hand. "I didn't know you were back. Is this one of your quick weekend trips?"

"That's right." His almost bald head gleamed in the sun as he patted her hand. "When the mood strikes me I just gotta move."

"Thinking about some big-game fishing this time around?"

"Funny you should mention it. I was just saying to my associate here that I only go for the big game."

"Only the big game." Scott Trydent turned around and pushed back his straw hat. "That's right, Clancy."

"Now don't turn around, honey." Ambuckle's fingers clamped over hers before she could move. "You're going to get on the boat, nice and quiet. We have some talking to do, then we might just take a little ride."

"How long have you been using my dive shop to smuggle?" Liz saw the gun under Scott's jacket. She couldn't signal to Jonas, didn't dare.

"For the past couple of years I've found your shop's location unbeatable. You know, they ship that stuff up from Colombia and dump in Miami. The way the heat's been on the past few years, you take a big chance using the regular routes. It takes longer this way, but I lose less merchandise."

"And you're the organizer," she murmured. "You're the man the police want."

"I'm a businessman," he said with a smile. "Let's get on board, little lady."

"The police are watching," Liz told him as she climbed on deck.

"The police have Manchez. If he hadn't tried to pull a double cross, the last shipment would have gone down smooth."

"A double cross?"

"That's right," Scott put in as he flanked her. "Pablo decided he could make more freelancing than by being a company man."

"And by reporting on his fellow employee, Mr. Trydent moves up in rank. I work my organization on the incentive program."

Scott grinned at Ambuckle. "Can't beat the system."

"You had Jerry Sharpe killed." Struggling to believe what was happening, Liz stared at the round little man who'd chatted with her and rented her tanks. "You had him shot."

"He stole a great deal of money from me." Ambuckle's face puckered as he thought of it. "A great deal. I had Manchez dispose of him. The truth is, I'd considered you as a liaison for some time. It seemed simpler, however, just to use your shop. My wife's very fond of you."

"Your wife." Liz thought of the neat, matronly woman in skirted bathing suits. "She knows you smuggle drugs, and she knows you kill people?"

"She thinks we have a great stockbroker." Ambuckle grinned. "I've been moving snow for ten years, and my wife wouldn't know coke from powdered sugar. I like to keep business and family separate. The little woman's going to be sick when she finds out you had an accident. Now we're going to take a little ride. And we're going to talk about the three hundred thousand our friend Jerry slipped out from under my nose. Cast off, Scott."

"No!" Thinking only of survival, Liz made a lunge toward the dock. Ambuckle had her on the deck with one shove. He shook his head, dusted his hands and turned to her. "I'd wanted to keep this from getting messy. You know, I switched gauges on your tanks, figuring you'd back off. Always had a soft spot for you, little lady. But business is business." With a wheezy sigh, he turned to Scott. "Since you've taken over Pablo's position, I assume you know how to deal with this."

"I certainly do." He took out a revolver. His eyes locked on Liz's. When she caught her breath, he turned the barrel toward Ambuckle. "You're under arrest." With his other hand, he pulled out a badge. "You have the right to remain silent . . ." It was the last thing Liz heard before she buried her face in her hands and wept.

CHAPTER 12

I want to know what the hell's been going on." They were in Moralas's office, but Jonas wouldn't sit. He stood behind Liz's chair, his fingers curled tight over the back rung. If anyone had approached her, he would have struck first and asked questions later. He'd already flattened the unfortunate detective who'd tried to hold him back when he'd seen Liz on the deck of the *Expatriate* with Scott.

With his hands folded on his desk, Moralas gave Jonas a long, quiet look. "Perhaps the explanation should come from your countryman."

"Special Agent Donald Scott." The man Liz had known as Scott Trydent sat on the corner of Moralas's desk. "Sorry for the deception, Liz." Though his voice was calm and matter-of-fact, it couldn't mask the excitement that bubbled from him. As he sipped his coffee, he glanced up at Jonas. Explanations wouldn't go over easily with this one, he thought. But he'd always believed the ends justified the means. "I've been after that son of a bitch for three years." He drank again, savoring triumph. "It took us two before we could infiltrate the ring, and even then I couldn't make contact with the head man. To get to him I had to go through more channels than you do with the Company. He's been careful. For the past eight months I've been working with Manchez as Scott Trydent. He was the closest I could get to Ambuckle until two days ago."

"You used her." Jonas's hand went to Liz's shoulder. "You put her right in the middle."

"Yeah. The problem was, for a long time we weren't sure just how involved she was. We knew about your shop, Liz. We knew you were an experienced diver. In fact, there isn't anything about you my organization didn't know. For some time, you were our number-one suspect."

"Suspect?" She had her hands folded neatly in her lap, but the anger was boiling. "You suspected me."

"You left the U.S. over ten years ago. You've never been back. You have both the contacts and the means to have run the ring. You keep your daughter off the island for most of the year and in one of the best schools in Houston."

"That's my business."

"Details like that become our business. When you took Jerry Sharpe in and gave him a job, we leaned even further toward you. He thought differently, but then we weren't using him for his opinions."

She felt Jonas's fingers tighten and reached up to them as she spoke. "Using him?"

"I contacted Jerry Sharpe in New Orleans. He was someone else we knew everything about. He was a con, an operator, but he had style." He took another swig of coffee as he studied Jonas. "We made him a deal. If he could get on the inside, feed us information, we'd forget about a few . . . indiscretions. I liked your brother," Scott said to Jonas. "Really liked him. If he'd been able to settle a bit, he'd have made a hell of a cop. 'Conning the bad guys,' he called it."

"Are you saying Jerry was working for you?" Jonas felt his emotions race toward the surface. The portrait he'd barely been able to force himself to accept was changing.

"That's right." Scott took out a cigarette and watched the match flare as he struck it. "I liked him—I mean that. He had a way of looking at things that made you forget they were so lousy."

That was Jerry, Jonas thought. To give himself a moment,

he walked to the window. He could see the water lapping calmly against the hulls of boats. He could see the sun dancing down on it and children walking along the sea wall. The scene had been almost the same the day he'd arrived on Cozumel. Some things remained the same; others altered constantly. "What happened?"

"He had a hard time following orders. He wanted to push them too fast too far. He told me once he had something to prove, to himself and to the other part of him. The better part of him."

Jonas turned slowly. The pain came again, an ache. Liz saw it in his eyes and went to stand with him. "Go on."

"He got the idea into his head to rip off the money from a shipment. I didn't know about it until he called me from Acapulco. He figured he'd put the head man in a position where he'd have to deal personally. I told him to stay put, that we were scrubbing him. He'd have been taken back to the States and put somewhere safe until the job was over." He tossed the match he'd been holding into an ashtray on Moralas's desk. "He didn't listen. He came back to Cozumel and tried to deal with Manchez himself. It was over before I knew. Even if I'd have known, I can't be sure I could've stopped it. We don't like to lose civilians, Mr. Sharpe. I don't like to lose friends."

The anger drained from him degree by degree. It would have been so like Jerry, Jonas thought. An adventure, the excitement, the impulsiveness. "Go on."

"Orders came down to put the pressure on Liz." Scott gave a half laugh that had nothing to do with humor. "Orders from both sides. It wasn't until after your trip to Acapulco that we were sure you weren't involved in the smuggling. You stopped being a suspect and became the decoy."

"I came to the police." She looked at Moralas. "I came to you. You didn't tell me."

"I wasn't aware of Agent Scott's identity until yesterday. I knew only that we had a man on the inside and that it was necessary to use you."

"You were protected," Scott put in. "There wasn't a day you weren't guarded by Moralas's men and by mine. Your being here complicated things," he said to Jonas. "You were pushing too close to the bone. I guess you and Jerry had more in common than looks."

Jonas felt the weight on the chain around his neck. "Maybe we did."

"Well, we'd come to the point where we had to settle for Manchez and a few others or go for broke. We went for broke."

"The drop we made. It was a setup."

"Manchez had orders to do whatever he had to to get back the money Jerry had taken. They didn't know about the safe-deposit box." He blew out a stream of smoke. "I had to play it pretty fast and loose to keep that under wraps. But then we didn't know about it either, until you led us to it. As far as Ambuckle was concerned, you had the money, and he was going to get it back. He wanted it to look as though you'd been running the smuggling operation together. When you were found dead, the heat would be off of him. He planned to lie low awhile, then pick up business elsewhere. I had that from Manchez. You were set up," he agreed. "So was he. I got to Merriworth, made enough noise about how Manchez was about to double-cross to set him off. When Manchez was snorkeling to your boat, I was on the phone with the man I knew as Clancy. I got a promotion, and Clancy came back to deal with you himself."

Liz tried to see it as he did, as a chess game, as any game with pawns. She couldn't. "You knew who he was yesterday morning and you still had me get on that boat."

"There were a dozen sharpshooters in position. I had a gun, Ambuckle didn't. We wanted him to order Liz's murder, and we wanted him to tell her as much as possible. When this goes to court, we want it tidy. We want him put away for a long time. You're a lawyer, Sharpe. You know how these things can go. We can make a clean collar, have a stack of evidence and lose. I've watched too many of these bastards walk." He blew out smoke between set teeth. "This one's not walking anywhere but into federal prison."

"There is still the question of whether these men will be tried in your country or mine." Moralas spoke softly, and didn't move when Scott whirled on him.

"Look, Moralas—"

"This will be discussed later. You have my thanks and my apologies," he said to Jonas and Liz. "I regret we saw no other way."

"So do I," Liz murmured, then turned to Scott. "Was it worth it?"

"Ambuckle brought thousands of pounds of cocaine into the States. He's responsible for more than fifteen murders in the U.S. and Mexico. Yeah, it was worth it."

She nodded. "I hope you understand that I never want to see you again." After closing her hand around Jonas's she managed a smile. "You were a lousy student."

"Sorry we never had that drink." He looked back at Jonas. "Sorry about a lot of things."

"I appreciate what you told me about my brother. It makes a difference."

"I'm recommending him for a citation. They'll send it to your parents."

"It'll mean a great deal to them." He offered his hand and meant it. "You were doing your job—I understand that. We all do what we have to do."

"That doesn't mean I don't regret it."

Jonas nodded. Something inside him was free, completely free. "As to putting Liz through hell for the past few weeks . . ." Very calmly, Jonas curled his hand into a fist and planted it solidly on Scott's jaw. The thin man snapped a chair in half as he crashed into it on his way to the floor.

"Jonas!" Stunned, Liz could do no more than stare. Then, incredibly, she felt the urge to giggle. With one hand over her mouth, she leaned into Jonas and let the laughter come. Moralas remained contentedly at his desk, sipping coffee.

Scott rubbed his jaw gingerly. "We all do what we have to do," he murmured.

Jonas only turned his back. "Goodbye, Captain."

Moralas stayed where he was. "Goodbye, Mr. Sharpe." He rose and, in a rare show of feeling, took Liz's hand and kissed it. *"Vaya con dios."*

He waited until the door had shut behind them before he looked down at Scott again. "Your government will, of course, pay for the chair."

* * *

He was gone. She'd sent him away. After nearly two weeks, Liz awoke every morning with the same thoughts. Jonas was gone. It was for the best. After nearly two weeks she awoke every morning struggling to convince herself. If she'd followed her heart, she would have said yes the moment he'd asked her to marry him. She would have left everything she'd built behind and gone with him. And ruined his life, perhaps her own.

He was already back in his own world, poring through law books, facing juries, going to elegant dinner parties. By now, she was sure his time in Cozumel was becoming vague. After all, he hadn't written. He hadn't called. He'd left the day after Ambuckle had been taken into custody without another word about love. He'd conquered his ghosts when he'd faced Manchez and had walked away whole.

He was gone, and she was once more standing on her own. As she was meant to, Liz thought. She'd have no regrets. That she'd promised herself. What she'd given to Jonas had been given without conditions or expectations. What he'd given to her she'd never lose.

The sun was high and bright, she thought. The air was as

mellow as quiet music. Her lover was gone, but she, too, was whole. A month of memories could be stretched to last a lifetime. And Faith was coming home.

Liz pulled her bike into a parking space and listened to the thunder of a plane taking off. Even now Faith and her parents were crossing the Gulf. Liz left her bike and walked toward the terminal. It was ridiculous to feel nervous, she told herself, but she couldn't prevent it. It was ridiculous to arrive at the airport nearly an hour early, but she'd have gone mad at home. She skirted around a bed of marigolds and geraniums. She'd buy flowers, she decided. Her mother loved flowers.

Inside the terminal, the air was cool and full of noise. Tourists came and went but rarely passed the shops without a last-minute purchase. Liz started in the first store and worked her way down, buying consistently and strictly on impulse. By the time she arrived at the gate, she carried two shopping bags and an armful of dyed carnations.

Any minute, she thought. She'd be here any minute. Liz shifted both bags to one hand and nervously brushed at her hair. Passengers waited for their flights by napping in the black plastic chairs or reading guide-books. She watched a woman check her lipstick in a compact mirror and wondered if she had time to run into the ladies room to examine her own face. Gnawing on her lip, she decided she couldn't leave, even for a moment. Neither could she sit, so she paced back and forth in front of the wide windows and watched the planes come and go. It was late. Planes were always late when you were waiting for them. The sky was clear and blue. She knew it was equally clear in Houston because she'd been checking the weather for days. But the plane was late. Impatient, she walked back to security to ask about the status. She should have known better.

Liz got a shrug and the Mexican equivalent of *It'll be here when it comes*. In another ten minutes, she was ready to scream. Then she saw it. She didn't have to hear the flight announcement to know. With her heart thudding dully, she waited by the door.

Faith wore blue striped pants and a white blouse. *Her hair's grown,* Liz thought as she watched her daughter come down the steps. *She's grown*—though she knew it would never do to tell Faith so. She'd just wrinkle her nose and roll her eyes. Her palms were wet. *Don't cry, don't cry,* Liz ordered herself. But the tears were already welling. Then Faith looked up and saw her. With a grin and a wave she was racing forward. Liz dropped her bags and reached out for her daughter.

"Mom, I got to sit by the window, but I couldn't see our house." As she babbled, Faith held her mother's neck in a stranglehold. "I brought you a present."

With her face buried against Faith's throat, Liz drew in the scents—powder, soap and chocolate from the streak on the front of the white blouse. "Let me look at you." Drawing her back, Liz soaked up the sight of her. *She's beautiful,* Liz realized with a jolt. Not just cute or sweet or pretty any longer. Her daughter was beautiful.

I can't let her go again. It hit her like a wall. *I'll never be able to let her go again.* "You've lost a tooth," Liz managed as she brushed back her daughter's hair.

"Two." Faith grinned to show the twin spaces. "Grandma said I could put them under my pillow, but I brought them with me so I can put them under my real pillow. Will I get pesos?"

"Yes." Liz kissed one cheek, then the other. "Welcome home."

With her hand firmly in Faith's, Liz rose to greet her parents. For a moment she just looked at them, trying to see them as a stranger would. Her father was tall and still slim, though his hairline was creeping back. He was grinning at her the way he had whenever she'd done something particularly pleasing to him. Her mother stood beside him, lovely in her tidy way. She looked now, as she'd always looked to Liz, like a woman who'd never had to handle a crisis more stressful than a burned roast. Yet she'd been as solid and as sturdy as a rock. There were tears in her eyes. Liz wondered abruptly if the beginning of the summer left her mother as empty as the end of the summer left her.

"Momma." Liz reached out and was surrounded. "Oh, I've missed you. I've missed you all so much." *I want to go home*. The thought surged up inside her and nearly poured out. She needed to go home.

"Mom." Faith tugged on the pocket of her jeans. "Mom."

Giddy, Liz turned and scooped her up. "Yes." She covered her face with kisses until Faith giggled. "Yes, yes, yes!"

Faith snuggled in. "You have to say hello to Jonas."

"What?"

"He came with us. You have to say hi."

"I don't—" Then she saw him, leaning against the window, watching—waiting patiently. The blood rushed out of her head to her heart until she was certain something would burst. Holding onto Faith, Liz stood where she was. Jonas walked to her, took her face in both hands and kissed her hard.

"Nice to see you," he murmured, then bent down to pick up the bags Liz had dropped. "I imagine these are for you," he said as he handed Liz's mother the flowers.

"Yes." Liz tried to gather the thoughts stumbling through her mind. "I forgot."

"They're lovely." She sent her daughter a smile. "Jonas is going to drive us to the hotel. I invited him to dinner tonight. I hope you don't mind. You always make enough."

"No, I . . . Of course."

"We'll see you then." She gave Liz another brief kiss. "I know you want to get Faith home and have some time together. We'll see you tonight."

"But I—"

"Our bags are here. We're going to deal with customs."

Before Liz could say another word, she was alone with her daughter.

"Can we stop by and see Señor Pessado?"

"Yes," Liz said absently.

"Can I have some candy?"

Liz glanced down to the chocolate stain on Faith's blouse. "You've already had some."

Faith just smiled. She knew she could depend on Señor Pessado. "Let's go home now."

* * *

Liz waited until Faith was unpacked, until the crystal bird Faith had bought her was hanging in the window and her daughter had consumed two tacos and a pint of milk.

"Faith . . ." She wanted her voice to be casual. "When did you meet Mr. Sharpe?"

"Jonas? He came to Grandma's house." Faith turned the doll Liz had brought her this way and that for inspection.

"To Grandma's? When?"

"I don't know." She decided to call the doll Cassandra because it was pretty and had long hair. "Can I have my ice cream now?"

"Oh—yes." Liz walked over to get it out of the freezer. "Faith, do you know why he went to Grandma's?"

"He wanted to talk to her, I guess. To Grandpa, too. He stayed for dinner. I knew Grandma liked him because she made cherry pies. I liked him, too. He can play the piano really good." Faith eyed the ice cream and was satisfied when her mother added another scoop. "He took me to the zoo."

"What?" The bowl nearly slipped out of Liz's hand as she set it down. "Jonas took you to the zoo?"

"Last Saturday. We fed popcorn to the monkeys, but mostly we ate it." She giggled as she shoveled in ice cream. "He tells funny stories. I scraped my knee." Remembering suddenly, Faith pulled up her slacks to show off her wound.

"Oh, baby." It was small and already scabbed over, but Liz brushed a kiss over it anyway. "How'd you do this?"

"At the zoo. I was running. I can run really fast in my new sneakers, but I fell down. I didn't cry."

Liz rolled the slacks down. "I'm sure you didn't."

"Jonas didn't get mad or anything. He cleaned it all up with his handkerchief. It was pretty messy. I bled a lot." She smiled at that, pleased with herself. "He said I have pretty eyes just like you."

A little thrill of panic raced through her, but she couldn't stop herself. "Did he? What else did he say?"

"Oh, we talked about Mexico and about Houston. He wondered which I liked best."

Liz rested her hands on her daughter's knees. *This is what matters,* she realized. This was all that really mattered. "What did you tell him?"

"I like it best where you are." She scraped the bottom of the bowl. "He said he liked it best there, too. Is he going to be your boyfriend?"

"My—" Liz managed, just barely, to suppress the laugh. "No."

"Charlene's mother has a boyfriend, but he isn't as tall as Jonas and I don't think he ever took Charlene to the zoo. Jonas said sometime maybe we could go see the Liberty Bell. Do you think we can?"

Liz picked up the ice cream dish and began to wash it. "We'll see," she muttered.

"Listen, someone's coming." Faith was up like a shot and dashing for the front door. "It's Jonas!" With a whoop, she was out of the door and running full steam.

"Faith!" Liz hurried from the kitchen and reached the porch in time to see Faith hurl herself at Jonas. With a laugh, he caught her, tossed her in the air then set her down again in a move so natural that it seemed he'd been doing so all his life. Liz knotted the dishcloth in her hands.

"You came early." Pleased, Faith hung on to his hand. "We were talking about you."

"Were you?" He tousled Faith's hair but looked up at Liz. "That's funny, because I was thinking about you."

"We're going to make paella because that's what Grandpa likes best. You can help."

"Faith—"

"Love to," Jonas interrupted. "After I talk to your mother." At the foot of the stairs he crouched down to Faith's level. "I'd really like to talk to your mom alone."

Faith's mouth screwed up. "Why?"

"I have to convince her to marry me."

He ignored Liz's gasp and watched for Faith's reaction. Her eyes narrowed and her mouth pursed. "She said you weren't her boyfriend. I asked."

He grinned and leaned closer. "I just have to talk her into it."

"Grandma says nobody can ever talk my mom into anything. She has a hard head."

"So do I, and I make a living talking people into things. But maybe you could put in a few good words for me later."

As Faith considered, her eyes brightened. "Okay. Mom, can I see if Roberto's home? You said he had new puppies."

Liz stretched out the cloth then balled it again. "Go ahead, but just for a little while."

Jonas straightened as he watched Faith race toward the house across the street. "You've done an excellent job with your daughter, Elizabeth."

"She's done a great deal of it herself."

He turned and saw the nerves on her face. It didn't displease him. But he remembered the way she'd looked when she had opened her arms to Faith at the airport. He wanted, he would, see her look that way again. "Do you want to talk inside?" he began as he walked up the steps. "Or right here?"

"Jonas, I don't know why you've come back, but—"

"Of course you know why I've come back. You're not stupid."

"We don't have anything to talk about."

"Fine." He closed the distance quickly. She didn't resist, though she told herself she would. When he dragged her against him, she went without hesitation. Her mouth locked hungrily to his, and for a moment, just for a moment, the world was right again. "If you don't want to talk, we'll go inside and make love until you see things a little more clearly."

"I see things clearly." Liz put her hands on his arms and started to draw away.

"I love you."

He felt the shudder, saw the flash of joy in her eyes before she looked away. "Jonas, this isn't possible."

"Wrong. It's entirely possible—in fact, it's already done. The point is, Liz, you need me."

Her eyes narrowed to slits. "What I need I take care of."

"That's why I love you," he said simply and took the wind out of her sails.

"Jonas—"

"Are you going to tell me you haven't missed me?" She opened her mouth, then shut it again. "Okay, so you take the Fifth on that one." He stepped back from her. "Are you going to deny that you've spent some sleepless nights in the past couple of weeks, that you've thought about what happened between us? Are you going to stand here and look at me now and tell me you're not in love with me?"

She'd never been able to lie well. Liz turned and meticulously spread the dishcloth over the porch rail. "Jonas, I can't run my life on my feelings."

"From now on you can. Did you like the present Faith brought you?"

"What?" Confused, she turned back. "Yes, of course I did."

"Good. I brought you one, too." He took a box out of his pocket. Liz saw the flash of diamond and nearly had her hand behind her back before he caught it in his. Firmly, he slipped the ring on. "It's official."

She wouldn't even look at it. She couldn't stop herself. The diamond was shaped in a teardrop and as white and glossy as a wish. "You're being ridiculous," she told him, but couldn't make herself take it off.

"You're going to marry me." He took her shoulders and leaned her back against a post. "That's not negotiable. After that, we have several options. I can give up my practice and live in Cozumel. You can support me."

She let out a quick breath that might have been a laugh. "Now you're really being ridiculous."

"You don't like that one. Good, I didn't care for it either. You can come back to Philadelphia with me. I'll support you."

Her chin went up. "I don't need to be supported."

"Excellent. We agree on the first two options." He ran his hands through her hair and discovered he wasn't feeling as patient as he'd thought he would. "Now, you can come back to the States. We'll take a map and you can close your eyes and pick a spot. That's where we'll live."

"We can't run our lives this way." She pushed him aside to walk down the length of the porch and back. But part of her was beginning to believe they could. "Don't you see how impossible it is?" she demanded as much of herself as of him. "You have your career. I have my business. I'd never be a proper wife for someone like you."

"You're the only wife for someone like me." He grabbed her shoulders again. No, he wasn't feeling patient at all. "Damn it, Liz, you're the only one. If the business is important to you, keep it. Have Luis run it. We can come back a half a dozen times a year if you want. Start another business. We'll go to Florida, to California, anywhere you want where they need a good dive shop. Or . . ." He waited until he was sure he had her full attention. "You could go back to school."

He saw it in her eyes—the surprise, the dream, then the denial. "That's over."

"The hell it is. Look at you—it's what you want. Keep the shop, build another, build ten others, but give yourself something for yourself."

"It's been more than ten years."

He lifted a brow. "You said once you wouldn't change anything."

"And I meant it, but to go back now, after all this time."

"Afraid?"

Her eyes narrowed; her spine stiffened. "Yes."

He laughed, delighted with her. "Woman, in the past few weeks, you've been through hell and out again. And you're afraid of a few college courses?"

With a sigh, she turned away. "I might not be able to make it."

"So what?" He whirled her back again. "So you fall flat on your face. I'll be right there falling down with you. It's time for risking, Liz. For both of us."

"Oh, I want to believe you." She lifted a hand to rest it on his face. "I want to. I do love you, Jonas. So much."

She was locked against him again, lost in him. "I need you, Liz. I'm not going back without you."

She clung to him a moment, almost ready to believe. "But it's not just me. You have to understand I can't do whatever I'd like."

"Faith?" He drew her back again. "I've spent the past weeks getting to know her. My main objective when I started was to ingratiate myself. I figured the only way to get to you was through her."

So she'd already surmised. "Afternoons at the zoo?"

"That's right. Thing was, I didn't know she was as easy to fall for as her mother. I want her."

The hand Liz had lifted to her hair froze. "I don't understand."

"I want her to be mine—legally, emotionally. I want you to agree to let me adopt her."

"Adopt . . ." Whatever she might have expected from him, it hadn't been this. "But she's—"

"Yours?" he interrupted. "No, she's going to be ours. You're going to have to share her. And if you're set on her going to school in Houston, we'll live in Houston. Within the year I expect she should have a brother or sister because she needs family as much as we do."

He was offering her everything, everything she'd ever wanted and had refused to believe in. She had only to hold out her hand. The idea terrified her. "She's another man's child. How will you be able to forget that?"

"She's your child," he reminded her. "You told me yourself she was your child only. Now she's going to be mine." Taking her hands, he kissed them. "So are you."

"Jonas, do you know what you're doing? You're asking for a wife who'll have to start from scratch and a half-grown daughter. You're complicating your life."

"Yeah, and maybe I'm saving it."

And hers. Her blood was pumping again, her skin was tingling. For the first time in years she could look at her life and see no shadows. She closed her eyes and breathed deeply before she turned. "Be sure," she whispered. "Be absolutely sure. If I let myself go, if I say yes and you change your mind, I'll hate you for the rest of my life."

He took her by the shirtfront. "In one week, we're going to my parents' farm in Lancaster, calling the local minister, justice of the peace or witch doctor and we're getting married. Adoption papers are being drawn up. When we settle in as a family, we're all having the same name. You and Faith and I."

With a sigh, Liz leaned back again against the post and studied his face. It was beautiful, she decided. Strong, passionate, patient. Her life was going to be bound up with that face. It was as real as flesh and blood and as precious as dreams. Her lover was back, her child was with her and nothing was impossible.

"When I first met you, I thought you were the kind of man who always got what he wanted."

"And you were right." He took her hands again and held them. "Now what are we going to tell Faith?" he demanded.

Her lips curved slowly. "I guess we'd better tell her you talked me into it."

From the *New York Times* bestselling author

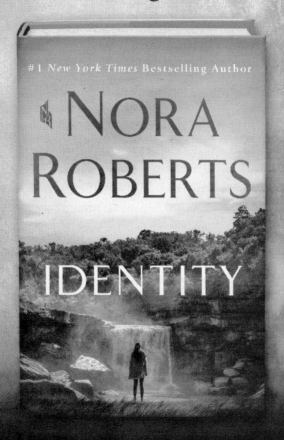

#1 *New York Times* Bestselling Author

NORA ROBERTS

IDENTITY

He stole her identity.
Now he wants her life.
How far will she go to take it back?